"HEADS UP, PEOPLE.
WE HAVE ACTIVITY!"

On the shots from the Hubbell, the Stony Man team could see the thrusters were firing on a dozen Thors, a lambent purple glow of ionized gas visible as the thick steel bars started accelerating toward the world below.

"Who are they attacking?" Tokaido asked anxiously. His hands itched to send out a warning to the target, maybe save some lives. But he knew it would be pointless. The Thors literally struck like lightning. There wasn't time for a warning.

"Somebody in the North American continent," Bear stated honestly. "Hell, maybe us." Reaching out, the burly man slapped a button on the console.

"Barbara, you better sound the alarm," Kurtzman said in a deceptively calm voice. "We may have incoming."

Other titles in this series:

DON PENDLETON'S

STONY

AMERICA'S ULTRA-COVERT INTELLIGENCE AGENCY

MAN®

SKY HAMMER

A GOLD EAGLE BOOK FROM

W★RLDWIDE®

TORONTO • NEW YORK • LONDON
AMSTERDAM • PARIS • SYDNEY • HAMBURG
STOCKHOLM • ATHENS • TOKYO • MILAN
MADRID • WARSAW • BUDAPEST • AUCKLAND

First edition February 2006

ISBN 0-373-61965-0

SKY HAMMER

Special thanks and acknowledgment to
Nick Pollotta for his contribution to this work.

Printed in U.S.A.

SKY HAMMER

PROLOGUE

Paris, France

Lightning flashed in the stormy sky as Alex Davis staggered through the filthy alley. Holding his right hand to his wound, he flinched at the burst of light and tightened his grip on the Beretta pistol in his left. But there was nobody in sight. The clouds opened and down came the rain. The NSA agent was drenched in seconds, the downpour of cool water slightly reviving him.

Coming out of the alley, the dying agent paused at the sidewalk, trying to focus his eyes through the torrential deluge. Only a few people were in sight, all of them racing through the puddles for the safety of a store or a cab. Nobody seemed to be looking his way.

Jerking his head, Davis forced himself awake. If he went to sleep now, he'd never wake up again. Leaving the alley, he lurched across the street and into another alley, a shortcut that kept him off the dangerous sidewalks.

When Davis had joined the NSA, he'd been told that field agents had a long life expectancy. But years of service had taught him the truth. Death stalked everybody in the intelligence game these days, and the only way to survive was to shoot first and ask questions later. He had paused, unwilling to take a human life without direct provocation, and now he was a walking dead man. Davis knew it in his bones.

That morning he'd arranged for a meet with one of his "groundhogs," somebody who could feed the agency news from the street. Not the public streets, but the back-alley gossip, the hushed news from the French underworld. Blackmail, weapons smuggling, kidnappings, arson and murder. The NSA agent did nothing about the crimes unless they affected America. He simply took in the raw data and wrote a report for his superiors. Machines could tap into cell phone calls very easily these days, the electronic warriors were doing most of work nowadays. But it was spies, moles, turncoats and stool pigeons who kept America safe. People talking. Old-fashioned spy work. Human intelligence.

Everything had seemed aboveboard when Davis met the snitch at the train station. The woman was mature, sixty, maybe seventy, but still maintained her good looks. She was demure in a pink dress with black trim. Only the smile was cold and impersonal. You'd never guess that she ran dozens of brothels across the great metropolis, establishments that catered to the criminal hierarchy, clients who liked to talk afterward. Davis had slipped the madam a book with money stuffed between the pages and she'd given him a newspaper. He'd barely had time to glance at the message taped to the book review page when a train arrived, somebody shoved a shotgun through the window in a crash of glass and opened fire. The madam hit the tiled wall of the station in a red spray, her ruined body crumpling to the ground. Taking cover behind a vending machine, Davis had withdrawn his side arm, but was unable to return fire because of all the civilians.

However, that hadn't stopped the dark-haired gunman, and Davis got hit twice before managing to escape by going through a plate-glass window. His agency vest had saved his life, but a block later he'd realized he was badly wounded. Dying. Somebody had tried to stop the madam from delivering the note he carried, so that made it a requisite that it be passed on. He pressed a hand to his jacket, but the cell phone was only bits and pieces, smashed during the brief gunfight.

Pausing to rest against a lamppost, Davis struggled to read the short note through the bad light and pouring rain. Could this be real? By God, that would mean...

Forcing himself into motion, the NSA agent continued his hopeless journey for the distant café. Come on, man, just one block more....

IMPATIENTLY, JOE SNYDER GLANCED at his watch. Half an hour late. Davis had to have been taking care of business. Ten more minutes and he'd start without the man. He had skipped breakfast this morning, and the CIA agent was starving. The two men lunched regularly and, more than once, one or the other was late.

Moments later a woman outside the café screamed, then a man sitting near the sidewalk jumped up, knocking back his chair. Coming out of the rain like something from a nightmare was a disheveled figure with a gun in his hand.

Snyder started to go for the Glock under his jacket when he recognized Davis.

"Good God, man, what happened to you!" Snyder cried, rising from his chair. Then he turned to a nearby waiter he knew. "Pierre, an ambulance! Fast!"

Pierre didn't waste a second in discussion. He turned and charged through the café, maneuvering through the maze of people and tables to disappear into the steamy back room.

"Joe, gotta tell…" Davis mumbled, staggering against the table and knocking it sideways, the plates and silverware flying everywhere.

Reaching out, Snyder caught the man as he collapsed. "Easy there, buddy. Easy. What happened? Are you shot? Stabbed?" Snyder demanded in a soft voice. There were no obvious wounds, aside from a lot of bruises and accumulated filth. Looked as though Davis had been wrestling alligators in the Parisian sewers.

Davis tried to answer but went into a spasm of coughing, spraying red dots onto his wet hand.

Grabbing a cloth napkin from the floor, Snyder wiped the red off the trembling man. Blood was on his lips, giving his breath a coppery odor. That meant massive internal bleeding. Not good. Then he noticed a crimson stain under the man's arm. Carefully peeling back the linen jacket, Snyder saw that the agent was wearing a nonregulation bulletproof vest. So that's why no blood showed, it was concealed under his vest! Releasing the Velcro strips on the side to let the man breath easier, Snyder frowned at the sight of the blood-soaked shirt underneath. There was a small bullet wound under the arm. An armpit shot. That was either a freak shot or else somebody knew that was a major killzone. And in their line of business, it was almost always deliberate. Stab or shoot a man there and, nine times out of ten, he died even if you got him to the hospital within minutes.

"Doesn't matter…" Davis whispered. "Couldn't reach HQ…cell phone smashed…traitor!…we have a traitor…"

"Easy now, don't talk."

"Have to!" he whispered. "Joe…demo today…new weapon…for sale to everybody…anybody! Going to hit…hit…"

"Who? Talk, buddy! Who are they going to hit?"

"Abacus…" he said softly.

"Abacus? Okay, what's that?"

Shuddering all over, Davis broke into a fit of coughing.

"Never mind the target, who's the traitor?" the CIA agent urged gently. "Tell me, and I'll personally squeeze all of the details out of their stinking hide." He paused. "Was Abacus a code name? Is that the traitor?"

Grabbing the other man's lapel with surprisingly strong fingers, Davis moved his lips, but no sound came out as the NSA agent slumped to the floor, his reserves of strength finally gone. Silently, Snyder lay his friend on the floor of the café where they had first met so very long ago.

"Goodbye," he said softly, using a fingertip to close the other man's eyelids.

The wailing siren grew steadily closer.

Suddenly an ambulance braked to a halt in front of the little café, and the side door slid back to reveal a group of people, all wearing black and carrying weapons. One of them a compact flamethrower, a hissing blue flame jutting out from the preburner angled underneath the ventilated main barrel. The heavy set of duel fuel tanks on her back gave the grim operator the appearance of a hunchback.

With a curse, Snyder dived to the ground as two of the men cut loose with shotguns. The café seemed to explode in blood as people near the entrance were literally cut in two by the discharges, then a machine gun racked the interior of the building as the flamethrower extended a fiery tongue of destruction that swept across the horrified crowd of civilians. Wine bottles exploded, people shrieked and a man dashed into the rain covered with jellied gasoline and dripping flames.

Rolling to his knees, Snyder pulled a Glock from under his jacket, racked the slide and fired a fast five times at the people in the vehicle. Two of the killers grunted from the impacts, but nothing more.

The attackers were wearing body armor, he realized, shoving over a table and taking refuge behind it. He had no idea who these people were, but they had professional hit squad written all over them. Probably the same group that iced Davis.

Now the strangers concentrated on Snyder, the barrage of incoming lead hammering the tabletop and punching through the ceramic tiles covering the wood. He tried to return fire, but screaming people were in the way.

Changing directions, the burning lance of the flamethrower went high and fire rained upon the patrons. Somebody threw a bottle at the ambulance and it smashed on the side of the vehicle with a shower of glass. This distracted the killers for a second and Davis emptied the Glock, trying to reach the pressurized tanks strapped to the back of the woman operating the flamethrower.

He missed and she aimed straight at the overturned table, the hellish column of flame hitting the flimsy barrier with audible force. The shaking table began to move backward, scraping across the floor, as the writhing fiery fingers reached through the bullet holes.

A second ambulance arrived with a flourish, parking in front of the first. As the French emergency medical team piled out, the rear doors of the ambulance opened and there came the dull thump of a grenade launcher. The windshield of the other vehicle shattered and the interior exploded, blowing off doors and sending out great plumes of thick black smoke.

Who were these guys? Snyder wondered as he quickly reloaded. The CIA agent knew he was outgunned here and decided it was time to leave. Davis was dead, and he was doing nothing to these people with the Glock. Might as well be throwing spit balls. That wasn't an ambulance, it was a tank!

A flashing blue light amid the fire caught his attention and Snyder eagerly snatched the cell phone out of the still hand of a dead businessman. Crouching, the agent tapped in a number. There was a short pause followed by a series of clicks as the scrambled signal was relayed to the Agency headquarters only a few blocks away.

"Hello," a voice said over the phone. It was flat, metallic, just a robot used to relay incoming messages.

"Snyder, Paris," he said, coughing, and then gave his identification number. "Under enemy fire. Alex Davis of the NSA is dead! Claims there is a traitor in the NSA or possibly the

CIA, I'm not sure which. Some sort of new weapon is going to hit Abacus. Repeat, Abacus is in danger!" He coughed again, longer this time. It was getting difficult to talk. The agent couldn't really hear the outside world anymore. He pulled into himself, trying to shy away from the incredible heat. He only had a few seconds more of life. He had to make them count.

"Repeat…" The cell phone crackled over the mounting inferno. It was a human voice. Somebody had been listening!

Trying to comply, Snyder broke into savage coughing and dropped the phone. It hit the ground and shattered, the pieces flying into the crackling flames. Bitterly cursing, Snyder decided to take a desperate gamble and insanely charged through the fire firing his gun at the dimly seen figures in the ambulance. There was a pay phone on the corner if he could just reach it…

The machine guns spoke in unison, then the flamethrower. Terrible pain filled Snyder's universe and everything went black.

CHAPTER ONE

An unmarked black helicopter moved across the Virginia sky. The single passenger onboard was a well-dressed woman with a top fashion model's flawless beauty.

Gazing out the small window, Barbara Price, mission controller of Stony Man Farm, could see nothing out of order on the grounds of the nation's premier ultrasecret antiterrorist installation. Yet something was going on that was serious enough to drag her back here from a three-day conference that she had been looking forward to for six months.

"Here we are, Ms. Price," the pilot announced over a shoulder as the helicopter landed on a wide patch of grass. "Right on time."

"Thanks."

Releasing the latch, Price slid back the side door and noted with satisfaction the assortment of men in work clothes lounging near the buildings. All of them had a hand out of sight, presumably resting on the butt of a loaded gun. She was expected, but they were trained to prepare for the unexpected.

As Price stepped to the ground, the men all smiled and relaxed their stances, returning to their cover work of painting and weeding.

When Price was a few yards away from the aircraft, the rush of air from above it increased dramatically and the helicopter lifted off again to head back to D.C. She decided to walk to the farmhouse. It was a beautiful day.

"Sorry to ruin your conference," Aaron Kurtzman said as she reached the porch.

"So what's the problem?" Price asked.

"There's trouble in Paris," Kurtzman replied.

Knowing he wouldn't divulge details within open air, Price hurried through the security process and made her way with him to the War Room, rather than heading to her office in the Annex.

"Talk," she directed him as she slipped into a chair. "What happened in Paris?"

Closing the door, Kurtzman took a seat and passed her a report on the café killings. "More importantly," he said gruffly, "do you know of any secret project or black ops named Abacus?"

Price took the page and read its contents. Her expression darkened with every passing second.

"Akira intercepted this message while on its way to Langley," Kurtzman said, referring to superhacker Akira Tokaido. "It wasn't earmarked for a 'please copy' to the NSA."

"So they're not sharing data, in spite of a presidential order to that effect," Price murmured.

"Exactly."

"Anybody crazy enough to hit both the CIA and the NSA is a major threat," she said bluntly, placing the paper aside.

"But it's this cryptic reference to Abacus that bothers me the most."

"That's why I called you back a day early," Kurtzman stated. "I really need your input. Do you know of anything with that code name? A satellite maybe, or a computer complex?" He paused. "Of course I know an abacus is an ancient Chinese device for making fast and accurate mathematical additions and subtractions. It's just a wooden frame with beads that move along taut wires. Sort of like a primitive slapstick. Yet the damn thing is so efficient and easy to use that three thousand years later Chinese shopkeepers around the world are still using it instead of mechanical cash registers."

"Something to do with money, then. Or perhaps the Chinese."

"Seems likely, given the name."

Placing an elbow on the desk, Price rested her jaw in her palm. "Well, there's nothing that I know about. Hal might have a better idea."

"I don't think we need the big boss for this. If there was known and confirmed trouble coming, sure. But not for a fishing expedition."

Price lifted the paper again. "Hmm, it says here the NSA agent was badly wounded at the time, dying in fact."

"Yes, he was. And…?" Kurtzman prompted, not sure where the woman was going with this. A dying report from a field agent was nothing new in their line of work. Terrible and tragic, yes, the death of a good man always was, but sadly, nothing new. Although it did make responding to his information a top priority. Officially they weren't in the revenge business.

"He might have been mumbling his words," she said,

thoughtfully. "Ab-ba-cus." Price tried it again, slurring the word, testing the syllables. Then she went pale.

Spinning in the chair, she checked a calendar. "Son of a bitch, that's today. Hell, it's going on right now!"

"What is? What's happening?" Kurtzman demanded.

Snatching the phone off the receiver, Price tapped in a string of numbers. It was answered before the third ring.

"Hello, Hal?" The mission controller spoke into the receiver. "You better warn the President. I think all hell is about to break loose in the Middle East!"

Abu Dis, Israel/Palestine Border

THE CLOUDS WERE THICK over the West Bank and everybody was thankful for the brief respite from the endless blazing heat of summer in the Middle East. Major Kushner approved. The rains weren't due for another month and the cooling shade added a festive touch to the milling throng filling the divided city.

Adjusting the compact, green, TAV assault rifle slung at her side, Major Adina Kushner of the Israeli Defense Forces inspected the decorative brick topping of the concrete barrier separating the city of Abu Dis. A single brick was missing from the array,

Walking along the edge of the scaffolding, the major breathed deeply, the smell of oranges from the nearby orchards almost overwhelming the traditional reek of gasoline fumes and camel dung.

On both sides of the concrete barrier, Abu Dis was filled with people, all of them singing, talking, praying, cursing, milling around and taking endless pictures. In spite of the concertina wire frothy on the ground, the Palestinian side of the wall was covered with graffiti and the Israeli side dotted with posters. The major sighed. Civilians! What could you do?

Situated on top of nearby buildings, television crews from around the world were already in place, their cameras sweeping the crowds on both sides of the concrete wall, doing background shots to be included into the news reports later. It seemed as if the entire world wanted to see the dedication ceremony of the wall. The famous wall. The hated wall. The "failing wall," as one BBC anchor had cleverly dubbed the barrier, the wordplay based upon the famous Wailing Wall of Jerusalem.

Started by another president of Israel right after the 9/11 al Qaeda attack on New York City in America, the wall was a desperate attempt to keep out the terrorist bombers that had plagued the West Bank, physically separating the nation of Israel from the Palestine territory. Although more and more people were simply calling it Palestine. These days, the hardcore Zion fundamentalists were grudgingly admitting that everybody deserved their own homeland.

Eight yards high, ten yards deep in places and 720 miles long, the imposing barrier had been built along the exact 1967 borders agreed upon by Israel and Palestine at the time. Of course, once Israel started building the wall, the Palestinians decried the construction in spite of the earlier accord. They took the matter to the World Court, which decided the construction should stop until the delicate political matter of whether the Palestinians should be forced to keep the treaties they signed was decided. Israel ignored the court order and continued building, although, they did change the borders ever so slightly so that the wall was a bit more on their property. The concession brought fury from the horde of Jewish settlers now trapped on the other side of the wall and from the few Palestinians still inside the barrier.

As a flight of Israel F-16-I jet fighters streaked by overhead, Major Kushner checked her wrist for the time, then looked at the position of the sun for confirmation. Only a few minutes to go. The wall had been finished for weeks, but this day was the ceremony of its completion. The last brick was to be officially laid today amid great fanfare, international press coverage and massive security. Why Abu Dis had been chosen for the ceremony, the major had no idea. Maybe because it was almost in the exact middle. Maybe not. Politics wasn't her forte.

Dressed in short pants and bulletproof vests, heavily armed Israeli soldiers moved through the crowd, smiling and polite, their sharp eyes checking everybody and everything.

A small child was delayed as the soldiers checked his shopping bag, but it proved to contain only foodstuffs and assorted sundries. A stumbling drunk was quietly escorted to a private room where the soldiers ascertained that the man really was intoxicated and that his bottle held whiskey, not nitroglycerin or some other form of dangerous liquid. A known terrorist was found photographing the scaffolding near the wall, and hit with a tranquilizer dart from a disguised camera held by a Mossad agent dressed as a taxicab driver. The unconscious man was caught by two pretty Mossad agents, who scolded their friend for being drunk in public, and the criminal was hauled away to a private interrogation room.

An elderly pickpocket tried working the crowd and, despite the massive security, actually got a couple of wallets from tourists before being apprehended. He willingly turned over the wallets, which were then surreptitiously returned to the owners, and the thief was thrown into a concrete cell for later trial.

Always in pairs, F-16-I jet fighters moved across the sky, while Yas'ur-class helicopter gunships hovered above the crowds, staying carefully out of range of the news cameras. Several of the huge helicopters were equipped for surveillance, while a few were armed to the teeth, their wings bristling with armament.

At strategic locations were brand-new Merkava-4 battle tanks; old Sho't army tanks stood guard at street corners. A dozen Zelda-class APCs full of troops patrolled both sides of the border. Radar swept the sky and chemical sniffers checked every bag for contraband. Video cameras swept through the crowd, relaying the scene to a massive bank of police computers in Tel Aviv where sophisticated software cross-referenced every face to a list of known terrorists. When one was spotted, he or she was deftly removed from the crowd for questioning. One man tried to escape and make a break for the hole in the wall, but was tackled by the soldiers guarding the entrance. Another pulled a grenade and was torn to pieces by concentrated gunfire from the silenced pistols of security forces.

Walking along the wall, Major Kushner reviewed everything. Flag poles adorned with the blue-and-white Israel flag flanked the platform on the north side of the wall, a precisely equal amount carrying the Palestinian flag on the south.

There was a podium with a speech prompter in place, and near the gap on top of the wall was a single brick lying on a white pillow like some ancient virgin sacrifice. Nearby was a battered bucket full of wet cement and a shiny golden trowel. All of which had been checked for bombs, poisons and anything else that could mar the ceremony or kill the PM.

At the base of the scaffolding was a full company of soldiers; six more in formal dress uniforms stood guard on the top of the platform. Only Kushner had no assigned post. She was the roving soldier ordered to walk everywhere, looking for trouble. But so far, so good. The military officer nodded in satisfaction. The area seemed secure. The Israeli Defense Force had done this sort of thing before, and there was nobody better. Everything that could be accomplished to secure the area had been already done in triplicate. This was an important occasion, and nobody was taking a chance of it turning into an international incident for some terrorist group out to grab some fast headlines.

Suddenly the radio receiver in her ear crackled with an announcement and a few seconds later, a civilian band, all in matching uniforms, swelled into the national anthem of the State of Israel. Just then, a motorcade of six armored limousines stopped in front of the scaffolding and the prime minister got out waving to the crowd, which roared in approval. Only a few people jeered the man's arrival, but their cries were lost in the overwhelming positive response. Cameras flashed continuously. Proceeding to the carpeted steps to the top of the platform, the PM moved to the podium and made the grand gesture of turning off the speech prompters. The people cheered in approval.

"On this historic day," the prime minister said softly into the microphone, the speakers amplifying his words until they boomed with biblical force across the entire city, "we lay the final brick in this modern day wall of Jericho. But unlike that ancient structure, this wall will be a symbol of peace and…"

The politician stopped as Major Kushner touched her earphone and frowned. On the ground, dozens of soldiers were charging around, the Zelda APCs began to disgorge armed soldiers as police vans started rolling toward the scaffolding, armed troops guiding civilians out of its way.

Removing a handkerchief from his pocket, the prime minister mopped his face and whispered to the officer, "Is there trouble?"

"Unknown, sir," Kushner replied. "But radar has picked up something odd."

"A missile?"

Scowling in concern, Kushner shook her head as lightning flashed in the cloudy sky.

Squinting into the clouds, the prime minster saw the flash again, but it seemed to come from the other side of the clouds and go right through to impact somewhere in the city only blocks away. But there was no explosion from a detonating warhead. He frowned at the sight. That didn't resemble a missile, rocket or a bomb. It didn't look like anything he knew.

Below the scaffolding, the crowd was growing nervous, its murmurs increasing in volume.

"Status report," Kushner snapped into her throat mike.

"Situation unknown," an IDF operative reported crisply. "Radar has something, or rather, they had something on the screens, but don't know what that was yet."

The flash came once more and something brighter than the sun smashed into the Palestinian side of the wall only a few yards from the platform. The concrete and bricks exploded in a geyser of destruction, the rubble flying for hundreds of yards into the air before raining upon the horrified crowds. A split second later a rolling thunder of a sonic boom arrived from the sky.

Turning to demand an answer this time, the prime minister was tackled by Kushner and she drove him to the floor, covering the politician with her body.

"Stay down!" she commanded, drawing a 9 mm Jericho pistol. "Control, I want air cover now! Do you read me, right now!"

"What's happening?" the prime minister gasped, his heart pounding in his chest.

The military officer didn't reply, but tilted her head as if listening to voices through her earphone. Clustered around the fallen politician, the honor guards had their assault rifles in hand, two of the soldiers thumbing 40 mm rounds into the grenade launcher attached beneath the barrels.

Everybody on the ground was screaming by now and running in panic on both sides of the barrier. Another flash of light and a second section of the wall exploded directly above the gate. The archway collapsed and dozens of civilians were crushed under the tons of falling masonry.

"Alert! We have civilians down at the Abu Dis gate!" Kushner reported, adjusting the transponder on her belt. "Convoy, I want a Merkava at the platform immediately! Get the PM out of here!"

"Confirm, battle tanks are on the way."

"What about the medics?"

"ETA, five minutes."

"Good. Where's our air cover?"

At that, a flight of F-16-I fighters streaked by and there came the dull heavy throb of a Yas'ur gunship. The tan-and-beige helicopter rose above the wall, then seemed to burst apart as another flash filled the air. The blades of the demolished craft spun free, skimming through the air in a blur, flying directly into a CNN camera crew. Bloody limbs sprayed everywhere.

Chaos reigned as sirens began to howl and more flashes rent the sky. A section of the wall exploded in a fast series of explosions. Rubble blew out like shrapnel and concrete dust clouded the atmosphere. Here and there machine guns chattered and another wing of jets streaked along the wall searching for the location of the enemy rockets or artillery emplacement. There was a burst of light and one of the jet fighters became a fireball above the city.

"Rockets, my ass, it's a goddamn meteor shower!" Kushner shouted into the throat mike, her ears ringing from the strident detonations. There was a tickling sensation on a cheek and she instinctively knew it was blood. "Repeat, this is not a terrorist attack! Not an attack! Meteors!"

"A what?" the voice in her ear demanded, confused.

Kushner started to reply when the clouds parted and a hail of brilliant flashes slammed into the wall. The noise was deafening. Debris shot out, smashing windows and peppering nearby buildings for blocks. Peals of thunder boomed, shrieks rent the air, weapons fired, a car exploded, a weakened building tilted and collapsed, sending up huge clouds of acrid dust. Now the major felt the ground shake with every triphammer blow. It felt like heavy bombing, but there was no report from distant cannons, only the sonic booms from the sky, then the savage hammering of the wall and helpless city. Dozens had to be dead, maybe hundreds. Where was the air cover?

Fiery darts rose suddenly from the horizon as the antiaircraft batteries and antimissiles answered the attack in a protective barrage. But it had no effect. The bright light bursts continued, the concussions growing to deafening proportions. Then they abruptly stopped. For a moment a thick silence covered the city. A cool breeze blew from the Palestinian side of the barrier, pushing the smoke and dust away to reveal a path of flattened destruction. Then the sirens, cries and gunfire returned with a vengeance.

"Move!" Kushner shouted, dragging the prime minster to his feet and shoving him toward the stairs.

As they hurried down the torn carpeting, avoiding the broken steps, Kushner could see that the entire section of the wall that went through the center of town was gone, reduced to smoking rubble.

"Incredible," a guard whispered.

Reaching the ground, Kushner shoved the prime minster toward the tank, and a Mossad agent helped the man inside. There were a dozen more of the agents nearby, their weapons drawn and hammers back. Kushner started to leave, but one of the men waved her inside and she obediently followed.

"Go!" a Mossad agent called down the hatch.

At the front of the armored vehicle, a driver started the massive diesels and the tank rumbled into motion.

"Are you all right, sir?" a Mossad agent asked, helping the politician to sit on a hard plastic seat. Her hands moved across the man, searching for wounds, but thankfully found nothing important.

"Hell, no. The Arabs are somehow going to blame us for this meteor strike," the prime minister proclaimed, brushing off his tattered clothing. "I don't know how, but they will."

"I always thought meteors burned up in the atmosphere," Kushner said with a frown, hanging on to a ceiling strap.

"Most disintegrate plummeting through the atmosphere, but not all," the tank commander stated. "The Gulf of Mexico was made by a meteor strike. As were all of the holes that make up the man on the moon."

Cradling a sore arm, the prime minister frowned. The officer was correct, yet this the strike had occurred just as the dedication ceremony began. No way that was a coincidence, which left one unnerving conclusion.

"I want a geologist," the prime minister announced, wiping dirt off his face.

"Sir?" Kushner asked, puzzled. Then she nodded. "Of course. Yes, sir." She touched her throat mike. "Control, we need a geologist with maximum security clearance at the grandstand immediately."

"A geologist?" a voice replied. "Did I hear that correctly?"

Kushner gave the prime minister a questioning look and he nodded.

"Confirm, control. A geologist. ASAP."

"Roger, we'll contact the university. Over."

Leaning to peer out a gunport, the prime minister scowled at the path of destruction cutting a swath through the borders of the two rival nations. Precisely, and exactly along the border, hammering the wall down to the ground for several city blocks. Buildings were riddled with shrapnel, streets smashed, cars burning, wounded people everywhere. A lot more laying motionless in the wrecked streets. The wreckage of a F-16-I jet fighter lay smoldering on the ground on the Israeli side of the crevice and a tank sat dead on the Palestinian side, an orange-hot hole in the roof armor clearly showing a direct hit from…whatever had done this.

"When the scientist arrives, have him check the residue at the bottom of each crater," the prime minister ordered brusquely. "Each and every single one."

"Why?" the Mossad agent asked bluntly.

"I don't think those were meteors," the politician stated.

CHAPTER TWO

Los Angeles, California

"Look, gentlemen, we can do this all night," the President of the United States said, lifting a carafe and pouring himself a cup of lukewarm coffee, "but I really don't think that—"

He stopped talking abruptly as the vice-president walked into the boardroom flanked by a cadre of grim-faced Secret Service agents.

"Sir, there is an important call for you from NORAD, sir," the VP said.

The President went still at the coded phrase. Any sentence that started and ended with the same word meant all hell had just broken loose somewhere.

"Sorry, gentlemen," the President said, wearily standing. "This is a matter of national security."

The gruff men in expensive suits murmured their understanding as the President left the room.

Moving along the corridor, a dozen Secret Service agents

closed around the President and more joined him from every doorway they passed. Soon, he was surrounded, and could no longer see where they were going. The leader of the United States had to simply follow wherever his bodyguards were leading.

Upon reaching the driveway, the Secret Service agents parted to reveal a line of identical black limousines, all of them with the exact same license plates. There were five of the vehicles, and the President was directed to the fourth in line. As he approached, the rear door opened and his personal assistant, Kevin Molendy, stepped out.

"This way, sir," he said, moving out of the way.

The man was wearing a bulletproof vest under his suit jacket, which was odd, but the President said nothing as he stepped into the limo and took a seat. Several people were waiting for him, four of them Secret Service agents. The rest were members of his Executive Council: Oswaldo "Oz" Fontecchio, his national policy adviser, as well as Hillary Hertzoff, his national security adviser, and Matthew Mingle, the current head of the CIA.

Thank goodness, Hal Brognola wasn't here, the President observed with a sigh. That would have meant real trouble.

As Molendy climbed inside, a Secret Service agent closed the door and the limo started to roll. The President knew that the vehicles wouldn't maintain formation, but rotate positions randomly, making it impossible for a sniper to know in which vehicle he was riding. An assassin would have to strike all of the limousines to even have a chance of success, and the plain black limos were all million-dollar cars, containing more armor than most light tanks, including the tires. Even if hit with a grenade, the rubber would blow off, but the limo would continue moving smoothly on the wide steel plates hidden inside.

"Okay, what happened?" the President asked as the limo took a corner.

"Sir, there has been an attack on the wall in Israel," Hertzoff said in clipped tones. It was as if every word was precious and she didn't want to waste any. "Hundreds are dead, perhaps more, with collateral damage in the millions."

"Missiles or car bombs?" the President queried.

Leaving his seat, Molendy opened a small wall panel and started making fresh coffee.

"Neither, sir. It was a meteor shower," Hertzoff replied.

"A what?" the President demanded as the smell of Jamaican Blue Mountain filled the air of the limousine. "A meteor shower?"

"Yes, sir. About a mile of the wall has been completely flattened in the border town of Abu Dis."

"A meteor shower," the President repeated slowly, leaning back in the seat. "How sure are you about that?"

"No confirmation as of yet, sir."

"And what does this have to do with the CIA?" he asked, accepting a steaming cup from the aide.

"We got a tip about the attack from an agent in Paris about ten minutes before it happened," Mingle answered with a frown. "The report said something about an attack on Abacus, or so we thought. It seemed like garbled data. Until Israel."

"And?" the President prompted. Then he frowned. "Wait a minute, wasn't the dedication ceremony supposed to be held today?"

"Yes, sir. Exactly."

No way in hell that was a coincidence. "Get the agent on the phone," the President commanded. "I want to talk to him direct."

Mingle shook his head. "Impossible, sir. He appears to have been terminated in what might have been enemy action."

"Appears? Might have been?" Fontecchio said, leaning forward in his seat. "Sir, the café was hit with flamethrowers and grenades! Twenty civilians are dead and the French government is furious!"

"We're checking further into the matter," Mingle replied smoothly.

"Did this meteor shower hit during the brick-laying ceremony, by any chance?" the President ventured as a guess.

Hertzoff nodded. "Yes, sir. Just as it began."

"Is the prime minister dead?"

"No, sir," Fontecchio answered. "Not a scratch. But the town is in shambles. The people are rioting and running back and forth across the border."

"The Israelis will stop that nonsense soon enough with some concertina wire," Fontecchio stated resolutely. "Not a problem."

"Good. I want a full report on the matter within the hour," the President snapped. "And contact the Joint Chiefs, I want our status raised to DefCon Three."

Fontecchio balked at that, but said nothing. DefCon One was peacetime, DefCon Five was war. After 9/11, the United States hadn't dropped below DefCon Two. Peace seemed to be a thing of the past, merely a notation on the war board, but nothing to do with the real world.

"Yes, sir," Fontecchio replied uncomfortably.

The passengers in the limo swayed slightly as the vehicle took a corner, the rear limo moving ahead of them as they dropped to a new position in the convoy.

Turning to his aide, the president asked, "Isn't there a ship christening tomorrow?"

"Yes, sir," Molendy answered without glancing at the personal computer sticking out of his pocket. "A new aircraft carrier will be launched from the San Diego naval shipyard."

"Don't cancel the ceremony," the President ordered. "Have the Secretary of Defense christen the ship."

"Yes, sir. And what should I tell the secretary?"

"Nothing."

"Yes, sir. And the press?"

"Same thing."

"No problem, sir."

"Then contact Space Defense, I want to know what's happening up there."

"NASA reports no unusual activity in space," Hertzoff reported. "If there was a meteor shower, it's over by now."

There came a soft buzzing and Molendy pulled out a cell phone. The device was huge, almost the size of a paperback book; it cost more than most small airplanes and contained some of the most sophisticated electronics in existence.

"White House," the aide said. Then he hit the mute button. "Sir, you have a call from a General Stone."

"Who?" Mingle muttered, his annoyance clearly discernable.

Placing down his empty coffee mug, the President took the phone. "Hello, General…yes, I…well, no…damn." Then the President was silent for a long time. "Okay, see you on the plane." As the line went dead, the President closed the lid on the cell phone, automatically scrambling the memory and sending a false signal to the White House library. There was no redial function on this cell phone. Especially not to Hal Brognola, head of the Sensitive Operations Group based at Stony Man Farm.

Molendy accepted the phone and tucked it away opposite his bulky journal.

"Is there a problem, sir?" Hertzoff asked in concern.

Trying to be casual, the President dismissed that with a wave. "Nothing of importance."

The others took that as a notice that the conference was over for the moment, and got on their own cell phones to check for any missed messages over the past ten minutes.

Outside the limo, police motorcycles rode along with the executive convoy, keeping people away from the line of limousines. Wherever the President went, traffic snarled and a major city ground to a halt for the duration of his visit. But his mind wasn't on maintaining good public relations right now. If Hal Brognola wanted a private meeting, then all hell had broken loose somewhere. Could be Paris or Israel. Maybe both.

Deep in thought, the President studied the city passing by outside, trying to recall the details of a scientific report he had read as a junior senator very long ago. Israel may have been hit by vaporware, something that was not supposed to exist. But very obviously did. Project Sky Hammer. If so, then nobody was safe, absolutely nobody, and there were going to be a lot more deaths real soon.

Pressing a button on the armrest, the President said, "Driver, maximum speed to the airport, please."

Instantly a siren started blaring from under the hood, and the convoy of limos surged with speed.

Computer Room, Stony Man Farm, Virginia

THE LARGE ROOM was very quiet, the air vents steadily exhaled a cool breeze and the silent keyboards made tiny patting noises from the hurried impact of fingers. A coffeemaker burbled at the kitchenette and muffled rock music could be heard coming from somewhere.

"What's this about a Thor?" Carmen Delahunt asked, lowering her glasses. "Okay, Aaron. Tell me we aren't looking at a Thor here. I remember reading about the project in a journal."

A virtual reality visor plugged into her console, ready to access the Internet anytime. But the million-dollar VR helmet was deactivated at the moment. After the Paris attack, the team had been looking for a possible traitor in the NSA or CIA. But then the attack on Israel occurred, and it had top priority.

Privately, Delahunt hoped the two incidences weren't directly linked.

Slim and well-built, the red-haired woman was a classic Irish beauty, but she was also one of the elite, the four Cyberwizards who composed the cybernetic division of Stony Man Farm. Her desk console was directly attached to the bank of Cray supercomputers under Stony Man's direct control.

"The display is coming up now," Aaron "The Bear" Kurtzman called from the small kitchenette along the wall, where he was filling his coffee mug.

Sipping and wheeling at the same time, he rolled back to his console, the chair fitting snugly underneath.

The console had several monitors. A few of them were dark, but the rest were busy scrolling with news reports from every agency in the world.

Impatient, Kurtzman tapped one monitor with a screen saver. Why was the file taking so long? Instantly the wooden glen disappeared to show the status of the top-secret download. Ah, here we go, almost downloaded from archives now.

"Okay, heads up," Kurtzman announced, tapping his keyboard.

Everybody else stopped whatever he or she was doing and paid attention.

"I'm afraid you're right, Carmen. The name of the thing is Project Sky Hammer," Kurtzman said as the big monitor at the front of the room came to life.

The plasma screen pulsed with light a few times, then cleared into a view of starry space, the blue-white globe of Earth low in the corner. The technical data flowed past the screen, showing power curves, field strengths and striking power. That end of the data nearly went off the chart. The Stony Man cyber team read the flowing data carefully.

Back in 1977, a research scientist named Dr. Gerald Mahone started thinking about weapons and what part of a bomb actually caused death and destruction. It wasn't the metal casing or even the shrapnel inside. As an example, he suggested taking a bullet and throwing it at somebody. A steel-jacketed, hollow point, .357 Magnum round would simply bounce off his or her chest and fall to the floor. The bullet, the casing, the metal, wasn't deadly, per se. It was the amount of force behind the projectile that made it deadly.

Anything was lethal if it moved fast enough. There were

hundreds of recorded cases where a tornado had driven a piece of straw into a telephone pole, or done the same thing with a bottle cap and a brick wall. Speed, raw velocity, made objects dangerous.

The space race was still strong back in the seventies, and America had been locked in a deadly struggle for supremacy with the Soviet Union. New weapons were needed all the time. So Mahone did some basic calculations and invented the Thor.

The idea was simple, as good ones usually were. Take a plain steel rod, eight feet long and twelve inches in diameter. Add a couple of inexpensive steering rockets, cheap wings and a limited-capability computer. The whole thing wouldn't have cost more than a couple hundred dollars.

Now place hundreds of these "spears" into orbit. A floating cloud of destruction waiting to be unleashed. When enemy forces were spotted, targeting information was sent to as many of the Thors as you needed to commit to the attack, and they would obediently jet out of space and into the atmosphere, constantly accelerating down the gravity hit, growing hotter and hotter from the friction with the atmosphere, until finally a white-hot, molten ball of steel moving at Mach Two arrived. There were few tanks, ships or gunnery emplacements of the time period that could have withstood the thundering impact of even a single Thor.

Even better, because of its speed and steep trajectory, a Thor should be impossible for missiles to track and blow out of the sky. The Thor was a cheap, deadly, unstoppable superweapon.

With a few flaws Space travel was still expensive back in

the seventies, and there was no way to accurately give a Thor the precise location of a target. It was quite possible that a swarm of Thors might drift off course and slam into your own tanks, annihilating your own troops instead of the enemy's.

The project was given the code name, Sky Hammer, and shelved in the deep top secret archives of the Pentagon. It was brilliant, but not feasible using technology of the time.

"So that's what we're facing," Kurtzman said, turning off the screen. "Sky Hammer, a plain piece of molten steel falling from high orbit. The only things holding back the project before were the cost of space travel and the inability to accurately pinpoint a target. But a dozen nations have relatively cheap access to space these days, dirt cheap if they use an illegal version of the new Spaceship One rocket plane, and with a Global Positioning Device—GPD—bought off the shelf of any electronics store…" The man shrugged. "You've seen the results."

"Everything old is new again," Huntington "Hunt" Wethers muttered, scowling.

"Son of a bitch," Delahunt whispered, reviewing the material again on her console. "And this is what hit Israel, a Thor."

"More likely it was several of them," Akira Tokaido stated grimly.

"Please bring up the TV news coverage of the wall," Kurtzman requested, taking a sip of coffee. "I want to check something."

Delahunt hit a macro and the CNN report appeared in a window within the view of space and started to play again.

"Hold," Kurtzman said after a minute, and the scene froze. "There, look at that."

Frowning, Wethers removed his pipe from his mouth. "The wall wasn't blown up, it was smashed down."

"Hit from above," Kurtzman growled.

Wethers turned to Tokaido. "Better check to see if anybody is looking for a geologist at one of Israel's universities."

"To analyze the residue at the bottom of the crater?" Tokaido asked. "Yeah, makes sense. And that is the only way to know for sure, isn't it?"

"Sadly, yes," Wethers replied. "If there is a lot of pure steel down there…"

"But why did they wait until the ceremony started?" Delahunt wondered out loud. "Just to kill the prime minister? But they missed him." Her head snapped up. "Paris!"

Biting back a curse, Kurtzman remembered the dying words of the NSA agent. He had said something about a new weapon for sale on the black market. Whoever was behind this had hit the wall as an advertisement. They probably announced in advance what was going to happen on the international arms market, and now that it had occurred right on schedule, they could start taking orders. With enough of them, anything could be smashed down by a Thor. Anything. The White House, Cheyenne Mountain, Hoover Dam… The targets were limitless and completely vulnerable. There wasn't a defensive system in existence that could stop a Thor. Nothing. Only solid bedrock—and a lot of it.

"A Thor could crush the Farm, and we couldn't do a damn thing except die," Tokaido said softly, glancing at the ceiling. There were only white foam tiles in sight, but in his mind the sky was falling at exactly thirty-two feet per second….

"Okay, how do we stop it?" Delahunt asked.

Kurtzman sighed. "We can't. The old figures were correct. Not a missile or antimissile, or antimissile laser can track and lock on to a Thor fast enough to do any significant damage."

"Then we have to go after the people controlling it. That's the vulnerable point, the operators."

"Yes," Kurtzman said, glancing at the world map. "Where they are."

"If this news hits the airwaves and Internet, there's going to be a worldwide panic," Wethers stated bluntly. "A Sky Hammer alert would make the Cuban missile crisis look like an ice-cream social! Thousands of people will die in the riots when they try to reach subway tunnels, bomb shelters, anything underground."

"And none of those would protect them."

"Exactly."

"It's possible that we might have to shut down the Net," Kurtzman stated. "Akira, prepare to arm the nexus point C-4 charges."

The young man stopped what he was doing and got busy. The entire Internet was relayed though sixteen junction points. If those were blown up, the Internet was gone, possibly for months. That would cause a loss of billions of dollars to corporations, and nobody had the authorization to do that but the Secretary General of the UN. And very illegally, Stony Man Farm. It had taken them months to get the firing commands for the remote charges, and even then, they'd had to have a field team infiltrate each nexus to add their own control elements. This was something they had talked about for years in dread. Blowing the Internet was a doomsday option, a last-ditch effort to hold back the news that could cause the death of countless people. Nobody sane wanted to undertake this action, but the cyberteam had to be ready. Just in case. On the other hand, if the news got on the cable news shows, then the cat was out of the bag and all hell would break loose anyway, and there really wasn't anything they could do about that event.

"Could Sky Hammer smash down the junction points?" Wethers asked suddenly.

Kurtzman nodded. "If the people controlling it know the locations, yes."

"I'll start a disinformation campaign about this," Delahunt said, slipping on her VR helmet. The best way to hide the truth was to bury it under half-truths and lies. With enough misleading rumors circulating, nobody would ever believe that Sky Hammer existed.

Kurtzman grabbed a telephone on his console. "Barbara? It's worse than we feared…yes, a Thor. It's got to be. We better recall the teams immediately. This is going to get real bad, real fast."

"I have them located," Wethers said, working a mouse.

The main screen switched to a map of the world, two glowing blue stars marking the precise location of the Stony Man field teams. They were on opposite sides of the globe.

Kurtzman hung up the phone. "Okay, Barbara is calling Hal, and we have recall authorization. Bring 'em back."

"We can't," Wethers stated. "See? They are both under radio silence."

"Why?"

"They found their targets much sooner than expected and have engaged the enemy."

Kurtzman narrowed his gaze. Damn! The teams were wasting valuable time taking out these minor dangers to America when the sky was literally about to fall down on everybody. Hours wasted. Time gone. Time they didn't have to spare.

Kurtzman clamped his mouth shut. He knew the current enemy action was merely "cleanup," but if the teams were in the middle of a firefight, any distraction at exactly the wrong moment could get all of them killed. There was nothing to do but wait, wait for them to finish the missions they were on.

"Come on, guys, shake a leg," Kurtzman whispered. "Move it."

CHAPTER THREE

Chicago, Illinois

The classic rock music of Peter Frampton was blaring over the wall speakers of the control booth. Lost in thought, the blurry DJ was staring out the window of the Sears Tower, and it took quite a while before he finally noticed the jingling instrument.

"Yellow!" he drawled, removing the handrolled cigarette from his mouth. The smoke was sweet and pungent, and highly illegal. "This is WQQQ, all radio, all the time. What can I do for you?"

"Pay close attention, Jew, or everybody dies," a garbled voice spoke.

The DJ went very still at that and dropped the joint into a nearly empty beer bottle on the sound board. It hissed out of existence.

"What did you just say?" he asked, flipping a switch to record the conversation. Having worked his way up through the ranks, the DJ had started in the news department and knew the sound of a scrambled voice when he heard it. Lots of kooks and nuts called up stations proclaiming everything imaginable, from women sighting Elvis on a UFO, to men claiming to be an alien's baby. But nobody ever had the coin to get a voice scrambler. That alone meant big bucks, and money plus crazy always spelled trouble.

"I said shut the fuck up, Moses, or we'll bomb your little shithole of a station just to make the other kike radio stations pay attention. Understand?"

In the control booth, a union technician perked up in his chair at the sound of the voice, and quickly started punching numbers into a red phone dedicated for outside calls only. The DJ tried to wave the man from calling the police, but the engineer paid him no attention.

"My apologies, sir," the DJ muttered. They thought the radio station was Jewish? The owner of the radio station was a Norwegian, Dave Linderholm, and he had no idea who owned the Sears Tower.

A crackle of static and the voice returned.

"Mind your betters, pig. Now, the wall in Palestine was destroyed by the American Liberation Strike Force," the distorted voice continued. "And we…"

"Do you mean, the wall in Israel?" the DJ asked, confused.

"Shut up! There is no such country!" The phone crackled. "All of that land belongs to Palestine!"

"Even the parcels they sold to the Jews?" the DJ asked quickly, pointedly trying to egg the caller into saying something that would be banned on the air. That always helped the ratings, and sweeps week was coming up.

"Zion propaganda! Now, unless American ZOG pulls all

of its troops back to U.S. soil, our next target will be the UN building!" There was a click and the line went dead.

Quickly shoving another recorded cassette of early heavy metal into the board, the DJ rushed into the engineering booth.

"What a freaking loon," the DJ exhaled, running nervous fingers through his wavy crop of hair. "Did we get everything?"

"Loud and clear." The engineer smiled, patting a digital CD recorder on the board. "By the way, what's a ZOG?"

"Zionist Occupation Government."

"What's Zionist?"

"Tell ya later. Did we get a trace on the call?" the DJ asked hopefully, looking at the bewildering display of read-outs, gauges, lights and meters. He was the talent, not a freaking atomic brain.

"Sure. It's useless." The engineer sighed. "The call came from a rest stop on Route 95, outside of Camden, right over the river in New Jersey."

Clever. Stop your car, make the call, drive away before anybody can get there.

"Could it have been a fake phone location?"

"For people with a voice scrambler? Sure." The engineer leaned back in his chair, the springs squeaking in protest. "So what now? Call the news director, or do we sell this directly to CNN?"

"We?" the DJ asked, stressing the word.

"I have the only tape, dude," the engineer said, patting the recording machine.

The DJ glared at the machine, then shrugged. "Fifty-fifty?"

"Done." The engineer grinned, extended a hand, and the two men shook.

"So who would you call?" the DJ smiled.

"The FBI, man," the engineer stated with a wave. "These crank yankers might be the real thing."

The DJ laughed, then he heard the reverberating drum roll of a Metallica song fading away and rushed back to his board to shove in a commercial for acne cream. When it was over, he shoved in the longest running song he could find, which bought him thirty minutes. Time to contact CNN and get a big check!

Heading back to the engineering booth, the DJ paused at the sight of the 9/11 wall poster of the Twin Towers. Vaguely he seemed to remember that everybody had lots of hint and clues about the forthcoming attack, but nobody had told the FBI.

"Aw, shit." the DJ sighed and picked up a phone. "Hello, Operator? Please give me the phone number for the Philadelphia division of Homeland Security." He paused. "Yes, ma'am, this is an emergency."

"What are you doing?" the engineer demanded, horrified, rushing out of the booth.

"Doing the right thing. We're ratting these assholes out, and I hope Homeland puts 'em in a cell down in Gitmo. With extra rolls of film."

The engineer rolled his eyes heavenward. "That guy on the phone was right. You're an idiot."

"That may be," the DJ said, feeling oddly patriotic. "But if you have any porn on the computer, better start purging. Homeland might check it out, and this dump needs you."

"Sure, who else would work for these wages?" The engineer snorted rudely. Then he returned to the booth and started hastily accessing files on the station's PC to delete them like crazy.

Trevose, Pennsylvania

"WHAT IS A ZOG?" Zdenka Salvai asked as her commander got behind the steering wheel.

"Something Nazis talk about," Bella Tokay replied, tucking away the voice scrambler, then starting the stolen car.

The vehicle had been obtained outside of a strip club on Admiral Wilson Boulevard in Camden, located just over the bridge from Philadelphia. Few people told friends that they were going to a strip club, thus they were safe to kill. The owner of the vehicle wouldn't be missed for a long time. Perhaps days. Eventually his body would be found; a corpse inside a plastic garbage bag soon filled it with fumes, and the bags often popped like balloons. It wasn't the optimum way of disposing of a body, but it was sufficient for today. They needed only a few hours.

The redhead lit a fresh cigarette. "I hate Nazis," she stated, puffing out every word. Her long fingers were stained yellow from the constant cigarettes and her teeth were the same. But few men ever noticed that, their vision rarely rising above her ample cleavage. Between her knees was a large object covered with a blanket. Some sort of metallic hose could be seen sticking out from underneath, and there was the faint smell of jellied gasoline.

Tokay laughed. "As do we all," he agreed, releasing the brake and heading north on Route 1. Bethlehem was far away, but they had plenty of time. On the seat next to the man was a newspaper, the checkered grip of a compact machine gun barely visible beneath it.

"Think they will take the bait?" Petrov Delellis asked from the rear seat. Cradling a bulky X-18 grenade launcher, the giant Hungarian seemed to fill the back of the sedan. There was a clean new bandage on the side of his neck, a gift from the stubborn CIA agent in Paris. A goodbye gift.

"Of course they'll take the bait," Tokay replied smugly, steering around a flatbed truck hauling steel beams. "And they'll waste precious time chasing us around, until the Castle is obtained, and then the boss lets us kill them."

"We can't kill them now?" Salvai said with a scowl.

Tokay smiled, cold and mercilessly. "Well, maybe one or two," he answered.

Sandy Hook, New Jersey

AS GRIM AS EXECUTIONERS, Able Team strode out of the rolling smoke screen, firing their weapons at every step. Ricochets zinged and threw sparks along the concrete wall separating the parking lot from the little museum, and people with guns ducked behind the stout barrier.

Still bodies sprawled everywhere on the asphalt between the rows of cars, including a state trooper without a face, a 9 mm HK pistol still in his hand, unfired. A former Los Angeles cop himself, Carl "Ironman" Lyons felt a visceral surge of rage at the sight, but controlled his temper for the moment and kept going. The dead and the dying didn't matter right now. Only killing the terrorist bastards who had invaded the beachfront park.

Unfortunately, Able Team had no counterattack plan, no clever tactics or fancy maneuvering. The numbers had fallen, and the three counterterrorists had arrived too late to stop the deadly assault on the vacation spot. Now all they could do was a full-frontal charge with guns blazing.

Moving from vehicle to vehicle, the three Stony Man operatives maintained a steady cover fire with their assault rifles and shotguns. Circling a bread truck, they caught one of the Red Star agents in the process of reloading his AK-47 rifle. The arming bolt had jammed, probably from overheating. The Chinese agent cursed at their sudden appearance and dropped the Kalashnikov to claw for a Norinco pistol at his side.

"Don't do it, bub," Hermann "Gadgets" Schwarz warned, leveling his M-16 assault rifle.

But if the Chinese agent understood the words, he made no sign, and the deadly Norinco .45 barely cleared leather when Gadgets sent a wreath of tumblers across the man's chest. The Red Star agent was thrown backward against a car, shattering the side windows with his splayed arms. Gurgling into death, the agent slid to the asphalt, leaving a trail of red across the car. But Able Team was already on the move, constantly trying to stay ahead of the terrorists. A split second later, a Chinese-made RPG streaked out from behind the souvenir kiosk and the Buick erupted into a fireball from the white phosphorus rounds.

Popping up from behind a concrete wall near the public restrooms, a Chinese operative fired a long burst from his machine gun, riding the chattering weapon in a tight figure-eight pattern for maximum killpower. The cars in the parking lot were torn apart by the hellstorm of incoming lead, windshields exploding, hoods buckling, tires bursting, and finally a stray ricochet got a gas tank and a compact car violently detonated into a fireball, spraying shrapnel across a dozen other vehicles.

Taking a stance, Schwarz pumped a shell from the M-203 mounted under the barrel of his M-16. The bomb tracked perfectly, arching high to land on the other side of the concrete seawall. The Red Star agents scattered as thick volumes of smoke rose from the hissing charge. But a salty warm breeze was blowing in from nearby coast, already thinning the protective cover.

"On three," Lyons said, readying the Atchisson autoshotgun in his arms. He had only a single 40 round drum with him, so every shot had to count. He hadn't been expecting a firefight! "Okay…three!"

The men broke around another SUV, got onto the dented hood of a station wagon and jumped to the top of the seawall. Two Red Star agents were crouching behind the barrier, their weapons aimed for the open section ten feet away, obviously waiting in ambush.

"Hey," Rosario "The Politician" Blancanales said softly.

The Communists started to turn and Able Team cut them down. Hopping to the terrazzo flooring, Lyon found a few more civilian bodies, mostly guards. Older out of shape men in clean uniforms, holstered revolvers at their side. This had been a part-time job for them, just something to help stretch their meager retirement pay.

On the nearby beach the corpses of several joggers dotted the shoreline, their blood still staining the waves as they washed over the still forms, giving them a horrible mockery of life.

"Look over there," Lyons told his teammates.

Through the thinning smoke, the men could see the long barrels of the old WWII cannons rising above the small museum and fast-food stand.

Originally, Sandy Hook had been a large brick tower resembling a lighthouse, a stony keep equipped with muzzle-loading cannons to attack any Imperial British frigates harrowing the guerrilla fighters in the Revolutionary War. During World War II, it became a concrete fortress armed with banks of sixteen-inch cannons that could blow open the hull of any German warship. During the cold war underground installation had been added and Sandy Hook became a Minute Man missile base, designed to knock down Soviet ICBMs. Sandy Hook had long been a bastion of defense for the east coast of the nation, and had seen a lot of fighting, including an invasion of German frogmen near the middle of World War II, saboteurs sent to blow phone lines, collapse bridges, burn down hospitals and movie theaters, and generally inflict as much harm and terror as possible upon the American people. Softening tactics for Hitler. A prelude to invasion. Paving the way. The big guns of Sandy Hook had fired upon the midnight invaders just as they got out of the rubber rafts, and not a Nazi agent reached American soil alive. Or even in one piece.

But that was sixty years ago. These days, the Minute Man missile base had been moved inland, away from the vulnerable beach, and the gigantic cannons had been disarmed, the barrels blocked with a concrete plug, the hydraulic lines removed, the firing pins gone. Once the guardians of the United States, the cannons were reduced to slightly rusty exhibits on public display, relics of the past standing alongside a small outside museum that told of the glory days, with a small gift shop. But the Pentagon Theoretical Danger Team had postulated there was a potential terrorist danger to New York at Sandy Hook. Long ago, when the cannons worked, they had a range of twelve miles, and Manhattan was just over the horizon, nine miles away. But the titanic weapons had been neutralized, disarmed, virtually disassembled. It would take a major undertaking to get them live again. So the Pentagon had placed the museum on the Watch Alert list and then promptly forgot about the place entirely. It was too nebulous a threat to be taken seriously.

Suddenly two men in greasy mechanic's coveralls appeared on the roof of the restrooms building and started firing assault rifles. Able Team dived for cover behind a painted wooden bench and came up returning fire. The chattering M-16 assault rifles held by Blancanales and Schwarz peppered the structure, driving the enemy under cover. When the firing stopped, they popped back and Lyon's Atchisson sprang into action. In a bull roar, the weapon discharged 12-gauge shotgun shells in a long burst. The Chinese agents were literally blown apart, their bodies shattered from the hellstorm of steel buckshot.

Even before the corpses tumbled to the ground, Able Team was on the move again.

Early that morning, the first indication that something was amiss had been a radiation sensor hidden in a tollbooth plaza on the Garden State Parkway. Considered the finest road in the world, the GSP actually received visitors from foreign countries to study its construction so that the builders could return to their homelands and try to duplicate the modern marvel. Tourists from New Jersey visiting Portugal, Argentina or Australia often found themselves experiencing déjâ vu as they encountered an exact duplicate of the New Jersey road cutting through the rolling hills of a foreign landscape.

When the cars stopped to pay the toll, one of many along the rather expensive GSP, every vehicle was probed for contraband. Chemical sniffers found a lot of drugs and sometimes a corpse in the trunk. But this day the hidden sensors spiked as weapons-grade plutonium was detected coming off Exit 9.

Quickly, computer records were checked, but since there was no record of such a radioactive source coming onto the superhighway, the state police tagged the report as a possible glitch. The police filed a copy of the report with Homeland Security and a minute later Stony Man knew about it. Since Exit 9 was dangerously close to Sandy Hook, Barbara Price had sent Able Team to do a recon. When the men arrived, they'd expected to find an ore truck full of pitchblende, or maybe a mobile health clinic. Portable X-ray machines used radioactive thulium and often set off detectors by mistake.

Instead, Able Team had discovered a parking lot full of dead tourists and an empty truck that had been full of greasy machinery. But not anymore. Grabbing weapons out of the back of their van, the team got hard and moved in fast. They didn't like the combination of murder, Sandy Hook and radiation. There was such a thing as nuclear artillery shell....

"Any heat?" Lyons demanded, checking the Atchisson on the run. He wished there were reloads for the hungry weapon, half of the shells were already gone, and this battle was barely ten minutes old.

"Bet your ass, there is," Schwarz said, firing a burst into some bushes. Leaves flew, but nobody tumbled out dead. Stealth wasn't a concern, the Red Star agents knew they were here. Schwarz was the electronics expert for the team, and his wristwatch was also a short-range Geiger counter. However, loud clicks during a battle could get a soldier killed, so instead the device vibrated as a warning. At the moment, it was going wild.

"They must be arming the shell," Blancanales repeated, pausing to roll a dummy grenade into the gift shop.

Inside the building, men cursed in Chinese and came bursting out, firing their weapons. Already in position, Able Team caught the Red Star agents in a withering cross fire and they died to a man.

Then a man and woman stumbled into view from around a corner. The man was carrying a wicker basket and the woman was holding a baby swaddled in blankets in her arms. Neither one was Chinese, they looked more Italian than anything else.

"Don't shoot!" the man yelled, stepping in front of his wife. "Please! I'll pay you whatever you want!"

"It's a trick!" Blancanales cried, raising his M-16.

Dropping the blanket, the snarling woman pulled a compact SDMG machine pistol from inside the plastic doll and started firing. Blancanales blew her away just as the man swung a Skorpion machine gun from behind his back. Schwarz shot the man in the chest to no effect, then Lyons triggered the Atchisson, the maelstrom of double-aught stainless-steel buckshot removing his face and opening the throat and lower belly like a can of spaghetti. Already dead, the Chinese operative spun, his hands instinctively tightening on the weapon, the deadly Skorpion spraying lead randomly as he toppled to the ground. Ricochets went everywhere and Schwarz grunted as a slug hit him in the stomach.

"Goddamn mercs," he muttered, rubbing his stomach. "The guy must have been wearing body armor."

"Still hurts like a bitch," Lyons stated, hefting the Atchisson. Only a few cartridges remained. After that, he was down to grenades and his pistol.

"Bet your ass it does," Blancanales agreed, checking their flank. Even the titanium and Teflon NATO body armor that the team wore under their shirts still occasionally broke bones when hit by large-caliber weaponry. But a week in hospital was preferable to eternity in the grave.

"Better bed than dead," Schwarz quipped. "Hey, how'd you know it was a trap?"

"She was holding the baby wrong. The kid would have been dead from strangulation the way she was doing it."

"Cover me," Lyons said, knotting a handkerchief around his face. Going to the museum, he checked the door for boobytraps, then swept inside, the Atchisson at the ready.

The place was a shambles, with two whimpering women bound and gagged in the corner. Hostages for the enemy agents to use as bargaining chips if necessary. He had expected something like that. Able Team had fought Red Star before.

Pulling out a knife, Lyon advanced upon them. The older woman fainted while the pretty teenager tried to wiggle away. With a slash, the ex-cop cut ropes from their wrists. Stunned, the teen looked at her freed wrists and then at Lyons, comprehension dawning in her face.

"Don't y'all worry none, ma'am, " he drawled, affecting a thick Texas accent. "We're Delta Force." Sheathing the blade, he snapped an ammonia capsule under the nose of the unconscious woman. She fluttered immediately and then awoke, recoiling in horror.

"It's okay, Mom!" the teenager said, pulling down her gag. "They're the U.S. Marines."

"Really?" the older woman squeaked, having trouble breathing.

"United States' Special Forces," Lyons corrected with a brief grin. "Now, y'all follow me outside. Quick, now."

With joyful tears on her cheeks, the teenager nodded agreement and slipped an arm under the other woman to leverage her off the floor.

"My husband…" the mother started.

Not having found anybody else alive, Lyons looked at the woman and said nothing for a long moment that seemed to last forever. The middle-aged lady went a little pale, then nodded in understanding.

"What about my daddy?" the teen asked, a quaver in her voice.

The mother touched her daughter on the shoulder. "Let's go," she said in a calm tone. "Now, dear, no time to waste."

Going to the door, Lyons whistled sharply. There came an answering whistle and he led the way outside. Schwarz and Blancanales were standing guard near the stairs to the beach, both of them with handkerchiefs tied around their faces.

"Thank you, all," the mature woman gasped, the cloth strip that had been used as a gag hanging around her throat.

"You're welcome," Blancanales said. "Now get!" Turning, he fired a burst at the open sea.

Livid, the two women jerked at the noise, turned and took

off at a run. Soon they lost their high heels and continued barefoot much faster.

"Alone?" Schwarz asked, glancing sideways.

Lyons pulled down his mask. "Husband."

"Damn."

"Let's finish this," Blancanales stated, starting toward the stairs that led to the outside exhibit.

But then he paused. The cannons were no longer visible rising from behind the museum, and just then the floor shook as heavy machinery buried below the ground came to life.

Without a word, Able Team charged. They still had a hundred feet of open ground to cover to reach the guns.

"WHAT IS HAPPENING, comrade?" the mechanic asked, both hands busy in the guts of the hydraulic pump. New lines were attached to the feed and snaked out the door to the middle cannon. More Red Star agents were installing the new firing pin into the weapon, and off by himself, the Beijing technician was unpacking a single artillery shell from a lead-lined picnic cooler.

"Nothing that concerns you," the colonel snapped, sweeping the sand dunes with a pair of powerful binoculars. "Get back to work."

"Yes, Commander."

The colonel knew that everything was going well, but was still unhappy. The parking lot had been cleared of civilians and the museum taken without losing a single man of his cell. The telephones were all disconnected in case they had missed somebody hiding somewhere, and the repairs on the guns were nearly completely. All well and good. But the colonel didn't like the fact that there was smoke rising from several locations. However, that might have been done to hide the police taking defensive positions, rather than to offer cover for advancing troops. It was highly unlikely that any of the American Special Forces could have arrived yet. This whole mission had been accelerated to lightning speed. Never pause, never rest, go fast, and the lazy Americans would trip over the red tape of their own government.

"Done," the mechanic said, laying down his wrench and throwing a freshly greased lever.

A light flashed, there was a snap of electricity, and the motor room concrete bunker shook slightly as a pair of ancient motors rumbled into life. The meters on the housing flickered alive, and the guns began to move as the hydraulic pressure reached functional status.

"Excellent." The colonel smiled. "Well done, Comrade." Then, drawing a pistol, he shot the startled man in the heart. The body limply collapsed onto the hydraulic hoses, the red blood pumping to spread along the lines between the tiles of the floor.

The colonel gave the corpse a salute, then holstered the pistol. At least the mechanic died well, from an honest Chinese bullet, rather than vomiting his intestines like the fools at the United Nations would soon be doing. The death of that many hundreds of diplomats would throw the world into chaos, and China had carefully laid out plans to take every advantage of the political turmoil. Every member of his cell knew this was to be a suicide assignment. There was no hope of returning home. Glory would be only earned if they accomplished the mission, so they would succeed or die trying.

By now, a man at the cannon was frantically turning guiding wheels to alter the elevation, while a second checked a compass in his hand.

"Left twelve degrees!" he commanded. "Hold! Now, up ten degrees! Hold!" He turned. "We're on target, Comrade."

Smiling, the colonel stuck his thumbs in his belt. "Load the shell!" he ordered.

Slowly the technician from Beijing stood, holding the artillery shell as if it were a priceless artifact.

A burly Red Star agent worked the latch and swung aside the breech to make ready. But there came an odd rattling noise from the cannon, as if something had broken loose and was moving freely.

Furious, the colonel advanced closer as three grenades rolled out of the open end of the cannon and landed on the sandy ground.

"Run!" a man screamed, turning to flee when the grenades exploded.

Thundering flame and hot shrapnel filled the area, teeth and broken limbs flying into the air as the hydraulic lines ruptured and pressurized red oil rose like blood from a cut artery. Not yet locked into position, the cannon impotently lowered its muzzle until pointing at the empty beach.

The colonel barely had time to react when the men of Able Team arrived, firing as they climbed over the seawall at different points. The last few Red Star agents collapsed, trying to fire their AK-47 assault rifles in response, but only getting off a few short bursts before falling on top of their weapons.

Pulling his pistol, the colonel shot the Beijing technician before he was torn apart by the incoming American lead, the hardball ammo going through the man to ricochet off the wall behind. As the technician dropped, he let go of the shell and it rolled across the sandy platform to bounce down a sand dune and come to a stop on the beach near some driftwood.

DROPPING A SPENT CLIP, Schwarz reloaded while the others stood guard. Then Blancanales replaced his exhausted clip as Lyons shouldered the empty autoshotgun and drew a .357 Colt Python from his belt. Moving to the edge of the gunnery bastion, Schwarz hopped down to the beach and walked over to the Chinese artillery shell lying near the water line.

"Clear?" Blancanales asked, looking around.

"Clear," Lyons confirmed.

"Oh, shit," Schwarz cursed, sitting on the piece of driftwood. "We're in trouble."

Weapons out, Blancanales and Lyons rushed over. By the time they arrived, Schwarz had already ripped open a Velcro pouch at his side and was placing electrical tools on the damp sand.

"What's wrong?" Lyons asked. "That thing can't possibly be live."

"Oh yeah, the shell is live," Schwarz said in a flat monotone. "The damn thing is designed to arm itself after a set number of revolutions after it spirals out a cannon."

"Rolling down the sand dune did the same thing?"

"Apparently so."

"Shit!"

"My word exactly."

"What can we do?" Blancanales said, leveling his M-16 at the shell. It was standard U.S. Army procedure that in case of a nuclear emergency, shoot the bomb. Once the uranium sphere was distorted, even slightly, the device could no longer detonate. One shot and the artillery shell would be dead. The same as Able Team after about ten days of slow dying by radiation poisoning.

"Your call, Hermann," Lyons said, aiming the .357 Colt Python at the red-and-green-striped shell.

"Make me a hole," Schwarz ordered, sorting through the tools.

Blancanales fired a burst from the M-16 at the beach, chewing a depression into the sand. Schwarz gently placed the shell into the hole and packed the loose sand around it.

Sitting on the damp ground, the electronics wizard wrapped his legs around the bomb to hold it tight and started working in the recessed side bolts.

"Thought you were supposed to go in through the top," Lyons said, watching his friend work on the nuclear charge. An explosion on the beach would boil the ocean for a hundred feet, the radioactive steam contaminating a hundred miles of New Jersey, killing thousands of people. There couldn't be a worse place to set off a nuke than the sea! His hand tightened on the checkered grip of his revolver. Three die, or three thousand. Hell, that was an easy choice. Another ounce of pressure on the trigger was all it would take to get the job done.

"The top? Not this model," Schwarz said, both hands busy. A sharp snap of breaking metal and Lyons and Blancanales both jumped slightly. The men held their breath as their teammate slid the casing off the nose of the bomb, exposing the complex internal mechanism.

"All the wires are the same color," Blancanales said with a scowl. "How the hell will you know which one to cut?"

Jamming his knife deep into the device, Schwarz stopped a tiny flywheel from spinning, then ripped out a handful of wires.

"Just got to know what you're doing," he said, casting away the circuits. "Whew, that was close!"

"Too close, brother." Blancanales sighed, raising the assault rifle. "You sure it's dead?"

"Oh, yeah. Deader than disco."

"Good."

"I happen to like disco." Lyons chuckled in relief. Touching his throat, the big man activated the radio link. "Stony Bird to Nest, all clear. We found a hot egg, but it will not hatch. Repeat, the egg is dead. What was that?" He frowned. "Roger, on the way."

"Take the bomb, we'll store it in our lead safe on the van," Lyons directed, startling briskly for the parking lot.

"We've been recalled to the Farm," Schwarz stated, lifting the core of the bomb out of the shell. It wasn't a question.

"Yep." Softly in the background, police sirens could be heard coming this way. The covert team paid no attention. Then the noise abruptly stopped.

"Sounds like they were also recalled," Blancanales said, glancing at the exposed workings on the mechanism swinging in his friend's bare hand. But Blancanales wasn't worried. If Hermann thought it was okay for them to travel with the nuke this way, that was good enough. He trusted the electronics expert with his life in battle, so why not now?

"Just a little diversion by Bear." Lyons grinned, hoisting the Atchisson to a more comfortable position. "As soon as we're gone, they'll be directed right back here, along with the FBI and Homeland."

"More Red Star?" Schwarz asked.

"Not this time," Lyons said, avoiding the civilian bodies. "We'll be briefed on the way to Bethlehem."

Schwarz balked. "We're going to Israel?"

"No, Phoenix Force is. We're going to see some Nazis in Pennsylvania."

Bethlehem, Pennsylvania, Steel Town U.S.A. Check. "Who's in trouble?" Blancanales asked, going around one of his own blast craters, misty smoke still moving along the ground.

Pausing at the entrance to the historic site, Lyons glanced at the clear blue sky. "Who's in trouble?" he repeated with a growl. "Hell, everybody is, this time."

CHAPTER FOUR

Edwards Air Force Base

The red Corvette hummed along the empty highway of the California desert. Dark clouds blanketed the early morning sky and heat lightning sizzled now and then. But no rain. Not yet, anyway.

Yawning behind the wheel, Mike Toddel was alternating sips of hot chocolate from a travel mug and bites of a cheese sandwich.

Taking a turnoff, he continued for a couple more miles until reaching the outer perimeter of Edwards. Glowing like a pearl against the rosy dawn, the air base was brightly illuminated by halogen lamps just inside the electrified fence.

Add a couple of Falcons and this would make a great postcard, Toddel thought with a chuckle.

Shifting gears, he slowed at the front gate and drove up to the guard kiosk. This separate section of the AFB was under maximum security, with armed men on station, guard towers, dogs patrolling the fence, gunship helicopters moving in the dim air and more SAM batteries hidden under concrete bunkers than even Toddel knew about. And he repaired their radar!

Stopping at the wooden bar blocking the entrance, he flashed the guard his access badge. "Hey, Harold." He smiled. "Looks like a hell of a storm coming, eh?"

"Sir, would you please show me you pass again," Sergeant Harold Adler demanded crisply, one hand resting on the holstered 9 mm pistol at his side.

He called me "sir"? That was when Toddel noticed another guard inside the kiosk wearing body armor and holding a massive M-60 machine gun, pointed his way. As the corporal in the kiosk worked the arming bolt, the linked brass dangling from the deadly weapon tinkled like distant wind chimes.

"Ah, sure thing, Sarge," Toddel muttered, doing as requested. "Something wrong? President here or something?"

Checking the pass against a list on a clipboard, the sergeant returned it and gave a salute. "Thank you, sir. Proceed to Hangar 19. They're waiting for you, sir."

Without comment, Toddel worked the clutch to shift gears and drove away, wary of the speed bump just inside the fence. What was going on here?

The base was full of airman, technicians and officers rushing around. A light burned in every window and there was a circle of black cars parked around the flight tower on the airfield.

Turning past a dark PX, Toddel headed toward Hangar 19 when lightning flashed, very bright and without thunder.

Suddenly a violent explosion obscured the hangar. Stunned, Toddel watched as a column of black smoke rose to form a spreading mushroom cloud. He panicked for a moment, then remembered that any large explosion would create that formation.

What the hell had happened? It looked as though lightning had struck the fuel storage tanks or maybe the munitions depot. He hoped everybody in the hangar was all right. The windows were bulletproof glass and the thick walls were solid concrete with brick on both sides. A bazooka couldn't dent that hangar.

Braking to a halt so hard it stalled the engine, Toddel could only stare agape as the desert wind moved the smoke to show the fiery hole in the ground. The hangar was gone. Completely gone! Along with all of the experimental F-22 Raptor antisatellite fighters stored there.

Yellow Sea, North Korea

GREASY WATER SLAPPED listlessly against the hull of the *Sargasso Queen*. Anchored five miles offshore, the vessel was large, a monster of its kind. Old, but still serviceable. She rested low in the ocean, clearly loaded down with goods to be delivered. However, the vessel was anchored into position with four chains, any one of which would have been sufficient for an oil tanker twice its size. The registry listed the *Sargasso Queen* as a cargo ship, but it was going nowhere. Ever.

Watching from the shore, David McCarter nodded with satisfaction that while the vessel was covered with rust spots, there wasn't a barnacle on the hull. Why remove one, but not the other? Maybe so that the ship was in good shape, but didn't look that way? Seemed likely.

While his team got the equipment in order, McCarter

counted six machine-gun nests along the deck, the weapon emplacements disguised with canvas sheeting to try to resemble lashed-down packing crates. The radar was brand-new, and there were depth-charge launchers, rocket batteries and a lot of searchlights. The ship was a fortress. During the day, McCarter had counted more than a hundred men on board, three times what a craft of that size needed, and all of them armed with AK-47 assault rifles. Not exactly standard issue for the merchant traders, even in Communist North Korea.

Just then a passing cloud blocked the moonlight and the Stony Man commandos quickly came out of hiding to slide into the waves. Adjusting their rebreathers, the team started swimming with the currents, slowly approaching the vessel. Visibility was only a few feet, but they knew from orbital photographs taken by NSA spy satellites that the underwater defenses were impressive. The sea floor around the ship was studded with sonar sensors, along with hundreds of chained mines. A submarine might be able to blow a path through those with torpedoes, but no enemy warship could possibly approach without being detected and destroyed. Only men could do that job.

Checking a GPD, McCarter stopped the team a safe distance from the mines, and Calvin James activated a box on his chest harness. The device vibrated against his ribs as it generated the sounds of a large school of tuna. That should fool the sonar, but now came the hard part. Switching on scooters, the Stony Man team started into the minefield, the small military waterjets in their hands pulling them along as silent as ghosts.

Slowly the murky depths resolved into a forest of mines, the huge metallic balls chained at different heights to form an imposing barrier. Up close, the spheres were festooned with seaweed that hung off them like Spanish moss on a tree. The dull surfaces of the mines were covered with trigger studs, and they swayed slightly to the motion of the ocean currents. Two of them clanged together, the noise unnaturally loud in the water. The men tensed, but then relaxed when there was no detonation. Obviously the mines were safe from contact with each other.

Something large flashed by them and McCarter bit back a curse at the sight of a pair of dolphins. The damn things had come hunting for tuna! Pickings had to be very slim in the sea for them to come this close to land. McCarter started to turn off the sound generator, but stayed his hand. If he did, that would expose them to the sonar. Damned if they did, and damned if they didn't. Only one chance, go faster!

Playfully swimming all around the team, the dolphins kept searching for the elusive tuna and bumped into the humans several times. Thankfully there was no explosion. Pulled along by the whispering waterjets, the men of Phoenix Force tried not to think about what would happen it they did that to a mine.

A last array of mines formed a dotted wall in front of the team, the spheres packed almost too close together for the scooters to traverse. Turning sideways, the Stony Man team shot through at full speed and reached clear water. A moment later the dolphins arrived, happily chattering to each other in their incomprehensible language.

James killed the generator and the dolphins paused in confusion, then rose to the surface for a breath of air and came back down to disappear into the minefield.

Ahead of the team loomed the cargo ship, the thick anchor chains extending into the dark depths.

Turning off their waterjets, the men let the scooters float in place as they climbed aboard and proceeded to the belly of the ship. Stopping there for only a moment, the men moved on to the rear of the ship. No video cameras were discernable; the zone was clear.

Reaching the propellers, Phoenix Force removed its swim fins and attached them to their belts. Swimming slowly upward, they moved among the huge propellers. If the blades started turning, the five would be chopped to pieces, chum for the sharks. But the propellers stayed motionless, and soon the team reached the hull of the vessel.

Opening bags at their sides, the men donned sophisticated climbing gloves. Slow and silent, the five shapes moved along the thickest part of the hull where the soft pats of the gloves wouldn't be heard by anybody in the engine room. Soon the surface shimmered above, the waves dancing with moonlight, and they rose like ghosts from the bay, moving hand-over-hand up the flat stern of the enormous vessel. Their wet suits were camouflage-colored orange, red and brown in irregular patterns. From a distance they should appear as just more rust spots. The effect was heightened by irregularly shaped backpacks and satchels that each man had strapped to his body.

The five men reached the gunwale, then paused as a sailor walked by smoking a cigarette. Pulling on night-vision goggles, McCarter turned on the Starlite function and clearly saw that the man was dressed in civilian clothing. But his boots were regular North Korean army, and an AK-47 was strapped to his back. As the disguised soldier threw the butt of the cigarette overboard, T. J. Hawkins gave a low whistle, the kind men use to get the attention a pretty girl.

Curious, the North Korean soldier glanced over the railing and looked down. Instantly Rafael Encizo rammed a Tanto combat knife directly into the man's jaw, pinning his mouth shut so that no possible cry of warning could be given. Drowning in his own blood, the North Korean flailed, clawing at his throat, then went limp. Carefully, he was dragged over the railing and tied with ropes to be lowered into the water without a splash. As the corpse reached the sea, the rope was released and the body sank from the weight of his boots and assault rifle.

Easing over the railing, Phoenix Force reached the deck and crouched, listening for any potential source of trouble. But the great vessel was silent; there was only the sound of the waves below. Everything else was still.

Staying in a bunch to keep a low profile, the team donned dry sneakers from their packs and opened water-tight bags to remove Heckler & Koch MP-5 submachine guns, each barrel tipped with an acoustical sound suppressor. The weapons carried a flip clip, bound together with the service man's best friend, duct tape. Warily, the men made sure that the clip carrying the half-load rounds was inserted into the machine guns. The reduced charge seriously lowered the firepower, but helped the suppressors do their job. The other side of the flip clip was standard ammo, armor-piercing, full charges. Just in case the suppressors failed.

The sound of soft footsteps came from around the housing and Phoenix Force dropped behind the canvas sheet covering a machine-gun nest.

Lightly resting a finger on the trigger of his MP-5, McCarter tracked the sailor strolling along the deck, an AK-47 on his back, both hands shoved into the pockets of his pea-coat for warmth. It was obvious to the former SAS commando that the North Koreans weren't expecting any trouble this night. Too bad for them.

It had been known for some time that Kim Jong-il, the dictator of North Korea, had been trying to manufacture biological weapons to use against the democratic people of South Korea and the hated United States. Several labs had been found by the CIA and blown out of existence by NATO. But Kim kept trying to duplicate his success with a nuclear weapons program. Half of the trapped population of impoverished nation subsisted on starvation rations, but their "glorious leader" spent billions on creating weapons that might never be used, for a war that only he wanted.

"Which way?" McCarter whispered, staying low.

Pulling a personal computer from a pocket on his thigh, Encizo checked the glowing map of the boat. It was a compilation made from the structural blueprints of the dockyard where it had been constructed and a lot of guesswork based upon orbital photos and passive thermographic readings from shore.

"Left," the little Cuban said, starting forward.

Proceeding along the deck, the five-man team kept close to the painted metal walls, pausing every now and then as somebody walked along the gunwale. The guards expected that any trouble would come from outside, and kept watching the sea, the sky and the distant shoreline, the small fishing villages and military slave camps twinkling patterns in the night.

Soft light came from a series of portholes and the Stony

Man operatives ducked low beneath them. Faintly, they could hear soldiers laughing and a television set blaring with a translated American sitcom.

Maneuvering past the cargo hold, Phoenix Force passed a couple of guards on patrol and a pair of soldiers out on errands, one of them carrying a silver tray covered with spotless white linen. The delicious aroma of roasted duck wafted behind the steward, lingering in his wake. Weapons poised, Phoenix Force watched the fellow cross the deck and disappear into the main salon a hundred feet away.

"That wasn't spam on a shingle like they feed the troops," Calvin James observed, easing his gun hand. "Guess it's good be to the king."

"Pity the general in charge is awake," Hawking quipped, checking the rigging on the cargo hoist for any suspicious motions. "But at least we now know that Le-Wan isn't belowdecks. That had to be for him."

James nodded in reply. Good point. Where ever Le-Wan was located, that's where Kim Jong-il would have the bulk of the troops to protect his nephew.

"Be nice if Yi was belowdecks."

"Amen to that, brother."

"Gary, over here," McCarter said, tapping an access panel in the wall.

Sliding the panel back, Manning found a fuse box, well protected from the corrosive salty air. Jimmying the lock, he swung the door aside. A bank of circuit breakers was inside, all of them clearly marked as to function. Opening the electrical panel, Manning exposed a complex nest of wiring. Checking the breakers, Manning clipped thin gauge wires to their backs, then snipped the bypassed circuits. The master console in the control room would still read the lines as live, but they would die the first time they were turned on and resetting the circuit breaker would do nothing to help. Manning pressed a gray-colored wad of C-4 to the back of the breakers and slid in a radio detonator. The whole ship might be protected by the Faraday Cage effect running through the hull, but this was located out in the open. Closing the board, he swung the door shut and pushed the access panel back into place.

Phoenix Force proceeded to the lower deck. Down here the air was much warmer, the smell of the sea was gone and there was the continuous sound of some sort of machine. Large steel gates were folded back against the walls, and arms lockers were everywhere. James and Manning hid more C-4 charges behind the weapons dumps as Encizo rigged a couple of the gates. Just a little insurance for the future. Hopefully, getting off the vessel was going to be just as quiet as it was getting on. But a wise soldier always planned for what an enemy could do, not for what he might do.

Loosening the light bulbs in the ceiling as they went along the hallway, Phoenix Force left darkness in its wake. That would be suspicious to a passing soldier, but far less revealing than actually spotting the team.

Hawkins took point while James read off the signs on each door. He was fairly proficient in Vietnamese, but only knew a few halting phrases in idiomatic Korean. However, it was enough. Sterile Room. Animals. Contaminate. Storage. Supplies. Laboratory.

Bingo!

Bending, McCarter softly scratched at the bottom of the lab door. After a few minutes, a grumbling person stomped over and threw it wide. The angry soldier was armed with a broom, clearly prepared to do battle with a rat. His face registered shock at the sight of the five intruders, and McCarter rose to hit him in the throat with an open-handed blow. The soldier dropped the broom and back away, hacking for air.

Moving fast, Phoenix Force stepped into the room and Manning closed the door while Encizo fired a single round from his MP-5. The weapon gave a *chuff* sound and the choking man crumpled into the corner.

Spreading out, the team secured the room, then did a fast search. The room was an office of some kind, containing desks, papers, computers, printers and tall green file cabinets. Double doors marked with warning signs in Korean filled the left wall and the air carried the antiseptic smell of a hospital.

Going to the desk, Manning checked, but every drawer was locked. Accepting that, he fixed a couple more blocks of C-4 from his dwindling supply onto the file cabinets and set the timers for twenty minutes.

"Make it fifteen," McCarter directed, stuffing some papers from the Out basket into a watertight pouch strapped to his chest.

Manning did as requested, as Encizo and James kept watch on the corridor and Hawkins checked out the double door at the far end. Through the round glass windows, he could see another set of doors. Past those he could vaguely discern some sort of a laboratory, but the angle was wrong for any details. Could be empty, could have a hundred armed troops inside. There was only one way to know for sure.

"Okay, it's showtime," McCarter declared, closing the pouch. "Let's find the professor."

Walking through the double set of doors, Phoenix Force found the inner room was indeed a full biological weapons laboratory. Two large tables were covered with bubbling experiments, the complex array of gurgling glassware reaching several feet high. Locked cabinets covered the walls, aside from the life-size portrait of Kim Jong-il. There was an autoclave, centrifuge, lots of cages for the test subjects and an Oriental man eating a sandwich. But no guards. The old man was tall and slim, with white hair and glasses. He wore a gold wedding ring. It looked like their target from behind, but could be a trick.

"Yi," McCarter said, announcing their presence.

The professor looked up from his meager repast and went pale. "No. No! I am loyal to our glorious leader!" he cried, dropping the sandwich and raising both hands. "Don't kill me! I love North Korean! Death to the Americans!"

"We are Americans," McCarter said, removing the night-vision goggles to expose his face.

The terror vanished to be replaced with joy. "Then get me the hell out of here, cobber," Yi stated, switching to English as he slid off the lab stool. "These people are bloody insane." He started their way, beaming a smile.

"Lift your shirt, please, Professor," Hawkins urged politely, aiming his MP-5 at the man.

Stopping in his tracks, Yi sighed and did as requested. The man's chest was marred by a large area of puckered scars, a gift from an early experiment in chemistry gone bad back at Perth University in Australia.

"Sorry, had to be sure," Hawins apologized.

Professor David Allen Yi lowered his shirt. "You thought I might be a fake? A stand-in or something?"

"Been known to happen," McCarter said, picking up a glass pipette used for drawing blood. Suddenly he threw the pipette to Yi and the professor caught the glassware with his left hand. Confused, he stared at the pipette, then frowned at McCarter.

"A good test," Yi noted with strained patience. "Autonomic responses are difficult to fake. Yes, I'm left-handed. Now, is that enough proof, or do you also want some blood and a stool sample?"

"Maybe later." McCarter grinned in spite of the situation. The old Aussie scientist was as tough as Barbara Price had said. It had to have taken a lot of men to kidnap him from the Woomera Military Hospital last year. Canberra was going to be delighted have the cranky genius back safe and sound.

James went over to an autoclave full of sealed bottles. Each was filled with a greenish fluid. "That it?" he asked.

"Sadly, yes," Yi said grimly. "Moonfire. The worst nerve gas I ever made, or even heard about. It kills, fast and horrible. Moonfire is not so much a war gas as it is a terror weapon. No solider who ever saw it work would ever risk going anywhere near again. Dear God, I must have killed dozens of people with the clinical test alone! But I…they…"

"Torture?" McCarter asked softly.

Yi turned away, unable to speak.

"Any man can be broken, Professor," James said gently. "It's nothing to be ashamed about."

The professor could only shake his head, obviously reliving the deaths of his unwilling test subjects. Kim Jong-il and his cruel nephew enjoyed finding new ways to dispose of their political enemies. His tests had thus served two purposes for the dictator: revenge and entertainment.

Opening a satchel, Manning started placing explosive charges around the room. Joining him at the task, James directed the placement of the C-4.

Keeping the inner door open with a foot, Encizo watched the outer set of doors while Hawkins stayed close to Yi. Pushing back the tight sleeve of his wet suit, McCarter checked his watch. Five minutes to go.

"Please hurry," Yi pleaded. "If they catch me with you, it'll mean the work camps at Pyongyang. Nobody lasts there very long." He frowned. "Although, I'm sure it seems like a bloody eternity to them."

"You're too valuable for that," McCarter stated bluntly.

"The hell I am. To be honest, I'm surprised at the rescue," Yi said, rubbing his face. "It would have been much easier to kill me."

"The incredible we do immediately," Hawkins said, "the impossible takes a few days."

"Besides," McCarter added, "you're the best man to make a counteragent to Moonfire."

A short whistle from Encizo caught everyone's attention. "Company," he said, working the bolt on his weapon.

The Stony Man operatives instantly moved into defensive positions behind the lab tables, dragging the reluctant professor along with them. McCarter slung his MP-5 and swung a Barnett crossbow from behind his back to load an arrow. It clicked into place just as the double doors to the sterile lab burst open and in walked a short, fat man surrounded by a dozen guards armed with AK-47s.

"Doctor, your work has been so excellent this past week, I prepared a special treat for you," Kim Le-Wan declared loudly, carrying the silver tray covered with a white linen cloth. But then his smile vanished at the sight of the armed strangers in the lab.

"Kill them!" Kim screamed, tossing aside the tray and diving behind a soldier.

The North Koreans and Phoenix Force all brought up their weapons and Yi moved between them. "Stop!" he screamed in Korean. "Fire those in here and we all die!"

The military guards paused, unsure of what to do, and McCarter fired. Across the lab, Kim rocked backward as the barbed arrow slammed deep into his face. For a moment he weaved drunkenly, only a tiny trickle of blood inching down his features. Then the miniature explosive charge detonated and the man's head exploded into a million pieces, bones and pink brains spraying outward in a ghastly cascade. Screaming obscenities, the guards raised their Kalasnikovs like clubs and charged.

Releasing their MP-5 machine guns, four members of Phoenix Force threw the knives they had been hiding. Three of the North Korean soldiers dropped to the deck, clutching their throats, while the fourth clasped a hand to the side of his head, teeth clenched in pain as blood poured from the horrible gash where his ear used to be located. The grisly object was pinned to the wall like some sort of demonic butterfly, still shaking from the impact. Then the two groups mixed, the green military uniforms of the North Koreans mingled with the slick rust-colored wet suits of the Stony Man commandos.

Assault rifle slammed against machine gun, the owners wresting for supremacy for a moment, then the men dropped the useless weapons and went hand-to-hand. Pulling out a curved knife, a guard threw the blade, but James deflected the incoming missile with his Randall fighting knife. The blade hit the floor and skittered away, and James advanced, slashing with the military knife, the spine of the blade tight against his palm.

McCarter fired again, feathering a guard's temple. The man went down with a sigh as if he were going to sleep. Hawkins kicked a guard in the groin, then opened the fellow's throat with a backhand slash. A muscular guard launched a Tiger Claw at Encizo, but he swayed backward out of the reach of the blinding martial-arts strike, then turned sideways and buried the heel of his sneaker into the man's solar plexus. As the air woofed out, the guard doubled over, and the Cuban brought down the edge of his hand in a Little Leaf strike, adding the full force of his entire body to the blow. The North Korean's neck snapped and he dropped to the deck dead, his twitching body only slowly accepting the irrefutable fact.

Loading and firing, McCarter killed a third, a fourth, then the Koreans were upon him, and he joined the battle. His hands dripping blood, Manning moved on to a new opponent, leaving a corpse behind, the empty eye sockets of the man staring at eternity.

Dropping to the deck with his face smashed apart, a dying guard fumbled for the pistol at his belt. Accidentally, he fired the weapon while it was still inside the holster. The round missed his boot and ricocheted off the steel deck to musically zing off a wall. Then there came a shattering of glass and a sizzling green mixture spewed onto a stainless-steel table, instantly discoloring the resilient metal.

"Masks!" James barked, slapping the emergency filter over his nose and mouth. Every member of the Stony Man team followed suit.

A second later the North Koreans started writhing in agony. Holding a spare mask, McCarter raced for Professor Yi, but it was too late. The old scientist began to violently shake. Turning, Yi grabbed a beaker and smashed the glass to slice open his own throat before the real pain began.

"There is no…counteragent…" He gurgled and fell to the floor.

Helplessly, Phoenix Force watched the scientist die, and in only a few moments they were the only people still standing in the misty green laboratory. Ever so slowly, the toxic fumes started thinning, moving with the air currents into the humming wall vent of the ventilation system.

"Okay, burn the place," McCarter barked, pulling out a fat canister. "Leave nothing behind for them to work with."

Moving to the double doors, the team pulled out grenades, yanked pins, released arming levers, threw and turn to run. They were in the office when the lab exploded into flames, the searing wash building into a roaring inferno as the thermite cooked. The metal tables sagged, the walls began to buckle. Sprinklers in the ceiling gushed to life, but the water only served to increase the fury of the chemical blaze, the thermite feeding off the oxygen in the water to fuel its rampaging endothermic reaction.

"That should do it," Hawkins said, wiping his face with a sleeve.

Somewhere onboard the ship, a siren started to howl, then abruptly stopped, the surge of power feeding the device causing the rigged wiring of the circuit breaker panel to blow.

"Okay, let's go," McCarter barked, slinging away the crossbow, and bringing up his MP-5. The team made the deck unchallenged.

A series of muffled explosions sounded from belowdecks and new sirens took up the Klaxon call of warning.

"Do it," McCarter ordered, sealing his wet suit closed and sliding the mouthpiece of his rebreather into place.

With a ripping noise, Encizo opened a Velcro-sealed pocket, pulled out a small cylinder. He flipped the top aside with a thumb, squeezed the body until a red light glowed, and pressed down hard on a small button.

A faint shiver went through the entire vessel as the two armor-piercing demolition charges that had been placed on the keel detonated. Hot gases bubbled up from below the on both sides. The ship gave a groan of tortured metal

Heading starboard, Phoenix Force fired at anything in its way. Guards were torn apart by the assault, flinging their rifles skyward in death. As the team leaped over the dead and the dying, the *Sargasso Queen* shook again, harder this time, and a gout of roiling flame rose from the main smokestack, brightening the mist for a full second.

Heading for the gunwale, McCarter felt the ship start to tilt to port. Yi was dead, the lab ruined, the Moonfire destroyed, files burned. The rescue mission was a failure, but they had destroyed the Moonfire lab. Now all they had to do was get out of here alive.

"Hello, Smoky. This is Bandit. Over," James said into his throat mike, one hand firing his MP-5, the other changing the frequencies on the box on his belt. "Smoky, this is Bandit, 10-45! Repeat, 10-45!"

"Roger, Bandit, copy. This is Uncle Smoky," Jack Grimaldi replied over their earphones. "My eggbeater is on the way to Check Point Charlie."

"Negative," McCarter snapped. "The Berlin Wall is coming down, hard and fast. See you at Bikini Zuma. Repeat, Bikini Zuma! Do you copy?" Check Point Charlie was the bow of the ship, where they were hoping to escape with Professor Yi. Zuma Beach was their hidden camp on the rocky shoreline.

"Check. Out," the pilot replied crisply, and the earphones went silent.

With a loud snap, one of the anchor chains broke, the length of links whipping out of the water to come crashing down across the forecastle, crushing men and machines alike. High-pitched screaming told of somebody still alive in the wreckage.

Grabbing the railing to hop over, Rafe grunted and fell to the deck as a North Korean shot him in the back. The rest of Phoenix Force retaliated with concentrated gunfire from their 9 mm machine guns and the enemy soldier went to his maker in several pieces.

"Shit, my rebreather is gone," Encizo cursed, releasing the chest harness. The device dropped off his frame and hit the deck to move away with a scraping noise.

"We can share," James offered, hefting his bulky rebreather.

"Got your six, brother," Hawkins confirmed, his MP-5 firing along the railing to take out soldiers coming their way. The men fell like bowling pins, several of them going overboard.

"Dump everything!" McCarter ordered. "Move it, people!"

As the deck continued to rise, the men removed their excess equipment. By now, every loose item on board was starting to sliding to port, and the shouting of the North Koreans was taking on a hysterical note. Another anchor chain broke, the whipping metal crashing down upon the rocket battery with thundering results. The *Sargasso Queen* shuddered.

Scrambling over the angled gunwale, the Stony Man commandos dropped into the water and started swimming across the surface. Speed was important now, not stealth. Everybody on board the sinking vessel was too busy to bother shooting at them now.

Minutes later, the five reached a pebble beach. Rising from the waves, McCarter turned just in time to see the burning ship do a death roll, water and flames blowing out of the gaping hole in its belly like a whale surfacing for air. Something in the engine room exploded, probably the boilers from all the steam mixing with the smoke, and the ship loudly groaned as it cracked in two to begin a short voyage to the bottom of the cold Yellow Sea.

CHAPTER FIVE

South Korea

Whistling between his teeth, Jack Grimaldi fed power to the Black Hawk's engines and the helicopter lifted off the ground, the tall grass of the desert field shaking from the powerful wash. Swooping past some trees, the Stony Man ace pilot checked his visual bearings before turning off his running lights and heading for the pickup point on the rocky coastline about two miles distant.

A thickening fog was hiding the moon and Grimaldi was thankful for the additional darkness. Every little bit helped when on a mission. The instrument board of the U.S. Army gunship cast a rainbow of lights across the cockpit, Grimaldi tried to watch for everything as he skimmed the treetops.

Just forty-eight miles to the north was the Korean DMZ, a strip of land that cut straight across the hundred-mile-wide peninsula and was peppered with land mines.

The fog was covering the landscape, and ace pilot was lost

in his dark thoughts when he alerted at a warning tone from the radar. Flying with his left hand, Grimaldi started flipping switches with his right as the tone came again. Yep. MiG 17s. Three of them and coming straight over the freaking DMZ. Over his headset, Grimaldi listened to Osan AFB warning off the MiG fighters, but they kept coming and dropped below the radar screen.

"This is not good," the pilot muttered to himself, trying to urge more speed from the Black Hawk. The Communists were violating South Korean airspace. Unthinkable! The North Koreans would never do such a thing and risk reprisals from the UN, unless it was on direct orders from the big boss himself. Grimaldi frowned. Somebody on the laboratory ship had to have gotten off a warning before Phoenix Force sunk the *Sargasso Queen*. What else could possibly have gotten the dictator so angry? Well, unless they killed his nephew. That would send Kim Jong-il into a blind rage. In the morning the Communists would claim it was pilot error, but Grimaldi knew the planes were after him.

Arming the weapons systems of the sleek Black Hawk, Grimaldi slowed his flight and turned to sweep the fog with everything on board. Okay, IR was picking up nothing, UV and radar were clean. Maybe they had turned back?

Just then something streaked by the American gunship and the wash slammed the Black Hawk. Spinning out of control for a moment, Grimaldi fought to regain command of the gunship as the radar started to beep again. He realized there had to be a whole wing of MiGs out there on a definitive search and destroy. The Stony Man pilot grinned as he dipped lower into the thickening fog. Well, the Commies could search all they wanted, but destroying him was another matter.

Squeezing a switch on the joystick, a hexagonal piece of plastic swung out from his helmet to cover his right eye. Closing the left, Grimaldi looked at the tiny screen and read the scrolling data relayed from an orbiting spy satellite. Nothing. The radar was still clean. The sons of bitches were jamming it with some new trick. No help would be coming from Osano Air Force Base then. Grimaldi was on his own.

Switching the tracking system to infrared, the ace pilot released a pair of Sidewinder heat-seeking missiles. The sleek missiles dropped away from the gunship, their engines caught at a safe distance and they leaped away into the fog on daggers of fire. Almost instantly, there came a radar warning on incoming enemy missiles.

Moving his head, Grimaldi coordinated the radar to the weapons system and matched up the two bull's-eyes on the eyepiece, the Gatling gun under the nose of the Black Hawk perfectly matching his movements.

"Come to Poppa," Grimaldi growled when the window pulsed as he got a confirmation.

Flipping a lever, he pressed a trigger and the Gatling ripped into the night, sending out a brief maelstrom of depleted uranium rounds. Somewhere distant, there came an explosion, and the radar screen cleared.

As if in response, a tremendous blast lit up the night and flaming wreckage fell across a rice paddy, spreading destruction for yards before finally sinking into the mud.

There came a loud clang as something hit the side of the gunship. The Black Hawk was hammered by incoming lead rounds and a MiG 17 shot by so close for a second he could see the sneering pilot.

Grimaldi banked hard and spun all the way around in a manner impossible for a jet plane. There she was! Taking a chance, he fired the Gatling and the MiG exploded, the fireball spreading outward in stages as the assorted ordnance onboard the deadly jet fighter detonated, adding their power to the payload of aviation fuel.

"Smoky, this is Bandit," a voice said in his ear on the private channel.

"Later!" Grimaldi snapped, rising straight up. Turning on full radar, he swept the foggy sky. The Commies knew he was here, so the hell with it. Let 'em come!

There was an answering tone of two aerial targets to the northwest and Grimaldi released a pair of Sidewinders and one of the new Pythons. But the missiles only got halfway to the targets when they disappeared from his screen. A second later a stream of fiery darts lanced past the Black Hawk, the 20 mm minirockets missing the gunship by the thickness of a prayer.

Dropping chaff, he performed an evasive maneuver. The MiGs were gone, but now attack helicopters had arrived. Time to rock and roll. Banking into a dive, Grimaldi waited until the last moment, building as much speed as possible. Then he sharply angled upward, the pitch of the rotors screaming from the effort. He swept the fog with guns blazing, the Gatling whining as the eight barrels spun to full speed. Nothing.

Rising his prow, the Stony Man pilot changed course and dropped his last Python. The radar-guided missile streaked away, angling in the fog until it locked on the nearest EM source. More 20 mm minirockets flashed from the darkness and Grimaldi answered with a burst of his own 35 mm minis.

Something exploded to his left and the fog momentarily cleared from the blast to let him see a damaged Hughes 530 helicopter spinning madly as it fought to stay in the sky. Leaking fluids like a man with his throat cut, the Hughes swung into the trees and erupted, rockets and missiles firing off in random directions.

Alarms flashed in the Black Hawk as shrapnel hit its armored chassis and something cracked the front window. As if in response, the radar went off again as the other Hughes got tone and lock. Releasing the last Sidewinder, Grimaldi dropped fast and swung around to rise again to face his unseen enemy.

A rocket flashed by and hit the misty ground, the blast showing the broken hull of a sinking ship. He was over the ocean already? Good. The blast ripped open the dying vessel, finishing the job started by Phoenix Force. Backtracking the flight path, Grimaldi adjusted for time on target, guessed at the evasive maneuvers and fired a long burst from the Gatling. The numbers fell on the digital counter as the minigun spewed a hellstorm of rounds into the fog. Grimaldi was almost out of ammo when something fireballed and the screen went clean.

"Gotcha," Grimaldi whispered, releasing his death grip on the trigger. Disengaging the helmet sensors, the eyepiece swung back and he looked upon the world of misty night with his own eyes again.

"Smoky to Bandit, do you copy?" the pilot said into the mike extending from his helmet like a silver wire.

"Roger, Smoky." McCarter replied. "Having some trouble?"

"Nothing important. We rondy in five at Zuma."

"Roger. Rendezvous in five. Out."

As the helicopter zipped along the surface of the Yellow Sea, the waves kicked up a wealth of salty spray onto the windshield and Grimaldi had to turn on the wipers. They squealed going over the crack, the rubber catching on every pass. Turning them off, Grimaldi risked going higher until he found the landing zone on the onboard GPD. Easing speed and power, he dropped on an even keel until gently landing on a flat pebbled beach.

Keeping the blades rotating slowly, he waited and watched, a finger on the trigger of the Gatling. The swirling fog was thick enough to hide a tank. Then five figures rose from the shadows and walked closer. He smiled.

"Welcome back," Grimaldi said as McCarter slid open the side door of the sleek helicopter. "Anybody hurt?"

"We lost Yi," McCarter replied solemnly, climbing inside the craft.

The pilot lost his grin. "Damn. Sorry to hear that."

"But we got Moonfire," Hawkins stated, dropping heavily into a jumpseat.

"Well, that's something."

"I see you had a little action yourself," McCarter noted, tapping a bulging dent in the chassis.

"It's those damn kids and their BB guns," Grimaldi said, trying to keep a straight face. "Oh, they'll ruin the paint job, I swear."

As the team smiled wearily, James frowned and touched his ear. Hastily he jacked into the communications system of the Black Hawk and started adjusting the radio controls on his web belt.

"Heads up, we just got an emergency recall signal from the Farm," James said, then touched his throat mike. "Acknowledged, Stony Man, we're on the way. Out."

"What's up?" Manning asked.

"No details yet," James said, turning to check the pilot.

Flying with one hand, Grimaldi looked over a shoulder. "You guys know what a Thor is?" he asked.

Washington, D.C.

A BRIGHT FLASH zoomed through the windows of the Pentagon, and the Joint Chiefs of Staff looked up from their conference table just as something exploded, the shock wave shaking the entire building to its core and shattering a hundred windows.

Cursing and shouting, the military officers dropped, several of them bleeding from deep gashes. Then another bright flash appeared, closely followed by a second explosion, a third...

By now, alarm bells were clanging on every floor and armed soldiers appeared in the corridors taking defensive positions. More men ran, carrying armloads of top-secret documents. Doors to secure rooms automatically closed and locked tight. A dozen files sizzled, then burst into flames to destroy themselves. The ceiling sprinklers came to life, the lights flickered and died.

After a minute, the sprinklers stopped their cascade of fire-retardant foam and the halogen lights came back on strong as ever. As the sirens faded away, a heavy silence descended upon the building, leaving only the sound of foam dripping off the furniture, running shoes and creaking doors.

Grabbing hold of the conference table, an Army general

pulled himself erect and listened hard. There wasn't any crackle of flames or rattle of machine-gun fire.

"All right, what the hell just happened?" an admiral demanded, levering himself back into his vacated chair. The Navy officer's normally spotless dress uniform was soaked with coffee from a toppled carafe.

Suddenly a lieutenant appeared breathless at the door. "Sirs, you have got see this!" As the officer dashed across the hall, the Joint Chiefs headed after the man, everybody shaking the broken bits of glass out of their hair and clothing.

The hallway was controlled pandemonium, every rank, of every branch, moving quickly but quietly. More armed troops were taking up positions at intersections and jet fighters screamed by overhead.

The door across the hallway was wide open and the Joint Chiefs entered the room to join the group of colonels and privates who stood in front of the gaping window frames, looking in disbelief at the quad situated in the middle of the five-sided building.

"All right, Lieutenant," a Marine colonel growled, pushing the lower ranks aside. "And just what are we supposed to be looking at…?"

His voice faded away at the sight of a huge smoking hole in the middle of the quad. Less than a minute ago, the enclosed park had been green and alive, filled with bushes and trees surrounding stone benches where personnel could eat their lunch away from the cafeteria. There had been small gardens of colorful flowers and an acre of manicured grass smooth enough to qualify for a professional golf tournament.

But that was gone. The glass in every window facing the

quad was gone, replaced with staring faces of military officers. Now there were huge mounds of steaming dirt that looked partially fused. Broken slabs of concrete dotted the mounds and exposed electrical wires were snapping and crackling below, casting a weird blue light over the deeper realms of destruction.

Craning his neck out of the window frame, an Air Force general could see down three levels.

An admiral grabbed a phone on the wall and cursed when there was no dial tone. The trunk lines had to have been severed from the impact. If the damage reached all the way to the bottom level, then the Pentagon was now completely offline. Deaf, blind and helpless.

"Lieutenant!" she barked.

An Air Force officer spun, the rattled man nearly saluting even though he was inside a building. "Sir, yes, sir!" he asked.

"Get me a secure line to the White House, and I mean now, mister!"

A dozen people reached into their jackets and produced cell phones.

"A secure line, the woman said!" a general barked, raising a clenched fist. "Now get moving!"

The staff swiftly left the room, heading for Communications.

Casting a last glance out the cracked window, an Air Force colonel felt a shiver run down his back at the rampant destruction. Thirty seconds. The barrage couldn't have lasted longer than thirty seconds.

"Well, whatever this was," an Army general exhorted, "I'm just glad they missed."

"Missed?" an elderly Navy admiral said through clenched teeth. "The bastards hit exactly what they aimed at!"

A lieutenant frowned. "The quad, sir?"

"The archives," a general said in sudden understanding. "When our war computers went off-line, it would only take a split second for NORAD command at Cheyenne Mountain to take over the job of protecting the nation."

"So this accomplished nothing," a colonel said slowly, worrying his jaw. "Unless the target was the deep storage files."

"But why attack those?"

"Only one possibility comes to mind," a general ventured. "To stop us from finding something in the records. Something we need to know."

"Or to stop us from seeing who had last accessed the files. To hide somebody's identity."

"A traitor?"

"Maybe."

"Wasn't there a recent report from the CIA about a NSA agent claiming he knew about a traitor?" a general said in an oddly normal voice. "Maybe he didn't meant the alphabet agencies, but the Pentagon."

With that, the room went oddly silent and the Joint Chiefs all looked at one another with suspicion, but said nothing.

Air Force One

IN A RAGGED TRIANGULAR formation, the three modified 747 jumbo jets streaked across the sky high above the North American continent. Oddly, all three planes had the exact same name and call signs: *Air Force One.*

This was a standard presidential convoy while he was in flight. Only one plane contained the President, and never the same plane twice. Their paths zigzagged along the continent, staying clear of all major air routes and away from major cities on the ground below. Their point of departure had all been the same, Los Angeles International Airport, and the destination was the same, Andrews AFB in Bethesda, Maryland. But their flight paths diverged as much as humanly possible.

Arriving at LAX, the President had been escorted onto the specialty built 747, along with his executive staff. The Secret Service allowed no members of the White House Press Corps onboard for this trip, citing security concerns. The reporters from the big news agencies were disappointed to lose the private time with the chief executive, and the luxurious accommodations, but glibly accepted the decision and tromped onto the Zoo, the standard commercial 747 full of freelance reporters. The Zoo was nowhere near as comfortable, but it was still free.

Once airborne, the President excused himself from the executive staff and went to his private office. Stepping into the room, he wasn't surprised to find somebody waiting.

"Good morning," the President said, locking the door behind him.

"Morning, sir," Hal Brognola said, standing as the President came over to shake his hand. "I'm just not sure how good it will be yet."

Looking like a middle-aged business tycoon, distinguished and somber, Brognola was the White House's liaison with the Sensitive Operations Group.

"Has this anything to do with the Paris incident?" the

President asked, going to a chair behind a modern-style desk. The wood top was supported by burnished steel legs, and there were no drawers. It was a work station, nothing more. With absolutely no place to hid a microphone or a bomb.

"Unknown as of yet, sir," Brognola said, taking the chair again. "But I would say, in all likelihood, yes."

Placing a briefcase in his lap, Brognola snapped the locks and withdrew a red folder armed with a small incendiary device. He thumbed off the device and placed the folder on the desk.

Opening the folder away from his face, the President started to go through the security documents. All of the pages inside were edged with red stripes, any attempt to photocopy them could turn the stripes blue. As he lifted a page, the paper under his fingers promptly turned brown from contact with human skin.

"Thor. My God, did we build this thing?" the President asked angrily.

Brognola shook his head vehemently. "No, sir. That would have violated a dozen international treaties."

"That's an evasion," the man said sternly.

"Okay, to the best of my knowledge, it isn't ours. How's that?"

"Acceptable," the President muttered. "But it is a Thor?"

"As far as we can tell, yes, sir."

"You don't know that, either?"

"Not for certain. But my people are working on the matter."

"Good." Sitting, the President took the sealed top off a carafe and poured himself a glass of mineral water.

"If you don't know anything for certain," the man said carefully, tasting the words, "then why did you want a meeting?"

Brognola scowled. "To see if you know anything that we don't. After all, under the 1994 *Security Act…*"

With a curt wave of his hand, the President cut the man off in midsentence. "Don't quote the law to me," he growled. "I helped write the damn thing, remember?"

"Which means you know how to get around it," Brognola reminded him. "Did we secretly build a Thor?"

"No." Then he added, "But we do know how."

"Not anymore," Brognola advised. "The Pentagon was hit an hour ago. The deep archives are gone. All technical data on Project Sky Hammer has been destroyed."

"Impossible," the President breathed. "No way in hell. Can't be done. Those files are fifty feet underground, locked in a vault surrounded by solid concrete."

Reaching into his briefcase, Brognola passed over an orbital photo of the Pentagon taken a few minutes earlier by a keyhole satellite, relayed by Cheyenne Mountain by the NSA, and copied by Aaron Kurtzman and his team. The President stared at the photo for a long time.

"All of the damage occurred in the quad. Foam has killed the smoke," Brognola said, loosening his necktie slightly. "So the building appears undamaged to any passing cars. You can only tell how bad things are from above."

"And nobody but the military is allowed to fly over the Pentagon anymore," the President finished. "Any idea why this was done? A warning, perhaps? Leave Israel alone, or this is what will happen to you?"

"No credible source has relayed a warning, sir. We have a lead in Chicago, and we'll check it out. However, I believe it was a preemptive strike to destroy all data about Sky Hammer and prevent us from trying a counterattack."

"Indeed."

"Luckily, we succeeded a copy of the file for Project Sky Hammer last year. Here is a duplicate, sir."

They raided the deep archives? What else has Stony Man stolen over the years? The President started to get angry, then broke into exhausted laughter. "Well, thank God you're on our side." He sighed. "Okay, old friend, give me the bottom line. How do we stop Sky Hammer?"

Brognola knew that that phrase well. *The bottom line.* That meant any evasion or partial truths would be meet with severe repercussions. The men were friends, but not always friendly.

"In space we can't," the big Fed said honestly, crossing a leg. "Not without a firewall."

"Are you sure? I mean, with all of our antisatellite missiles, the F-22 Raptors and that new ASL—"

"Useless. All of them," Brognola interrupted. "Sir, Sky Hammer is just a bunch of thick steel bars floating in space. There is no space station, battle platform or central control element to hit. Firing missiles at Sky Hammer is like trying to kill flies with an ax. Oh, you're going to get a few, but not enough to make any difference." He frowned. "If we sent up every Raptor, there might be a fighting chance. However…"

"A 'meteor shower' took out Hangar 14 this morning," the President added, pouring another drink. "Along with a similar aerospace research facility you don't know about."

"Nellis AFB in Nevada."

The politician popped the stopper back into the carafe. "Gee, Hal, is there anything you don't know?"

"Only who's behind these attacks," the big Fed said wearily.

"And why they're being done."

"The who part almost always tells us why they did it," Brognola explained brusquely. "Okay, if Sky Hammer is nearly invulnerable in space, then we have to hit it on the ground. Take out the installation sending targeting signals to the Thors."

"Along with the people who built the thing."

"Exactly. But they could be located anywhere in the world. Might even be mobile. Send a command and run."

"Well, finding people is what you do, Hal. That's what Stony Man was created for," the President acknowledged. "May I take it that your people are already handling this?"

"Not yet. We had to recall them first. The teams were disposing of other matters." Brognola glanced at his wristwatch. The watch was old and bore the Great Seal of America. It was a gift from a former president many years ago. "They should be back in communication with the Farm at any moment."

"So what's our first move in tracking down the fanatics behind this…" The President frowned. "No, that doesn't make any sense. This must have taken years to set up, and most terrorists don't have the patience for that kind of long-term operation."

"Nor the billions of dollars necessary to launch something into orbit."

"Maybe China? Their Red Star agents have been causing us a lot of bother lately."

"No, sir, not the Red Star. The group doesn't have the re-sources to pull an operation like this one."

"Accepted," the President said. "Then who can it be? This had to be done by a major power, with access to space. But England, France, Germany, Japan, Australia…everybody with launch facilities are friendly nations these days."

Except for China. "Some nations are less friendly than others," Brognola reminded him. "Maybe we have a traitor who stole the files, and somebody else has a traitor within their space agency." Just for a moment, Brognola felt that he was close to something very important, but the idea slipped away into an ocean of possibilities.

"An international spy ring?" the President stated, rolling his glass back and forth between his palms.

"There have been others."

"Not for a long time," the politician drawled, starting to take a drink. Then he frowned and placed it aside. "Georgia?" The President spoke into an intercom. "Coffee, please. Ser-vice for…" He glanced at Brognola who shook his head. "Service for one."

"Right away, sir," his executive secretary replied. "Decaf?"

"Hell, no, I have work to do, not a nap."

"You have an emergency meeting with the Joint Chefs as soon as we land at Andrews."

The President could guess what the Joint Chiefs wanted to talk about. "Then sandwiches, too. Anything but tuna."

"Five minutes," Georgia stated, and the intercom gave a click.

"Couldn't run the country without her," the President mused, templing his fingers.

Leaning back, Brognola smiled. "My PA is the same. Once a year she reminds me of that and I have to give her a raise."

Rising from behind the desk, the President started to pace the office. "Okay, if we are indeed facing a spy ring," he started, clasping both hands behind his back. "Then we know why Israel was hit during the opening ceremonies. Advertising."

"Check." Brognola nodded, placing his briefcase on the floor. "That's our estimation, as well. The only reason to hit a ceremony being broadcast to the world is to spread your message that the wall could be hit and that you did it."

"Advertising implies something to sell," the President said slowly. "They can't sell the Thor itself. Maybe the blueprints... No, the buyer would still have to launch the Thor into space."

"That only leaves target acquisition," Brognola conceded, turning in the chair to face the man. "By God, sir, that's it! They're going to sell hits like old time mafiosi! For X amount of dollars they'll have Sky Hammer take out the Kremlin, or the Vatican, whatever. Anything above ground is vulnerable."

"At least we have one point in our favor," the President said thoughtfully. "Sky Hammer has limited resources. There can only be so many Thors in orbit. Fifty, maybe a hundred, at the most. And they must have used half of them by now. After those are depleted, the danger is over."

"There could be thousands, sir," Brognola stated grimly. "They might have been smuggling Thors into space for years before going into business."

Walking back to the desk, the President reclaimed his

chair. "I sincerely hope not," he said, leaning both arms on the wood surface of his desk. A thousand Thors. God alone knew how many millions of people could be slain. Murdered in their sleep. It was unthinkable. "Okay, if somebody else had a Thor program, maybe Russia, could we turn one against the other?"

"No, sir, these are kinetic energy weapons. In space they have no speed to generate any punching power. They only work hurtling through the sky. In space, they would just be hunks of metal banging together. Wouldn't do a damn thing, sir." Brognola spread his hands. "And that's not even considering the difficulty of hitting a steel rod a foot across, with another steel rod of the same size, six hundred miles in space. That's not pinpoint flying, that's a freaking miracle."

"Even if we knew where they were located in the first place."

"Exactly."

"Which leaves a firewall, if your people fail."

"And we're not even sure a firewall would work completely," Brognola continued doggedly. "Each Thor operates alone. We could detonate a hundred nukes in space, polluting half of the world's atmosphere, and might still miss a couple of them. Even one of those things aimed right could knock down a hospital full of civilians."

For a moment the President felt the old dread from the cold war coming back strong. Death from above. No defense. Vulnerable. Helpless.

"Can we jam it somehow?" the President said suddenly. "Block the signal from reaching Sky Hammer?"

"I'd be delighted to hear how."

"Just spitballing here."

"Sorry, sir. A nuclear firewall is possibly the way to attack Sky Hammer, and that would shove America into a war with every major nation on the planet."

"Which could be the goal of this thing," the President added, glancing out the window. There were clouds below the 747, and hidden somewhere within the swirling mists, lightning flashed.

The President hoped it wasn't an omen for the future.

CHAPTER SIX

Paris, France

"This is it," the CIA agent said, parking the sedan at the curb. "Get hard, people."

The old vehicle bore no unusual markings, the sides a little scratched, the bumper slightly dented, one of the tires bald, and the license was duly registered. Bland and dull, almost nondescript, the sedan blended into the busy Parisian traffic perfectly. Which was exactly as it should have been.

Dutifully, the four big men inside the vehicle checked their weapons. They were CIA agents that even the Agency refused to admit existed to other departments of the intelligence organization. This was a wet work team. They only had one function—to terminate enemies of America with extreme prejudice. But this day was different, one of their own had been killed in an ambush, and they wanted more than revenge. They wanted payback.

The neighborhood was more rundown than expected. Not

merely old, although every part of Paris was old, but poor, the grinding heel of poverty leaving permanent sour expressions on the local people. Garbage and graffiti were everywhere. And even at this hour of the day, prostitutes rested against the sides of buildings, near the mouths of alleyways, ready to do business. A man lay in the gutter, asleep or dead, it was impossible to tell from a distance. The air smelled of cabbage and urine. This was a section of the town that tourists never visited.

"Should we alert the local police?" an agent asked, checking the clip in his Beretta.

"There's no time. We move now, or the trail will be cold," the CIA section chief said, checking the notebook in his hand.

They had parked two blocks away from the brothel of the dead NSA agent, and a CIA recon team was already sweeping the neighborhood, making sure that this wasn't a trap. The NSA didn't have any field agents in Paris, so the mission fell to the CIA alone. But that was the way they liked it. The NSA was tops at breaking codes, but not the best at brutal retaliation.

Loosening their clothing, the agents liberally poured bourbon on their jackets and rumpled their hair. Appearing to be drunk businessmen, the CIA agents staggered out of the old sedan and wandered toward the brothel. They moved here and there, singing vulgar songs and trying to get a freebie from the streetwalkers until finally reaching the steps of the prewar mansion.

The house was large and Gothic, the window curtains closed, a universally understood red light burning discreetly near the front door.

Climbing the front steps, the CIA assassins gathered

around the door and started laughing while one of their members whipped out a keywire and shot the lock full of stiff wire. It was a professional locksmith's tool, favored by burglars, and owning one without the proper documents carried a ten-year jail sentence.

The lock disengaged, the agent pocketed the device and the team stumbled inside, mumbling greetings. Then one of the assassins went stiff and, slapping a hand over his mouth, shoved the others outside and down the steps.

"M-m-mustard gas," he wheezed, barely able to drag a breath. "Know the smell…Gulf War…" Judiciously, the agent exhaled hard, emptying his lungs before daring to take in a breath. He did so gingerly, and when there was no stabbing pain, he allowed himself to relax and breath normally. Thank God, he had recognized the odor. One good whiff and they all would have been coughing out their lungs onto the pavement in bloody chunks.

"Mustard gas?" the section chief rasped, rubbing his chin. "I think we can forget about this lead." There was a yellowish cloud rising from around the door.

"Somebody has gotten here ahead of us," the other agent agreed, watching the windows for any movement. But the building seemed to be still.

"Okay, I want a hazmat team here in five minutes," the section chief ordered curtly. "I want that brothel gone over with a fine-tooth comb, and then do it again! They probably think using gas was a clever way to kill all of the prostitutes, but I'll bet that—"

The entire building shook as mirror flashes of light came from the cloudy sky. Then with a splintery crash, the structure collapsed. When the smoke finally cleared, there was only a smoldering hole in the ground, a few broken pipes spewing water as if they were ruptured arteries.

The enemy had used the mustard gas to kill all of the prostitutes, and had probably expected the fumes to fade over time. Then the CIA team would discover the ship of death and bring in more people to do a forensic sweep and they'd all be slain in the…whatever the hell this was. It had seemed more like a meteor strike. But that was flatly impossible. Only the good condition of the old house kept the gas intact until the agents opened the door. The mustard gas that had killed everybody in the brothel had saved their lives by driving them into the gutter.

A freak mistake had accidentally saved their lives. By all rights the CIA team should be dead. Maybe they could turn that to their advantage? Nobody paid attention to the deceased. So his team wouldn't call in to headquarters and they'd play dead for a while until he could find out who was behind this. Then the assassins would show the enemy their special skills. Over and over again. Until hell itself wouldn't accept the tattered remains of the once human bodies.

Turning, the CIA chief led his team through the growing crowd, away from the demolition site. Anonymity first. Then all that remained was for his team to answer to the original question that had brought them here in the first place.

Who could have done this?

The Morning Star

ONBOARD HIS LUXURY YACHT, the *Morning Star,* Attila Meternich was having a splendid time. Almost four hundred feet long, and more than fifty-two feet wide, the massive vessel consisted of five decks, fifteen suites, a swimming pool, a seventy-foot launch, a helipad and several secret rooms that weren't on any engineer's blueprints or inspector's manifest. In spite of its size, the diesels were able to obtain a cruising speed in calm waters of nearly twenty knots. Absolutely amazing for a ship of its tonnage.

Although not the largest yacht in the world—that honor went to the Turkish registered *Savarona*—or the most luxurious—the Greek-built *Alexander*—the Hungarian *Morning Star* was truly impressive, and noticed wherever it sailed or moored.

On the forelock, several well-endowed young women were relaxing on chaise longues. Their bikinis were hardly noticeable and left little to the imagination. Oddly balanced, there was a redhead, a blonde, a brunette and a raven-haired beauty. The last was Japanese, Susie Wu, and as she walked, the flowing tresses of deepest midnight brushed against her tiny waist. Her thong was the color of cherry blossoms on Mt. Fuji in the spring, and shone against her skin like freshly polished sin.

Stretching catlike, Terry Lynn fluffed her red hair and dipped a painted toe into the warm swimming pool, the water so clear that she could see the mosaic tiles on the bottom forming some sort of symbol or logo. What it meant, she didn't know, but it was beautifully done.

The woman were strangers to one another, recruited from the endless swarm of hopeful wannabes who walk the golden sands of the French Riviera hoping to catch the notice of somebody rich and powerful. A fast marriage, and an even faster divorce, with a large settlement was the ultimate goal. Although many would settle for being a mistress. A lot of the new money millionaires, and quite a few billionaires, quickly learned never to walk the beach. The refined women stayed in the casinos and out of the wrinkling sunlight. Only the doxies walked the burning sands, showing off their assets and hoping to find a lonely fool with a Swiss bank account. The French, who were normally quite relaxed about social indiscretions, dunned these sexual predators "the little sharks."

Leisurely taking a bottle of sunblock from a nearby table, Terry Lynn filled her hands and began to massage the protective screen into her long legs, starting at the small tattoo of a butterfly on her ankle, and working her way slowly up to the minuscule strip of emerald-green cloth that composed her revealing bikini. Then she started on her other leg, taking her time, performing to an unseen audience. The young woman was always acutely aware that she could be spotted by a potential lover at any time, and was always performing, always posing.

It was quite a show, and several members of the yacht crew had gathered on the second deck to take seats at the bar and watch the display. The bar was mahogany and brass, the swivel chairs bolted to the deck as an aid for the more serious drinkers.

Sensing that she was being eclipsed by the redhead, Elizabeth Ashe brushed the blond hair from her pretty face and sat up on the lounge to deftly reach behind and remove her string top, freeing her breasts to the warm sunlight. Running stiff fingers tipped with electric-blue nails, Elizabeth tousled her windswept hair. The ocean breeze felt wonderful on her skin, and she enjoyed the male attention. She hated them, but enjoyed the enraptured looks of lust. The fools.

Lifting a dew-covered drink from her table, Elizabeth sipped the cocktail through a straw, leaving the marks of her lipstick behind. A poor girl from a poor village, Elizabeth knew how beautiful she was, and that no ridiculous show was necessary to make her the center of attention for every man on the sleek vessel. There were many yachts moored at the slips of the Riviera, but this one was oddly the most important. Not the biggest, oh, no, but it was the ship that everybody wanted to visit.

The elusive Attila Meternich was rich, naturally, but most people on the southern coast of France were that: millionaires, billionaires, technocrats, playboys, royalty, movie stars. More importantly, the man was powerful. Many claimed he was dangerous, but never very loud and never more than once. Elizabeth liked that. Power meant strength, and that was security. Strangely he also held some sort of a position in an international company. Yet he wasn't the president or CEO. Most unusual. She assumed it was a hobby, or the family concern.

Rising languidly from her chaise longue, Kimberly Stone shook her wild mane of brunette curls and walked over to Susie Wu.

"May I?" she asked in rich tones, as warm as honey from the island of Thebbes.

Smiling, the Japanese girl rolled over onto her back and the olive-skinned Greek girl began to rub the slippery sun-block into her skin.

Yawning in contempt, Elizabeth slipped on her sunglasses and ignored the others. These were the kinds of sluts that millionaires slept with for a weekend, but she was class, the type of woman they took for even a second wife. Briefly, she wondered where Meternich was.

At that moment, Meternich wasn't paying attention to the scantly clad women posing alongside his pool. Standing at the aft railing, he was sliding on a pair of kid leather gloves, wiggling his fingers and making fists to get them as tight as possible. The sobs of a prisoner had he brought on board were barely audible.

When he was satisfied, Meternich extended an arm and a small automatic pistol slid into his waiting palm. The barrel was extra-long from the homemade sound suppressor attached to the end, a simple affair of steel wool packed into a hollow tube. It was crude, but worked well for one or two shots. Then it became useless.

Clicking back the hammer, he aimed the .32 at the bound man weeping on the deck. He hadn't personally killed a man in years. This promised to be quite interesting.

Impeccably dressed, Meternich was in white linen pants and jacket, a shirt of raw silk clinging to his massive chest. Gold rings gleamed on his fingers, and a Rolex Presidential watch shone on his left wrist. The gold combined with the stark white of the suit only made the olive-skinned man seem darker, which was the general idea. Diamonds bored him, they had no color, only stole what they could from light. But gold was alive, heavy and delicious in your palm like a young woman's breast.

Although a large man, Meternich moved with an almost feline grace, and it was the slow motion of controlled power. His body was hard, and he exercised every day. His custom-tailored suits were barely able to contain his Herculean form, and a decent fit over his thighs was always a problem.

"Use the knife," Mikhail Abelovsky chided, shaking the prisoner by the scruff of the neck like a terrier attacking a rat. "Make it slow. I want to hear him squeal."

Smiling slightly, Meternich said nothing, knowing the speech was more for the prisoner than him. Mikhail was a true sadist, a distant cousin that he had helped escape from a brutal lunatic asylum outside Budapest. Under the Communist regime, it had been a hellhole, unfit for animals. Even if Meternich hadn't needed the unique services of his knife-wielding cousin, he and his brother would have busted the poor fellow out anyway. Once their family had been nobles, dukes and counts in the Hungarian court. No Meternich would ever be allowed to serve time in a common prison, no matter what they called it: penitentiary, insane assembly or debtor's work camp. Unacceptable.

"Please. No…" the kneeling man begged. "I only wanted a picture… I wasn't hurting anybody…."

Mikhail cuffed his ear. "Shut up!"

Shaking with fear, the man on the teakwood deck was handcuffed at the ankles and wrists. His face was badly bruised from the recent beating he received when the deck crew found him hiding in a lifeboat. A tooth was missing, one eye was swelling shut and his shirt was covered with blood. The remains of a 35 mm Nikon camera hung around his neck, the lens smashed and the delicate roll of film inside already burned to ashes and tossed to the winds.

"No, please," the reporter pleaded, raising his bound hands.

"Why?" Meternich asked politely, leveling the silenced pistol. "Are you now renouncing your career as a tabloid journalist?"

"Yes, please, anything you wish!"

In a rush of anger, Meternich's face darkened. "Liar," he whispered, and shot the bound man in the throat.

Blood gushed from the ghastly wound and, as the reporter started drowning in his own blood, Abelovsky shoved the gurgling man off the rear of the speeding yacht. He hit the wash with a small splash, hardly noticeable, then began to paddle furiously in a desperate effort to stay afloat even as he drowned internally from his own blood.

"Pity there are no sharks." Abelovsky chuckled, watching the show. The girls at the front of the yacht were very pretty, but tits and ass could never compare to this.

Left in the wake of the yacht, the reporter slipped below the glistening waves and sank from sight.

"You like American movies too much," Meternich growled. "A thing should be admired for what it is, not what it could be. He annoyed me, and he died. Isn't that enough?"

"No," he stated, the salty wind whipping his dark hair forward to cover his pockmarked skin.

Shoving the slim .32 up his left sleeve, Meternich felt it click back into place inside his tailored linen jacket.

Noting a tiny speck of red on his deck shoes, Meternich slipped them off and handed them to his cousin. The man was an expert on removing bloodstains. If that witness hadn't testified in court, the man never would have gone into the insane asylum in the first place.

"Maybe after this, I can see if one of the girls is also a news reporter," Abelovsky said hopefully.

Casually, Meternich looked forward at the crew of his yacht. They had sauntered to the railing to watch the girls below.

"I want the blonde, you can have the Greek girl," he stated. Then raised a hand to lower his sunglasses. "But only later, cousin, after we have come to…know…her better."

"Of course, my lord," Abelovsky said, giving a small bow.

"Our family is no longer royalty," Meternich stated coldly. "The Communists saw to that. Please do not call me by that title again."

Dutifully, Abelovsky nodded. "Yes, baron."

Savagely, Meternich grabbed his cousin by the throat, then released him with a chuckle. "You have always been a pain in the ass, cousin."

There came a polite cough and the two men turned.

"Professor Meternich?" a steward asked. He approached, carrying a cell phone on a silver tray covered with an embroidered white linen cloth. "There is a call for you, sir."

"Tell them I shall call back later," he replied.

"Sir, it is the red line, and you told me to always interrupt you during anything, anything at all, if there was a such a call, sir."

Meternich waved a hand. "You are correct, Zema, my apologies. I'll take it in my office."

Abelovsky sneered at the man, who scurried away in fear, even though he was quite safe. Attila Meternich knew that mercs and paid assassins were easy to find. A good butler was irreplaceable. If he ever had to choose between the two, it would be quite a difficult choice. Unless it became a business matter, then the servant died. Nothing was more important than business.

Padding barefoot along the warm teakwood deck, the big

Hungarian pressed his palm to a steel plate on an unmarked door. There was a buzz and the door slid into the wall.

Stepping out into the delicious warm sun, Meternich wiggled his stubby toes in the thick carpeting as the door automatically cycled shut and locked.

The room was sumptuous in a dignified manner that took generations of wealth to achieve. Not even the clever interior designers of New York or Milan ever really got it quite right. It was a feeling that came from within, impossible to achieve without the sure knowledge that you were better than anybody else in the world.

The walls were lined with bookcases bearing scientific journals and university tomes. Maps of the stars were framed above the wet bar, and a wooden gunrack behind the desk was filled with various models of illegal assault rifles. The metal shone with oil and the wooden stocks gleamed with polish.

Sadly, this was the last few square feet of his family's fortune. What the Communists hadn't stolen, the new government had taxed away in their mad effort to bring equality to the peasants. Even the *Morning Star* was mortgaged to the hilt, and his desk was covered with overdue bills from a dozen collection agencies. But if all went well, all of that would change soon. His family would be wealthy enough to buy back their title, their honor, and never again would a Meternich have to soil his hands with work.

Touching a hidden switch on the wall, Meternich watched a section of the paneling slide back to reveal an array of American LAW rocket launchers, Russian RPG launchers and a South African X-18. Closing the panel, he knew it was silly, but the sight of the heavy ordnance always seemed to put him in the right frame of mind to deal with terrorists.

Sitting at his desk, Meternich activated the controls and swept the room for any electronic listening devices or hidden optics. After a minute, a light flashed green and only then did he turn on the new laptop. No cash down, easy monthly payments. Bah! The clerks should have given him the machine as a gift, and been thankful for the honor.

He watched closely as the plasma screen swirled with colors and then cleared to display numerous incoming e-mail messages. Excellent. A little business before lunch and then perhaps a swim with the girls. One last morning of pleasure with that annoying brunette before turning her over to Mikhail and his little games.

The first e-mail was a confirmation of the transfers of funds from the PLO to his numbered Swiss account for the destruction of the Israel wall. Hamas knew that payment on time was all that stopped Meternich from leveling all of Palestine. Not that he cared about their politics. Jews, Arabs, whites, blacks, only money mattered. Well, money and family.

The amount of the transfer wasn't very much, but then, it was a bounty. If Meternich succeeded in taking down the wall, then, and only then, did he get paid. Fair enough. If he was able to make a little money, and advertise his product to the terrorist organizations of the world at the same time, so much the better. What did the Americans call it? Oh, yes, double dipping. Quite amusing. Of course, they had taken extra-special precautions that there would be no mistakes on this strike, it had to be perfect. But everything had gone off without a hitch. There now was a minor danger from the direction, but Meternich didn't believe it was of significant value. Besides, there was an element of danger in doing anything, even crossing the street. Why should this be any different?

Switching the funds from the secret account in Switzerland to another in Barbados, Meternich then relayed them again to a bank in Luxembourg, and finally back to Switzerland. Nobody could trace the funds now. There were too many walls of silence between his Arab contact and himself.

Lifting a sterling-silver dome off a marble plate, Meternich found ice tea and ham-and-cheese sandwiches for lunch. Ghastly. Caviar was for the guests. In private, he suffered eating such muck to save a few dollars. Money. It was always about money.

Deleting some spam, Meternich found a large file waiting for authorization. A video file? Curious. Clicking to open it, Meternich suffered through some old German offer of ten million dollars for a strike on the American White House. The money was good, but Meternich hated all Germans after what Hitler and his goose-stepping murderers did to his beloved homeland of Hungary.

"Declined," he said, a scrambler changing his voice into crackling monotone.

A flashing icon on the screen showed somebody was waiting in the conference room. As per the instructions of his computer expert, Meternich switched formats constantly. Something called a flick box constantly switched his ISP, and did a lot of others things he could only barely understand. Computers were magical as far as Meternich was concerned.

He understood people, but not machines. Switching the Web cam to silhouette mode, Meternich joined the meeting, which was already in progress.

"There you are!" a featureless man snapped in Mandarin, the Hungarian translation scrolling along the bottom of the screen. "We have been waiting long enough!"

"Then wait some more," Attila said with a smile, and turned off the screen. There! Let the impatient fools stew for a while before returning. The Asian Dawn were madmen, dedicated to destroying their own people for reasons too complex for Meternich to ever comprehend.

The next e-mail was a genuine offer. Again the money was small, two million dollars. Pitiful. But Meternich was willing to take anything at this point.

With a sigh, Meternich removed the silver cover and started into the disgusting sandwich when he was interrupted by a voice message on-line.

"Talk," he said without any preamble, watching a red light flash in the corner of the screen to show the voice scrambler was working. Even with his own people, security stayed tight. Only fools trusted. The wise man hoped for the best, but prepared for the worst.

"We are secure," the scrambled picture said, showing a moray pattern endlessly changing and flowing. "The birds of Edward are gone, as are their children."

"And the archives?"

"They are history."

How droll. "Good," Meternich said, clumsily typing in a few commands, then double-checking the syntax before hitting the send button. "We have a new client. The integers are small, but I'm sure that larger figures will be forthcoming."

"Data received," the other said. "Anything else?"

"No," Meternich said calmly, hitting a button. "Goodbye."

"Goodbye, Caesar."

As the screen went dark, Meternich felt the thrill of a kill and decided to do it right now. Why wait? Unlocking a side drawer, the big Hungarian pulled out a small device resembling a TV remote control. Thumbing a button, he brought up a map of the world on a wall screen, then zoomed onto the relatively unimportant city of Murzuk. He had never heard of the place, but that hardly important. For the right price, he would blow up an orphanage for cripples. Who cared? As long as they weren't fellow Hungarians. That he would never do.

Working a tracking ball, he pulled up a more detailed map of the area, chose the target, found out when Sky Hammer would be in range, then pressed the activation code.

Done. Two million dollars made with the press of a button. Suddenly feeling expansive, Meternich tossed the partially eaten sandwich into the trash can and left to join the women by the pool. A worker was worthy of their dues, correct?

Besides, there was baked crab for lunch, and he could afford such luxuries now.

CHAPTER SEVEN

Libya Oil Fields

The wrench fit securely over the nut and Abis Hassan pulled with all of his might. Nothing happened.

Stretching his sore back, the Arab oil technician groaned a little, but not enough so that the other workers could hear. He had read once that the Chinese were very worried about saving face. Well, that was nothing in comparison to the delicate public honor of an Arab man working for the National Oil Company.

Wiping his hands clean on a rag, Hassan looked around to make sure he was alone, then wearily sat on a thick pipe and leaned back into the cool shadows of the feeder pipe just above.

Ah, better than the kiss of a new melon.

Taking a water bottle from the shadows, he took a sip of its warm contents, carefully sloshing the fluid in his mouth before allowing a swallow. Water wasn't precious in Libya anymore, not with the new viaduct running from Bette. But long life was. A Thermos would keep the water cool, and that would only make you sick. Warm water was the answer.

This new oil field was deepest in Libya, and promised to be a boundless source of wealth. Once this oil field began producing, the government's coffers would be overflowing with wealth, and some of that would trickle down to the people. Khaddafi treated the people right.

On the horizon, set dangerously close to one another, were the massive storage tanks, five huge globes holding more than six million gallons of processed fuel. Already, the Spanish had placed a standing order for more than a million gallons a month, and that was just the tip of the iceberg.

Resting his eyes for what he thought to be a moment, Hassan awoke to the sound of snoring and realized in rank embarrassment that he had dozed off.

Hurrying back to work, the man slipped on his sturdy canvas gloves and tackled the stubborn nut again. This time he followed his wife's suggestion and spit on the crusted center first, then banged on the nut with the wrench for a few minutes as if it was a stubborn jar of salt before applying his full weight.

With a snap, the nut moved and Hassan was thrown to the sandy ground. "It worked!" he gasped in delighted surprise. "Praise God!"

Happily returning to the task, Hassan easily moved the locking nut until it came off. With the impediment gone, the master feeder value turned freely. As it clanged into the open position, Hassan placed an ear on the metal pipe. Any second now....

It started as a trickling noise, built to a gurgle and soon

was a steady rush as four thousand gallons a minute flowed along the pipe to descend into the new underground storage tank. Success!

Whistling a tune, Hassan started to pack away his tools when something flashed in the sky. Worried, he looked up, dreading to see the contrail of an incoming missile. The endless Libyan wars with the hated Chad were over, but feelings still ran strong with their stupid southern neighbor. Chad had been the main reason to build to these new underground storage tanks. Just a bit of protection from the possible strike by the Berber madmen. Hassan actually hated them more than Egyptian television, and there was nothing worse than that.

There was anther flash. Raising a hand to his face to shield his eyes from the blazing sun, Hassan tried to see what was happening. Bright lights in an oil field made everybody nervous, especially… Merciful God!

In stark horror, the technician actually saw the side of the globular storage tank dent inward before flame shot out the side. He threw himself at the ground and a split second later, an earthquake of titanic proportions shook the entire Murzuk area. The shock wave arrive a moment later and Hassan risked a quick look. Incredible. He could see that the entire area was now a writhing ball of fire. Wordlessly, he blinked at the astonishing sight of men still airborne, tumbling through sky as if they were sand fleas shaken off the back of a dog. The sight was so horrible, he couldn't comprehend it at first. There were no thoughts in his mind, no emotions, no reaction from his heart.

A small sand storm was spreading out from the explosion, a perfect circle of dust rushing across the barren flats, swamping over buildings, men and machines. Seconds later the rolling thunder of the detonation arrived and he was buffeted by the stentorian sound of destruction.

Blinking against the hellish wind, Hassan felt his heart stop at the sight of the next tank in line go up as expected, then the third, the fourth, the fifth…

He covered his head again, suffering through the bombardment of explosions, whispering childhood prayers. Gone. In the blink of an eye. They were gone. A billion dollars' worth of processed fuel, gasoline, kerosene, the wealth of his nation vanished into nothingness from a freak lightning storm.

He scowled as a thought occurred. Had it been lightning? There were only a few cirrus clouds in the sky. Nothing that could support lighting. Had it actually been a missile strike? If so, where was the contrail?

"Chad," he muttered, making a gut decision. Those stinking bastards had struck without warning. Again! This was going to cripple his nation.

Spinning around, he grabbed the feeder valve and turned it with all of his might. The fire had to be spreading through the network of pipes! It would be here soon and rip the new facility into atoms, and him along with it!

The winds of destruction buffeted the swearing technician as he struggled to completely close the valve. As it squealed to a stop, sealing off the new underground tank, he saw a wave of flame sweep across the Idehan Sand Sea, coming straight his way. Wearily, Hassan dropped the wrench and didn't even try to escape. He was an oil tech and knew fire, in all of its many forms. There was no escape. He was a dead man.

But how could this have happened? How did those Chad bastards reach this far inside Libya airspace without being stopped by the air force? Their Russian-bought planes and American missiles were the best in the world! Certainly better than anything those impoverished southern dogs could afford. How could this have been done? How?

Then the rushing flames arrived, the world seemed to explode and Hassan ceased to exist.

Stony Man Farm, Virginia

"OKAY, PEOPLE," Aaron Kurtzman said, slapping his big hands together and rubbing them vigorously. "Able Team is on the way to check out the Nazis, and Phoenix Force is headed for Israel. Let's find Sky Hammer."

"Why Israel?" Akira Tokaido asked.

"The Shin Bet have somebody in custody who claims to have known about the attack on the wall before it occurred. If true, he could be a link to the people behind all of this. Barbara wants David and his men on the spot to handle the interrogation personally." He frowned. "The Shin Bet also have a reputation for accidentally beating prisoners to death. That can't happen this time."

"Radar's clear," Akira Tokaido called, "although we really don't have the equipment to locate something only six feet long in outer space. Never needed to before. At that size, objects burn up before reaching the ground."

"Or at least melt," Kurtzman corrected grimly, adjusting his wheelchair under the console.

"Jamming is ready to go," Carmen Delahunt said, not

moving. Her hands were encased in VR gloves, her face encased in a virtual reality helmet. "I have a network of communication satellites around the world ready to start pumping out megawatts of hash. That should block any radio transmission from reaching the Thors with targeting commands." She turned her mask toward the others. "That is, once you the find the damn thing."

"Where brute force fails, guile prevails," Hunt Wethers said, flexing his fingers before typing. "This is a matter of deductive logic."

"Thank you, Sherlock Holmes."

"Now, we know the Thors are in orbit and don't have the spare fuel in their tiny rocket engines to move around. Once they reach a section of space, they stay there until ordered to attack." A vector graphic of the world appeared on Wether's monitor. "Now SETI has a listing of all known satellites, so we remove these from consideration…"

"Why not use the NSA list?" Kurtzman asked, then frowned. "Oh, yes, right."

"There's a traitor somewhere," Wethers stated grimly, working steadily. "We can't trust the NSA list. It is too obvious a way of finding the Thors. Hopefully, whoever is behind this didn't think about the SETI program."

"And if they did?"

Hunt said nothing in reply, but kept working. "All right, matrix is ready. Now, assuming a line-of-sight descent for maximum striking power…" His voice failed away, his eyes locked the graphs and mathematics crawling along the screen. Only the motion of his fingers and the occasional movement of his pipe showed the former university professor was still working.

Leaving the man to his work, Kurtzman accessed the master feed lines of NASA control in Houston. Once they were secure, he slipped a special disk into his console and let the system automatically seize control over the Hubbel space telescope.

The Hubbel had once been the wonder of the ages, the greatest marvel of space exploration ever. Humanity had learned a great deal about the formation, and creation, of the universe because of the amazing invention. The basic idea had been simple. The atmosphere of Earth was full of moisture, and dust blurred the light from outer space. So why not build a telescope in space where there is no air? The results had been astounding.

In spite of several upgrades in computers, and a couple of lens replacements, the Hubbel was rapidly reaching the end of its useful life. Oh, it still worked, and would for some time. But a new supertelescope was being built, the Space Telescope. This one would tag along behind Earth in its orbit, protected from the blinding rays of the sun by the penumbra shadow of the planet. Cooled by liquid nitrogen, the Space Scope would have the same thermal signature as the universe. Free from any possible distortion, the new device would be able to see a thousand times farther than the Hubbel, with a hundred times greater clarity. If trained upon Earth, it would literally be able to read the time on a wristwatch. Turned outward toward deep space, who knew what marvels it might uncover? Which was why Stony Man made sure it also had access to the new Space Telescope, in case they ever needed it for national security reasons. However, that was still being constructed. The Hubbel would have to do for today.

"And…we're on-line," Kurtzman announced with a flourish.

"Already?" Tokaido asked, looking sideways as he slide a new CD into his stereo.

"Readiness is all," Kurtzman stated, pausing to take a sip of steaming coffee.

Kurtzman grinned as the main monitor cleared to a view of near space, the shiny blue-white Earth filling the lower left corner of the screen.

"Won't somebody notice the Hubbel looking in the wrong direction?" Delahunt asked in a worried tone.

"It's being registered as a malfunction," Kurtzman answered, blocking a request from NASA for the Hubbel to run diagnostics. "We have control of this baby anytime we want. Remember a couple of months ago, NASA lost control of the Hubbel? Made all of the newspapers? That was us."

Kurtzman leaned into the keyboard and monitor. Okay, this was the tricky part. Finding the damn thing. There was no platform, like a missile base in space, that contained the Thors. The Thors would be floating free, attached to nothing, held in placed only by their own inertia. Naturally, the enemy had painted them a flat black to hide against the ebony of space, that was a given, and even if America had a mass proximity detector that could reach that high, the Thors would probably be spread out over hundreds of feet… yards…miles? A needle in a haystack was child's play compared to this. You could always burn down the haystack and sift through the ashes. This was a little bit more complex.

Time passed slowly, an hour, then two.

"How are you searching for them?" Delahunt asked, flexing her shoulders. An itch was impossible to scratch when wearing VR gloves. "Infrared at dawn?"

"Exactly," Kurtzman replied, rubbing his eyes. "There's no other way." To keep the Thors cheap, they would be made out of simple steel bars. Painted black, yes, but not coated with any thermal insulation, like the tiles on a space shuttle. Thus, when the sun rose, the metal would get warm and radiate a small but detectable thermal signature against the absolute cold of space.

Of course, any tremendous amount of orbiting junk would also do the same thing—dropped tools, jettisoned waste material frozen solid, wreckage from the secret satellites... Plus, the Thors were only vulnerable to detection during the terminus, the dividing line when night became day. Eventually he would find them. But this was going to take some time...

"Son of a bitch, I found them!" Kurtzman swore in surprise, then his face darkened. "The Thors are at three hundred miles, and there are only a dozen of them. Hmm, and there are another dozen a hundred miles away at 310 miles. Oh, crap. They're in clusters."

At her post, Delahunt whistled. "These folks don't miss a trick. The bastards sent up groups of Thors to strategic positions and parked them until needed. No sense moving the rods around. That'd use up their limited fuel capacity."

"What kind of fuel?" Tokaido asked, his eyes closed. His headphones vibrated from the thunderous rock music. To the others, it was a tinny voice from another room. "Maybe we could do a spectrographic reading of the sky and find the exhaust that way?"

"Won't work," Wethers declared, removing his pipe to

examine the well-chewed end. "There is no way the Thors have a LOX/LHO engine. Liquid oxygen and liquid hydrogen are the best chemical fuels pound for pound, but that requires a lot of heavy insulation. I would more tend to believe they're using a boron plasma drive."

"A what?" Delahunt asked, her hands pausing. "Are you making that up?"

Wethers threw back his head and laughed. "Good Lord, no. It's what NASA uses as a retro rocket for the shuttles. A boron plasma drive is just a solid block of elemental boron and a small microwave beamer, similar to what you have in the kitchen. The microwaves tear the boron apart on the surface and a boiling plasma jet blasts out with tremendous force. There are no moving parts, and the boron block will last indefinitely."

"Why wasn't this in the Mahone report?" Tokaido asked, craning his neck for a better view of the world map.

"The technology didn't exist back in 1970. NASA developed it around 1994 or so."

"Okay, we get lemons, we make lemon beer," Kurtzman said, cracking his knuckles. "We found a handful. Let's see what we can find out about them."

The view on the screen zoomed forward with dizzying speed, and there they were, dark shapes in the rosy dawn. Cycling through its menu, the Hubbel probed with radio waves, visual light, IR, UV and X-ray, feeding the data stream to the banks of Cray supercomputers. Slowly, the computers delivered an enhanced image of thick steel bars, six feet long and painted black. There were a few discolorations near the middle, denoting the receivers and targeting system—it was too primitive to be called a computer—and four stubby wings at the end. But the earlier estimation had been wrong. There were about a hundred Thors in the cluster.

"And we've already found four other clusters," Kurtzman said, recording the scene and sending a copy to Price and Brognola. "Christ, there's enough of the things up there to fight World War III."

"Any HK sats nearby?" Tokaido asked hopefully.

"Wouldn't matter if there were," Kurtzman growled. "Hunter-killer satellites destroy other satellites by firing small missiles or by exploding themselves and sending out a halo of shrapnel."

"Neither of which would do anything against a foot-thick steel bar."

"Exactly," Kurtzman said, wheeling away from the console to refill his mug. "But these things must have a flaw, a weakness somewhere. Everything has an Achilles' heel, and I'll find theirs." He just had to find it before the builders noticed the unwanted attention and retaliated.

"I'm ready to go," Delahunt reported, a finger poised above a macro key.

"Not until I say so," Kurtzman warned, returning to the console. He placed his mug onto a piece of paper. "Ah, there's a British Excalibur spy satellite sitting nearby, less than a thousand miles way. I'll try to hack into a Thor… Damn!"

"What?" Tokaido asked.

"The Thor is blind-coded."

"Damn," Tokaido agreed vehemently. The Thors didn't have radio receivers. They got their targeting data from a maser. The Farm was absolutely state-of-the-art when it came to electronics, but they didn't have a laser cannon, or access to one, capable of firing a modulated beam into space. There had never been a need before.

"Can we still jam it somehow?" Delahunt queried, releasing the civilian satellites. "Flood it with enough bright light that the maser can't reach them?"

"Got a couple of arc lamps in orbit?"

"No."

"Then we can't do it."

Removing his pipe, Wethers started to suggest using an ASL, antisatellite laser. The MIRACLE project, midrange chemical laser, used a ethanol reaction to produce a seventy-second burn. That was enough to kill any incoming ICBM, if they could hit it. But it was useless against a decentralized weapon. Maybe the laser could burn out the receptors on each Thor? No, too many of them. Besides, Sky Hammer would have polarized lenses as protection against solar flares.

"Oh, hell," Kurtzman said, his voice rising in timbre. "Heads up, people. We have activity!"

On the shots from the Hubbel, the Stony Man team could see the thrusters firing on a dozen Thors, a lambent purple glow of ionized gas visible as the thick steel bars started accelerating toward the world below.

"Who are they attacking?" Tokaido asked anxiously. His hands itched to send out a warning to the target, maybe save some lives. But he knew it would be pointless. The Thors literally struck like lightning. There wasn't time for a warning.

"Somebody in the North American continent," Kurtzman stated honestly. "Hell, maybe us." Reaching out, the burly man slapped a button on the console. A submonitor came to life with a picture of Barbara Price on the telephone.

"Yes, Aaron what is it?" Price asked, covering the receiver with a palm. The remnants of lunch, or possibly dinner, were scattered around her desk at the bottom of the screen.

"Barbara, you better sound the alarm," Kurtzman said in a deceptively calm voice. "It's possible that we'll have incoming."

Hanging up the phone, Price pulled a 9 mm Glock pistol from her desk. "What kind of invaders?" she demanded, working the slide to chamber a round for immediate use.

"Sky Hammer," Kurtzman stated bluntly.

The woman went pale at that, then flipped the cover off a button on her intercom and pressed.

Instantly a red light began flashing above the door to the Computer Room and warning sirens began to howl. Stony Farm was about to go hard.

CHAPTER EIGHT

Norfolk, Virginia

Sitting in the warm gray waters off the coast of Virginia, the USS *Hawes* was surrounded by a hundred other warships, and nobody was paying much attention to the frigate.

Only 450 feet long, and displacing less than five thousand tons, the *Hawes* wasn't a very big ship, yet the frigate packed phenomenal firepower. Named after Rear Admiral Richard E. Hawes, the hero of Manilla Bay, the warship was equipped with numerous aircraft, MK-46 torpedoes, a 76 mm rapid-fire, and a Phalanx-class 40 mm Vulcan minigun that moved in perfect synchronization with the radar dish. Very impressive. But its main weapon was a honeycomb of launch tubes filling the middle of the craft, a deadly hive containing a wide assortment of missiles: ship-to-ship, ship-to-air, ship-to-underwater, several nuclear cruise missiles and four ASM, antisatellite missiles.

Near the end of the cold war, America and the Soviet Union had raced to develop a satellite killer. Then the soviet bloc collapsed, and antisatellite weapons were banned during the SALT talks. However, just in case, the U.S. Navy had kept a few squirreled away in storage, and now their paranoia was paying off.

"Captain on the bridge," a lieutenant called as the officer appeared in the hatchway.

"At ease, gentlemen," Captain Winterborn said, walking briskly to the command and control board. "What's our status, Lieutenant?"

"All systems are go, Skipper," Lieutenant David Jones said crisply.

"We have a green light, Mr. Donaldson," Captain Winterborn stated, studying the readout panels. "Ready the hive." Working the control board, the lieutenant opened the hatches on four launch tubes, released the inner locks and opened the exhaust vents. "Good to go, sir."

"Fire, Mr. Ridley, let 'em jump," the captain ordered.

The first officer of the missile frigate pressed the button on the fire control board. Amid ships, a white column of fire and smoke rose into view. The stabilizing fins snapped into position, lifting quickly into the blue sky. A few moments later, the first stage disengaged and fell away as the liquid-fueled second stage kicked in. The ASM streaked into the sky with breathtaking speed.

"Again, Mr. Ridley," Winterborn ordered.

"Aye-aye, sir," the first officer replied, hitting the next three buttons.

A trio of satellite killers erupted from the honeycomb of pods, darted into the blue and out of sight.

"Report, Mr. Miller," the captain requested, clasping both

hands behind his back. Incredibly, an amateur astronomer in Duluth, Minnesota, had spotted something eclipsing Ursa Minor and reported it to a UFO club. After that, how the information got into the hands of the Pentagon, the naval officer had no idea. Probably the NSA and their snoops listening to cell phones. That was all the snoops were good for, actually. But their keyhole-peeping paid off today. Now they were going to destroy this terrorist battle station with one salvo. These birds were Skywalkers, the newest model of the old ASM-135. Humorishly named after that kid from the sci-fi flick, these Skywalkers could reach four hundred miles straight up, and carried a warhead of explosive bomblets. A trick the Navy stole from the Air Force after how well it worked in the Gulf war. Soon, there was going to big a great big hole in space where nothing existed anymore, except for a billion dollars' worth of wreckage.

"Our birds are five-by-five skipper," a specialist mate reported sharply, bent over a radar screen. "The first bird is at…ten miles and climbing. The first stage was just separated, second stage is live and fine. The others are close behind."

"Very good, carry on."

"Aye, sir!"

Studying the radar screen, Winterborn watched with pleasure as the four blimps climbed into space at Mach Two and steadily accelerated. The higher they went, the faster they moved as there was less gravity and air to get in the way. Fifty miles now. Sixty. The second stage of the missiles dropped away, and the third and final stage assumed the work of driving the deadly birds far beyond the atmosphere, past Earth's gravity. A hundred miles now, 120, 160. The radar echoes were only shadows, of course. The missiles projected a radar ghost of themselves, making it virtually impossible for them to be tracked or shot down. Of course, nothing was perfect, but a detection hadn't occurred yet.

Thoughtfully rubbing his jaw, the first officer couldn't shake the uneasy feeling that they were sailing into a mined harbor. This was all too easy, too predictable. "Sir, request permission to arm the antimissiles."

The captain swung around and started to demand a reason why, then frowned and nodded. The XO started to bark orders and sailors rushed to obey.

Just then, the four blimps on the radar screen vanished.

"What the... Sir, our birds are dead!" a rating announced.

Winterborn snapped around. "How many?" the captain demanded.

"All of them, sir. Orders?"

Damn and hell! Crossing the room in a stride, Winterborn grabbed a hand mike and thumbed the switch. "Engine room? This is the captain speaking. Give me emergency power! Full speed, hard a port. And I mean now!"

"Aye-aye, sir!" a sailor replied.

As the ship began to change direction, heading for the open sea, the radar started to beep, the tones coming closer together every instant.

"Fire in the hole!" the XO announced, pressing a series of buttons.

Four boxes in the honeycomb burst open and a stuttering stream of fiery flashes streaked skyward as the fourteen Sparrow antimissiles took off, searching for anything that didn't broadcast a recognition code. Then six Standard antimissiles joined the fight. But even as the Sparrows and Standards spread out in a protective umbrella, the Thors flashed past them and hit the *Hawes* like the hammer of God.

A white-hot bolt grazed the side of the frigate, setting off the Phalanx gun, the automatic weapon systems firing a long burst of 40 mm shells in an effort to kill the invader. But the molten Thor was deep underwater by then, setting off the sonar alarms for the entire bay.

Then the rest of them arrived, punching holes through the deck armor as if it were paper. The frigate shook as sirens howled. In hammering fury, the USS *Hawes* was brutally torn apart, pieces of hull flying from the staggering impacts of the suborbital rain. Sailors vanished in fiery explosions.

Lolling from side to side, the crippled warship started to slow down when the fuel tanks ruptured. The explosion ignited the missiles, and the ship seemed to rise slightly from the water, then vanish in a deafening thunderclap.

The concussion spread outward across the Atlantic Ocean, heading for the other warships docked at Norfolk base, but before the reverberation reached anything, wreckage began to rain from the sky. A few moments later, there wasn't any sign that the USS *Hawes* and her brave crew had ever existed, aside from a faint trace of oil and blood on the choppy water.

European Space Agency Headquarters

TOUCHING HER HAIR, the pretty young secretary checked herself in the compact mirror, liked what she saw and practiced a gracious smile. Yes, that would do nicely.

Tucking the compact into a drawer of her desk, Valerie

Carlson rose and gathered a thick report bearing the ESA logo. Walking across the reception area, she could hear the murmur of a hundred voices from the secretary pool and the endless tapping of computer keyboards. Every time they completed a project, it was exactly the same, rush-rush-rush. Then a small celebration that they had pulled it off, as if a battle had been won against overwhelming odds. Then again, the financing was very complex, with a dozen countries sharing the monetary responsibility, and each paying a different percentage. Depending upon their involvement and interest.

Strutting down a hushed corridor full of bustling people, Valerie slightly crossed her legs with each step to put a well-practiced sway in her hips. More than a few heads turned her way and she paused to playfully check the rear seam in her old-fashioned stockings, relishing the attention it garnished. Especially when her short skirt rode up to a dangerous level.

Beautiful and young, healthy and full-figured, Carlson could type a hundred words per minute, and held minor degrees in electronics and chemistry, plus spoke four languages. But she had turned down jobs across Europe to work for the project coordinator for the European Space Agency. The middle-aged man wasn't very wealthy, most top executives at the corporations he worked with earned ten times his salary. A hundred! But when she had seen him at an international conference about space exploration, she'd fallen instantly in love with him. Silly, yes. Stupid, ridiculously so. But true nonetheless. For weeks she had hoped the feelings would go away. He wasn't rich but twice her age. She didn't care. Carlson wanted him with a burning hunger, and the more reluctant he was, the more it intensified her desire to have him.

Pausing in front of the door to his office, Carlson moistened her lips and softly knocked. Then quickly undid a button on her blouse, then another. Then nervously did one up again. She was out to steal the man's heart, not seduce him for an evening of sex. Bed partners she could get anywhere, and at any time, day or night. Although they probably would be involved, sooner or later. Hopefully sooner. Much sooner.

"Come in, please," a deep voice replied.

Pushing open the heavy door, Carlson walked into the cool room, the clicks of her high heels vanishing as she moved from the marble floor of the hallway to the soft carpeting of the private office.

"Good morning, sir." She smiled.

Reviewing the recent death tolls, Attila Meternich glanced up from his computer screen and watched her approach in genuine pleasure. The hot little bitch was mad for him, wild with desire, and he had done nothing to encourage such a response. It was all very amusing. He ran, she pursued. A delightful little game.

"Good morning, Miss Carlson," Meternich said. "I'm so sorry, Ms. Carlson."

"Valerie," she corrected softly.

"Valerie, such a pretty name. Is that a new skirt?"

She dimpled and turned around, making the soft fabric swirl and rise slightly, briefly showing her silk panties.

"Lovely." Meternich chuckled.

"Here is the report, sir, on the new space transport," Carlson said in a sultry manner. "I tried to follow the mathematics but it was so…complex. Maybe we could get together some time and you could…" She smiled. "Explain it to me. Alone. Maybe in my apartment. Tonight."

"That would be improper," Meternich said, as if slightly shocked. "Then again…"

"Yes," she asked, her eyes filled with the sight of his handsome face.

Making no reply, he accepted the report and started to turn the pages, reading about fuel consumption and aerodynamics chain tests. The shock diamonds were up on the new boron engine. Very nice.

After a few minutes the secretary realized that he wasn't going to respond, and turned from the office, closing the door behind.

"Whore," Meternich muttered, putting the worthless report into the trash basket. My God, his grandfather would kill peasants like her just to test the edge of a new sword.

Getting back to his real work, Meternich accessed the files of Sky Hammer and reviewed the recent kill list. Very nice. Every time they used the system it became more accurate. First they had done ranging shots, and some tests in the South Pole and Borneo, where nobody ever noticed. Then a public attack to catch the right attention of all the wrong people. So far, the bidding for their services had been thin, so he accepted a modest payment from the impoverished nation of Chad to hit their northern enemy. That had done the trick. Now the board was filled with offers, each larger and more lucrative than the rest. The American Pentagon had been bothersome, but Sky Hammer quickly put an end to their nonsense. No files meant no chance of his partner's discovery. He was safe and secure inside the American government. And if the pesky American military tried anything else, their White House would be the next target, and he'd grind it down to the bedrock just to prove his point. After that, he'd hit a major amusement park. Yes, splendid idea. Maybe they could do that anyway…no. He shook his head.

"No. Business first," he muttered. "Stay the course. Keep to the plan. Mistakes lead to failure."

Such a pity it would all be over soon. But Meternich didn't consider himself or his partner fools. Greed was what got most criminals caught. There were specific goals, and when they were reached, Sky Hammer would be destroyed, and he'd retire, a proper Hungarian nobleman once more, with many, oh, so many, pretty young ladies to play with in his dungeon.

A chime broke his reverie and Meternich read the latest proposals. A Greek billionaire wanted his ex-wife removed. Good Lord, the alimony had to be truly stupendous for the man to risk committing murder over the Net. Of course it was done through multiple layers of people, so that Interpol and the local police would never be able to get anywhere near the fellow. Hmm, the timing was perfect. Meternich accepted the deal, a partial payment was sent to the numbered Swiss account, and a coded command was sent to his partner. A minute later, a small glowing symbol appeared at the bottom of his screen.

"Done and done," he chortled. The wife was dead, her mansion in Peru destroyed with her inside talking to her ex-husband on the phone so that he could hear the destruction. Meternich informed the billionaire of the matter, and the rest of the funds flowed into the account. Then the software automatically switched the funds from bank to bank, under a bewildering array of names, until it was safely washed and hidden away.

Meternich smiled. Five minutes, five million dollars. Excellent. This put them at the break even point, everything from now on was pure profit. He had mortgaged everything, and borrowed even more, to be able to build the Thors and pay off enough ESA personnel to get them launched into space. Their deaths swiftly followed at the hands of Bella Tokay, and the fiendishly talented Mikhail. But now, everything was coming to fruition, and soon he would have the family estate back.

Kicking off his shoes, Meternich wiggled his toes on the soft carpeting and reviewed more offers. Most were rejected because of lack of funds, or simply because he couldn't trust the people involved to keep their mouths shut. Commoners had no sense of honor. A man's word should be his bond. He never promised to set a victim free and then didn't. That would be rude. Ungentlemanly. He always cut their throats and set them free. Attila Meternich was a man of honor, and none could say any different.

A winking flag signaled new e-mail. He scanned it before opening, and read the offer. So the Colombian drug lords had finally entered the market, eh? Good. He didn't care where the funds came from, as long as they kept coming. The money was acceptable, so Meternich agreed to the deal and assigned four Thors to level a rival drug lord's cocaine labs in Mexico.

Hmm, the IRA wanted to hit Buckingham Palace. Meternich gave them a price, they tried to haggle, and he terminated the call. Was he a rug merchant to be bargained with? Besides, he really didn't like killing fellow royalty. And this was the second time the Irish rebels had tried this foolishness. Using a light pen, Meternich wrote a note on the screen that the next time the IRA placed a bid, to level the source of the call no matter where it was, the isolated Isle of Man, or busy downtown Dublin.

"Idiot peasants," he muttered.

In the corner of the screen was the number of Thors in orbit, thirty-eight. Then the number blinked to thirty-six.

Suddenly a call came in from his partner. Hastily, Meternich donned a pair of headphones and activated the VOX microphone.

"Caesar," a scrambled voice said.

"Mr. Hyde," Attila Meternich replied into the microphone.

"Our financial backer wanted to renegotiate."

The Hong Kong bankers were never satisfied! Meternich raged. What were they going to do, blackmail them? Intolerable.

"Indeed?" Meternich said without emotion. "How very curious."

In their private shorthand, that meant kill the people involved. There were numerous intelligence agencies around the world that monitored communications, and their computers listened for specific keywords. Avoid the words and you were safe to discuss anything. Metnich knew that for a fact. His partner had helped build the very network spying on them right now.

"Agreed. I sent him two flowers."

Two Thors.

"I hope he is not allergic."

Any reaction?

"Sadly, he was."

Meternich noticed the past tense. *Target destroyed.*

"How sad."

Excellent. Well done.

"Agreed. By the way, do you like the color green?"

That confused Meternich for a moment and he struggled to recall what that meant. Green… yes, as in the color hunter-green. Somebody was hunting them?

"Not personally, no."

Are they after us personally, you and I?

"I should have known that."

Not yet.

"However, I do like green flowers."

Can we kill them with a Thor?

"I do not, they are often too large."

Unnecessary overkill.

"Perhaps some other kind of gift?"

What do you suggest?

"I'll buy something appropriate."

Mercenaries.

"As long as it is not very expensive."

Pay any price.

"Agreed. Goodbye," his brother said, and disconnected.

Reclining in his chair, Meternich scowled. He wondered who was searching for them? Perhaps the CIA. He toyed with the notion of destroying their headquarters in Langley, Virginia, then vetoed that idea. An attack on their headquarters now would reveal an information leak at the highest levels. That could be trouble. Sending in mercenaries was the perfect solution. Their own people were dealing with the FBI in Pennsylvania at the moment, keeping the federal agents far away from anything important. But Meternich felt sure that his brother would find somebody to do the job. Perhaps a trade-off, eh? Al Qaeda killed these new hunters, and Sky Hammer destroys Teheran. Quid pro quo. Nice and simple, and totally untraceable. Stay low. Give nothing away. That was the key to success.

Removing the headset, Meternich smiled. There, another problem solved. It was all so easy when there were trustworthy people working alongside you. All of their conversations were like this. No personal chitchat, no jokes, nothing but business. There were old criminals, and there were bold criminals, but there were no old, bold criminals. The brothers had arranged everything to stay as low-key and covert as possible. Nothing could go wrong if they kept to the plan and didn't get greedy. Kill a few million people, make a billion dollars, fake their own deaths, retire to live like kings. Better, as Hungarian barons. Noblemen from the noblest house in all of Budapest. The plan was flawless.

Returning to the bidding, Meternich rejected an offer from North Korea to strike Osano AFB is South Korea. He wasn't interested in petty squabbling. Besides, he hated Communists. What they had done to Hungary was a sin and a crime. If only the Soviet Union still existed, he would happily destroy the Kremlin for free. Ah, well.

Meternich was about to go off-line when an offer came in that he couldn't refuse. How very amusing! Happily, he accepted a down payment and sent the kill command. There in a few hours, he and his brother would be fifteen million euros richer, about seventeen million U.S. dollars. Now that was more like it, a proper fee! The world didn't yet fully understand the raw power of Sky Hammer.

"But they soon will." He laughed out loud.

LISTENING AT THE DOOR, Valerie Carlson had trouble catching her breath. He…he considered her a whore? The word stabbed deep into her heart and she felt numb, as if something had died inside. How could he do this to her? He had to know how she felt!

Fighting back tears, Carlson left the door behind and walked down the marble hallway. And why in the world was Meternich talking in code? Who was this Mr. Hyde? She was familiar with the English novel, and could guess that it was a fake name. Did that mean his real name was dangerous to know? That was very suggestive. Were they doing something illegal? Gambling, maybe, or smuggling drugs. Perhaps even selling proscribed space technology from the ESA files to Communist countries!

Lost in thought, she never even noticed the usual smiles and leers coming her way, her mind a whirling storm of emotion and a slowly building rage over the casual betrayal. Briefly the woman wondered how she could get a glimpse of what was on his computer.

CHAPTER NINE

Pelagosa Archipelago

Leaving Osan AFB in South Korea as quickly and quietly as possible in the C-130 Hercules, Phoenix Force contacted the Farm and arranged for a supply drop at Pelagosa, a small island in an archipelago on the Adriatic Sea, about halfway between Italy and Yugoslavia. Nobody would see them land there.

Israel was a long way from South Korea, halfway around the world, and the Stony Man team was low on supplies. The quartermaster of Osan AFB would have gladly given them anything needed, but most of their equipment wasn't standard issue. Bullets that carried no manufacturer's mark, disposable garrotes, false passports and such weren't typical items in stock at the airbase. Even this close to the DMZ.

Cleaning the salt off their weapons, the Stony Man team chowed down on MREs, affected some minor repairs on cuts and bruises, and got some much needed sack time. Then they rose and ate again. Grimaldi was at the controls of the Hercules C-130.

The hours passed peacefully. Moving with the world, it was still night when the Hercules dropped from their cruising height of thirty thousand feet and started a gradual descent toward the Adriatic Sea. But in spite of the moonlight, there was nothing visible below except endless open water.

"Okay, got them on screen," Grimaldi announced. "Jeez, some of these are so tiny they wouldn't make a decent putting green!"

Standing in the open doorway, McCarter kept an hand on each side of the hatch to steady himself.

"We're headed for Little Pelagosa," McCarter said, looking over the pilot's shoulder.

Behind McCarter, there was a flight of metal stairs leading to the main cargo area. A couple of Hummers were lashed down in place for use in Israel, and the rest of Phoenix Force was buckled tight into jumpseats lining the bare walls. The Hercules was basically a flying truck, and could carry a hundred armed soldiers, tons of supplies, or an APC.

"Ah, sorry, but that's not where we're going," Hawkins corrected. "That's Pelagosa, the big island. We want Little Pelagosa, over there." He pointed to the north.

"Show me," Grimaldi directed, and followed the headings.

Ahead of them, islands appeared on the dark horizon, dots of gray and green lost in the night. Then a blinding light swept the sea, from an island to the south, and Grimaldi corrected his course. Okay, if the lighthouse was Pelagosa, then two islands to the north was Little Pelagosa.

Warily, Grimaldi eyed the land mass with disdain. That

was the big island? God have mercy on them all. He was going to try to land a Mack truck on a postage stamp.

"Do we really have enough room to make a landing?" Hawkins asked, not sounding so confident anymore.

"Two thousand feet exactly," Grimaldi read off the flight plan. "No problem."

"Ahem," McCarter said, behind them. "I thought a bloody Herc needed three thousand feet to stop."

"Well, technically, sure," Grimaldi said, easing the controls forward. The Hercules followed, slowing descending as they went into a gentle dive.

"Hey, trust me," Grimaldi said, checking the hydraulic pressure in the landing wheels. "I once landed a Hercules on an aircraft carrier."

"Bull," Hawkins snorted. "This monster wouldn't fit on the carrier."

"Sure as hell didn't," Grimaldi agreed enthusiastically, lowering the flaps. "Lord, you should have seen their faces when my wings brushed a couple of Hornets into the soup, then I followed right along." He grinned like a madman. "Just said I landed on a carrier. Didn't say I stayed there for very long."

"How long?" McCarter asked, fighting back a laugh.

"Oh, two, three seconds. Now, once I crashed a Raptor on a carrier—"

"Heard it," Hawkins said, cutting off the old tale.

"Half speed," Grimaldi ordered, thinning the fuel mix. The propellers took on a new tone.

"Cutting to half speed," Hawkins repeated, adjusting the controls. Lights blinked everywhere, the flight deck was a Christmas display of high tech. "Landing gear down."

"Gear down, check," Grimaldi confirmed. Then over a shoulder he added, "David, would you like to grab a seat, or have you always had a desire to taste windshield?"

There was no time for a proper reply, so McCarter turned, closed the flight deck door, then trundled down the metal stairs to grab a jumpseat.

On the flight deck, Grimaldi and Hawkins were busy throwing switches and adjusting trims.

"Want to do a pass first?" Hawkins asked, feathering the props to reduce their air speed more. The ocean moved below them in a blur.

"No need," Grimaldi replied confidently. "We're going in!"

Moving low across the azure sea, the Hercules slowed until almost reaching stall speed. The low waves started smacking the landing gear and, for a moment, it looked as though the massive plane was going to crash on the sandy beach. Then the shoreline vanished underneath and the wheels touched dirt.

Violently thrown against their seat harnesses, the two men fought to keep the Hercules on course as they applied the brakes and killed two engines. Rocking and bumping, the aircraft fought to go airborne again, then finally dropped below threshold speed and started to roll along the uneven ground until finally coming to a halt about ten feet from the opposite shoreline and open sea. Perched on a nearby rock, a monk seal stared at them and honked loudly in displeasure before diving nimbly into the water and vanishing.

"Told ya, no problem at all," Grimaldi boasted, forcing his cramped hands off the controls.

"Right," Hawkins drawled, unsnapping the harness. "And my mother is a virgin."

Chuckling, Grimaldi flipped some switches on the control board and started lowering the rear cargo ramp. As it thumped on the flattened grass, the men of Phoenix Force got out and stretched their arms. In the streaming light they cast giant shadows across the tiny landmass. The salty air was crisply clean, and the smooth sea was the only thing in sight.

"Welcome to Little Pelagosa," McCarter said. "Population, us."

"And a couple of lizards," Manning added, motioning at a rock.

The reptiles stared at the humans with huge eyes, their scaled tails lashing about with a scuttle noise.

"Well, we're too damn close to Serbia for my taste," James stated, narrowing his eyes in remembrance of a bloody battle they had there not so very long ago.

Just then a light silhouetted the Hercules and moved across the group. Instantly the men drew side arms and dropped into combat positions. As they reconned around the plane, the team saw a scattering of bare rocks dotting the calm water and near the horizon a rocky mesa rising from the sparkling waves. Situated on top of a craggy bluff was a squat white lighthouse, the oscillating beam sweeping the vista for uncountable miles.

"Must be a Parnel Four, maybe a Five," Encizo said, rubbing the scar on his chin. "Very nice."

"You know about lighthouses?" Grimaldi asked in surprise, standing in the open hatchway. A military flashlight was in his hand, the brilliant beam pointed at the grass.

"I'm navy," Encizo said, tapping his chest with a fist. "If it's docked, we know how to take it. If it floats, we know how to sink it."

"And if it pours, we know how to drink it," James added with a grin. "Come on, swabbie, let's find our stuff and get out of here before the lizards stage a revolt."

Getting additional flashlights from the equipment lockers, Phoenix Force spread out across the dark landscape, Grimaldi staying with the plane, an M-16 cradled in his arms. Soon enough, the team found the stacked crates of supplies at the north end of the tiny island where it would have been impossible to land a helicopter, much less a gargantuan Hercules. The goods had been deposited there by persons unknown, only Barbara Price knew the details. But that was part of her job, getting the teams reequipped in the field. The mission controller had gotten desperately needed ammo airdropped to Phoenix Force in the middle an arctic blizzard when even snowballs wouldn't fly because the weather was so bad. She was the woman behind the men behind the guns, and the team was damn thankful they had somebody as good as Price covering their backs.

Unpacking a Hummer would have taken too long, and afterward the team would only have to store it away again. So the men carried the crates back to the Hercules by hand. Occasionally they would have to drag the bigger boxes along behind them with rope. The amazing Ms. Price had thought of everything but a handcart.

"Maybe she read how Marines are supposed to be half pack mule," Encizo quipped, throwing a packing strap over a crate. Going to the other side, he feed it through the buckle and cinched it tight. Then put some muscle to work and made it tighter. A loose box careening around a plane in flight could be deadly.

"More muscle, less mouth," McCarter directed. "We've got business in Israel."

"Ah, Tel Aviv." Manning sighed, resting an arm against the fuselage of the plane. "Now I know a little bar where the beer is cold, the gaming tables are honest, and there's this belly dancer, Autumn Jade…"

"Too plump," Hawkins snorted, wiping his forehead with a sleeve. "I like little Japanese women who barely reach this high." He held his hand out at a rude level.

Crossing his arms, McCarter gave the big Texan a stern glance he had learned from a SAS air marshall, who in turn claimed that he had learned it directly from the devil.

"All right, cut the horseshit, T. J.!" McCarter bellowed in his best drill sergeant voice. "Now drop and give me twenty, boot!"

Everybody broke into laughter.

"Hey," Encizo said straightening. He stood still for a moment and glanced around, his face a hard scowl. "Something's wrong."

Everybody stopped laughing and studied the well-lit interior of the Hercules. Nothing seemed to be amiss.

"You sure?" Hawkins asked pointedly.

Encizo nodded. "Can't tell you what it is," he said slowly. "But something has changed, and I don't like it."

"Bloody hell, the lighthouse!" McCarter snapped, and strode to a window. Gazing in the direction of Pelagosa, he counted to sixty under his breath. But there was only darkness.

"Could the bulb be burned out?" Grimaldi hazarded for a guess, scratching his head. "Or whatever it is that a lighthouse uses?"

"Cut-crystal refractors with an electric arc lamp," Encizo stated from memory. "Ten million candlepower. And no, they don't burn out. They last forever, as long as there is power."

"Or until somebody turns it off," Hawkins said with meaning, cracking his knuckles.

"Heads up, people! We got company coming!" McCarter barked, snatching an MP-5 machine gun of a wall hook and working the arming bolt. The lighthouse had been sweeping its beam across the Hercules regularly. When it stopped, they had almost missed the subtle difference.

Quickly, the men of Phoenix Force armed themselves. Everybody grabbed a Heckler & Koch MP-5 machine gun, except for Gary Manning. He opened a gun case and took out a Barrett .50-calibre rifle. Draping a bandolier across his chest, he worked the bolt to slide a cigar-size cartridge into the breech. The Barrett was a sniper's weapon, capable of shooting through brick walls or accurately reaching a target more than a mile away. However, the recoil was bone-breaking if the rifle was held wrong. There were very few men in the world who handled the dire weapon better than Manning.

Killing the interior lights, the team walked onto the grassy island and studied the calm sea. Maybe it was just a blown fuse. Or maybe they were already surrounded.

"How could they have found us?" James asked in hushed tones. "If it is the Sky Hammer people, why not just hit us with a couple of Thors?"

"Maybe they're low on ammo. Or maybe we're not in

range at the moment," McCarter whispered, feeling that he was shouting in the quiet. "Or maybe they can't hit anything this small. Who knows? Jack, how soon can we take off?"

"We're good to go," Grimaldi answered. "But first I have to taxi the plane around to face into the wind. This ain't a Cessna, ya know, where four of us can lift the thing and walk it into position. And we're going to need every foot of distance to get off this rock."

"Get back to the flight deck and wait for my signal," McCarter ordered tensely. "But if the balloon goes up, get this crate into gear fast."

The Stony Man pilot nodded and moved back into the pitch blackness of the aircraft, both hands stretched out to feel his way.

"Hawkins, James, sweep the island," McCarter directed, slinging the MP-5 over a shoulder. "Ten-meter spread."

The men moved into the night like ghosts and were gone.

Gently, McCarter worked the slide on his 9 mm Browning Hi-Power, trying to make as little noise as possible. The rest of Phoenix Force did the same, the clicks and clacks sounding like a colony of robotic crickets.

"Gary, get the heavy weapons ready," McCarter added grimly. "Rafe, stay by the control to the rear hatch. Don't close it until we know there is trouble. The bloody thing is louder than the engines."

Suddenly two bright lights flashed into existence across the island and started heading their way. There was no sound of engines, only a whirring noise like an electric fan. Then bright flowers of flame flickered in the night and something hit the open ramp to ricochet off, but then ricocheted again off the Hummer.

"Silenced weapons!" McCarter cursed, raising the MP-5 to started hammering the darkness. "Close the bloody door!"

Lurching into motion, the men got moving just as the huge engines on the wings gave a plaintive whine, coughed, then roared into life. A hurricane swept the little island from the Hercules's massive turboprops. Outraged Falcons nesting in the scrub bushes screamed at the rude awakening and took off into the starry sky.

Riding the weapon into tight figure-eight pattern, McCarter heard the recognizable chatter of another MP-5 come from the south, and then a third spoke from the north side of the island. Manning and James were setting up a cross fire.

As the loading ramp began to raise, a low whine became noticeable above the engines of the trembling Hercules. Then McCarter saw the headlights of the enemy coming straight out of the sea and onto land without slowing.

"Hovercraft!" McCarter barked, firing in controlled bursts. Ignore the machine, aim for the men.

But in the light of the enemy guns, McCarter could see sand bags were placed around the crafts and draped over the vulnerable power plant. Damn! What a clever idea. His bullets patted into the bags and didn't penetrate.

The crew of the hovercrafts abandoned their silenced weapons now that the element of surprise was gone, and opened up with AK-47 assault rifles, the familiar deep thumps of the 7.62 mm rounds filling the night.

Dropping a clip, McCarter reloaded, then moved to a new position in the flapping grass so they couldn't get his range. For a moment the Briton saw the face of the enemy and recognized them instantly. Serbians.

Firing an entire clip, McCarter took out a halogen head-light, but another came on, replacing it instantly. He grunted at that. Okay, no way this was the Serbian militia. That rag-tag collection of warlords and thugs could barely afford ammo. This kind of hardware was impossible for them. Which meant it belonged to a private concern, and that spelled mercs. Yeah, it had to be the Sky Hammer people. For whatever reason, they decided not to get their hands dirty this time. McCarter made a mental note to look further into that, if he was still alive five minutes from now.

Hawkins and James maintained the cross fire, and an-other Serbian crumpled. Staying side by side in attack for-mation, the two Serbian hovercrafts came straight-on, the crews wearing flak jackets, steel helmets and firing Kalash-nikovs. There seemed to be gimbals present for mounting large caliber machine guns, but those were empty. The mercs had to have spent all of their money on the hovercrafts. Fool-ish.

Coming out of a side paratrooper door on the Hercules, Manning dropped to the grass, aimed the Barrett and fired. A lance of flame stabbed out the muzzle, and a Serbian on a hovercraft threw up both arms and went flying backward off the craft, with a gaping hole in his chest.

Now the crews of both hovercrafts returned fire, their AK-47 assault rifles peppering the area in return, the lead boun-cing off the loading ramp, but punching holes through the wings. Fuel started to flow, then stopped. The self-sealing tanks repairing the damage in a heartbeat.

Going wide, the Serbian mercs separated and tried to cir-cle the taxiing plane as it shook along the uneven ground. But

Phoenix Force drove them back into the sea by firing non-stop and replacing clips as fast as they were exhausted. The team was going through ammo like crazy, and only the fact that they had just been resupplied allowed this unorthodox tactic. Spent brass covered the ground, glinting among the grass like fairy gold, smoky and unreal.

There came a thump and something sailed over the Hercules to splash into the sea before detonating. Grenade launcher! Thankfully, the wind from the engines was making it difficult for the mercs to aim, but the plane was slowly turning, and soon they'd be out of the slipstream. The 30 mm Kalashnikov grenade launcher spoke again, and a chunk of ground blew up, sending loose dirt everywhere.

Releasing the MP-5 to hang from its canvas strap, Mc-Carter pulled the pin from a grenade and threw the bomb hard. The sphere hit the side of the hovercraft and bounced off the apron to rebound into the shallows. Seaweed and rocks sprayed out, and stone hit the sandbag armor with the smack of a fist. The Serbians jumped at that, then broke into laughter, and concentrated their guns on McCarter.

As the loading ramp closed with a muffled boom, Encizo stepped out the other side of the aircraft, holding a long tube in his arms.

A string of bullets hit the fuselage of the Hercules, the armor-piercing rounds punching through the reinforced skin of the aircraft until reaching the paratrooper door. The bullets ricocheted off the armored panel without a leaving a scratch.

Reloading McCarter didn't feel cheered by the action. The plane had only a few hardpoints: the flight deck, fuel tanks, galley... The rest of the fuselage was as thin as possible to save weight. This wasn't a combat vehicle to fly into hot zones. Small-arms fire could take out a Hercules with a little luck. He had seen it done.

Throwing another grenade, McCarter missed again, the sphere rolling underneath to be spewed out by the wash of the pinning turbines. The grenade exploded in midair, forming a bright fireball for a second, but harming nothing.

Gunfire was pandemic now. The Serbians threw grenades, but the wash of the Hercules was shoving the spheres back at them. The plane was a hundred feet from the shore, and starting to make its turn, exposing the vulnerable windshield of the flight deck.

Shifting position to track the moving targets, Manning fired again, and another men flew off a hovercraft. The Serbian tumbled underneath, and red blood sprayed out from below the louvered skirt, then came a pair of drenched combat boots.

More explosions shook the dark island, grenades from Hawkins and James. Then smoke puffed from a hovercraft and a fiery dart streaked toward the side of the turning Hercules. An antitank rocket!

Walking alongside the lumbering Hercules, Encizo knelt and fired the fat tube. Wintry nitrogen snow blew out the aft end of the Armbrust as it boomed, and a hellstorm of fléchettes expanded through the air, tearing the rocket to pieces. It exploded twenty yards away from the Hercules, only shrapnel reaching the craft to rain impotently against the fuselage.

Staying with the Herc, Encizo dropped the Armbrust and pulled a LAW from behind his back. Pulling the arming pin, he extended the tube, making the sights pop up and exposing the launch button. Kneeling, the Stony Man warrior took aim and hit the button. Smoke whooshed out the aft end, flame from the front. A split second later a hovercraft erupted in thunder, ripped bodies and broken machine parts flying straight to hell.

Converging from different directions, Phoenix Force poured on the lead in a unrelenting attack.

Moving fast, the remaining Serbian hovercraft slid over the smoky turbulence of the blast zone, charging at the nose of the Hercules, obviously trying to reach the pilot behind the windshield.

Tracking his chattering MP-5 after them, McCarter almost grinned at that. Bad move, boys.

Disappearing from the pilot's seat, Grimaldi reappeared at a gunport on the lower level. Now a Bofors cannon was raised into attack position, and the 40 mm weapon ripped a long burst of explosive shells. The stream went high, but he pushed it down and the shells hammered the hovercraft as they passed, blowing men to pieces in spite of their flac jackets, and smashing equipment. Sandbags exploded, filling the air with loose material. The Serbians kept firing, but so did Grimaldi. Then the Bofors stopped, out of ammo.

But it was enough. Crippled, the hovercraft buckled in the middle and the prow crashed into the ground, plowing a mound of dirt. There came a crash of metal, an explosion, a piercing scream, and the wildly shaking machine flipped over, smashing the crew underneath. Then belly turbines broke loose from their shafts and went spinning free. One went out harmlessly to sea, but the other flew across the island like a buzzsaw. Phoenix Force dropped flat as the impeller slashed by overhead, then it came apart into a thousand pieces of steel that spread out in every direction. Shrapnel hit everywhere like the wrath of God.

"Take any survivors alive!" McCarter bellowed over the crackling flames.

CHAPTER TEN

Stony Man Farm, Virginia

"Understood, Hal. Goodbye." Slowly lowering the receiver, Barbara Price stared at the telephone for a long moment, then rose and left the office quickly. Her relief at not being the focus of a Thor attack was blown away by this latest development.

A minute later she walked into the Computer Room of the Annex. Aaron Kurtzman and his team were busily tapping away, their consoles softly humming.

"Shut it down," she ordered. "Shut it all down!"

Curiously, Kurtzman raised his head. "What was that?"

"Shut it down! Phoenix Force just got attacked by mercs in the middle of the ocean," Price stated, walking closer, her eyes snapping with fury. "Somebody knew exactly where they were and when they would be there."

All work stopped.

"We've been hacked?" Tokaido asked, his voice rising on the end of the last word. "Us?"

Price nodded. "Somehow security has been compromised. The teams can no longer trust any information coming from the Farm. As of this moment, there will be no further communications with the field teams until the matter is resolved."

Kurtzman opened his mouth to speak, then snapped it closed and nodded. Hacked! Well, any system was vulnerable. His team knew that better than anybody else in the world. But the Farm? How was it possible? They had the most sophisticated security system in existence.

"On top of which," Price added, crossing her arms, "I want you to find these guys and burn them to the ground!"

But she said that to the backs of their heads. The Stony Man cyberteam was already at work accessing files and running trace programs, diagnostics and everything else they could think of doing.

Unnoticed, over in the lower left-hand corner of Wethers's console, the automated search program continued analyzing and comparing, adding this new data to the matrix, the red area on the world map for the possible source of the Sky Hammer maser getting smaller and smaller....

Bethlehem, Pennsylvania

TRAFFIC WAS HEAVY on the main streets of the old town, mostly from large trucks hauling rolled steel on flatbeds, the metal going to foreign factories where it could be made into a spectrum of marketable items, to be sold back to America again. Old dented cars mixed with sleek new sedans, the people inside dressed in work clothes and imported suits.

Bethlehem was a city in transit, destination unknown at the moment. But there was always hope.

Keeping both hands on the wheel of the van, Carl Lyons looked around, more angry than saddened by the urban decay. The megacorporations bought the local industry, then broke it apart and sold the pieces for a massive profit overseas. The town was left without source of income for the locals, and that started the downward spiral. The only good thing that could be said was that the air was cleaner now that the coke plants for the steel mills were closed. Very little fresh steel was made anywhere in America these days. The old-fashioned, costly, coal-burning hearths replaced with efficient minifurnaces that used microwaves to melt old steel and purify it into new bar stock. Old rusted cars, corroded metal beams from demolished buildings, bath tubs were the new wealth of America. The corroded material flowed in one side of the microfoundries and clean pure steel come out the other.

After a few years, the air of the once infamous "black fog" capital of the world was now better than Aspen, Colorado, whose burgeoning electronic industry was filling the city with a thick layer of deadly ozone that clung to the ground like swamp mist. But there would be no more Black Christmas for Bethlehem. Now the folks could really breath easily on their way to the welfare office.

At the moment Able Team was driving through one of the poorer sections of the former steel town. The buildings were dirty and the sidewalks in disrepair. Plywood covered the windows of many of the stores, and the cars parked along the street didn't appear as if they had in years.

"We've seen worse," Gadgets Schwarz said, removing the

safety tape from the handle of a gas canister and placing it next to the others on the worktable. The surface was lined with ammo clips, grenades and other items for the upcoming job.

"Sure thing. Beirut," Rosario Blancanales agreed. "After the bombings."

Turning a corner, Lyons almost hit another car as he swerved to avoid a large pothole. Weeds were growing out of the depression showing quite clearly the state of local government. There was always more important things to pay for, and as the roads crumbled, the traffic took their business elsewhere, and the stores closed, the tax revenues dropped, and there was less money to repair the roads. A vicious cycle with no end in sight. Lyons found the situation intolerable, Not new, just intolerable.

"A couple of new stores are opening," Schwarz commented, glancing at the strip malls along the road.

"Local economy seems to be improving," Blancanales said, checking the action on his M-16. "They have a new major, I hear. Must be doing some good."

"Hey, they can't all be crooks," Schwarz agreed, slipping a laptop into a canvas shoulder bag. "Although it does seem like it sometimes."

"Welcome to the twenty-first century."

"What happened to all the flying cars and jet packs we were supposed to have by now?"

"Melted them down to make DVD players."

"Well, at least it was for a good cause."

In spite of himself, Lyons grinned slightly at the exchange. He had no formal training in the military, but even in police work, sometimes the job got so hard the only way to stay sane was by cracking jokes. Lyons had heard tales of officers in combat forbidding any wisecracks. Those were the kinds of officers who kept losing battles and wondered why. Morale was more important than firepower nine times out of ten. That tenth time, however, you better have some really big damn guns or else truly enjoy the smell of polyurethane body bags.

"Done, ready to go." Closing the flap of the bag, Schwarz slid it over a shoulder and adjusted the strap. The bag originally came with a Velcro seal, but that had been removed because it made way too much noise. The laptop was a U.S. Army combat model, sheathed with enough titanium to let it withstand a .357 Magnum bullet at point-blank range. More than once it had saved his life in combat. Plus, it contained an arsenal of high-tech surveillance tools. In battle, as everywhere else, knowledge was power, and Gadgets Schwarz had a bag full of lightning.

"Try this instead," Blancanales suggested, passing over the loaded M-16.

"Got one, thanks." Checking the video probe, a flexible cable that let him see underneath doors to the other side, Schwarz felt his hip vibrate and unclipped the cell phone to take the call. Last one before the mission. No live phones in combat. It was a text message, and his features got hard.

"Heads up," Lyons said, pulling the van to the curb near a sagging mailbox eaten away by rust. He set the parking brake, but left the engine running. "This is it, 264 Alberta Drive."

"Doesn't look like the headquarters for an international spy ring, does it?" Blancanales asked, glancing through the tinted windows. The building across the street was a dump. There was no other word for it. Filthy walls, cracked windows, and the door couldn't be clearly seen under the overlapping layers of graffiti and dirt. A homeless person slept near a basement window, and what looked like a dead cat lay on a brick windowsill, flies buzzing thick around the furry corpse.

"I imagine that would be the whole point," Lyons said dryly. "Can't exactly hang a medallion on the front door for the Local 101, Villains, Thieves and Scoundrels Union."

"Close enough," Blancanales said, pointing skyward.

Curiously, Lyons leaned onto the dashboard and craned his neck to look up. On the roof was a fluttering American flag with the stars replaced by Nazi swastikas.

"You sure we can't kill them, Carl?" the Latino asked hopefully. "Just a few?"

"Tempting, isn't it? But that's not against the law."

"Damn well should be," Blancanales said, slamming the receiver home on the assault rifle.

"Hermann, run a—" Lyons started to say, swiveling around his chair. But he paused seeing that the man was on the phone. From the expression on his face, it wasn't good news.

"Rosario, would you do a scan of the building?" Lyons asked, stepping into the back of the van. "Passive only. We don't want them to get wise, in case they have detection equipment. I'll check the mikes."

"Don't think anything could register through all the grime," Blancanales replied, turning to a small table full of elaborate equipment. "But I'll see what I can get." His hands moved across the electronic devices with a sure knowledge. Ironically, the thermal scanner took a few minutes to warm up. That always amused the hell out of the soldier.

Getting a dish microphone from a locker, Lyons lowered a side window a few inches, and checked to make sure the area was clear before swept the building. At first the mike only got snoring from the homeless man and buzzing from the flies. Increasing the sensitivity, Lyons then heard gurgling water pipes and faint footsteps. Nothing more. Okay, there was somebody there, but he would have expected better soundproofing from people with the technical knowledge to command a Thor.

Or could he be listening to a tape recording, the way divers used the sounds of whales to sneak past sonar nets? Maybe. Nobody in the Justice Department had ever heard of the American Liberation Strike Force, but Brognola had a small file on the group. They were neo-nazis, viciously brutal, and wanted in ten states for assorted crimes, mostly bank robbery and rape.

However, the ALSF was considered small-time and no real danger to America, barely worth noticing. But Lyons knew that the files had been wrong before, and Able Team carried the scars to prove it.

"Okay, the Pentagon just got hit with a Thor," Schwarz reported, a hand touching the receiver hidden in his ear. "Several in fact. They blew a hole in the quad you could drop Rhode Island through."

"Went after the archives?" Lyons asked, packing away the mike.

"That would be the logical guess."

"How many dead?" Blancanales asked over a shoulder. On the infrared screen the building was merely a silhouette. The homeless man was brightly radiating heat, but the cat was thoroughly dead, and the building wasn't registering at all. It was either totally empty or else very well shielded. He didn't like the sound of that.

"One hundred thirty-five are confirmed dead," Schwarz replied slowly, as if disbelieving the answer. "After the Pentagon got hit, the Joint Chiefs had a frigate launch missiles at Sky Hammer." He frowned. "The Skywalkers hadn't just gotten out of the atmosphere yet, when a dozen Thors came down a minute later and hit the frigate. You can guess the rest."

"Skywalkers?"

"Guess we had a few left over somewhere."

"They do any damage?"

"None of them reached space."

Lyons scowled. "What a minute, that's impossible," he growled, sitting on top of an equipment trunk. "The reaction time doesn't jibe. The Thors must have launched before the Skywalkers did to hit the frigate that fast."

"The enemy knew the strike was coming," Blancanales said softly, raising his head. "They were tipped off."

"Well, the CIA said we had a traitor somewhere," Schwarz muttered. "Guess they were right."

"Tell the Farm," Lyons ordered brusquely. "Trust nothing we hear over uncoded channels. Better yet, trust nothing we hear period. If the mole, traitor, spy, whatever, is in the NSA, then every line of communications is compromised."

With a nod, Schwarz got busy.

"Skywalkers, jeez, the damn fools should have known that wasn't going to work," Blancanales sighed, assembling his weapon and sliding in a fresh clip. "Well, the Raptors will handle it from this point."

"Bet your ass they would," Schwarz said grimly, tapping on the cell phone. He finished and closed the lid. "One small problem."

"They hit Edwards," Lyons guessed, "and took out the Raptors."

Tucking away the phone, Schwarz nodded. "Leveled the hangar to the ground. With every F-22 Raptor and the ground crew still inside."

Without comment, Lyons went into the rear of the van and opened an ammo trunk to pull out the Atchisson autoshotgun. Checking the drum full of 12-gauge cartridges, he placed the bulky weapon into a cardboard box and folded the top shut. Then he stripped and got into his uniform. The others did the same. Able Team was going in dressed as city garbage men. Nobody ever paid refuse collectors any attention, and a plastic garbage bag could hold a lot of weapons.

Grimly, Lyons racked the slide of his .357 Colt Python. The Farm wanted these people alive. But alive didn't mean undamaged. People often talked better than ever with a few teeth removed.

"We getting anything off the building?" Lyons asked, tucking the pistol into a holster under his shirt. It was too warm for a work jacket. Missing small details like that often tripped up an undercover officer and blew the arrest.

"No readings. Could be empty."

"Hmm, not likely," Schwarz said, checking a monitor on

the workbench. "Somebody just ordered pizza. Lots of them."

"How many?"

"Ten."

Shaking his head, Blancanales gave a low whistle. "I sure hope all of that is for one big fat guy."

"More likely ten to fifteen skinny ones."

"Don't want to wait thirty minutes," Lyons said carefully, weighing the options. "Somebody is bound to notice us by then." The decision made, he lifted the cardboard box containing the Atchisson. "Okay, we go now. Ready hard, people."

Swinging down a disguised panel in the ceiling of the van, Blancanales removed a couple of specialty items and stored them in the pockets of his uniform. "Ready," he said, lifting a plastic bag full of C4 and handcuffs.

"Hold it," Schwarz said, jerking his chin at the front windshield. "I think this is one of them."

Pulling out binoculars from an equipment bag, Able Team studied the fellow striding down the street. He was young, maybe twenty, with a shaved head and a lot of tattoos. A couple of young women on the corner stopped talking as he came into view, and he swayed in to rudely bump one, sending her into the wall. She came back furious, met his glare, then hung her head and left quickly. Her friend followed right behind.

Laughing, the young man crossed against the green to the Nazi headquarters. At his approach, the sleeping man awoke and raised a foam cup and shook it, obviously rattling coins hoping for a handout. Contemptuously, the youth spit at the homeless man and slapped the cup from his grip, sending loose change across the sidewalk, and kept walking. The raggedy man did nothing and started crawling along the broken concrete, picking up the scattered coins.

"Fun guys," Schwarz muttered, putting down the binoculars. "Can't wait to meet them."

Going to the door of the old building, the fellow knocked, paused, then knocked again, constantly checking over his shoulder as if afraid of being seen. He glanced at the unmarked van sitting near the mailbox across the street, and looked away, paying it no attention.

A minute later the door was swung open by a big man with a shaved head and a bristling mustache, wearing a plastic net shirt that showed a lot of muscles and tattoos. The interior of the building was too dark to scan with the binoculars, but the sideways view of the door showed that it was more than a foot thick, made of several layers of material, shiny steel sandwiched between wood, and other things.

"Glad we decided to make this a soft probe," Blancanales said, holstering his own weapon. The flat Colt .380 pistol fit snugly into the belly holster under his stained shirt, the tails hanging loose. "We'd need a battering ram to breach that baby."

"Can do," Schwarz stated, tucking a handful of incendiary charges into a pocket. Then he placed a hand on the door. "Let's go."

"Hang on, we've been made," Lyons said, stowing away the binoculars and getting behind the wheel. "Let's move to another location, before we go for a visit."

Driving the van into a vacant lot, Lyons parked behind a

burned-out truck chassis, the incongruous windshield the only thing not rusted and broken on the entire wreck. Setting the automatic defenses, Able Team exited the vehicle into the weeds, and left the rear door unlocked in case they needed a fast entry. Normally, pushing the button on the outside handle opened the door. But not this van. It had been modified by Cowboy Kissinger at the Farm, along with some help with Schwarz. Doing that now released a small electric charge. Not sufficient voltage to knock a person unconscious, just enough to make them go away. Anybody who opened the door in spite of the charge got a special mix of tear gas in the face. After that, things got more serious.

Taking some loose dirt from among the glass and weeds, Able Team rubbed the smell of compost into their clothing for an added touch of realism, then took their bag and boxes and walked over to the front door.

As they approached, the homeless man rattled his cup and Blancanales paused at the sight of a U.S. Marine Corps tattoo on the man's skinny arm. Shit.

Leaving Lyons and Schwarz scowling at the front door, Blancanales went over to the homeless man and took away the cup.

The dirty man stared, both hostile and afraid. "Hey…" he started.

Hiding the action from anybody passing by, Blancanales stuffed a wad of bills in the cup and threw it back at him as if he had taken the change. "You don't want to be around here, friend," Blancanales whispered, his black eyes deadly serious. Pretending to scratch, he opened his shirt slightly to show the checked butt of the Colt pistol. "Savvy?"

"R-Roger," the man stammered, staring at the cash.

Blancanales made a motion to slap at the man's face, missed, turned away, laughing. To anybody watching it was just another moment of random cruelty, and nothing of importance.

Clutching the foam cup, the wretched Marine hurried away, his shoulders hunched over as if expecting to receive a blow from the cruel universe.

Watching from the sidewalk, Lyons and Schwarz felt an indescribable sadness as they watched the man depart. Once he had been a warrior for America, now he was starving on the streets. In ancient Rome, a veteran received farmland and a horse when they left the service of the state.

"Sometimes I think we're fighting on the wrong front," Schwarz said, barely above a hush as Blancanales joined them.

Blancanales nodded, too angry to speak.

"Shouldn't have done that," Lyons said honestly, glancing sideways the building. "You might have been seen. But then again, screw 'em," Lyons growled, and went to the front door to knock loudly.

Clustering around the door, his teammates shielded Lyons as he pounded on the wood again, raising a cloud of dried paint from the layers of graffiti. Normally, they would simply knock politely on the door, and when somebody answered they would then shove an electronic stun gun against the metal doorknob to zap knock the other person unconscious, then pick the lock and sweep inside. But that wouldn't work here. The handle was wrapped with duct tape for God alone knew what reason. It would take far too long to get the metal clear, and even then, the inside handle might also be wrapped. Nobody had thought to notice when the door was open before. Entry had to be done the hard way, face-to-face.

"What?" a voice shouted from within.

"Garbage inspector!" Lyons called, knocking loudly on the door. "Have you been recycling?"

"Fuck off!"

"Should I talk to your mommy instead, asshole?" he shouted back.

There was a stunned pause. Then the sound of a bolt disengaging, and the thick door swung open.

"What did you say?" the muscle man in the skimpy see-through T-shirt demanded hostilely, a crowbar in his hand.

Smiling broadly, Lyons kicked him in the crotch with a steel-toed work boot.

Squealing for air, the fellow staggered backward into the building and Able Team followed right behind. Subtlety. Worked every time.

Schwarz snatched away the crowbar, while Blancanales bolted the door. Lyons kept advancing and placed the heavy cardboard box on a table repaired with duct tape. The mystery of the door handle was explained.

"Gonna cut you mother…" the beefy man croaked, clutching his groin and looking up to see the three Able Team commandos leveling silenced handguns. Three black eyes of death.

"Speak and you die," Lyons vowed, thumbing back the hammer to drive home his point.

Incredibly, the doubled-over man tried to run away. Switching hands, Schwarz shot him in the back. The twin barbs of the stun gun went through the plastic mesh T-shirt and delivered a parlaying jolt of 40,000 volts and not many amps. The man convulsed, every muscle straining, tightening hard, then the current cut off and he collapsed unconscious to the threadbare carpet.

Retrieving the Atchisson, Lyons stood guard while Blancanales bound the fallen man's wrists with disposable police handcuffs, and then Schwarz slapped a strip of duct tape from the table across his mouth, leaving the nostrils clear.

Opening the plastic garbage bag, the men reclaimed their weapons, but left the assault rifles slung over a shoulder, and proceeded with their silenced pistols in hand.

Sweeping across the room, the team soon saw that the building used to be some kind of a factory. The carpeting ended where walls used to exist, beyond that was bare concrete, stained and roughed from years of heavy work and machinery. Broken pipes jutted from the floor where something was once connected to the city water supply, and rusted drains were scattered everywhere. Lyons recognized the layout as a cutting room, where ingots were sliced into slabs. Once this had been a busy workshop, thriving with energy, full of people earning a living. Now it was a hovel, reeking of excrement and hate.

A door marked Toilet in spray paint was situated under a flight of stairs leading to the next floor, there was louvered metal door for a loading dock chained into place, and the only door in sight was barred and partially bricked as if the owners expected an armed attack. The windows were covered with plywood with tufts of pink fiberglass insulation sticking out, the ceiling tiles were the same, giving the factory an odd appearance of a stuffed toy coming apart at the seams.

The brick walls were covered with Nazi posters, some of them replications from World War II. A few had been decorated with markers, adding obscene slogans to the rigid German soldiers. Part of a poster was eaten by cockroaches and a squashed silverfish lay smeared on Hitler's stern face.

Catching a whiff of ammonia, Schwarz waved a chemical snuffer around, carefully watching the indicator. The other members of the team waited with guns in had. Ammonia was the prime ingredient in a lot of cheap explosives; the place could be mined to blow.

"Clear," he announced, gesturing at a stained corner of the wall. "It's human, not industrial ammonia."

Going to the bathroom door, Lyons knocked politely, and after a moment the door swung open and out walked a skinny woman drying her hands on a towel. The blonde had close-cropped hair, almost a Marine buzz cut, but her eyebrows were brunette, showing the color was from dye, not nature. She was braless, and really didn't need one, the sleeveless T-shirt bulging from overdeveloped muscles instead. Her thick arms were covered with barbed-wire tattoos and naked laughing very-male demons, while a Nazi Iron Cross hung around her throat. More importantly, the lady weight-lifter was packing a Ruger on her left hip, with the grip reversed for a crossdraw.

"Say nothing," Lyons ordered, pointing the massive barrel of the Atchisson at her face.

The woman gasped in surprise, then went for the Ruger. Not bothering to shoot, Lyons flipped over the Atchisson and rammed the stock into the women's left temple. She crumpled to the stained concrete with a sigh.

The bathroom proved empty, and hadn't been cleaned in years. Lyons understood now why somebody had used the corner of the factory as a makeshift latrine.

"No way these people are running the show," Blancanales stated, standing straight. "Maybe knocking over a fruit stand, or mugging an old lady, but attacking the Pentagon with a Thor?"

Lying on the floor, the skinny blonde was trussed like the other man, her hawkish nose sucking in air to show that she still lived.

"Could be a cover," Schwarz said, placing tape across the woman's thin-lipped mouth. She had a tongue-stud and he didn't know if that would hinder her breathing, so he poked a hole in the middle with a knife to help. "City inspectors, and cops might see down here, so they try to make it as disgusting as possible. While upstairs it's the War Room with top computers, and a SAM missile."

"Sounds like a trap to me," Lyons said, going through her scant clothing. He found nothing except a spare ammo clip for the Ruger and a man's wallet full of credit cards with a variety of names. Then one of the credit cards moved under his fingers and out slide a wafer-thin razor blade. Sticking the deadly little blade under a boot, he snapped it off, then returned the disarmed credit card to the wallet.

"A trap, eh?" Blancanales said, scowling at the fluffy ceiling tiles. "Let's find out."

Starting for the stairs, the team paused as footsteps could be heard tromping above, gray and pink dust raining from the stuffed ceiling tiles.

"Hey, Thor, who was at the door?" somebody called from above.

The Stony Man operatives registered surprise at that name, then moved swiftly to the wall under the stairs and took positions. Heavy boots could be heard on the steps, and when a pair of pants came into view, Lyons jabbed them with a stun gun. Gasping in pain, the man stumbled and fell down the rest of the stairs as if he'd slipped and tumbled.

Tossing his gun to Blancanales, Schwarz caught the man as he rolled off the stairs, checked to see he was still alive, then dragged him aside and bound him securely. He retrieved his Taser.

Keeping to the edge of the steps where the old wood was less likely to creak, Able Team proceeded upstairs, guns at the ready. A scrawny man appeared from an open doorway as they reached the landing, and Schwarz raised the stun gun when he saw the fellow was wearing linked chainmail for a shirt. Switching hands, he fired the Beretta, and the men crumpled, groaning loudly as he clutched his stomach. But there was no blood in sight.

Stepping close, Lyons touched the neo-Nazi's neck with the stun gun, and the man went silent. A brief check showed there was no blood, only a stretched area where the 9 mm slug had hit the chainmail, but failed to penetrate. He grimaced at the thought of what the sledgehammer blow had to have felt like, and moved on. The building was like a crack den—then it hit him. That was why the layout downstairs was so familiar. He had seen similar designs before as a L.A. cop. This was just the East Coast version. An old factory converted into a crack den. More and more, this was feeling like a waste of time. But something in his gut, honed in a hundred battles on the mean streets of the nation, told him there was something more here. Something they were going to miss unless they stayed sharp.

The second floor was mostly a big screen TV with five loungers in a curved line. Sheets covered the chairs, and Schwarz looked underneath each, then moved on.

This seemed to have been the employee lounge at one time. There was a refrigerator filled with junk food, an unused kitchen in one area, along with another toilet worse than the one downstairs if that was possible. The cracked plaster walls were covered with downloaded pictures of Internet porn stars, most of them Latino, Asian or black. Some male, some female, a few of both sexes.

"I thought these guys were supposed to be racists?" Schwarz asked, puzzled by the bizarre pornography.

"Love thy enemy," Lyons muttered, feeling as though insects were crawling over his body. "But with these fools, I think they took that literally."

Going to a closet, Blancanales found it locked with a brand-new, shiny Vische lock. He whistled softly as he picked the lock and swung open the door. The closet was actually a small tiled room, completely filled with guns. None of which seemed to have ever been fired, some of them thick with dust and cobwebs.

"Some of these were fired and put away dirty!" Schwarz said in disgust, touching a rusty M-1 rifle hanging from a shower nozzle with his oiled Beretta. "Half of these would jam the next time they're fired."

"These guys can't spell Thor, much less build one," Blancanales agreed. This room had once been a shower for the workers to wash in before donning their street clothes. It had to have been hotter than hell in the cutting room downstairs.

"Let's finish the sweep and get out of here," Lyons decided, pushing aside a plastic curtain covering a shower stall. A dead rat lay covering the drain, ants carrying away the carcass bit by bit. He let the plastic drop back into place.

"Okay, this is a bust," Lyons declared. "Just some local creeps who heard about the attack on the wall and tried to grab some glory for their organization."

"Doesn't feel like that," Schwarz added, closing the door behind them as they left. "But I guess we're wrong this time. It happens."

"Yeah, guess you're right, Mr. Stone," Blancanales said, gesturing at the toilet door across the room. It was open a crack, but had been closed tight before.

"All right, guys, let's go," Lyons added.

Instantly the toilet door slammed open and out came the skinny man they'd seen on the street, firing a pair of revolvers at the head of the stairs. It took him a second to realize there was nobody there, and he spun to track after the three invaders.

The slugs went wild, as if he'd never used a handgun before, and Able Team returned the favor with the stun gun. The young neo-Nazi groaned loudly and dropped the guns, but stayed standing for a moment before sagging to the linoleum floor.

"Tough guy," Blancanales said, prodding the body with his pistol to make sure the fellow wasn't faking. "Must be the leader."

"Brains, not brawn, how original," Schwarz said, applying handcuffs and duct tape.

Checking the reeking stall, Lyons noticed that the toilet-paper roll was off center and prodded it with his Python. It fell away to reveal a series of mirrors set inside the wall to afford an upside down view of the toilet downstairs. The pervert had been spying on the skinny woman. That's how he'd known the team was here.

"Leave him for the cops," Lyons said, pulling out a cell phone. "We'll place a call and hit the road. This was—" He stopped just then and closed the cell phone with a snap, pocketing it.

It was faint at first, then the telltale throb of heavy rotors could dimly be heard. Four—no, six, blades. The sound was unmistakable. Standard police helicopters used three, SWAT used four, only the military used more.

"It's a trap," Blancanales whispered, holstering the Colt and unslinging the M-16. He worked the arming bolt. "Somebody arranged for this just to see how we'd come after them."

"You mean to kill whoever came after them," Schwarz corrected grimly, yanking out the shell from the breach of the M-203 slung under his M-16. He shoved the stun-bag round into a pocket and took a 40 mm fléchette shell from the canvas bag at his side.

The throbbing got louder as the team freed the prisoners, and hauled them downstairs before waking them with snap capsules of smelling salts under the nose. The fellow wearing the chainmail shirt didn't rouse, and Schwarz had to inject him with a NATO Hot Shot, a combination of powerful drugs guaranteed to get a soldier moving again no matter how bad the wounds. The aftereffects were considerable, but that wasn't Able Team's problem.

"Who are you?" the skinny man demanded, holding his throbbing head. The effects of the stun gun were still strong.

"Friends," Lyons said, helping the youth to stand. "Get your people out of here fast. The Feds are on the way."

"Feds?" he slurred, then adrenaline hit and he woke hard. "Shit! We always knew this going to happen someday."

"We'll stand with you," the blond woman slurred, rubbing a aching temple. "We got a lot of guns, real expensive ones, too."

"And Molotov cocktails," another boasted, going to a lounge chair and throwing off a sheet. The middle of the cushioned chair was gone, the hole filled with bottles topped with oily rags.

The throbbing stopped then, and silence filled the factory.

"They're here." Lyons cursed, then turned and put a round from the Atchisson into the floor, blowing a hole in the linoleum.

"Move!" he commanded. "Run and don't stop, or we'll do you next!"

Under the threat of the three weapons, the amateur Nazis shuffled toward the stairs, then their will broke and they charged out of sight below.

"Captain Softhearted," Blancanales said with a hard grin.

Lyons shrugged. "Innocent until proved guilty."

"Enough chitchat," Schwarz said, flipping the selector

switch on his assault rifle to full-auto. "Let's go meet our hosts for this party."

"Same as before," Lyons directed. "We want them alive."

"If possible," Blancanales added as there came the sound of splintering wood from above.

CHAPTER ELEVEN

Barcelona, Spain

The body had washed up on an isolated length of shoreline in Spain. It was bloated from a long immersion in the water, and had been nibbled upon by numerous fish, but the corpse was still recognizable as having once been a beautiful young woman.

The small boys who found it were horrified, and ran home screaming to their parents about a dead mermaid in the tide pools. After lunch, the weary father had gone for a look. He returned in less than an hour and called the police.

In due time, a constable arrived with a van and took a lot of photographs, just in case this was some rich person fallen overboard. The French Riviera wasn't far away, and the drunken fools who owned priceless yachts, but could never be called sailors, liked to power around throwing wild parties and causing trouble. Many times before there had been bodies on the beach where the tide and currents deposited them unceremoniously.

The Barcelona morgue attendants chilled the body to firm the softened flesh, then took fingerprints and sent them off to Interpol, hoping the woman was a wanted criminal and there was a huge bounty for her death. But alas, she merely soon turned up as a missing person—a Kimberly Nia Stone from Athens, Greece, missing these past few days, last reported seen on the French Riviera.

The body was covered with marks that couldn't be disguised as fish bites or coral damage. She had been tortured before death, slice and burned. Possibly raped, but after a few days in the sea, that was impossible to tell. Bruises were literally everywhere on the battered body. The morticians in Greece would have to repair the damage and handle the grieving family. Reverently, the morgue attendants packed the body into a refrigerated coffin to retard further decomposition, and arranged for the body to be sent home by air. Just another lost soul in the ocean of human misery.

Bethlehem, Pennsylvania

THE STOLEN CADILLAC sat idling in the alley, while its passengers quickly performed one final check of their weapons. There was not going to be another mistake like in Paris.

Many years earlier, several men met inside a jail in Algiers, and were surprised to discover they were fellow Hungarians. Cutting a deal with a guard, the prisoners escaped during the next full moon, killing another guard who had been sleeping with the wife of the first guard, thus paying for the loan of a knife, a brass key and a map. Broke and hunted, the escaped prisoners had to steal clothing, food, cars, then guns, and rob a bank to eventually reach home alive.

But by now the pattern had been set: a strong distrust of the vagaries of authority, and a liking for the dark freedom of criminal activities. The four banded together, forming the Blue Moon, and set about forging a criminal empire.

Twenty years later, their children sat in a stolen El Dorado, assault rifles in hand, watching the back door of the ALSF headquarters. Stealing things for profit had been their fathers' business, but it wasn't a solution to poverty. The real money came from killing. First the aristocrats who cruelly ruled Hungary, then the Communists, then the military, and now it was anybody who hired them. The Blue Moon team didn't ask reasons, just who and how much.

"God, I miss Budapest," Petrov Delellis rumbled, checking the .44 derringer in his hand. Shoving it backward there was a click and the gun vanished up his sleeve.

"I know what you mean," Bella Tokay agreed from behind the steering wheel. "America is like green beer. Too young to have any flavor yet."

"Look at this place," Delellis scoffed. "Not a single building older than a hundred years. Bah. The stones still weep from the cutting in the quarry." Casually, the big man ran a hand across his coal-black hair, making sure it was still in place. The thick crop of curls was plastered flat by an odorless pomade, the same brand his father used when he did special assignments for the hated KGB.

"Alert, there's the helicopter," Zdenka Salvai said, pointing upward. "It's landing on the roof, right now."

"Then the fools should be coming out at any second,"

Tokay said softly, flicking off the safety on his AMR-69 assault rifle.

The compact weapon fit snugly under his loose coat, and the Russian-designed sound suppressor fit smoothly to the satiny-black steel. This wasn't the huge cumbersome model given to ground troops, but the compact, lightweight killing machine designated for special airborne troops, the best of the best in his mountainous homeland. There was a rail along the side for a laser-pointer, and the AMR-69 carried its trademark flip clip—one carrying a full load of 7.62 mm rounds and the other holding only five of the blunt-nosed rounds reserved for special use.

"I'm looking forward to this," Salvai agreed, minutely adjusting the Hungarian-made flamethrower with her scarred hands.

The preburner hissed softly, the tiny blue flame in the ventilated barrel casting an oddly cold light on the ceiling of the luxury car. It was an old weapon, designed for killing troops inside concrete bunkers. But there were a lot of caves in her country, and nothing was better for flushing out hidden enemies than a stream of jellied gasoline under high pressure.

Grenades could sometimes cause a cave-in, and then you'd never know if you got the enemy or if they'd escaped. That kind of mistake could get a person killed with a knife in the back ten years later. Flame did the trick, setting off the ammunition the hidden soldiers carried. Afterward, she had learned to simply count the boots and divide by two to get the kill number. Heads often cracked and shattered. But military boots were tough and survived intact. Her first pair of shoes as a child had been Russian boots stuffed full of newspaper for her much smaller feet. Salvai still had them in a closet at home. A treasured memento of the years with her father, learning the family business.

The windows were down and the mercenaries tried not to notice the reeking piles of garbage around their vehicle. The car had been stolen only hours ago, the body of the owner not yet discovered by the efficient American police. The vehicle was an older model without a low-jack or automatic theft devices. The faceplate for the radio didn't even come off to discourage thieves. There was no alarm and the steering wheel didn't lock into place. It was just an old car, large enough for six, and quite valueless. Which made it perfect for the three Hungarian killers and their cargo of illicit military ordnance.

"We could get hot goulash in Tatabanya, or better yet, lovely Budapest," Petrov muttered softly. "Red wine and fresh sour cream."

"Old gold and young girls," Tokay added with a half-smile.

"That goulash we got in Bluestone was wretched and the women even worse."

"Shut up," Salvai snapped irritably, lighting a fresh cigarette off the preburner. The tobacco tasted odd for moment, then was fine, and she blew an impatient smoke ring out the window. Any second now.

A man in a dirty overcoat but polished shoes shuffled along the street. Warily, he approached the parked car, then spread open his coat to display the items strapped to his body.

"Candyman." He chuckled. "I got 'ludes, bennies, zooters, whatever ya want."

"How nice," Tokay said without emotion, and the bulbous end of a silenced Kalashnikov pistol came out of the side vent window and pointed at the drug dealer. The startled man had only enough time to gasp before subsonic lead punched through his stomach, blowing his life red and hot onto the nearby brick wall. He collapsed onto a garbage can in a ringing crash and they both rolled into a still pool of scummy water near a sewer grating.

"Police?" Salvai asked, not even looking up as she pulled on insulated gloves.

"Just a peddler."

"Ah. Why do you still carry that antique pistol? It must be fifty years old."

"Why do you collect boots?" Tokay replied, his sharp eyes sweeping the street.

"I hate this country," Delellis sighed, shifting the heavy weight of the X-18 grenade launcher in his hands. Let the others enjoy the Hungarian-made guns; that was just patriotic foolishness. He much preferred good, solid, South African craftsmanship. There had been a lot of runaway Nazis living in South Africa, and nobody knew weapons like the Germans.

The short-barrel weapon had a rotating clip that held eighteen 30 mm grenade rounds. More than enough to level most small villages in Asia and Africa. Delellis had the deadly weapon filled with a scenario load, a series of projectiles placed in the predicted order of the mission. Shotgun charge, then high explosive, then a thermite, and so on. It took a seasoned professional to guess the reactions of an enemy correctly. The wrong round could get the gunner killed. An HE round didn't arm until traveling thirty feet from the grenade launcher. But the round would still kill one man if fired directly into his face. Delellis smiled faintly at the glorious memory. The KGB agent had taken a full day to die, and he'd sat there and watched, enjoying every minute of the Soviet fool's slow, lingering death.

Lighting a fresh cigarette, Salvai blew a smoke ring at the exit door. "Come to me, pretty babies," she whispered.

Suddenly the metal door was thrown open and several people came charging out, three men and a woman in front, all of them young. But each carrying a pistol of some sort.

Funny, the guns looked rusty. These were the American secret police? Pitiful.

"Kill them," Tokay said, stroking the trigger and releasing a hellstorm of lead at the running group. The others followed suit and the rear alley was filled with the muffled thunder of heavy-caliber ordnance. Then the flamethrower spoke and hell filled the alley.

THE DIM INTERIOR of the abandoned store was still, the dust thick on the counters. A desiccated rat lay on the crunchy carpeting, untouched by ants or cockroaches. The final act of the departing tenant had been to fill the store with bug spray strong enough to kill any living creature. Some of the stink still lingered and the air was murky, thick and heavy. Cobwebs filled the corners and the front window was soaped to translucency.

With a strident blast, a wall blew into the store, busted bricks and motor flying loose. Out of the smoking gap came Able Team, their weapons held at the ready.

The helicopter-on-the-roof trick had almost worked, when Lyons had wondered why anybody was trying to sneak into a building by using a helicopter loud enough to hear through soundproofing. Realizing that they were caught in a trap, the Stony Man team did the only sensible thing and went sideways in a flanking maneuver.

Walking through the smoky store, they heard the sounds of combat and tried to feel some sympathy for the young Nazis, but there was only contempt. Nobody had held a gun to their heads when the teenagers chose which side of the war to support in the battle for civilization.

Going to the front door, Lyons held up a closed fist and the others froze. Then he nodded and raised a finger. Firing from the hip, Blancanales put a short burst from the M-16 into the window, the 5.56 mm rounds blasting it apart.

Stepping into the empty street, Able Team raced around the corner and took cover behind a rusty car. Three people holding military weapons were inspecting several charred corpses sprawled on the ground.

"Bah, these are not the secret police," Tokay said with a sneer, kicking the leg of the skinny blonde. She moaned slightly, then went still forever.

"Which is why we killed them," Salvai said. A rivulet of excess flame dribbled from the barrel of her flamethrower.

Tokay frowned. This had been too easy, and anything easy was a trap, in life as well as in battle. Nothing had value unless it was taken by force.

"Real, fake, what difference," Delellis said with a shrug, hefting the grenade launcher. "All flesh dies."

"This I do not like," Tokay muttered in Hungarian, checking the roof. Right on time, the rented helicopter lifted off the roof and slipped away, heading to the south. Its part of the hit was completed.

"Could this have been be a diversion?" Salvai demanded suspiciously, looking around with the flamethrower in both gloved hands. Then her face registered shock.

"There!" Delellis shouted, pointing down the alley.

"Surrender!" Lyons boomed, rising from behind the wrecked car and leveling the Atchisson. Then Blancanales and Schwarz popped into view and worked the bolts on their M-16 assault rifles.

Outflanked? Impossible! Even as Tokay fired his weapon from the hip, both hands held low, the merc grudgingly increased his respect for the American police. This was an enemy he would enjoy killing. Pity they had to be kept alive.

Heavy 7.62 mm rounds pounded the old wreck and Lyons replied with a single round from the autoshotgun, aiming for the legs.

Crying out in pain, Salvai dropped to a knee, then swung around the flamethrower and unleashed a burning column of flame.

As the jellied gasoline washed across the abandoned car, Blancanales pumped a 40 mm HE round into the Cadillac behind the mercs. The vehicle looked like a getaway wagon. It was best not to take any chances.

The grenade shattered the windshield and the car lifted from the ground with the force of the explosion. Schwarz added a short burst from his M-16 across the chest of the giant holding the bulky X-18 grenade launcher. Delellis staggered, but didn't drop, the holes in his shirt showing the burnished tone of body armor underneath.

Now, everybody started to shoot and the alley was filled with a prolonged fusillade of the noise and death. But nobody fell. Soon it became apparent that both sides were deliberately missing. Able Team wanted the mercs alive for questioning, while Blue Moon wanted the Americas to chase after them and waste time going in the wrong direction.

Bella Tokay started to grab something from the bag at his side, then stayed his hand. There were only a few of the objects. Best to save them for later.

"Blue Moon!" Tokay commanded angrily.

Raising the X-18, Delellis smiled at the change of goals and now happily started pumping out rounds as fast as he could pull the trigger. Still firing, Able Team jumped as a hole the size of a fist punched straight through the wreck. A deer slug! Then they ducked as a hailstorm of steel buckshot shook the vehicle. Next, the rear brick wall of the nearby building exploded with fire, and sticky flames dripped down. Napalm!

Throwing themselves backward, the men of Able Team hit the ground, frantically rolled over to crawl to cover behind the wall. As expected, a split second later the car exploded. The X-18 kept going. More buckshot peppered the edge of the burning building, then a canister bounced along the ground, spewing out yellow tear gas, followed by another canister that filled the alley with the searing heat of thermite, the thermal charge bubbling the tar out of the pavement.

"Okay, we aren't going to take these Blue Moon clowns alive," Schwarz stated, loading an HE shell into his M-203.

Lyons agreed. "We kill them. We'll search their bodies for clues to Sky Hammer."

"Now you're talking," Blancanales growled, rubbing his bruised chest. He had caught a couple of bullets back there from the man who seemed to be in charge of Blue Moon, and only the NATO body armor had saved his life.

Going around the building, Able Team couldn't hear the X-18 anymore and feared the worst. As the men arrived a few moments later, they found the rear area empty of any living opponents.

"Follow the blood," Lyons directed, pointing to a trail of red dotting the pavement and heading past the burning car.

Able Team swept down the side street, moving from one protective cover to the next. Turning the corner, Lyons cursed to find the area blanketed with smoke, and an old man lying in the street next to a torn bag of groceries, the cans and boxes spilled across the road. There was no sign of the mercs.

"They jacked a car," Lyons said bitterly. "Cover me."

Lyons's teammates stood guard while he checked the body for any signs of life, but the hole in the back of the man's head told the story. He never even saw it coming.

Going through the old man's pockets, Lyons found a wallet and pulled out the insurance card.

"Watch for a green sedan," the former L.A. cop said, pulling an earplug from his grimy uniform and turning on the radio. "Bear, this is Stone Bird One, I need a lowjack activated for a—" Lyons scowled, then turned off the radio.

"Son of a bitch," he muttered, standing. "Okay, back to the van, double time!"

"What's wrong?" Schwarz asked, racing alongside.

"I got a react recording from Hal," Lyons stated, barely able to believe the news himself. "The Farm has been hacked. It's off-line until further notice."

"So we're on our own, then?" Blancanales queried.

"Until further notice."

A crowd had gathered around the burning corpses, but everybody hastily scattered at the approach of the heavily armed Able Team.

Crossing the street, the Stony Man commandos headed directly into the lot, disarmed the van and climbed inside.

"We're looking for a dark green, 1995 Saturn LX," Lyons said as he started the engine.

"Triple A member, license plate number Delta Alpha Zulu, 439," Schwarz read from the insurance card.

"Try heading south," Blancanales suggested. "In the same direction of the helicopter."

"Hell is where they're going," Lyons stated, throwing the transmission into gear and hitting the gas.

The van pulled away in a spray of loose gravel, leaving the burning factory behind.

CHAPTER TWELVE

Luxembourg City, Luxembourg

"Did you say cash?"

"Cash."

"Sir, surely a cashier's check would be much more—"

"Cash."

Placing a Closed sign in the window of his cage, the bank teller sighed. "Very well. A moment please. Guards!"

Several large gentleman in spotless uniforms approached the teller instantly. They had witnessed him having a heated discussion with the customer and were prepared to intervene.

"Would two of you please stay with this gentleman until he leaves the grounds?" the teller directed, gesturing at the middle-aged man standing at the window. "He is withdrawing a rather large amount in cash and bank rules necessitate protection."

"Thank you," George Meternich smiled. "Much appreciated."

An hour later Meternich left the bank carrying two large suitcases stuffed to capacity.

Going to the corner, he waited for the light to change, then hurried to the Chase International Bank. Walking into the cool marble interior of the bank, he went directly to the head cashier. The woman looked up in surprise at his approach.

"Good morning." She smiled hesitantly. "If this is a new account…"

"Old account," Meternich stated firmly, placing one of the two suitcases on the counter. "My name is Adam Smithy, and I wish to make a substantial deposit. Call your guards, please."

By the end of the day, Meternich threw away the empty suitcases. The break was done. Nobody could track the funds now. Going to a train station, he purchased a ticket for Budapest and prepared for the final part of his assignment.

Abu Dis, Israel

THE MOOD OF THE CROWD was ugly, and Major Adina Kushner tried not to show her nervousness as she stood her post near the ruin of the wall. In front of her were wooden sawhorses, and steel drums full of sand and coils of razor-sharp concertina wire. The crowd stayed clear of that. Behind her was half a kilometer of destruction.

More camera flashes came from the tourists in the excited crowd, the Israelis among the foreigners merely looking and filing the memory away to discuss later. There were helicopters in the air on patrol, and squads of soldiers and Shin Bet agents were going through the destruction checking everything for anything. Kushner had seen bombings before, and missile strikes, but this destruction was caused by neither. To be honest, the major couldn't really say what had happened here, and was almost ready to believe the wild story that a meteor swarm had hit the wall.

Already protestors from both sides of the divide had gathered and were waving placards and shouting about this and that in several languages. The Arabs wanted the wall destroyed, the Israelis wanted it back up, the settlers wanted it moved ten blocks, and everybody wanted a piece as a souvenir. Dourly, the major fully expected fake pieces of the Israeli wall to appear for sale soon on the Internet.

Cradling her assault rifle, Kushner sighed. The only thing people liked more than watching violence, was owning a piece. As a combat soldier, she had seen quite a lot of violence, none of it pretty, and so found that civilian fascination quite puzzling.

"Excuse me," a plump woman said, shoving to the front of the crowd.

The major tried not to frown. The Hebrew was flawless, but from the attitude, Kushner pegged her as a rich foreigner. Those were the worst. She could be American, but lots of countries spoke English, England for one. Plus the Dutch, Australians, South Africa, Belize. Lots of people.

"Move along, please," Kushner stated, gesturing slightly with the assault rifle. That usually did the trick, but not this time.

"Excuse me, miss, but my son would like one those rocks, please," the woman said, waving a fistful of cash. The denominations of the euros was large. "Is that okay?"

Kushner frowned. Being stupid was one thing, offering a

bribe was insulting. "No. Move along. Now." The "please" was gone.

The plump woman fanned that aside with the cash. "So we have to haggle, do we? Just like in the marketplace. You people, I swear…"

You people? That did it. Keeping both hands on her rifle, Kushner whistled sharply and two men stepped out of the crowd and took the civilian by the elbows.

"What is going on here?" she shrieked.

"Excuse me, ma'am, but there's a problem with your credit card," the Mossad agent said with a tolerant smile. "If you could just come this way, please."

"The card? What's wrong with my card?" she declared loudly. "I'll have you know that my husband…" Still complaining, the tourist disappeared into the milling throng.

Switching the positions of her hands, Kushner sighed. One down, ten thousand idiots to go. Why did they always came to her? There were hundreds of soldiers along the barricade, but most talked to her. Did she looked like an easy mark? Was there a sign she didn't know about?

A horn blared in the background and Kushner mentally logged the driver as a new reporter. No tourist could have gotten this close to the site and no Israeli would ever bother using the horn. But the horn continued to blare, and now the crowd started to shift, edging away, separating as the armored Hummer crawled through the mob of people, gently nudging aside those too stubborn to listen to reason.

Wary, the major clicked the safety off her rifle and watched closely as the unmarked Hummer stopped in front of the barricade. The engine was turned off and an English officer stepped down. He was wearing the uniform of the British SAS, but the others in the Hummer were an odd mix: a German, an African, a Spaniard, and one tall fellow so obviously American he was probably from Texas.

"This is a restricted zone," Kushner said politely but firmly.

"We have authorization," David McCarter replied, handing over a folded piece of paper from his breast pocket. And so his team did. The Stony Man operative just didn't say from whom it came. As cover, they were all dressed in the uniform of different combat or intelligence agencies. Basically, bored and polished.

Warily, the Israeli leveled her weapon. "Unfold it first please, sir," she directed firmly.

Doing as requested, McCarter handed over the form. Accepting it, Kushner gave perfunctory glance. Hmm, it seemed okay.

It was common knowledge that any document could be easily duplicated, along with the signatures. So it was the style of the form that mattered. Older forms were refused, and Military Intelligence changed the styles randomly to keep one step ahead of the forgers.

"I'll have to phone this in," Kushner said, handing the paper back.

"Of course, Major," McCarter said, tucking away the bogus form away once more. "Should I wait in the Hummer?"

"Here is fine, sir," Kushner said politely, and unclipped the microphone from her shoulder. "This is Post 34, I need a check on a pass, Number 79-79-160, Code Euclid."

As he waited, McCarter had to admit that in spite of his personal feelings, the woman seemed to be on her toes. He could see it in the major's face that she corporal didn't buy the Intelligence story. Very smart. But then the Israelis dealt with infiltrators on a daily basis.

"Sir, permission to pass is granted," Kushner stated, giving a salute. Slinging the assault rifle over a shoulder, she grabbed a sawhorse with both hands and lifted it aside to allow the Hummer full of men through, then she walked it closed again behind them. Naturally, the crowd made cries of favoritism, secret police and injustice. She ignored them.

Driving the Hummer over the bumpy field of broken debris, T. J. Hawkins parked it near a large tent covering the location where the scaffolding had once been. Pieces of it were all around them. The bodies had been removed, but chalk outlines showed where the people had fallen. The area more resembled a homicide investigation site than anything else, aside from the helicopter gunships and armed troops.

Armed guards in body armor stood along the entry flap of the tent. They stood with the easy confidence of front line troops, and watched Phoenix Force arrive with hard expressions.

As Hawkins killed the engine, the flap whipped aside and out walked a small, lean man with a pencil-thin mustache. He was in duty fatigues and carried no insignia. McCarter instantly pegged the fellow as Shin Bet.

"What's going on here?" the man demanded, placing fists on hips.

"NATO, Special Investigations," McCarter said, his British accent replaced with the flat twang of the American

Midwest. He climbed down from the Hummer and offered a sheaf of papers with a commission booklet. "My papers."

The Shin Bet agent ignored the documents. "Looks like we'll get some rain today," he said impatiently.

"I prefer it dry," McCarter answered.

"Until there is a drought."

"And then we need the rain."

"Uri Weingate," the agent said, extending a hand. "I hate these code word exchanges, but they're necessary. So you're NATO security, eh. Welcome."

McCarter took it and they shook. "Thank you. I'm Colonel Obsidian. These are my men."

"Obsidian?" Weingate asked, tilting his head. "A code name?"

Stoically, McCarter gave no reply.

"Accepted." The Shin Bet agent laughed. "We all have secrets. Well, come inside. The man you want to see is here. We shall leave the dusting for fingerprints to the Mossad."

"He's here?" James repeated, stepping to the rough ground.

Walking into the tent, Weingate paused, standing half in the shadows. "And who would like him in a bomb crater?"

Inside was cool, but dusty. The tent had been erected over a wide field of debris, and the members of Phoenix Force trod carefully through the loose rubble. Here and there were craters, yards deep with dull pools of lumps of metal at the bottom. Direct hits from the molten rain of Sky Hammer.

There was a second tent set on a flat area, with neatly dressed men and women in civilian clothing standing around. The held clipboards and had pencils behind their ears. But the Shin Bet agents were fooling nobody. They wore their profession on their faces like a badge of honor.

The double interior should have been dark, but powerful electric lanterns filled the tent with soft illumination. A couple of Shin Bet agents carrying shotgun were standing behind a small, toothy man sitting on a chair. The man was wearing a ratty burnoose and dirty sneakers, his face discolored and puffy from a recent beating.

A couple of tables had been set along the canvas wall, covered with electrical equipment, a laptop and a water cooler that was steadily dripping onto the wooden boards. There was also a small metal box lying on a foam static-free mat.

The prisoner looked up at the newcomers, hope on his face, then sagged at their hard appearance. Just more cops. There were always more cops.

"His real name is Akhmed. No family name, and no family, a war orphan," Weingate said, standing in front of the prisoner, looking down as if the man were a specimen in a jar. "But everybody calls him Benny Zero."

McCarter knew that "Ben" meant "son-of." Benny Zero, the son of nobody.

Weingate started walking around the prisoner, hands clasped behind his back. "Now, Benny here was working the crowd with a friend, Sholomo Tashar, dead by the way. They found a parked car and broke into the trunk to steal the luggage. Didn't you?"

Akhmed nodded glumly.

"Ah, but instead of suitcases, there was only a metal box bolted to the floor. When Sholomo tried to force it open, he was hit the face with some sort of yellow gas, mustard gas according to the autopsy report. He died quite horribly according to Benny here."

The man in the chair said nothing, his head bowed, waiting for judgment. At least the Jews would only beat him and put him in jail. The Arabs would have cut off his hands. That's why he did so much business in the other side of the wall. What's the use of a thief with no hands?

"This was where Benny used his brains for the first, and probably last, time in his whole life," Weingate said, making a dismissive gesture at the prisoner. "He left the box alone and stole the car instead. Well, he tried to, but Benny can't drive and crashed it into the side of a tank."

"And that's how you got him and the box," Hawkins said, rubbing his chin.

"And the crash damaged the box," Manning stated. "It's a homing beacon, isn't it?"

The Shin Bet agent blinked in surprise, then shrugged. Very good. But then, would NATO have sent fools for the assignment?

"Yes, it is a radio beacon. Very old, but powerful. Obviously for...well, whatever hit the wall." Weingate scowled at the prisoner. "He knows nothing about it, of that we can be sure. Benny is just a thief at the wrong place, wrong time."

McCarter walked to the table and looked at the box, which had already been opened. Using a finger, he swung aside a service panel and looked at the complex maze of wiring. Most of the room was taken by a pressurized cylinder for the mustard gas and a stack of batteries. He stared. No, those were fuel cells, the kind designed by NASA for use on the space shuttle and in orbiters. Most space agencies used them. They had a very limited life, but generated a lot of power.

"We'd like a few minutes in private with the prisoner, please," McCarter said, touching the transmitter with a fingertip. Good it was cold. Nobody had been stupid enough to test the device.

"Of course. Take as long as you wish." With a wave of his arm, Weingate departed with the guards leaving Akhmed alone with Phoenix Force.

"Door," McCarter snapped, and Rafael Encizo took a position near the flap to kept a watch outside.

Pulling out tools, Hawkins and Manning went to the box, while James brought Akhmed a cup of water from the cooler. The man gulped it so fast the Stony Man operative thought it might come back up again.

"Thank you," Akhmed gasped.

"More?" James asked.

Akhmed nodded eagerly. "Yes, please. I have not had a drink in days."

Days? Right, since they caught him just before the strike. "Freakin' Shin Bet," James muttered. He knew their job was hard, but there was no need to go down to the level of the PLO with a prisoner. Israel was supposed to be the good guys!

As Akhmed gulped his second cup, James considered the fact that the CIA had been caught doing similar things to their own prisoners. Why were so many people in the intelligence community so stupid? Where they watching too many spy movies?

"Akhmed," James started, "we're not going to hurt you, but we need to know, is that what really happened?"

"Yes, yes," he burbled, almost weeping. "I am just a thief. I steal. Should I be a terrorist and throw bombs? I don't hurt people, I steal from the rich. I take radios and cameras…"

"Is what the Shin Bet agent said true?" McCarter demanded from across the tent.

"He…was Shin Bet," Akhmed asked, his eyes going wide. "Then why am I still alive?" In spite of the handcuffs attached to the chair, the little Arab spun and stared at the box. "What is that thing?" he demanded in horror.

That was enough for McCarter. Nobody was that good an actor. Akhmed knew nothing about its real purpose. "Guard!" he shouted.

A moment later Weingate appeared with a quizzical expression on his face. "Already done?" he asked. "I would have thought that several hours were necessary to cover everything."

"Under the power invested in me by the United Nations, I am dismissing all charges of espionage, and will be turning Mr. Akhmed over to the Israeli police for the crimes of car theft and restless endangerment. Nothing more."

"What was that?" Weingate asked, his voice low and dangerous.

"You heard me," McCarter whispered, stepping closer. "One of my men will escort the prisoner to the local jail, and if I hear of him disappearing in the night, or anything else mysterious happening, I will come back and shoot you in the heart. Do we understand each other, or should I use smaller words?"

The Shin Bet agent bristled and actually started to go for the gun on his hip when there was suddenly a room full of automatic pistols all pointing in the wrong direction. At him.

Snarling a curse, one of the guards stroked his shotgun to chamber a round and suddenly Hawkins appeared behind the man and pressed the barrel of his Beretta 93-R into the back of his head.

"That wouldn't be a wise career move, bub," he stated.

The guard froze, then slowly removed his finger from the trigger. Hawkins stayed where he was; Encizo took the shotgun and aimed it at Weingate.

"Your move, Peewee," he stated. "We don't torture prisoners."

Weingate looked as if he were going to explode, then burst into coarse laughter.

"Fine, keep the pile of dung. He is yours. I make him a gift. But I will take the box and—"

"What box?" McCarter asked, sliding a grenade from his pocket and pulling the pin. Then he lifted two of the four fingers holding down the arming lever. "You sure there's a box of some sort in here?"

They locked eyes for a long minute, then, without comment, Weingate turned and left, taking the guards along with him.

"Jail?" Akhmed asked hopefully, tears in his eyes. "Really?"

"Fuck it, set him loose," McCarter muttered, putting the pin back into the grenade. "He's had more than enough punishment."

"I'll walk him to the perimeter," James said, kneeling to release the handcuffs. "Then you're on your own. Good enough?"

"These sons of whores will never catch me again,"

Akhmed boasted, rubbing the raw skin on his wrists. Libya was nice this time of year. And he heard there was a lot of new construction in the southern oil fields.

Encizo tossed the shotgun to James. He caught it and waved at Akhmed. "Come on, master thief, let's go."

Smiling widely, the Arab touched fingertips to his heart, then his lips as a goodbye to the team, then left with James.

"We ever need a snitch in this area, there's our man," Hawkins stated, holstering his service piece.

"Think he'll be okay?" Encizo asked gruffly.

"I think that Benny Zero has never been caught by anybody before," Hawkins said, holstering his weapon. "So yeah, he'll be fine."

"As long as he doesn't steal any more cars," Manning added, smiling in spite of himself.

"I'm more worried about us," McCarter said, sitting at the worktable. So, this was a targeting beacon, eh? The Sky Hammer people probably wanted to make sure the advertising strike went as planned, so to hedge their bets, they planted a homing beacon. A GPD broadcast unit.

"Now if only there is a serial number on the parts, we can trace the sale," Hawkins said, turning another chair around and sitting on it backward at the table.

Encizo grunted. "Be tough to do with the Farm off-line."

"I still have a few friends is the SAS," McCarter stared, rubbing his chin. "And maybe the Shin Bet can help. They owe us."

"Big time," Hawkins agreed.

Outside, somebody stomped a boot on the ground in lieu of knocking, then entered.

"Did he buy it?" Weingate asked, looking around the tent.

"Absolutely." McCarter smiled, offering a hand. "America gets a little good press in the underworld, and Akhmed will spread the word about the toughness of the evil Shin Bet. People will avoid you like the plague."

"A strong enemy is all they respect," Weingate said with a shrug. "I dislike such games, but they save lives."

"Which is why we went along with it," Hawkins drawled, shooting the Israeli agent with a finger.

"So where did he get the marks?" Encizo asked curiously. "From when the wall came down?"

"Exactly. As you said, we do not use torture." Then Weingate smiled. "But we do spread the lie that we use torture. It makes many difficult people more…agreeable…to negotiations."

Just then, people started screaming outside and suddenly the ground shook as if a giant had stomped Earth. Then there came a fluttering noise as if a million bats had flown by overhead.

"That was no explosion," Encizo declared, looking at the canvas ceiling. Raw sunlight seemed to be hitting the tent, peeking through every hole, creating cathedral lighting.

"It can't be them," Weingate stated fearfully. "Why hit the wall again? There is nothing here anymore. No prime minister, no TV cameras…"

McCarter turned and stared at the open electronic beacon.

"Just that box," Hawkins finished, rising to his boots. "Let's move, people!"

Lurching into action, Weingate and Phoenix Force burst out of the tent at a full run, the beacon tight under McCarter's left arm.

Outside, the team saw that the large tent was gone, sky was clear above them. Suddenly there were multiple flashes of light and the entire world seemed to explode.

CHAPTER THIRTEEN

Paris, France

Watching the computer, Attila Meternich sat back in his office chair and smiled. And...there, done. The wall had been hit again, exactly when the PLO said it would happen. Now they can claim all the credit for the original attack, and that missing beacon was doubly assured to have been destroyed. Meternich had been paid to cover his ass. How nice. A win-win scenario. Besides, a little misdirection never hurt.

Thank God the beacon had proved unnecessary in the first place. It had gone dead just before the attack, and the Thors still hit perfectly on target. On the other hand, they were almost out of Thors. But that eventuality had been planned for.

Using the mouse, Meternich placed all future orders for strikes on hold for twelve hours, then glanced at the wall clock. In sex and combat, timing was everything.

Any second now....

Cheyenne Mountain

THE WAR ROOM was the heart of NORAD, the nerve center of the North Atlantic Defense. The front wall was a triptych of screens, The left showed Europe, the middle screen showed the North American continent and the right showed whoever was considered a threat. For thirty years that had been the Soviet Union. Nowadays it was sometimes North Korea, sometimes China, and for a brief few months it had shown Iraq.

The ceiling and walls were a flat-black, the floor dark reflectionless terrazzo. Banks of consoles curved in front of the three screens. There were a dozen of them in each line, three layers deep. Busy technicians from every branch of the armed forces were working away at the twinkling controls, constantly whispering into their throat mikes to keep a moment-by-moment running communication to the duty officers, who in turn relayed the info to the Joint Chiefs of Staff and the White House. The right wall was covered with clocks showing the precise time in every major city around the world. The left had a scattering of screens showing the worldwide weather, and the Stick, the indicator that showed the status of America. Only a few hours ago, the President had ordered it moved up to DefCon Four. DefCon Five meant open warfare.

Since its inception, the war room had always been noisy and busy, endlessly full of people coming and going, delivering reports. But that was good. Noise meant personal conversations, yawning, jokes. The louder the room was, the more peaceful and secure was America.

At the moment, the war room of Cheyenne Mountain was dead silent.

Located at the rear of the huge room, General Hall Overton and Rear Admiral Roger Sullivan were standing behind the visitor railing where tourists used to come to gawk at the technological might of America. That wasn't allowed anymore for security reasons, but the facilities were still in place, and now congressmen and senators took tours and stood behind the railings, while armed guards stood by and watched everyone's movements.

Overton and Sullivan were readings reports from NSA listening stations from around the world, when a duty officer handed them a priority report.

"They hit it again?" Sullivan frowned. "What in bloody hell for?"

Before Overton could speak, a technician on the floor raised her voice.

"Alert," she said loudly, crouched over a console. "We have multiple bogeys come in on course…47 degrees and zero by zero."

Lowering the report, Overton scowled. "What? Impossible," he snapped. "That is almost a vertical attack vector…Oh, hell, Thors!"

"Here?" a major gasped, going white.

"But those things can't possibly hurt us," Sullivan replied smugly.

"Sky Hammer just sent a dozen to Israel," Overton retorted hotly. "The craters reach a hundred feet in places. Countless more are dead from the crowds who wanted to see the destruction."

"Still not enough," the admiral stated firmly, then frowned. "But we have a hundred people on the outside!"

Oh, hell. "Red alert!" Overton commanded, leaning on the rail. "Get all external personnel into the mountain!"

"Then close the blast doors!" Sullivan added grimly.

"This isn't a nuke attack," Overton chided.

The admiral frowned. "Next best thing."

A siren started to howl outside, and everybody paused in shock, then dropped whatever they were doing and raced into the brick-lined tunnel that lead into Cheyenne Mountain. Armed guards left their kiosks to frantically herd people inside. The guards were shouting at the top of their lungs, but not a word could be heard above the wailing sirens.

Nuke attack! The words sent cold adrenaline through hearts of everybody, solider and civilian.

But the years of training paid off this day, and the last civilian technician dived through the slowly moving blast door just before it slammed shut. Large enough to drive an APC through, the door was a truncated cone thicker than a person could reach with both arms extended wide, and was layered with tungsten steel, compressed lithium fibers, titanium, depleted uranium and enough lead to line a nuclear reactor. When the blast door closed, the concussion felt through the floor for three levels rattling pencils and knocking pictures askew. Then the locking bolts engaged, fourteen metal shafts a foot thick, went a yard into the jamb all along the circular door, sealing off the mountain from the world.

"Status, please," Overton demanded softly, in forced control.

"All personnel accounted for, sir," a major crisply reported. The door is shut, bolts home."

Admiral Sullivan was watching the radar screen now filling the third monitor at the front of the room. A dotted line reached from space above and came almost straight down, advancing blink by blink, faster than anything should be able to move through the atmosphere.

"Here they come," a colonel whispered from a console.

Nothing happened in the war room. There were no tremors, no shorted-out consoles, not a flicker in the ceiling lights.

However the video cameras showed hell up on the surface. The sky flashed, as if shooting stars were coming out during the day, and then the forest covering Cheyenne Mountain exploded in a dozen spots. Pine trees went flying and flames erupted across the landscape. The parking lot vanished and the Visitor Center was slammed deep into the ground. A dozen video cameras went dead. Multiple flashes smacked the entry tunnel to the underground citadel, and it collapsed for a hundred feet. Loosened from the pounding impacts, boulders started rolling down the sides of the mountain and crashed through the electrified fencing and out into the Colorado wilds.

Then the flashes stopped, and as the dust air cleared, the people in the war room could see only desolation and destruction. Bricks were still falling from the sky as gravity finally caught up with the escapees. The manicured landscape of the nation's fortress now looked like Hiroshima after the bomb.

"Damage report!" Sullivan demanded, laying aside the unread reports.

"Minimal, sir," reported a technician. "Only cosmetic. We are fully operational."

The civilian staff cheered, but the officers frowned.

"No, we're not fully operational," Overton declared, pointing at black screens dotting the wall. "Look there! The satellite uplink dish is gone."

"Hell, son, they're all gone," Sullivan corrected angrily, making a fist. "Along with the link to our backup dish and tertiary array out of state."

"Impossible!"

"True, nonetheless. Somebody knew exactly where to hit."

Overton looked down at the floor full of people at their consoles. "What about the hard-line?"

"Those are fine, sir," a man reported, without turning. "We're in full contact with the Pentagon, SAC and Washington. But we're off the air."

"Start the repair crews digging us out, and get those dishes up and running!"

"Work crews are already starting to dig the tunnel clear," a woman replied. "Additional help coming from all over the state."

"Good," Sullivan stated. "How long until we have eyes again?"

"Half an hour, sir."

"Make it twenty minutes."

A colonel gulped. "We'll do our best, sir."

"Do better than that," Overton directed, then walked over to Sullivan. "Thirty minutes. What the hell good is that, Roger?" he demanded softly, turning his back to the command staff. "What can Sky Hammer possibly do in thirty minutes?"

"A hell of a lot of damage, is what it can do," Sullivan replied, trying to control his fury. "But I don't think that's the problem. They could have hit anything on Earth. Why us? Why right now?"

"What do they not want us to see happen in this window?" Overton mused, rubbing his chin. "Okay, what's the worst thing you can possibly imagine? Hitting the White House? The UN building in New York?"

"No, it has to be something dangerous to their survival. Something…" Sullivan glanced upward. "Oh, hell."

"They're rearming." Overton cursed. "Launching more Thors from their secret base."

"Then we got 'em by the balls if we can find it," Sullivan agreed. "Duty officer! Call Washington! Have the Pentagon contact SAC…shit! Their computers are down for another day."

Of to the side were banks of monitors that normally would show satellite pictures from space. The Keyhole sats watched for missiles launches, the WatchDogs tracked troops and ships, and so on. But the screens were dark green; live, but receiving no information.

"Then we're blind," the general said simply.

Guyana

A WARM WIND BLEW in from the sea, shaking the fronds on the palm trees and making the monkeys chatter and scamper around madly.

Just over a low hill, a massive Zenit-class rocket stood poised at a gantry in the middle of a flat plain of concrete, white mists escaping from the fuel lines pumping the main tanks full of liquid hydrogen and liquid oxygen until the very last second before launch. Along the sides were four solid state boosters, slightly canted inward to maximize their thrust potential.

"Ten…nine…" Loudspeakers boomed the words from a series of poles established around this end of the tropical island. "Eight…ready for preignition!"

From the bunkers a half mile away, technicians and scientists watched video monitors as telescopic cameras showed the brick-lined blast pit underneath the giant Zenit rocket. Electric motors spun to operational speed, clutches engaged and then grinding wheels spun to power and lowered onto slabs of steel to start howling as they threw off coronas of white-hot sparks.

In the old days when rocket science was brand-new, occasionally the fuel pumps would operate out of order and raw fuel would pour into the blast pit and form pools before igniting. This caused massive explosions. Nowadays, the danger was easily removed by filling the pit with white-hot sparks first. Any fuel spilled would ignite instantly and never have a chance to pool and detonate with enough force to do any damage.

Most rockets these days used solid propellants that were mass produced. The Zenit used both, and was the workhorse of the Russia space agency. There were even factories that sold the preassembled rockets to anybody who had the cash. There was no danger of improper use. Owning a rocket was one thing, building the facilities to launch it was another matter entirely. Those couldn't be disguised in any way and were easily located from space by spy satellites. If NATO found an illegal site being constructed, they would wait until it was most nearly finished, then destroy it. A million dollars of weaponry ruining a billion-dollar launch facility in under an hour. After the first illegal space base was destroyed in Jordan, nobody had ever tried that approach again. Is was simply too costly, even for the oil princes of the Middle East.

But preburn explosions and illegal launch sites were in the past. These days, space flight was no longer an adventure, but was mostly the placement of satellites for cable TV, cell phones, pharmaceutical research and storm tracking. Nothing special, not anymore, just a business. International treaties signed by every nation capable of reaching space forbid the placement of weapons in orbit.

There were no illegal space sports anymore, at least, there were none known to exist.

"Seven…six…five, go internals!" the loudspeakers continued. "Three…two…one…ignition!"

In rumbling fury, the blast pit underneath the Zenit-class transport exploded into roiling flame as the trembling rocket vehicle strained against the locking clamps, rapidly building power.

"Disengage all feeds! All systems locked. Release!"

Huge locking clamps slammed back with a bang as loud as artillery, but the noise was completely lost in the thundering fury of the LOX-LOH engines, then the solid boosters came alive. In rumbling fury, billowing clouds of steam and vaporized concrete spewed forth across the launch site as the Zenit rose majestically skyward.

"Lift off. We have lift off," the loudspeakers announced.

Turning, the rocket began to travel against the rotation of the Earth, making the planet recede even faster and thus cut its trip into space shorter by hundreds of miles.

Inside the command bunker, a score of technicians tracked the rocket on their instruments while eating sandwiches. This was the tenth launch this month. The things never really lost their magic, but it was becoming routine magic, and most of them knew all of the secrets of the magician.

"Flight path is good," a man said, watching the radar. "Rollover successful. Five by five."

"What is the payload this time?" a woman asked, fighting back a yawn. There had been an all-night poker game in the basement, and most of the staff of the ESA were exhausted.

"Commercial stuff. A new satellite for WorldNet and parts for the new space telescope."

"Parts?"

Swiveling, he shrugged. "Big steel rods. Something for the support frame, I suppose."

Suddenly the door to the control room burst open and in rushed a man waving a French newspaper.

"Hey, did you hear about Israel?" he panted, coming over. "This just arrived on the ferry with our supplies."

"I listen to the BBC radio news," the woman stated. "Old news, I know all about it. Terrorist attack."

"Another one?" the technician at the console asked, taking the paper. Italian, the scientists struggled with the French headlines, but could get the gist of the story. Somebody had blown up the wall of Jericho? How sad.

But that had nothing to do with the European Space Agency.

Stony Man Farm, Virginia

"CASH?" DELAHUNT ASKED, peeking out from under her VR helmet.

"Cash," Tokaido said, frowning at the computer screen. "Somebody made a massive withdrawal in hard currency from the First Royal Bank of Luxembourg. The figures are confidential, but they only assign guards to special customers, and they just ordered two replacement suitcases. The kind they give to special customers for holding stacks of cash." The Luxembourg banks had excellent security, so the Stony Man team had hacked their personnel files and monitored their business purchases. To a clever hacker, those told everything.

"Damn," Kurtzman muttered, thumping the armrest of his wheelchair. There was absolutely no way to trace where the money went, even if they had the serial numbers. There were a lot of banks in Luxembourg, banking was their main source of income, that and the casinos.

"Sky Hammer?" Wethers asked pointedly, crossing his arms.

"Possibly," Kurtzman agreed. "It has been awhile since this last happened. Most terrorists are stupid enough to handle all of their deals electronically, thinking the anonymity of a computer transfer would be sufficient protection against identification. Interpol caught a dozen of them every year. Some of them even tried to hide the arms shipments as commercial traffic. Occasionally, that worked. But this…"

"Indeed," Wethers said, chewing on his pipe. "If these Sky Hammer people don't act foolishly, then we will never track them down by following the money."

"Thousands, maybe millions dead," Tokaido observed. "Just so that they can lay on a sunny beach somewhere and drink margaritas."

"Exactly."

"Unacceptable," Kurtzman declared. "How are we coming on the trace?"

"Almost finished," Delahunt said, sliding her VR helmet back into place. "If we've been hacked, I'll find it."

"Need any help?" Tokaido asked, massaging his face. The

man was tired, totally exhausted. But still willing to keep working.

"Not really." Delahunt's gloves caressed the air as she cybernetically opened programs and altered data streams.

"Hit a bunk in the farmhouse for a couple of hours," Kurtzman directed. "I'll call you if something big happens."

"But—"

"That wasn't a request, Akira. Sleepy minds make mistakes. We're walking the razor's edge here. Get going."

Wearily, the young man stood, groaning from the tremendous effort. "Maybe a couple of minutes," he mumbled, shuffling for the door.

Tokaido was almost there when it opened and Buck Greene rushed in.

"Cheyenne Mountain has been hit by a Thor," he announced. "The White House has done a total blackout, but Hal relayed the news to us."

"Over the phone?" Kurtzman asked, wheeling his chair around.

"No, he flew out in a helicopter. This is fresh, less than two hours old."

Wethers snapped his head up and removed the pipe to gesture with it angrily. "They're rearming!" he observed. "By God, we're idiots. We should have seen this coming!"

"Akira, get me the Hot Bird list!" Kurtzman demanded, sliding under his console.

Already at the kitchenette, Tokaido poured himself a mug of black coffee, then added three teaspoons of sugar. Slurping the thick sludge, he felt the exhaustion slip away from his mind and he sat, ready to go again. He knew it wouldn't last long, but hopefully long enough.

"Okay," he said, fingers dancing across the keyboard. "We have…a… Nothing happening at Tangegashima space port in Japan. Russia has a launch scheduled for tomorrow, and NASA sent up a shuttle early this morning. Hmm… Spaceship One did another trail flight in the Mojave Desert…"

"Too small," Kurtzman stated. "The prototype can't carry more than five or six Thors maximum."

"Hardly worth the effort of expending fifty on NORAD."

"Exactly."

Seeing that he wasn't needed, Greene slipped out of the room and left the electronic warriors to their assignment.

"Australia is doing trail test today at Woomera, India delayed a launch in the afternoon for tomorrow, and Guyana Island has a launch scheduled for…right now." Tokaido glanced at the clocks on the wall showing the different time zones. "No, correction, they had a launch scheduled. It lifted off two hours ago. Their bird is already in orbit."

"Two hours?" Kurtzman mused. "That could be a coincidence, but I hate coincidences. They give me stomach cramps. What was the manifest on that bird?"

"Checking," Tokaido said.

The hacker hated this. If the Farm was compromised, then all data coming in could be false. Everything had to be checked with independent sources. Price had arranged for the Library of Congress to place a research librarian standing ready at the phone just in case the team needed some data verified. Under the guise of national security, of course. The librarian thought she was partitioning in a dry run for Homeland Security. But the incredible delays were infuriating. Six, sometimes ten minutes to confirm information that normally he would have found in a matter of seconds. Sometimes even faster! It was like running a marathon with one foot in a bucket.

"Okay, the ESA headquarters in Geneva and Paris had nothing on file."

"Nothing?"

"Zero."

"Strange," Wethers muttered, chewing his pipe furiously. "Very strange, indeed."

"But the launch facility in French Guyana did," Tokaido reported in grim satisfaction. Most of this info was public knowledge. A person just had to know where to look for it. "The payload consisted of a new telecommunications satellite for WorldNet, an ISP service for Tasmania and…" Grinning, he looked up from the console. "Bingo. There was also a load of construction material for the new space telescope. A hundred and twenty steel bars."

"They spent fifty to get 120," Kurtzman said in false calm. "That more than doubled their reserve of Thors."

"'Fraid so."

"Notify the ESA…no wait, they might be in on this," Kurtzman stated. "Send this news to the White House via a blacksuit messenger."

Tokaido tapped a button. "Done." he announced.

"So the people behind this must have been smuggling Thors into space in small batches over the years," Delahunt said from behind her mask. "That's mighty long-term thinking for a grab-and-run operation. Sounds personal."

Revenge? Could be. "Akira, get me a full security dossier on everyone involved with the launch today at the Guyana base. Hunt, do the ESA, the astronaut training base in German, the headquarters in Geneva and the operational center in Paris."

"Didn't the NSA lose a man in Paris recently?" Wethers said softly, his hands busy. "Something about a traitor?"

"They sure as hell did." Kurtzman grinned ferociously. "Start there, work down from the very top, the project manager. That could be our guy."

The room became quiet again, there was scant movement and little sound, but tremendous activity.

Meanwhile, on a subsystem, Wethers's search program ground on, analyzing every Thor strike from several different perspectives. One had been in the Southern Hemisphere, while the next was in the Northern. Two had occurred simultaneously in different countries. The line of sight into space of every strike was dutifully recorded and torn apart. Vectors and planetary curves were taken into account, cloud formations to block a maser, as well as mountain ranges, storms, airplanes in flight, buildings and low-orbit satellites. Everything was being cross-referenced, compressed, digested, and a million points of possible maser sources carpeted the globe. But with every strike, a few more were removed, the vector of access grew smaller and smaller.

Soon, the maser could only have been located on half of the planet, then a third, a fourth, a fifth…

Almost there.

CHAPTER FOURTEEN

Kremlin, Russia

"Tell me," the president of Russia commanded, filling a glass of tea from the steaming samovar on his desk.

"It is called Sky Hammer," the director of the Federal Security Bureau said, handing over the translated report.

Taking a sip of the tea, the president placed aside the glass and accepted the folder. Wetting a finger, he then flicked through the pages, speed-reading all of the data in less than a minute. His parents had forced him to learn how to speed-read as a child, preparing him for government service. He had cursed them then, but praised them now. His ability to go through a hundred reports a day was the saving grace that kept him sane in this mad job of running a complex country full of equally complex people. Russia, a nation with a hundred million people and five hundred million opinions.

"This report is three decades old," the president stated, tossing it onto the desk. Aside from the silver tray holding the samovar, there was nothing else on the desk but two plain telephones. One went to the supreme general in charge of the russian rocket Forces, the other a direct line to the American President. One for war, the other for peace. War and peace, the humor of the matter did not escape his notice.

"We stole it as soon as possible," the director of the FSB said by way of apology. The FSB was one of the organizations that had taken over when the dreaded KGB fell out of power. The Federal Security Bureau operated like the Scotland Yard in the United Kingdom, handling national crimes, unusual cases beyond the resources of local police, and special circumstances. This matter came into the latter category.

"So this is what destroyed our base at Minsk," the president muttered. "A swarm of comets, bah."

"Minsk?" the director asked curiously. "I do not know of any secret military bases in Minsk. Are you sure that wasn't Pinsk?"

"No, it is…was Minsk," the President declared. "And you should not have known about it as your security clearance does not reach that high a level, Red Flag Nine."

Nine! "B-but you just told me that—"

"It does not matter now." The president sighed. "The secret installation of our antisatellite laser is gone, along with the laboratory building the new Gryazno Paka fighters."

"Which are…" the director prompted, fascinated.

"Which were," the president continued, "jet fighters capable of launching a nuclear warhead into orbit."

"But that is exactly what we need!" The director beamed in delight, then paused. "And that is why Sky Hammer took them out."

"Yes."

"May I, sir?" the director asked, pointing at the samovar.

The politician gestured in permission, and the director poured himself a glass of black tea.

"So the Gryazno Pakas are totally destroyed?"

"Totally. It will take us years to replace them, at a cost of billions of rubles."

"Ahem," the director said. "Sir, please."

"Millions of euros," the president corrected. A world economy, that would be next? World peace? The politician sipped his hot drink and glanced out a window that showed Red Square. It was full of people now, laughing, singing, children playing with kites. Formerly the area had been a place of public executions, overlooked by a giant bronze statue of a very dour Lenin. The Great Liberator was only a hated memory these days, and he wouldn't have approved of the changes in Red Square, or of Russia in the European Commonwealth. But that was merely just another good reason to join.

A flashing red light on the desk caught his attention and the president scowled at the phone for a long minute before lifting the receiver.

"Yes?" he answered gruffly, then paused, listening to the man on the other end. "No, sorry, our own laser cannon has been destroyed… What? So you know about the Gryazno Pakas? Well, they are gone, too… No, not everything… We have one disassembled in a dozen laboratories undergoing tests for metal fatigue and such." He lowered his empty glass. "No, even if we reassembled it, the GP would be nonoperational."

"I know that France is working on something similar...they canceled the project as too expensive. Typical. England..." The Russian president frowned. "The entire airbase? This is very grim, yes, my friend. Is there anybody with an illegal method of delivering a nuclear charge into space? Perhaps, the NSC, CDTI, JAXA or the ESA?"

"I see." The president sighed. "So be it. Farewell, my friend. Goodbye."

"Nobody?" the director said as a question.

"Nobody," the president answered, hanging up the phone, then reaching for the other. There was a buzz, a click and a voice answered.

"General Vastrov? Me. Please prepare a flight of Vostock missiles armed with a thermonuclear warhead, the biggest we have. Call when you are ready... Um? The target?" The president sternly looked at the ceiling. "Straight up, my dear general, straight up into space."

EVER SINCE BETHLEHEM, the Blue Moon mercs had been slowing down suddenly, then speeding up, taking a U-turn twice and so on, to shake any tails. Using every trick in the book, then inventing a few out of sheer necessity, Able Team had been doing its best to keep tabs on the mercs in the stolen sedan, and it hadn't been easy.

Zigzagging their way south, the two vehicles finally hit Interstate 80, and played a deadly game of tag for two hundred miles, before finally turning south on Route 79.

Where they were headed, Able Team had no idea. And without the help of the Farm, they couldn't arrange for aerial surveillance, get a fuel drop, or even hold off the police. Near the state line to Ohio, the team had to watch the mercs kill a motorcycle cop who pulled up alongside with his lights flashing. A sound suppressor poked out the window, there was a puff of smoke and the cop went flying, blood spraying out the other side of his head. The policeman and machine went off the embankment and tumbled down into the marshland below, both disappearing among the thick weeds.

Muttering curses, Lyons almost lost it then, but gripped the steering wheel harder and concentrated on the mission. If they lost the mercs, tens of thousands, possibly millions, of civilians might die before Sky Hammer was stopped. Because of the communications blackout, Able Team had no idea how Phoenix Force was doing on its end of the problem, and Lyons had to operate on the assumption that they were alone. Millions lived, or millions died, on their actions. The team couldn't stop to help a wounded cop, or even to use a cell phone to call for a local react base to send an ambulance. The traitor might be monitoring their phones for activity, and that would reveal Able Team's position. Which could have been the reason why the Blue Moon mercs started speeding for a few miles, and abruptly stopped after a traffic cop arrived to pull them over to issue a ticket. They lured him to his death to try to see if anybody was trailing them. It was cold-blooded murder of the worst sort, and Lyons made a solemn promise, that he would remind the mercs of this slaying just before he blew out their hearts.

"Can you change the frequencies?" Blancanales asked, holding up his phone.

"Not in time to do anything," Schwarz stated sadly. "And I wish to God that I could."

"How about the CB?" Lyons demanded, glancing at the unit on the rear equipment table. "We have enough stuff to build an atomic cyclotron, and we can't do anything?"

"Not if they have tracking equipment on board." Schwarz said firmly. "Then we might as well fire off a flare to announce our position as well as send a radio message."

"How likely is it that they have stuff to do that?" Blancanales asked, tucking the useless phone away.

Schwarz shrugged. "I dunno, say, fifty-fifty."

"Then place the call," Lyons decided. "Right now."

Reaching for the CB radio, Schwarz switched it on, grabbed the mike and thumbed the switch. "Breaker one-nine, break, break. Emergency, repeat.." He coughed for a while. "E-emergency! I'm a fisherman, down in the Ala…genny R-river near I-79… I tripped, got cut bad on a bottle in the water… Oh, Jesus, there's blood everywhere… break, break, please help me…Allegheny River Inter…Interstate seventy-nine…"

He released the transmit switch, and for a moment, it seemed as if the attempt hadn't worked, then the CB speaker crackled into life.

"Come on back, breaker!" a gruff voice demanded. "Breaker? Kick 'er back, son… Damn it, man, if you can hear me, help is on the way. Lazy Sue and the Dark Savage are calling a local react base right now. Copy, breaker? Put pressure on the wound, and hold on. Breaker, do you copy?" The call continued, and after a minute Schwarz turned the CB radio off.

"Okay, that's the best we can do," Schwarz said glumly, casting a glance at the U.S. Army field surgery bag on the rear shelving of the van. "God, I hate leaving a man behind."

"Can't be helped," Blancanales said, staring at the distant green sedan rolling along the roadway. "I just hope it hasn't cost us too much."

"It already has," Lyons stated, his hands knuckle-white on the steering wheel.

"ARE THEY STILL following us?" Tokay demanded, shifting gear.

"I have no idea," Salvai snorted, the flamethrower filling her lap. "They are nowhere in sight, and we lost the radio tracking equipment in the other vehicle."

"Lucky we had a med kit with us," Delellis said, looking at her bandaged leg. There had been way to get the steel flé-chettes out, so he had washed the dozen small wounds with alcohol, smeared on antibiotic cream and wrapped them tightly with clean bandages. Unfortunately there had been no painkillers aside from some aspirins, and he could only guess at the agony Zdenka was going through.

"Want two more?" he asked, offering the tiny bottle.

The woman sneered at the gesture. "They don't help." She grunted. "And my ears are starting to ring. Any more and I may bleed to death inside from them."

"How soon do we reach Bluestone?" Delellis asked, tucking the container back into the med kit.

"An hour, maybe more," Tokay said, glancing at the fuel gauge. They were low, but it would be enough. If he stopped for fuel, the Americans might decide to attack them at the station. Unacceptable. This was becoming a race against time, in more ways than one.

AN HOUR LATER the green sedan rolled over the Pennsylvania state line and entered West Virginia. The landscape had been getting steeper with every passing mile. Now, the world rose sharply in ragged stages, steep hills forming deep valleys and the majestic Allegheny Mountains rising high in the distance.

"If they start heading west," Blancanales said, crumpling an empty MRE envelope and stuffing it under the seat, "we'll be heading directly for Shenandoah National Park."

"Think that's the goal?" Schwarz asked, pulling an M-16 assault rifle into his lap. "Maybe this is some sort of tactic to try to trick us into revealing the location of the Farm."

Blancanales pulled out his Colt pistol and racked the slide. "Sure as hell hope not," he stated. "That would mean they know more about us than we do them."

"Okay, we're now officially on the empty mark," Lyons announced. "At the first blink of the red light showing the tank is dry, I'm going to charge before we stall, and everybody start shooting. Maybe we can get them busy in a firefight and they'll come back to kill us."

"And we shall steadfastly thwart them," Schwarz said, placing an AP round into the grenade launcher.

"Thwart?" Lyons asked, looking in the rearview mirror at the man in the back of the van.

"I also said steadfast."

"We're not impressed, Hermann," Blancanales stated, swinging down a ceiling panel to get his own M-16.

Since Lyons was driving, Schwarz took the Atchisson autoshotgun and attached a fresh 40-round drum to the big-bore weapon.

"Heads up, people, this could be it," Lyons announced, dropping back a little as the green sedan turned off the main road and took a side road.

Warily, Able Team followed after a few minutes, trying to give the mercs enough distance to stay hidden, but not enough to lose them completely. It was a gamble either way, but the Stony Man commandos had little choice, aside from a direct attack, and that time was rapidly coming as the fuel gauge fell.

They lost sight of the sedan for several minutes, and Lyons accelerated in pursuit. The dashboard light suddenly came on as he spotted a smoking car by the side of the road and three still bodies sprawled in a spreading pool of red blood.

In an instant, the men of Able Team took in the scene. The make of burning car was different, and the three people on the ground were all carrying Kalashnikov assault rifles. There was no sign of the X-18 or the flamethrower.

"It's a trap!" Lyons shouted and spun the wheel hard, sending the van shooting off the road and crashing into the bushes.

A split second later the road behind them violently detonated.

CHAPTER FIFTEEN

Jekyll Island

A warm salty breeze blew in through the open window of the cottage, and the gentle rhythmic sounds of ocean waves cresting on the beach could be heard.

The walls of the beachfront cottage were lined with smooth plaster, the floor bare pine, and the spacious basement was hermetically sealed and filled with humming supercomputers.

To the side of the isolated property was a fenced-in area containing a cable TV dish of unusual size. Behind some tall hedges was a swimming pool, with a retractable sheet of canvas covering its contents. On the beach were a couple of speedboats and a yacht, but then, this was a rather exclusive neighborhood. If you had to ask how much the houses cost, then you couldn't afford to live here.

Unless you were a government hardsite.

The melodious strains of a Franz Liszt concerto was playing on a stereo, the dulcet tones filling the NSA listening post as the owner sipped a glass of port. But then the stereo stopped playing in the middle of a note and a faint beeping could be heard coming from the office.

Rising from the comfortable chair, John Meterson padded barefoot down the hallway. Dressed in loose cotton pants and shirt, Meterson was a small, stocky man, with pale blond hair but dark eyebrows, which gave him a faint movie star appearance. His nails were manicured as befitting a resident of Jekyll Island, and his wristwatch was a gold Rolex that weighed more than a PDA. The man hated the stupid thing, but accepted the necessity of its presence as part of his role as a wealth recluse.

Sliding back the parting doors, Meterson entered the office. The room was dimly lit and coolly air conditioned, unlike the rest of the cottage. The walls were lined with bookcases and an expensive Persian rug formed a soft island in the middle of the hardwood floor. A wooden desk stood in one corner, and a flower-print sofa in another. The desk was antique, the chair was leather, and the computer beeping. There was no phone.

Placing the glass of port aside, Meterson sat at the desk and flipped a few switches hidden in a drawer. With a hydraulic sigh, the windows closed and locked, the office door did the same, and the stereo started playing Rhapsody #2 again, slightly louder to cover any possible conversations or keystrokes.

Accessing files, the man briefly read a scrolling message from his brother. Ah, the new shipment had arrived and been deployed. Excellent. One hundred and twenty Thors; they could smash Tokyo off the map with that many, even withholding the twenty reserved for their escape.

In reply he sent the good news that the family estates had been reclaimed. The Meternich castle was their property once more, obtained through a dozen fake corporations and false identities, until there was no way the purchase could ever be traced back to them. Once Sky Hammer had finished its job, the brothers could retire, never having to worry about a knock on their front door and opening it to find a CIA wet-work team with guns drawn.

A soft knock sounded on the door and Meterson quickly killed the computer link, then unlocked the door.

"Come in," he said, smiling.

The double doors parted and a bikini-clad woman walked into the office. She was deeply tanned, except for where the bikini covered her pale skin. A silver bracelet jingled around her ankle and long red hair cascaded to her slim hips.

"I heard the music stop and start," she said sleepily. "That usually means you're in the office working."

"Just taking care of some family business, my love." He laughed, internally furious that she knew so much. Was he becoming predictable? That could be very dangerous.

Slipping into his lap, the redhead gave him a kiss on the cheek. Her full breasts rested heavily against his shirt and he could feel the heat of her skin through the thin cotton.

"Was it your brother?" she asked, stroking his hair. "I know that you haven't seen him for a long time."

Meternich's face didn't register a thing, but his eyes grew colder. "Brother, my dear? Whatever do you mean?"

She giggled. "Oh, don't play that game with me, silly. I got curious last week and started looking through your stuff until I found a note from you brother, Attila." She laughed. "What a name! Although, I guess it is common enough in Hungary. Why are you so secretive about him? Did he—"

Slamming a fist into her smooth stomach, John "Meternich" stood and dumped the gasping woman onto the hard floor. Going swiftly to the couch, he took a cushion and hurried over to spread her flat on her back. He then sat on her stomach, placing both knees on her arms, pinning them to the floor. She started to wriggle uncomfortably then, and he ruthlessly rammed the pillow onto her face, pressing hard.

It only took a split second for her to realize that this wasn't some sort of rough foreplay, and started fighting back. But it was hopeless. She was taller, but slim. Meternich was a gorilla and twice her weight in sheer muscle. Hysterical, the redhead started screaming into the cushion, but that only hastened her demise. The cries for help got softer and weaker, and eventually stopped altogether.

Pressing down for a couple of extra minutes to make sure she wasn't faking, Meternich finally got off the woman's still form and checked her pulse. Yes, dead.

"Curiosity killed the cat, my dear," Meternich admonished, returning the cushion to the sofa. God, what a waste. The man felt just terrible about this. She had been a wonderful lover!

He really hadn't planned to kill her until the following week.

West Virginia

CAREENING OFF A TREE with a strident crash, Lyons slammed on the brakes and grabbed the Atchisson to dive from the vehicle even before it ceased rocking back and forth. Out of gas, out of time. Get moving!

The men of Able Team hit the ground running and were only a few yards away when the van was rocked by a salvo, the rifle grenades smashing through the bulletproof windows and detonating inside the vehicle. Wisely, the Stony Man commandos kept swiftly on the move. A few moments later the stores of munitions in the armored van cooked off and a staggering series of explosions lit up the West Virginia countryside, shrapnel rustling the leaves, tracer rounds sizzling by dangerously close overhead. Then the C-4 satchel charges went off and the area rocked under a deafening triphammer blast.

"Count off," Lyons said into his throat mike, switching to a encoded channel. The transmissions couldn't be understood, but the radio signals could be located by triangulation. Especially, if there was a lot of the enemy out there. All communications had to be short and constantly on the move.

"One," Blancanales said softly.

"Two," Schwarz replied, coughing.

"Any breakage?"

"None," Schwarz coughed. "Landed on a rock. The hard kind."

"Twenty in thirty," Lyons ordered, clicking off.

"Confirm," Blancanales answered, and cut power to the radio.

The Stony Man commando understood the message: get twenty yards away, call back in thirty seconds. That should give them a safe zone from enemy fire and radio surveillance. Hopefully. Crawling through the thick brambles, the Latino replayed the attack inside his head. There had been a hard bang before the first grenade arrived, not a hard thump. For a brief moment he was back in boot camp with a drill sergeant screaming in his face that the difference between a thump and a bang from the enemy could mean life or death in the battle-field.

This second group had hit them with rifle grenades, so there were at least six of the enemy out there. Possibly more. A lot more. He hoped they weren't clever and had brought along dogs. Things would get real ugly, real fast, if they had dogs. Then again, Blancanales remembered the fight in the alley. Maybe the mercs wanted them alive for questioning just as much as Stony Man wanted them alive.

Only Stony Man didn't want them alive anymore, that gave the team an edge. Rolling to his knees, Blancanales checked his weapons. The M-16 carried one clip of thirty rounds, no reloads. The Colt .380 was still tucked inside his windbreaker, two clips, and he had a knife and— His hands found only fabric in the pockets of the jacket. Damn it, no grenades.

Dull machine-gun fire tore through the leaves overhead, rattling off the thicker branches of the trees and snipping off the smaller ones, sending them tumbling to the ground like green snow. It sounded like an AK-47, but a trifle different. It had to be the Hungarian AMR-69. He tried to recall any important difference, and couldn't come up with anything. Basically, it was just a rip-off version of the Kalashnikov that Hungary made so they wouldn't have to buy them from Russia.

An explosion came from the west and machine guns tore up the forest to the east.

"They're trying to flush us out with bracket fire," Blancanales said to himself, tugging on his earphone and activating his throat mike. "Carl, Hermann, you there?"

"Loud and clear," Schwarz replied. "These assholes are mighty serious about removing us from this plane of existence."

"So let's return the favor," Lyons growled, "Check the frequency, Gadgets."

There was a brief pause as more explosions thundered around the woods, followed by crashing tree limbs. Very soon, the mercs would come after them personally. Then things would get interesting. The hunters had become the hunted.

"All clear," Schwarz reported. "Nobody else is listening in to us at the moment."

"Good," Lyons said, scanning the top of the forest. "Can anybody see the big pine tree with the bird nest on top?"

"Sure."

"No. Wait a minute. Okay, I was underneath it."

"Good. Meet me there in five," Lyons directed as the enemy machine guns started shooting again.

The ground was sloping, and soon he realized that they were in valley. Faintly he could hear the sound of a rushing river. A few minutes later the big ex-cop breached a wall of laurel and found his teammates waiting with guns at the ready. Both had leafy twigs mixed into their clothing and dirt on their faces to soften skin tones.

"Okay, I'm down to the Atchisson, no reloads," Lyons whispered sharply.

"About the same," said Blancanales.

"Ditto."

"Then we do this fast and dirty," Lyons continued, switching to an uncoded channel on the radio. "Is…anybody still alive? Count off!"

"One," Blancanales replied, smiling.

"Two," Schwarz said. "But my arm is broken."

"Don't move," Lyons said earnestly. "Just stay put and we'll find you. Out."

Swiftly moving away from the clearing, Able Team did its best to mask any trace of its presence, then settled in to wait. It wasn't long before three men crept toward them wearing forest camouflage fatigues, AK-47 assault rifles in their hands. Black bags slung over their shoulders were bulging bulky objects that looked like Soviet Union rifle grenades.

Probably just leftovers found in a warehouse somewhere. The Soviet army left a lot of munitions in the field when the Communist party lost favour. A lot of it showed up on the black market, but some of it didn't and was stored away by civilians, police and some criminals in case of future trouble.

Looking at Blancanales, Lyons mouthed, "Mercs?" The Latino nodded.

Good. Then these were just more mercs armed with old weapons. Better and better. That only left the question of where the others were, the three mercenaries Able Team had followed all the way down here. Hiding in another ambush? Or had they already escaped?

Schwarz patted his arm to get the attention of the other men, then made a circling motion with the barrel of his M-16 rifle. After a few moments the others agreed with the plan and slipped into the bushes, leaving the three mercs in fatigues behind.

Retracing their steps to the wreck of the van, Able Team used binoculars to check for any watchers. It seemed clear, so they inched to the road, the sound of a river getting noticeably louder. The flipped-over car had been spray-painted dark green, although it was a very good match. However, the three corpses were all men, one wearing a dress and wig to make him appear to be the female merc. Under his dress was the uniform of a West Virginia park ranger. Somebody had even wrapped his leg in white masking tape to simulate bandages. The Kalashnikovs were fake, plastic toys painted to look real from a distance. The blood was genuine.

"So we got the flamethrower gal," Lyons said with some satisfaction. "Next time, I'll blow her head off."

"Cold, man, very cold," Blancanales stated. "They capped three civilians to try to get us."

"Nothing in sight," Schwarz declared, sweeping the woods and road with the binoculars. The road they were on went across a river, or some sort of major waterway, at least, and he could see far along the other side. "No sign of the sedan, or any other mercs."

Turning to ask the man a question, Lyons was startled a see a red dot moving across his friend, then disappear, then come back and settle into place above his heart.

"Snipers!" Lyons shouted, kicking sideways.

Schwarz was shoved out of the way as a stream of high-velocity rounds poured through the space he'd just occupied.

Sweeping the treetops on the opposite shore through the telescopic sights of the assault rifle, Blancanales caught a flash of light in the low-power scope and raised the barrel high to fire a full clip. The distance was pretty far, almost too far. But he had aimed high, and the decelerating lead patted through the lush needles of the pine tree. The Stony Man commando doubted that the rounds had enough punch left in them to kill, but the thirty bullets had to have done something right, because a voice cried out in pain. Then a body tumbled into view from its perch, dropping out of the tall tree, bouncing sickenly from branch to branch like a broken rag doll until it went out of sight.

"One down," Schwarz muttered, moving behind an oak tree for cover and leveling his assault rifle toward the burning car.

"Five to go," Lyons agreed, doing the same.

Drawing his pistol, Blancanales took a position behind the others just as three men in fatigues appeared from behind the thick smoke rising from the burning vehicle. All three were carrying their AK-47 assault rifles at the ready, one of them with a Soviet rifle grenade stuffed into the barrel.

Switching from single shot to full-auto, Lyons still wanted one of them alive. Blending in with the forest, the Stony Man operatives stayed hidden, letting the others come closer, until a merc snapped a head in their direction.

Then Able Team opened fire.

"Petrov!" Salvai demanded, shaking the limp corpse. "Petrov!" But even through the blinding pain of her throbbing leg, the woman could tell he was dead. The body had thumped to the ground like a pile of wet newspapers, the limbs flailing loosely. She strongly doubted that there was an intact bone in the entire man's body.

"Leave him," Tokay said, resting the heavy barrel of the X-18 grenade launcher on a shoulder. "We will drink to his memory later, but let's finish this assignment first."

"The brothers wanted us to capture one alive," Salvai muttered, swaying slightly as she awkwardly stood using a tree branch as a crude crunch. "Make the others waste time on a rescue, keep them away from Jekyll."

Radiating fury, Tokay started to raise a hand, then let it drop. Salvai didn't know what she was saying. The woman was babbling. Along the car trip, the wounds had to have gotten infected and she was feverish. A fight was out of the question now. So be it. But the combat zone for the ambush had been chosen well. Baron Meternich always thought ahead, and had a contingency plan ready in case of trouble.

Whipping out a cell phone, Tokay dialed an emergency number and let it ring three times before hanging up. With no conversation, the call couldn't be monitored or traced. But the number of rings were the message. A request for death.

"Back to the car, my friend," Tokay said, letting the X-18 hang by its strap at his side.

Slipping an arm under the shoulder of the trembling woman, Tokay helped her hobble along to the SUV driven by the three hired gunners. They called themselves mercenaries, but they were only grunts, muscle for hire. Well-meaning, but not overly intelligent, which made them perfect cannon fodder for this mission. Besides, the stolen sedan was almost out of fuel and the grunts wouldn't be needing the SUV anymore.

Pressed against the woman, Tokay could feel the temperature ravaging her body, but she had said nothing, refusing to let the others down. He felt proud that she was Hungarian.

"What happened?" Salvai asked in a blur, her head lolling. "Did we win?"

Pausing in the shadow of a tall tree, Tokay looked at the clear sky. "Oh, yes," he whispered grinning. "We killed them all. Every single one."

"KILL ME," the merc groaned, clutching his bloody chest. "Go ahead, do it."

"Not quite yet," Lyons said, crouching alongside the man. The Colt Python was in his hand, the barrel warm. Able team had caught the mercs dead to rights. They killed one in the first second of combat, the next, soon after that.

"Yeah? Well, why don't you go f…f…" He slumped and the blood stopped oozing from the wounds.

Keeping his gun ready, Lyons checked for a pulse, then peeled back an eyelid to double check. The man was dead.

Rifling through his clothing, Lyons found nothing but a wad of cash. It was probably the mercs' fee for this assignment. Men like this didn't have secret banks accounts, they preferred cash, something tangible. They called themselves mercenaries, but they were disposable soldiers. The Blue Moon trio liked to use others in their missions: the helicopter, the ALSF and now these fools. They were extremely careful and utterly ruthless. That made them very dangerous opponents.

Taking off the man's camouflage cap, Lyons placed it over his face, then stood and looked over the Kalashnikov rifle he had gotten from the so-called merc. The weapon seemed well cared for, with no silly orthopedic modifications. Professional target shooters used those to fine tune the weapon and marginally increase their accuracy in contests, and the modifications did work. But just for that specific person. In the heat of combat, if a comrade had to use that weapon, maybe to protect his or her life, then the alterations worked against him or her, lowering accuracy. It was a rich man's toy, unnecessary and unwanted by professionals.

Removing the clip, Lyons checked the ammunition. Blunt-nosed specials, half-charges to be used for the rifle grenades. Four rounds left.

"These are very bad for the barrel," Lyons said out loud, tossing away the clip and replacing it with one containing standard ammunition. Working the bolt, he paused as a tree hit by a rifle grenade earlier gave a loud splintery noise and came crashing down across the road, almost hitting the burning car.

"Carl, you killed a tree with that blinding glimpse of the obvious," Schwarz said, standing guard. "Well done."

Almost smiling at that, Blancanales continued going through the personal items of the other two mercs. There wasn't much. The wallets were probably in their vehicle somewhere, being driven by Blue Moon by now, as well as their wedding rings, and any other jewelry that could reflect light during a fight and give away your position. Paper money and cell phones. That was all.

Giving the cell phone to Schwarz, Blancanales went through the wads of cash carefully, then smiled as he extracted a slim piece of white paper with faint blue printing.

"And we have a winner," Blancanales whispered in triumph. It was a receipt for three breakfast specials from a restaurant called the Bluestone Inn, and it was dated that day.

"There's only this group," the Latino announced, tucking away the slip and cash. People did that sort of thing all the time, even an experienced soldier. You paid for a meal, the cashier gave you a receipt with the change, and it got stuffed with the money into a pocket. Out of sight, out of mind, forgotten completely.

Disassembling another Kalashnikov, Lyons grunted in reply. Good news. They were down to the original three again. Checking inside the weapon, the Able Team leader noted with satisfaction that these were civilian models, illegally modified for automatic fire. A simple procedure, he had done it himself while on assignments. Using a piece of paper, Lyons took a rubbing of the serial number and folded it away carefully. When the Farm, came back on-line, hopefully soon, this would tell them exactly where the guns had been purchased. It might be near the Sky Hammer ground base and the all-important maser.

Going over the cell phones for traps, Schwarz hit the re-dial button and one of the other phones rang. He pressed that one, and the third one rang. Okay, a daisy chain. How nice. He pressed the third and somebody answered.

"Are they dead?" Tokay asked, the sound of a racing car faintly in the background. "Or is this one of them?"

"We're waiting for you," Schwarz said in a hard voice, then turned off the phone and stuffed it into a pocket. Let the bastard chew on that for a while.

"Was that them" Lyons asked.

"Yeah, and it sounded like Elvis has left the building."

"I expected as much."

"Maybe yes, maybe no, but I'm still not too keen on crossing that bridge," Blancanales asked, working the bolt on another Kalashnikov and ejecting a spent round jammed in the port. The dented brass came free and flew away. The mercs had carried lot of spare clips, so the team was well equipped again. He didn't like Kalashnikovs—they were heavy and had a much shorter range than the M-16—but the assault rifles were certainly better than throwing rocks.

"Not on foot, anyway," Lyons said, looking through binoculars. "But I guess we have to. That's where the Blue Moon people are located." There were a couple of wooden posts sticking out of the ground on the other side of the river. Looked as though a sign had been there and crudely removed. Why remove a sign?

Following his gaze, Blancanales marked the missing sign. Odd. Very odd.

"Now, it sounded like they were driving away fast," Schwarz said, squinting at the bridge. A hundred feet of wide-open space with nowhere to take cover. "But they could have just been revving the engine to sucker us into thinking they were long gone."

"Just their style," Blancanales said. "Get the wonder boys here to charge, and we retreat across the bridge into range of another sniper."

"Most likely, the first guy was supposed to wait for us to reach the middle of the span, and then cut loose," Schwarz said, rubbing his chest where the laser mark had been located. "But he got impatient."

"Then he got dead," Lyons added without humor. No car, low on ammo, and the only way after the mercs was an obvious deathtrap. "Let's go check the tires on the van. If they're still intact, we can smear them with brake fluid, set them on fire, and roll them across the bridge. The smoke will give us cover."

"Better than nothing," Schwarz said, then blinked. "Hey, what was that?"

A bright flash appeared in the sky, like a shooting star or heat lightning.

With his heart pounding in his chest, Lyons traced the path of the streak to the right, and turned northward to see an expanse of gray concrete barely visible above the tree line. An explosion sounded, followed by a tremendous crackling noise, like hot glass dropped into cold water.

"It's a dam," he said as a second flash streaked by and a thundering crash echoed through the valley. "They're smashing the dam!"

Without a word, the Stony Man commandos turned and raced up the access road for the highway. They were in a valley with steep sides right now, a perfect venue for a flood.

My God, that was what the missing sign had to have said, Blancanales realized in shock. Welcome to such-and-such dam. No wait, the receipt had said Bluestone Inn. The Bluestone Dam? He had never heard of the place, even though it was this close to the Farm and had to be pretty big to see over trees this far away. Say, two hundred feet high, and the valley was maybe a half-mile wide, and the river flowing under the bridge was about a hundred feet wide, so that would roughly yield a trillion tons of water coming this way.

"Move faster, guys!" Schwarz urged, pelting around the fallen tree and along the sloping roadway.

"City! There's a city nearby somewhere," Blancanales breathed, running. "Gotta warn them…"

Whipping out his own cell phone, the Stony Man commando hit the last button, preset for emergencies.

"You have reached 9-1-1," an operator announced calmly. "Please state the nature of your—"

"The dam has cracked!" Blancanales shouted. "Call the chief engineer if you don't believe me, but it's cracked, lady, and coming your way. Sound the alarm!" With a snap, he closed the lid, terminating the call.

"Didn't say which dam," Lyons added, banking along a curve in the road. The main roadway was ahead of them now, maybe a thousand yards away.

"Can't be very many in the valley."

"Sure hope not!"

More explosions came from the dam, sounding like field artillery. Suddenly a strong wind pushed against their backs.

"We're not going to reach the road," Lyons said cursing, glancing around for a safe haven. "There! Into the ravine! The access ramp will shield us!"

"Sure, until it comes apart!" Schwarz added, staying with the big ex-cop. "We don't know how much water is coming this way! Could be larger than Lake Mead!"

The wind increased until the men were nearly lifted off their feet, running on tiptoes, almost flying.

"Then I'll see you in heaven!"

"As if St. Peter admits people like us!" Blancanales retorted, jumping off the road.

The men hit the sloped side and slid down the loose gravel, ripping their clothing apart, tearing the flesh from their hands. The team landed ankle-deep in muck that filled the bottom of a concrete ditch meant for handling rainwater. Under the access ramp, there was a culvert going through to the other side. The rushing deluge would funnel through that and come out faster than an express train, and just as unstoppable. But suddenly, Able Team realized that this was their chance for life.

Dropping their weapons, the men went flat to the layered stonework on either side of the opening and held on tight, splaying their legs for traction. The rugged layers of stone offered good hand grips, perfect for climbing. The Stony Man team only hoped it would be enough. There was nothing to anchor themselves to. Muscles and brains were all they had.

"Been nice knowing you, Hermann," Blancanales said, his heart pounding.

"Ditto, Rosario," Schwarz replied solemnly, a cheek pressed against the granite. He could smell the mud beneath their boots, and the sweet pine trees. "Pol, after you're dead, can I date your sister, Toni?"

"Forget it!"

He grinned. "Hey, it was worth a shot."

"Here it comes," Lyons shouted over the building roar.

Then the wind stopped and the thunder arrived, an endless crashing of trees, and water pounding like a thousand surfs combined into one maelstrom. It shot over the access ramp forming a solid ceiling of chaos, then it lanced out of the culvert, moving with such tremendous force that the Stony Man team remained untouched for a few moments, only the stinging spray pelting them hard. Holding on for dear life, they saw trees uprooted and boulders smashed aside, the topsoil, leaves and gravel gone in a heartbeat. Everything imaginable was inside the tumultuous flow, chunks of concrete, items of clothing, pieces of boats, fish, men and death.

Going flat to the rock, they dug in their fingers, straining from the effort to hold on tight. The backwash arrived and the water rose to their knees, then their waist, then chests. It was cold, stealing the strength from their muscles. Beyond comprehension, the noise was like an anvil, conversation was impossible, even breathing was difficult, and the ground currents tugged on their legs, swirling the muddy residue beneath their work boots.

Then the asphalt cap was pried off the roadway, long strips and short pieces tumbling into the rush and breaking apart. A slab bigger than an intersection crashed behind Able Team, missing by inches, the impact almost shaking them loose. But for a precious second the lethal currents tugging at their legs eased. When the piece of road flipped over, vanishing into the raging torrent, the riptide returned with a vengeance.

Bare ground was above them now, and dirt clouded the flood making it a murky brown. A stone shot of the wall near the top and more swiftly followed. Without a protective covering, the flood was eating away the ramp, the water undercutting the stones and mortar like a mining sluice. More stones shot away and the erosion began to accelerate, getting lower and lower with ever-increasing speed.

With wet faces, the men grimly watched doom approach. There was nowhere to go and nothing to do. If the team lost its grip for an instant, the cascade would rip them off the stone wall and send them smashing along the valley, hitting everything along the way. At least death would be mercifully swift.

The savage pounding seemed to last forever, Able Team simply concentrating on holding tight. Their whole world becoming the irregular stone facade of the access road. Breathing was reduced to frantic sips stolen from the gaps between the jutting rocks, their legs were as cold as columns of ice, hands numb, their faces bleeding from pressing so hard against the decorative granite, and the stonework above them kept breaking away and descending closer. The moment it reached the level of their heads, it was all over.

And then it was gone, like the flipping of a switch.

As the noise and madness faded away, the men of Able Team forced open their eyes and watched the river water drop away until it was only inches deep around their shaking legs.

It took an effort, but Lyons forced his fingers to relinquish their hold and stiffly turned to see the tidal wave recede along the valley, leaving nothing standing in its wake. There was only muddy desolation studded with splintery tree stumps for as far as he could see. The forest was gone, the bridge, the car wrecks, everything had been removed, washed clean by the rampaging flood.

"E-everybody okay?" Lyons asked, staggering from the stone wall. His legs felt dead, and the big man slowly bent his knees a few times to try to force the return of circulation.

"Never better," Schwarz answered, wiping drool from his mouth with a shaking hand.

"Same here," Blancanales said hoarsely. The man felt as if he'd been run over by a truck, and his ears were ringing so loudly that everything the others said seemed to be coming from the bottom of a well. Hopefully that condition would go away quickly.

Just then, distant thunder roared from farther down the valley. Sloshing in the muck, Able Team turned in that direction.

"I only hope that Hinton can say the same thing five minutes from now," Lyons stated, holding his aching side.

"THANKS, DALE, pay you tomorrow!" Mrs. Johnston called, leaving the grocery store.

The clerk waved. "No prob, Mrs. J.!"

The sidewalks were busy in the little town, fishing season had just started, and the campers had arrived to buy everything they forgot to bring from home. The temptation was strong for some of the merchants and storekeepers, but prices on items remained the same. This was the heartland of West Virginia, and the folks here didn't do the questionable things merely accepted as good business in wicked cities like Fayette and Richmond.

Shuffling to the corner, Mrs. Johnston smiled at friend walking his dogs along the gutter, then looked up and frowned at the sight of some heat lightning to the north. Now that was odd. There really didn't seem to be enough clouds to support lightning. She would have to check on local weather on the Internet back home. Maybe a big storm was coming.

When the traffic light changed, she stiffly walked across the intersection, her new titanium hip moving much easier now that the swelling had gone down from the recent operation. Soon she'd be walking better than ever!

Awkwardly stepping onto the curb, Mrs. Johnston politely hid a smile as she let some big-city tourists go by first, their hands full of cameras and film, their hats covered with fishing lures.

Everybody came to Hinton this time of year. The Bluestone Dam was surrounded by a hundred miles of the best fishing in the state, which was really saying something for West Virginia. There were countless cabins and hunting resorts all along the banks of the reservoir, and even more along the new river feed by the great sluice gates. The dam was the marvel of the county, and she kept promising herself to go see it one day. Maybe when her hip was better. Yes, that was it. There was no rush. After all, the dam wasn't going anywhere!

Everybody looked up as the tornado sirens went off, building to a strident howl.

Puzzled, she looked around. What was going on? Was it a test and they forgot to mention it at the Sunday services? There was hardly a breath of wind today, so how could there possible be a tornado coming their way? It wasn't even tornado season!

Just then, a big truck passed behind her and she turned around to see that the roadway only had a few cars in sight. But there had been a truck. She'd felt it!

Nervously, she felt a touch of panic and hobbled into a music store, taking refuge behind the glass-topped counter. Several people were already there, and she knew them all by name.

"Bob, what the heck is happening?" Mrs. Johnston asked, her voice quavering a little, old spotted hands clutching the counter.

"Damned if I know," he answered nervously.

"Look!" a woman screamed pointing out the window of the store.

A muddy mountain of debris was sweeping along the

peaceful new river. Reaching from side to side, the wall of churning water filled the entire valley, pushing houses and cars and bodies ahead in foaming destruction.

Whispering a prayer, Mrs. Johnston felt her blood run cold at the nightmarish sight. Thunder could be heard and the ground was shaking worse every second. Items danced off the walls and displays toppled over, spilling goods onto the tiled floor.

"The dam has busted!" the priest announced through a bullhorn, standing in the church tower. "Run for your lives!"

Suddenly the bell started to clang in warning, barely heard above the keening siren. Then hell arrived as every window in town exploded from the onrush of compressed air. The woman standing in front of the music store window was cut into pieces, blood spraying everywhere. The clerk started to get sick and the old woman closed her eyes, bracing for death.

The flood hit Hinton like a crashing moon, flattening everything it touched, tearing up the road, crushing homes, flipping over cars and hurtling bodies skyward. The priest kept ringing the bell and shouting his warnings even as the tidal wave slammed into the church. The bell came free, crushing the priest, but the building stood as the floodwaters flowed around on either side, uprooting trees. Then a cornerstone came loose, the whole church trembled and came down in a rain of debris that vanished into the deluge.

On through the town it crashed, taking out homes, schools, the police station, fire department and the hospital. Nothing withstood the hammering fury.

When the waters left Hinton, there was nobody alive to see it leave, and very little to show that the town had ever existed.

CHAPTER SIXTEEN

McGuire Army Base, Minnesota

Edged by scrub brush and weeds, the closed Army base was in the middle of a cow pasture that stretched to the horizon. A tall wire fence enclosed the base, and the top of the fence was a mix of barbed wire and concertina wire. Twenty low buildings were inside the barrier, and dozens of warning signs outside. Two presidents ago, a lot of military bases had been closed in an effort to save the country money and balance the budget. It had failed, and soon there was a new president who opened up as many of the closed bases as possible.

But not McGuire.

Suddenly the sleepy cows became agitated and started to moo. Then a U.S. Army truck appeared, racing through the pasture. The cows lumbered out of the way, and the ones that moved too slow, the driver of the truck went around. His hand kept going for the horn, but the private restrained himself.

"Covert, quiet and clandestine" read the mission orders, and who was he to argue with the White House?

With a squeal of brakes, the big 4x4 truck came to a halt, causing a cloud of dust to rise, and two soldiers jumped off the back carrying heavy equipment bags. A lot more soldiers were inside, all of them carrying similar bags. Everybody not armed with an M-16 assault rifle was wearing a web belt with a holstered side arm. A couple of soldiers carried Stinger missile launchers.

"Okay, you two, we'll pick you up tomorrow," a sergeant said from the rear cargo area, hanging on to a ceiling strap. "Good hunting."

"Thanks, Sarge," the corporal said, giving a salute. "You, too."

The burly veteran grinned. "Bet your ass, kid." Then the sergeant turned his head. "Driver, move on to the next location!"

As the utility truck drove away, the corporal and the private slipped the straps for the bags over their shoulders and started to walk along the perimeter of the rusty fence until finding a big gate. The three keys the corporal used to open the series of padlocks all looked as if they had never been used before, and he knew that might be correct.

"What a dump," the private said, entering the base. He paused to pull out a pack of cigarettes and to light a smoke. "I've seen bombed-out villages that looked more hospitable."

Locking the gate behind them, the corporal had to agree. McGuire looked as though the whole base had been ridden hard and put away wet. There were twenty buildings, and each was worse than the other. The glass in the windows was cracked, weeds covered the streets and the base sign hung by only one end, the other in the dirt. McGuire had been deserted for years and looked it. The only incongruous element was a second fenced-off area containing four huge satellite dishes, each facing a compass point.

Then again, as the two got closer, the corporal could see that the main support for the cluster of dishes was covered with spiderwebs, and there was a bird nest in the southern dish. A couple of newborn chicks were inside the collection of mud and twigs, peeping to beat the band, demanding more food.

"Birds," the private said in disdain, blowing a stream a smoke at the tiny creatures.

The corporal scowled. "Hey, I like birds."

"Oh, don't get me wrong, so do I!" The private smiled. "A little olive oil, some breadcrumbs…" The man kissed his fingertips. "Delicious!"

"Get the crowbar, St. Francis," the corporal ordered. "Let's get this over with as soon as possible."

"Roger, wilco." The private grinned. "Sir!"

Setting down the utility bag with a clunk, the private opened the flaps wide and pulled out a crowbar. Taking a stance, the corporal jabbed it a few times into the dirty street until locating the manhole, then he wiggled the edge into place and heaved. The cover came free with an exhalation of stale air, exposing a steel ladder that led down into the dark.

"Whew!" the private said, dropping his cigarette and grinding it under his boot. "I've smelled worse, but only in New Jersey."

Sliding on air masks, the soldiers got their bags ready and started to climb down, the corporal going first.

After a few yards, he had to turn on the halogen lantern

hanging from his belt, and a brilliant blue-white light filled the corroded shaft.

"Snakes. Why did it have to be snakes?" the private mumbled. "Very dangerous. You go first."

"Put a cork in it, boot."

Reaching the bottom, the soldiers found themselves in an iron compartment with a Navy-style hatchway as a door. This one wasn't locked, but it took the strength of both men to get the stubborn wheel turning and finally undogged the hatch.

Beyond was only blackness.

Turning on the second halogen lantern, the men walked into a brick-lined tunnel filled with insulated cables. Somewhere far off, they heard dripping water, and their footsteps echoed along the passage as if they were the only people left in the world.

After a hundred yards, the dank tunnel branched out in a dozen directions, each of the passages identical to the first.

"Your tax dollars at work," the private snorted behind his air mask. "Okay, which one do we check?"

"All of them," the corporal said, sighing, and set down his bag to pull on a pair of gloves. "I'll take the first, you do the second, and so on."

"Ah, is it too late to join the Air Force?"

"Get humping, boot."

"Sir, yes, sir!"

Entering the first tunnel, the corporal started to wonder if the private hadn't been right about the Air Force. This passageway smelled horrible even through the mask.

Hey, nice clean planes, snappy uniforms, he thought dourly. Okay, occasionally you got a missile up the butt and bought the farm, but nothing was perfect.

Getting on his hands and knees, the corporal crawled along the sticky concrete, fondling every foot of the repulsive cable. The general had said to use bare hands, but he wasn't down here in this cesspool.

Hours passed, and the corporal finished the first tunnel feeling as if he'd crawled through the bowels of some prehistoric beast.

The third also proved clean, but in the middle of the third, the corporal stopped and double checked the concrete under the huge cable. There was nothing wrong with the cable itself, aside from a million years accumulation of rat crap, but the moorings were odd. Different. Bringing the light closer, he inspected the area under the feeder cable from the satellite dishes. Yep, the color of the concrete didn't match here. If he didn't know better, the soldier would have sworn that somebody had patched a section.

Sitting on the damp floor, he pulled off his gloves and shifted his side arm to check the blueprints stuffed inside his duty uniform. Nope, no work had ever been done along this length. This could be it, all right.

Taking a screwdriver, he started stabbing the concrete. It crumbled easily and soon the blade hit something metallic. Bingo.

Trying to get the object free, the corporal found there wasn't enough room, so he reluctantly removed his gloves and dug bare fingers into the gooey morass. He didn't know what his hands were immersed in, and didn't want to know. Come on, you big bastard, move already!

With a wet sucking noise, the object came free and the corporal stared in wonder at a rectangular box sealed inside a transparent plastic bag. Through the plastic, he could see that the metal box seemed to have been welded shut. Weird. But this couldn't possibly be what they'd been sent to find. It wasn't even touching the communication cables, just located very close.

Scraping off the reeking muck as best he could, the corporal wrapped the box in a spare shirt and started directly back to the surface. The sarge would definitely want to see this.

Stony Man Farm, Virginia

EVEN BEFORE THE Black Hawk helicopter had landed on the grassy lawn, Hal Brognola was out and running for the farmhouse, not waiting for a drive from one of the Farm's Jeeps.

Charging onto the porch, the big Fed tapped in the access codes and shoved the armored door aside. Blacksuits didn't react to the intrusion as they were aware of his imminent arrival.

Panting slightly Brognola took the steps two at a time and hurried to the Annex. He went directly to the Computer Room and hastily entered, announcing, "We found the tap!"

Everybody looked up from their work.

"Excellent! Where?" Kurtzman demanded, rolling out from under his console.

"Minnesota, McGuire Army Base," Brognola replied. "It was buried under a feeder line for the satellite relay station for the entire Midwest region."

"A lot of our stuff is routed through that link."

"Yes, I know."

"May I see the tap?" Price asked, walking over.

"Sure." Hal tossed her the box.

As she inspected the tap, Brognola gave the woman a hard look. Price was clearly exhausted. Normally she looked more like a high-fashion model than the mission controller for an antiterrorist organization. But today Price looked the job. He would guess that she hadn't eaten properly, or gone to sleep for at least two days. He'd have to do something about that. The numbers were falling, and his people had to stay sharp for when a break occurred. If one ever did.

"This is a standard NSA model," she said slowly, turning it over in her hands. "I've installed a hundred of these taps myself on embassy hardlines, and such."

"Only, the NSA has absolutely no record of it being installed at McGuire," Brognola stated gruffly, staring hatefully at the alien device. "It isn't one of ours."

"A rogue agent?"

Brognola grabbed a spare chair from the kitchenette and sat.

"I would have called you to save time," he stated, lacing his fingers. "But I could have been anybody using a voice modifier."

"And with our lines of communication breached," Price added, hefting the box, "we couldn't trust the usual ID codes."

"Exactly."

"Do you trust the people who found it?" Price asked, hefting the box in her palm. It couldn't weigh more than a pound.

"I had the President issue an executive order," Brognola explained. "We used soldiers, not intelligence agents. If the enemy has spies in every platoon, then they've already won. So, yes, we can be reasonably sure this is legitimate, and the only one."

"Why is that?" Tokaido asked curiously.

"Doubling the numbers of taps means tripling the risk of exposure," Price explained loquaciously. "If nothing else, these people are professionals, they would only have used the one tap."

"But I'm keeping the Army on the hunt until every line, every cable, every goddamn thing has been checked and double checked until we're absolutely sure our comm lines are clean," Brognola stated. "I don't care if it takes a year. We have the human resources, and they'll keep at it forever if necessary."

"Let's hope they're good enough," Price stated, tossing the box to Kurtzman. Striding over to the intercom on the wall, the mission controller pressed a few buttons.

"Greene here," the speaker replied. "What do you want, Bear?"

"It's Barbara," she corrected. "We've found the leak."

"That's great!"

"Yes and no. We still can't contact the field teams because they have no way to be sure it's us."

"Oh. I see."

"I need you to send a couple of blacksuits in civilian clothes to find the teams, and tell them face-to-face that we're back in business."

"No problem," Greene replied. "Where are Carl and David?"

"Unknown," Kurtzman replied. "We have deliberately not been keeping track of them in case our internal lines were compromised."

"Last known locations?"

"Bethlehem and Abu Dis."

"Then how do we contact them?" Price demanded, scowling.

Glancing at the map of the world on the main monitors, Kurtzman shrugged. "Beats me." He sighed.

Price went over and placed a hand on his shoulder. "Find them, Bear," she urged. "We have to let them know that—"

"Let me know what?" Lyons said from the doorway.

"Carl?" Price gasped, spinning.

Resembling drowned rats, the men of Able Team made their way to the kitchenette and started helping themselves to coffee. Their garbage collector uniforms were tattered and torn, and the men moved stiffly, as if covered with bruises.

"Sorry we're late," Schwarz said, trying to hide a slight limp. "We stopped for a wash."

"Actually, we had a little trouble over in Hinton," Blancanales said, adding milk and sugar to the acidic brew. He had experienced Kurtzman's powerful coffee before. "Since we were so close, we came here to rearm."

"What happened to your weapons?" Brognola asked, then added, "From the look of you three, I'd say a mountain fell on you."

"Close enough," Schwarz sighed, taking a sip. He shuddered, and took a longer drink.

"How did you get here?" Delahunt asked, raising her VR helmet.

"We took a bus," Lyons said, dropping into a chair. "Lots of cash, but no cabs in that part of West Virginia. We thumbed a ride to Skyline Drive. Blacksuits let us in the main gate." He took a long drink, finishing the coffee, then went back for more. "Okay, we heard the last part. You found the tap, and the Farm is back on-line. Great." Reaching into a pocket, Lyons turned and passed a couple of crumpled papers to Kurtzman. "Here, trace these, please. One is a cell phone, and the other is the serial number for a Kalashnikov hunting rifle."

"Done." Kurtzman passed them on to the others. Tokaido took one, Delahunt took the other, and they got busy. Sitting pensively, Wethers was still holding the box, turning it over and over in his hands, his expression unreadable.

"Okay, what happened?" Price asked, crossing her arms. "Were you hit by a Thor?"

Sipping coffee, the men of Able Team told the sequence of events.

"So the Nazis were a trap," Price said. "Yeah, we expected that."

"You guys need a week in the hospital," Brognola observed dryly. "I haven't seen you look this bad in years."

"What we really need," Lyons said grimly, a touch of steel in his voice, "is a van, guns and a name."

"The people you faced, Blue Moon," Kurtzman said, reading off his screen, "are based in Hungary, the descendents of freedom fighters. Now they're freelance mercs. So much for ideals. They're listed by Interpol as extremely vicious, which we now know to be extremely true, but honest to a contract. They never take the money and run. If they agree to kill you, they'll keep at it until you're history. Three known members, Bella Tokay, Zdenka Salvai and Petrov Delellis." He read off descriptions of the mercs, along with their signature weapons.

"That's them," Blancanales said, nodding.

"Well, you can scratch Zdenka or Petrov," Schwarz stated, nursing his drink in both hands. "Pol got one, but we don't know which. Too far away."

"Excuse me," Wethers said, then he stopped and started again, "but I know this box. I helped make it."

In unison, everybody in the room turned.

"What are you talking about, Hunt?" Brognola demanded curiously. "You were never in the NSA."

"No, Hal, I wasn't. However, I used to do some design work for them," the former professor said, unable to take his gaze off the box. "God, it was so long ago. But I helped create this, model C-57-D. It was back when I was at Berkeley University, I was doing some freelance work for the NSA. A young student helped me with the feedback circuits. A very clever fellow."

"Give me a name," Kurtzman demanded, turning, his hands poised above his keyboard. "That's all I need, a name."

"Joe…Jim? No, it was John something," Wethers said slowly. Then he shook his head. "Sorry, it was just too long ago."

"Then access the university files and find every student named John who took your class," Price ordered brusquely.

"Certainly," Wethers replied, placing the box on top of his console where he could keep an eye on it, and got to work.

"First, a dying NSA agent claimed there was a traitor. Now we find an NSA tap, on an NSA feeder line."

"So you think the traitor is a CIA agent?" Schwarz asked.

Tactfully, she ignored him. "Bear, get me the duty roster for the NSA, live, dead and retired, for the past twenty years.

No thirty, back to when Mahone first wrote his report about Sky Hammer."

"Done."

"Now, if Hunt delivers a name, we can do a comparison, and if our luck holds…"

"Then we can go to work," Lyons finished. Draining the mug, he stood. "Okay, we're going to wash up, get some food and clean clothes. Then we'll commandeer some bedrooms in the farmhouse. Let us know when you find something."

"A moment, Carl," Brognola said.

Schwarz and Blancanales walked out of the room, but Lyons turned from the open doorway.

"Good job."

As hard as stone, Lyons gave no response and walked from the room, quietly closing the door behind him.

"How many people used to live in Hinton?" Price asked softly.

"Five thousand twenty-eight," Kurtzman replied, a submonitor alive on his console with details of the destroyed town.

Price took in a deep breath and let it out slow. "They're going to remember this for a long time."

"A soldier's burden." Brognola sighed. "In war, good people die. I wish it wasn't so, but that's just how it is."

"Well, the cell phone is a dead end," Tokaido announced over a shoulder. "The number is listed as nonfunctional, but reserved, and the phone isn't even registered as having ever been sold."

Kurtzman whistled. "Impressive. That took a lot of high-powered hacking to secretly activate a cell phone."

"Agreed."

"Who reserved the number?" Price asked, pacing the floor.

"A Mr. John Smith."

"Ah, him again. Of course. Any address?"

"Yes, 479 Sherman Oak Drive, Atlanta, Georgia."

"A fake, naturally."

"Actually there is a Sherman Oak Drive, but it doesn't reach the 400 series of numbers."

"Smart," Brognola said in grudging admiration. "They're not fools, these people, I'll give them that much."

"They're also ruthless mass murderers."

"And we will stop them. Somehow."

Delahunt kicked her chair around from the console. "Okay, the Kalashnikov came from the Happy Hunter gun store," she reported, glancing at a printed page still warm from the laser copier. "It was purchased for hard cash by…surprise! A Mr. John Smith. What an amazing coincidence."

"Got an address?" Price asked.

"For the buyer? No. For the store, sure. It is at…" She paused, then smiled. "Peachtree Plaza Mall, Cordele, Georgia."

"Where? Show me," Price demanded, walking over to the large monitor.

There was some keyboard activity and a map of Georgia appeared, then two glowing red stars blossomed into existence, showing the origin of the cell phone and the guns.

"That's two links to Georgia," Brognola stated, walking over to join Price. "Any NSA offices in Georgia, maybe in Atlanta, or Cordele?"

"Shouldn't be, but I'll check," Kurtzman said, tapping away. "Okay, no offices. Nothing NSA-related in the whole state." He paused. "Except for a small listening post on Jekyll Island, an island off the East Coast." The map of Georgia moved to the east and zoomed upon tiny dot, until it swelled into the picture of an island.

Marina on the left shore, beaches on the right, lighthouse at the top, it looked like a thousand other islands along the coast of North America.

"Got any background material?" Price asked hopefully.

Kurtzman hit a switch. "Sure."

Reading the scroll, Brognola and Price frowned at the news that scrolled along the bottom of the map. Jekyll Island was famous and infamous. Back in the 1930s it was a playground for the superrich, and at one point boasted that its visitors owned a one-sixth of the all the wealth in the world. Now Jekyll Island was a national park consisting mostly of sandy beaches, a cypress forest and a wildlife preserve in a marsh, plus a couple of incredibly expensive hotels.

"Along with a secret NSA listening post," Delahunt added, massaging her temples. "Didn't the President go to the International Finance Conference last year on Jekyll Island?"

"Yes, that was one of the reasons for the listening post," Brognola said, worrying his jaw. "Keep a watch on things. Everything going in or out of the island feeds directly to the NSA."

"So they must have really big computers there," Delahunt said, lost in thought. "Better and better. Any chance the post has a maser cannon?"

"Not as standard issue equipment, no," Price said, almost

smiling. "On the other hand, this is too much of a coincidence. Is there a roster of the duty personnel?"

"Sure." Kurtzman tapped a few keys. "We have Phil Foglio, Sue Johnson, Scott Benson, Nick Smith, Ignatus Salvatore and John Meterson."

"Meterson!" Wethers cried, looking up quickly. "That was the name. Johan Meterson, but everybody called him John."

Thoughtfully, Kurtzman looked at a submonitor on his console. "Looks like a match, all right."

Wether's console beeped. "Surprise, surprise," he stated, moving the pipe from one side of his mouth to the other. "Meterson was my student during the right time period, and Berkeley University oddly lists him as deceased."

"What else did he study aside from cybernetics?"

"Telemetry systems."

"Long-range controls," Kurtzman stated, grinding his teeth. "Son of a bitch! I'll bet my ass he specialized in optical controls. Maser!"

Wethers checked the screen. "Your behind is safe, Aaron."

"Good, I'm rather fond of it," Kurtzman said. "Okay, people, let's get Able Team some air transport to Jekyll Island. They can sleep on the plane."

"Now how do we locate Phoenix Force?" Delahunt asked, sliding her VR helmet back into position.

"Watch the news," Price stated. "Wherever NATO sends troops, our guys would have just left the area."

"Heads up," Tokaido announced, adjusting the controls on his console.

A plasma screen became alive with the breaking story of the PLO hitting the hated wall again. The death toll was staggering, bodies were still coming out of the rubble. The UN was having NATO send in troops to try to bring some order to the hot zone, but Israel was preparing for full war with Palestine.

"Things are getting out of hand," Brognola stated, loosening his necktie. "Find Phoenix Force, people, and tell them about the NSA connection. We need to wrap this up fast before World War III starts."

CHAPTER SEVENTEEN

Erbutz Mountains, Iran

A dry wind, warm from the nearby desert, blew across the top of the ridged stone walls, carrying along the dust of a thousand years past the hidden oasis.

It was cool inside the depression, and a natural spring bubbled out of the living rock to create a small lake with green plants growing along the edge. Long ago, fig trees had been planted, and now the secret oasis was a paradise, hidden deep within the deadly desert and forbidding mountains.

For a terrorist camp it was more than perfection. The desert wind hid the thermal signature of the people and machines from NATO planes and American satellites. A natural fortress, the walls of the crater were yards thick, proof to even tank cannon, and the only opening was a crooked crevice that would only admit a single person at a time. Attack for a large force was flatly impossible.

Briefly, during the Iraqi war, Sadaam Hussein had stayed

here as a sanctuary, paying millions for a single week of safety to hide from the hated Americans. But then the bounty on his head became too great, and the former dictator had been forced to flee, or else be captured and turned over to the United States by his own men. He had taught them that money was the only thing of importance in the world, and they had learned the lesson well.

At the north end of the crater was a small cave that led deep into the mountains. The interior had been reinforced with concrete and brick, the opening partially closed off with sand bags. Bearded men in turbans stood guard with AK-47 assault rifles, and behind them was another sand bag wall forming a redoubt inside the cave.

Past the redoubt, several men were cooking food over a small campfire, the frying pans resting on rocks. The food had to be turned often to prevent it from burning on the inside while the outride stayed raw, but that was a minor inconvenience.

"Women should be doing this," an al Qaeda terrorist muttered unhappily. "Cooking is not the work of men."

"Women lead to fighting," another replied unhappily. "We are too few these days to afford the unnecessary loss of a single fighter."

A flickering glow came from deeper inside the cave and the two men glanced up from their cooking. They had no fear of invasion from that direction. The labyrinth of tunnels went on for miles, but they were all dead ends. There was only one entrance to the underground fortress.

"Fools! Idiots!" the al Qaeda commander cursed, marching into the light of the campfire. "We have been refused. Refused!"

"Refused what?" one of the cooks asked, turning over the browning meat.

Walking over to a bucket, the commander shoved the torch into the dirty water. Pulling it out again, he placed the torch to dry on a flat rock next to several others. The pitch was reusable again and again, and dried soon in the open air. Torches worked well, and more importantly, they could be made by hand. Since the loss of Afghanistan, the resources of al Qaeda had been serious curtailed. And then again when Hussein was ousted from power. Now, most of their equipment came from the Third World black market and occasional contributions of second hand military equipment from the Saudi royal family.

"The Sky Hammer people," the commander raged, going over to the fire and squatting. Pulling a knife, he stabbed a slice of meat from the frying pan and began to gnaw. "We offer them fifteen million euros to level Baghdad. That could have completely destabilized the nation. Before control was returned, our agents would have seized all of the key locations."

"Cowardly fools," a cook agreed.

"Bah." The other sneered. "You should have offered more!"

The commander nodded at the words of his friend. This was true. He had been hesitant, and lost a priceless opportunity for others to do his dirty work. Sky Hammer didn't negotiate prices. You told them the target, they said a price and you either agreed or said no. There was no haggle. He assumed they had to be Dutch with a strange attitude like that. After all, it was only money. It flowed from the ground in an endless stream like tears from an old wife. Fifteen million, fifty million, what difference did it make?

"Or perhaps they have bigger cows in another pasture," the first cook suggested, forking the meat. The smell was starting to fill the cave, a delicious miasma that set mouths watering.

"That may be true," the commander admitted. "But their lack of respect annoyed me greatly. I threatened to expose them to the CIA if they did not accept our next offer."

"You did what?" the second cook whispered.

Grandly, the commander gestured with his greasy knife. "The CIA has many wet work teams and would—"

"Idiot!" the first cook screamed, throwing aside the frying pan. "You have slain us all!"

"How dare you address me in this manner!" the commander said hoarsely, a hand going to the curved knife on his belt.

"Make the call," the cook snapped, pulling out a cell phone. "Tell the CIA everything. We're already dead, but even a corpse can bite the living with a message."

"Use that here?" the commander gasped. "You are insane. That would reveal our position to the Americans!"

Just then something streaked across the sky, leaving a glowing contrail. A moment later, a nearby hill violently detonated, rock dust and molten lava spewing out like the charge from a shotgun barrel.

"Too late," the cook sobbed, stepping deeper into the cave.

The terrorists turned to run, and that was when the light flashed down directly into the tiny oasis, and the world abruptly came to an end.

Cologne, Germany

THE UNMARKED C-130 Hercules landed at the United States AFB in Cologne, Germany, around midnight. Unconcerned, the locals paid little attention to the military craft as the U.S. had several bases in Germany and personnel were constantly coming and going, day and night.

Following directions from the tower, Jack Grimaldi taxied the Hercules directly into a waiting hangar at the far edge of the airport, the open space held in reserve in case a stalled plane had to be rammed off the landing strips to make room for an emergency landing. This gave them privacy from prying eyes and a little elbow room in case a firefight broke out. After unloading its one remaining Hummer, Phoenix Force changed from desert togs into civilian clothing, while Grimaldi arranged for immediate refueling. Hopefully, a quick exit wouldn't be required this time. But it was better to have, and not need, than the other way around.

Trapped in Israel, the team had dived into the original blast craters from the first attack, hoping the Sky Hammer wouldn't precisely hit the exact same spots twice. Incredibly, it worked, Phoenix Force emerged battered, but alive. Unlike Weingate, Benny Zero, and everybody else they had met in their brief sojourn. All of them dead. Most of them civilians.

Stripping the Hercules bare, the men donated all of the medical supplies on board to the swarming crews of doctors and nurses dealing with the wounded and the dying along the edge of the strike zone. The medics didn't seem to care if the bleeding person in front of them was an Arab or a Jew, they were only concerned with the severity of the wounds.

Helping with crowd control, the Stony Man commandos wished that more people felt the same way as the physicians, but sadly knew the world would never be like that. Man had evolved from a plains ape to a snarling carnivore who attacked antelope from behind, and sometimes ate their own kind. Humanity had only seemed to have gotten more sophisticated in technique, but not much else. Man was a killer. End of discussion.

When finally relieved by the Red Cross, the team went to the airport and reclaimed the Hercules. Once inside the aircrafts, the Stony Man team carefully disassembled the beacon with tweezers and a microscope, trying to find anything that might lead them the builder, and then in turn, the people who controlled Sky Hammer. The men got a lot of fingerprints, along with some grains of a fine white sand. But since the beacon had been planted in the middle of the desert, the sand didn't necessarily mean anything. The device could have been built near a beach or the particles might have been carried along the Gaza wind.

Taking a gamble, McCarter broke cover and risked faxing a copy of the fingerprints to a buddy in the SAS. But that came up zero. The prints weren't on file in the Interpol criminal database. Once again, that wasn't significant. That only meant the prints weren't on file. But then, neither were the fingerprints of the Stony Man team. Unfortunately, without the massive resources of the Farm, that was about all they could do for the time being.

There was no serial numbers on any of the parts, or even the fuel cells. But a microchip carried the manufacturer's logo, Telerex Electronics, Cologne, Germany. Ten minutes later, they were in the air heading north.

"It's a beautiful city," Hawkins said from behind the wheel of the big Hummer. "Old and new at the same time."

Watching the busy traffic and happy people stream past the Hummer, McCarter lit a cigarette and firmly agreed. Cologne was the new heart of Germany, the past and the future coming into one hell of a present, and full of hope. Cathedrals rose alongside sleek office buildings, and gargoyles snarled down from glass-enclosed markets. Beautiful.

"Not that there's anything wrong with the Big D," the Texan at the wheel quickly added, flashing a grin. "Dallas kicks ass."

"Every been to Montreal?" Gary Manning asked, reclining in his seat, hair in the wind. "Now there's a city for you!"

"Now, the Montreal Symphony is excellent," Encizo chimed in. "But they're light-years away from the glory of the London Philharmonic."

"Bloody right." McCarter smiled, releasing a stream of smoke out the side of his mouth. "Although that classical stuff gives me a severe pain in the arse."

"Here we are," Hawkins announced, turning off the busy street and into a brightly lit parking lot.

And a lot of fire trucks.

"Son of a bitch," James stated. "Didn't we just leave this party?"

Beyond the parking lot was a field of ash, with twisted steel girders rising obscenely from the smoking remains of the electronics plant. There were only a few fireman spraying water over the charred remains of the structure, the police and crowds gone. Only the neon sign bearing the company logo still remained, untouched and undamaged, blazing away in the dark,

McCarter hailed a passing fireman. "Excuse me, sir," he said in basic German. "When did this happen, please?"

"Last night," the fireman answered politely, his face so black with soot his race was a matter of sheer conjecture. "Some fool set off fireworks on the roof, then something exploded and the whole building was ablaze. The blast was tremendous!"

"Thank you," McCarter replied, and the man shuffled away, too tired to lift his boots from the pavement.

For a few minutes, Phoenix Force sat in the Hummer and looked at the desolation. A pile of bricks collapsed, sending up a flurry of red embers.

"There might be an off-site data dump," James said, frowning. "But it could take us days to find it. Maybe weeks."

"If ever," Encizo quipped. "Start driving. We don't want to be seen around here."

"I hear that," Hawkins muttered, shifting into gear.

"The bastards knew we were coming," Manning said in barely controlled fury. "Damn it, the Sky Hammer people are always ahead of us!"

"Then it's time to play leapfrog," McCarter said, throwing the butt out of the car. "Or better yet, move sideways."

"Meaning?" Hawkins asked, interested. "Come on, David, you have something in mind."

"Damn straight I do," he said, pulling out another cigarette, then stuffing it back into the pack. He smoked too much lately. Got to cut down more. "A Thor, it's tougher than a nickel steak, but how do the Sky Hammer people know that? They weren't going to risk millions on a gamble this big."

"But they did test shots in the Antarctic," Manning said, then he smiled. "You mean, before they went up. Bench tests."

McCarter nodded. "Exactly."

"How the hell can you bench test a Thor?" Hawkins demanded. It's just a slab of solid steel."

"With a few electronics shoved up the rear. Now, the boron jets were probably copied from the NASA designs. That's old tech, proved reliable under the worst conditions. But the GPD directional circuits, those were new."

"Sure. That only makes sense," James added. "Nobody is going to make hundreds of these things, and then ship them into space until they know for certain they worked."

"So if the electronics were assembled here," McCarter continued softly, looking at his reflection in a passing store window, "then maybe, just maybe, mind you, the rest was tested here. In case the electronics needed to be modified."

"The shorter the supply line, the least chance of discovery."

"Exactly."

"Any steel mills in Cologne?" Encizo asked, his eyes brightening with the hunt. "I mean, around Cologne?"

"Not anymore," Manning said, holding on as the Hummer took a corner. "They all closed years ago."

"Closed, or were they demolished?" Hawkins asked pointedly, shifting gears. "If the furnaces still exist…"

"Demolished," McCarter replied bluntly. "I checked back at the airport. Gerweiller, Ajax, all the big mills are gone."

"Damn."

"Except for two," McCarter added. "One is a working mill, Suda Steel, open twenty-four hours a day."

"Kind of hard to sneak a six-foot long Thor into there to run a thermal test," James stated. "Okay, what's the other?"

"The Museum of Science down on the boardwalk along the waterfront," McCarter answered. "But with a working microwave blast furnace to do demonstrations for the tourists."

"Museums close at night," James observed dryly.

"Why yes, they do."

"And it's night right now."

"Absolutely. How clever of you to notice."

"David, you do realize that this idea is thinner than a stripper's G-string?" Encizo stated, shaking his head.

"Utterly transparent," McCarter agreed. "Damn near nebulous. A shot in the dark. Total madness."

"But since we're in town." Hawkins suddenly grinned without any trace of humor. "Then we might as well see the local sights."

Taking a sharp right, Hawkins cut off a taxicab and headed for the nearby Rhine River.

THE MUSEUM PROVED to be a bust. The furnace was dusty, the advertised demonstration proved to only be red light bulbs and a sound-effects machine.

"That leaves Suda Steel," Manning said, getting back in the Hummer. He tossed the kit bag of burglar tools into the rear cargo area and draped a blanket over top.

Without comment, Hawkins started the vehicle and drove away from the boardwalk.

Opening an equipment bag, James ruffled through an assortment of leather identification booklets. "Let's see. We have Interpol, the Peace Corps and BBC News."

"When did we get those?" McCarter asked, raising an eyebrow.

"Last week."

"Thanks for telling me. Okay, we'll do Interpol," the man decided, accepting a fake ID. McCarter checked and the picture was of him five years ago. Nice, that made it more realistic. "Since nobody seems know exactly what Interpol does, we can get away with just about anything we like."

"Unless this is another trap," Hawkins reminded harshly.

Encizo pulled out a .38 Walther PPK pistol and worked the slide, chambering a round. "Sure as hell hope so," he said grimly.

AN HOUR LATER the Hummer was streaking through the night, heading back to the Cologne airport.

"A replacement shaft for his yacht, my arse," McCarter raged. "The balls of the man!"

"Why should anybody think different?" Encizo added. "It sounds reasonable enough, unless you check the figures."

"Damn right we did! A Thor takes five to nine minutes to travel through the atmosphere and reach its target. Temperatures hit about 2,600 degrees Fahrenheit before impact."

"And the thermal tests for this new propeller shaft for his yacht just happened to last nine bloody minutes," Hawkins finished. "And at 2,600 degrees. If this isn't our man, then he knows who they are."

"Meternich," Rafe read off the credit card slip. "Attila Meternich. Never heard of the guy."

"According to the Internet," James said, "the global ship registry lists an A. Meternich as owning a yacht, damn big one, called the *Morning Star*."

"Registry?" McCarter asked.

"French Riviera," James said, then double clicked on a small picture of the ship. "Wow, she's a beauty. Ah, we have a bingo."

"What is it?" McCarter demanded.

James passed over the laptop. "Read the bottom line."

It was a newspaper shot of the yacht, covered with smiling men in white suits and dozens of women in skimpy bikinis. "'ESA executive Attila Meternich and several guests celebrating the Cannes Film Festival,'" McCarter read out loud. "Jesus, the ESA? He's an executive at the European Space Agency?"

"That explains the NASA fuel cells in the beacon," Encizo observed. "This might be our guy. Best bet, so far, at least."

Rocking to the motion of the speeding Hummer, Manning asked, "Does the ESA have any offices in France? The clerk said he spoke with a thick French accent."

"Could be a fake."

"Hopefully not."

Taking back the laptop, James diligently surfed for a few minutes until finding the Web page for the ESA.

"There an ESA complex in Paris," he announced. "Astronaut training camp, executive offices, the whole shebang. Paris is their headquarters."

"Any launch facilities?"

"Nope. Those are down in Guyana."

McCarter scowled. "Didn't an NSA agent recently die in Paris talking about a traitor?"

"We got them," Hawkins said, turning into the airport. "Now all we have to do is find the guy and have him turn off Sky Hammer."

"I'm betting that ol' Attila won't want to do that," James said.

"Then we'll have to insist," Manning replied.

For the hundredth time, McCarter started to reach for radio under his windbreaker, but stayed his hand. Until he knew better, anything said to the Farm was going directly to the enemy, to this Meternich.

But maybe there was a way around that.

SIX-FEET LONG black metal rods floated in the velvet of space high above the turning world. There were clouds to the left, but clear sky to the right, and the vast ocean directly below.

Then land mass came into view and several Thors spurted brief bursts of boron steam from the directional rockets to align properly, then darted forward, rapidly building speed. The on-board computer briefly checked with the GPD satellites, minutely changed their attack vectors, then committed at full speed until their small engines were exhausted and gravity took over.

Missiles rose from the four corners of the world and detonated into fiery blossoms, but the Thors punched through the shrapnel without damage. Soon, their blunt noses turned red-hot from traveling through the thickening atmosphere.

Then orange-hot, yellow and finally white-hot and started to melt. The computers died at this point, but the Thors were already committed to their target and guidance was no longer needed. Gravity would do all the work now.

The Gray Wolf mercenaries in Turkey ordered a Thor strike on the downtown headquarters for State Security, destroying all government files on their wide-spread criminal activities and killing countless innocent bystanders.

Bolivian rebels hit the capital city, smashing bridges and tunnel causing massive riots and the deaths of hundreds of civilians.

The Karen rebels hit Myanmar.

Meanwhile, the world kept turning....

CHAPTER EIGHTEEN

Paris, France

In the privacy of his office, Attila Meternich was in the middle of accepting a bid from the Uyghur terrorists to hit Beijing, China, when a flashing symbol appeared in the lower corner of his screen. What? Canceling the sale, Meternich turned on the silhouette function and the voice scrambler before answering the priority call.

A featureless form filled the screen, the background a moray pattern. There were no details to reveal anything about the caller.

"Caesar," John said.

"Mr. Hyde," Attila answered, wondering what was wrong.

"Sorry, but I have been looking for you."

The ESA project director went cold at that. Somebody had been searching the Internet for him—by name?

"Do you have a surprise for my birthday?"

Have we been discovered?

"Who celebrates birthdays anymore?"

Unknown.

"What about all of my presents?"

We have many bids for Thor strikes.

"Just blow out the candles and make a wish."

Destroy all files and run.

"I can always make a wish on a star."

Is the yacht Morning Star *safe to use?*

"I sometimes make wishes."

Possibly.

Meternich bit a lip. Damn, that wasn't what he wanted to hear. "Well, it's late, see you back home."

Meet you in Hungary.

There was no reply, just a buzzing click to show the call hadn't been tapped or traced, then the line disconnected.

"Damn," Meternich swore, running fingers through his hair. "Damn, damn, damn!" So it was over already. How very inconvenient. But they had made enough to pay off all of the family bills, buy back the castle and lands and set aside a sizeable amount in several unnumbered Swiss and Luxembourg bank accounts that would keep the brothers living comfortably for the rest of their lives. He wanted more, of course, who wouldn't? But prudence was wisdom. Then Attila and his brothers would vanish into a maze of false identities already established, dying and being reborn with new faces and fingerprints, until they returned to the beautiful misty mountains of Hungary a year later as millionaires and free men. Winners.

Starting to turn off the computer, Meternich paused, then slowly smiled. Nobody was knocking at his office door yet, so there should be enough time for one last deal. A big one, for the largest fee offered. Just a little extra to change their life-style from comfortable to luxurious. Yes, just one more fast deal.

Reviewing the bids, he rationalized that this final strike was going to be in America. Most people hated the United States, because they were winners. An intolerable condition to the rest of the world. He and his brothers would survive such a condition though, because nobody comes hunting after dead men.

With the clock ticking, Meternich finally accepted the bid simply offering the most money, and authorized a strike using every unassigned Thor. A few had been placed aside for spe-cial purposes. The funds were transferred and the target codes sent to the hidden maser. There, all done. Time to leave.

Opening the bottom a desk drawer, Meternich pulled out a sealed bottle, twisted off the cap and poured the contents over the files. Instantly the treated papers started to turn brown and crumbled into pieces. Closing and locking the drawer, he then open the top drawer, set the timer on a pow-erful incendiary device, then also closed and locked that drawer.

Glancing around the room that was no longer his office, Meternich felt a twinge of nostalgia as he did an inventory of possible dangers, and decided there was none. He had been extremely careful for many years. There hadn't even been a publicity shot taken of the *Morning Star* for over a decade.

Going to the desktop computer, Meternich started a S&D program that would delete everything twice and then over-write the blank harddrive with random keystrokes. His brother promised that nobody alive could retrieve the files then. Well, maybe his old teacher from Berkeley, but the professor had dropped out of sight years ago and was presumed deceased.

Picking up his personal laptop, Meternich stood and cast a smile at the triptych on his desk of the three of them, himself and his twin brothers. Now, Attila didn't know about George, but John would be very impressed by the new laptop. It was sheathed in titanium and was bulletproof. The device was a gift from the U.S. Army for helping NASA, and was unavailable on the market.

He tucked the laptop into a bag and slung it over a shoulder. Well, soon enough they would be together again. Very soon. There was a lot of work ahead of them rebuilding the family estate, the buildings were crumbling with age, but now they had the funds to get it done properly. Father and mother would have been pleased, maybe not at the methods, but certainly at the results.

Squaring his shoulders, Meternich strode to the door, paused, put on a smile and casually walked into the hall, surreptitiously locking the door behind him.

Smiling politely, Meternich nodded at everybody he passed along the way, stopping to sign a birthday card for a young Belgium astronaut who had just joined the training program, and giving a couple of euros toward a gift for a janitor who was going to retire next month.

Bad timing, old man, Meternich thought, signing the card with a flourish. "By the way, where is Valerie? I haven't seen her all day."

"Oh, she left, sir," a secretary replied, taking the card and pen. "Something about not being able to work here anymore. It was very strange. She left without any advance notice. Just emptied her desk, and went."

"I'm sorry to hear that, she was a credit to the ESA," Meternich said amiably, then moved toward the elevators swinging the laptop casually at his side as he did every day. So the sexed-up little bitch ran without notice. He didn't like the sound of that. If she had heard something, or seen something that she shouldn't have and was telling everything to the police, worse....

Pulling out his cell phone, Meternich hit a redial button and ordered the limousine to meet him at the front door. His brother may have called too late. He had a bad feeling that this was now a race against time.

Exiting the building, Meternich had a hand resting on the pin of a grenade sown into a pocket, half expecting Interpol or NATO intelligence agents to leap from the bushes and tackle him to the ground. I'll never go to jail. Death first!

But there was nobody in sight, aside from the usual ebb and flow of scientists, technicians, secretaries and clerks hustling around the busy complex of buildings. A few moments later, the limousine stopped at the curb and Meternich climbed inside to thankfully close the door.

"Where to, sir?" the driver asked, removing his cap to brush back his wild crop of curls before setting it back into place.

"That new tonic working for you, Eric?"

"Like a dream, sir. More hair than ever! Many thanks."

"My pleasure, old friend. Now please take me directly to the dockyard," Meternich directed. "I'm rather late for an appointment."

Shifting gear, Eric grinned. "You'll make it, sir, I promise that!"

"Good man," Meternich replied, swinging out a small hinged work board and setting down the laptop. There was just one more little chore to do.

As the limousine pulled onto the main thoroughfare, Meternich hit the send key. There, in about twelve hours, the United Nations building would cease to exist. That would start a world war of unprecedented magnitude. But as long as Hungary remained neutral, what did he care happened to the rest of the world? Most of them were only peasants, anyway. Not worth pissing on if they caught fire.

Starting a search and destroy program on the computer, Meternich noticed a black Hummer turning into the access road for the ESA headquarters. The powerful vehicle was filled with large, dangerous-looking men, probably new security personnel. They had the look of guards about them, stony faces and sharp eyes. For a split second, Meternich looked directly a fox-faced man smoking a cigarette and felt a cold shiver run down his spine. God help the poor thief who had to go against that monster! Then the Hummer was gone.

Closing the laptop, Meternich set it aside and gave Paris one last loving look as he left forever. Soon, it would be all over. Pity he couldn't stay to watch the fun.

"ODD FELLOW," McCarter muttered, puffing on his cigarette as the Hummer drove onto the road leading to the ESA complex.

"Somebody you know?" Hawkins asked from behind the wheel.

"Not bloody likely," McCarter growled. Those had been the eyes of a killer, worse, of somebody to whom taking a life meant nothing. Thrill killers always tripped themselves up, doing one more murder, always one more, until they were caught. The cold, unfeeling killers were the backbone of the criminal world, hit men, mercenaries, they were all the same. Dead men with no hearts, taking lives in an effort to make their own lack of feelings seem more normal. If it wasn't so horrible, they almost would be sad.

"Not bad," Manning said, craning his neck at the tall buildings rising around them.

The headquarters of the European Space Agency was a modernist's dream, full of mirrored structures edged with cool stone to take off the harsh look, lushly trimmed with green bushes and flower beds, a center pavilion full of fluttering flags from half the nations in the world, everybody who participated in the ESA efforts.

"That's where they train the astronauts," Encizo said, pointing out a building surrounded by a small lake. "Over there is the executive offices and computer complex."

Where Meternich worked. "No launch facilities?" McCarter asked checking the Interpol ID booklet in his jacket pocket.

"Those are in Guyana," James stated, loosening the Beretta in his shoulder holster. "Down by the equator."

"Why so far away?" Manning asked curiously

"Saves fuel," James said simply.

Manning started to ask for more details, then dismissed the matter. He'd find out why later. If there was a later.

"Any chance Sky Hammer might be using a magnetic railgun to launch the Thors?" Encizo asked.

"Not in the confines of a major city," Hawkins retorted, swinging around a tour guide leading a group of people. "The magnetic field would scramble computers, televisions, cell phones, everything electronic for miles."

"No way to hide that kind of disruption," Encizo stated.

"Good enough," McCarter said, grinding his cigarette into the ashtray. Then his cell phone started to vibrate.

Curiously, he checked the return number and smiled. So his message had been delivered.

"Pull over," McCarter ordered. "I have to take this."

Stopping at a parking kiosk, Hawkins took a ticket from the machine and drove into the parking lot until finding an empty space.

"Who is it?" Encizo asked.

"The Farm," McCarter answered. "I hope."

The picture on the phone cleared in a view of Barbara Price in the Stony Man Computer Room with Kurtzman, Buck Greene and everybody else in attendance.

"Flowers?" Price asked, crossing her arms. "The blacksuits at the main gate wouldn't let the delivery person onto the grounds. She almost left with them."

"The florist claims that they would deliver them anywhere," McCarter said carefully. The room looked right, but he had heard of computer simulations that were impossible to tell from the real thing. If the Farm had been breached by a traitor, then nothing was to be taken at face value.

"By the way, what kind of flowers arrived?" Hawkins asked.

"Fourteen carnations, six roses and one yellow daisy," Price said crisply. "I always liked those, and the card was a nice touch. 'Give my teacher a call, Achilles.' Now how was

I supposed to know that according to Greek mythology the teacher of the legendary Achilles was a man named Phoenix?"

"Because you're a smart lady," McCarter grinned. "Okay, I know it's really you. And since you called, I'll assume our leak has been patched."

"Yes, a mole in the NSA, somebody named Meterson."

"What was that name again?" McCarter demanded sharply, his every nerve alive. "Meter…what?"

"Meterson."

"Not Meternich?" Encizo asked over a shoulder.

Brognola replaced Price. "No," he snapped. "Why?"

Briefly, McCarter explained.

"Another coincidence?" Price asked sternly.

"Like hell," Brognola rasped.

"The files are downloading right now," Tokaido said off to the side. "Okay, here we go, Attila and John were born one year apart. Both men are left-handed, born in Budapest, Hungary, and according to the NSA and ESA medical files they have the same blood type and…they're brothers. Gotta be."

"Makes sense," Brognola said, rubbing his jaw. "Okay, find this guy fast. He must have the command codes for the maser. Or at least know where the damn thing is located. If we can find it before the next strike—"

"Got a recent picture?" McCarter interrupted. "We found one from a newspaper ten years old, and it was fuzzy enough for me to pass for the guy."

"No problem," Kurtzman announced, and the cell phone screen dissolved into a portrait shot of a smiling dapper man in an expensive business suit.

"Wait a goddamn minute, we just passed him on the road!" McCarter cried, glancing at the city traffic outside the complex. "He just left the ESA grounds."

The screen joggled and Price appeared. "Run!" she ordered. "Move it people! Get as far away from there as fast as possible because if I were him—"

That was as far as the mission controller got before something flashed mirror-bright in the sky. Phoenix Force jerked up their heads, hearts pounding.

"No," Manning whispered. "Not in downtown Paris."

Another flash came, two, three and then the salvo of Thors slammed into the side of the ESA headquarters building cutting the structure in two and blowing out a hundred windows. Tons of glass sprayed across the complex and was still twinkling in the air when the entire structure groaned like a dying giant. Then in ghastly slow motion the top half of the building began to move sideways along the diagonal cut. Then the lower section crumpled, and the twenty story building collapsed upon itself, driving out a thundering gray cloud of concrete dust and human screams.

Caught in an open vehicle, Phoenix Force moved fast. As the cloud rolled over the parking lot, blotting everything from sight, Hawkins killed the engine to keep the air intake from blocking solid, and the men covered their faces with handkerchiefs to keep from choking.

A moment later, midnight arrived and a hellish wind buffeted the team, rocking the Hummer as if it were a toy. A dozen car alarms went off, but the noise was lost in the crashing fury of the crumbling skyscraper.

CHAPTER NINETEEN

Jekyll Island

The Cessna SkyKing touched down on the long strip of smooth pavement, bounced once, then landed properly, the tires squealing as the brakes were applied.

Coasting along, the blacksuit pilot directed the two-engine plane to the very end of the runaway, then off onto the smooth grass.

Watching from the windows, Lyons could see that there were a couple of other planes parked in the shade of towering cypress trees, a Beachcraft and an Elite, the expensive single-engine planes lashed down with nylon ropes against the ocean breeze.

"Be it ever so humble," Schwarz said.

The airport, if it could be called that, was little more than a section of pavement roughly three thousand feet long. Just enough to handle a small personal plane, but nothing of commercial size.

There was no control tower, fuel depot, machine shop or coffee shack. There certainly weren't any airport police. No customs, no cops, no cameras. Just the pavement and neatly mown grass. A perfect spot to land equipment and smuggle it into a NSA listening post without a soul being the wiser. Unfortunately, what worked for the NSA would also work for the people behind Sky Hammer.

"Anything I can do help?" Madison DeForrest asked, sliding off her headphones. The ex-cop from Philadelphia turned out to be one terrific pilot, and Able Team sometimes flew with her at the controls whenever Grimaldi or Charlie Mott wasn't available.

"Not in those clothes," Lyons said. The pilot was still in her Farm garb of a red flannel shirt, denims and work boots.

Knowing they would have to travel among millionaires on this island, Able Team had gotten into white linen suits, pastel-colored shirts open at the neck; very lightweight material perfect for strolling along the beach holding a drink. The deck shoes were practically worthless, they offered less protection than a decent pair of sneakers. But the jackets hid their shoulder holsters. However, the angular NATO body armor had been out of the question.

"You'd stand out a mile in those," Blancanales agreed, slinging a golf bag over his shoulder. "Plus, your nails aren't done, and you don't have any jewelry."

The clubs sticking out were only six inches long and attached at a false top. Inside the bag was an M-16 assault rifle.

"I'm your caddy?" Madison asked hopefully.

"Should have brought along a bikini," Schwarz said, smiling, toting another golf bag. The pockets lining the outside of the bag for tees and balls were bulging with ammo clips and grenades. "I'd loan you mine, but the color is just all wrong for you."

"Next time for sure," the woman agreed, then solemnly added, "Watch your ass, boys. These people are insane."

"Then it's a good thing we're just as crazy," Lyons replied, giving a rare smile as he lifted a wicker picnic basket. It was oversize, the largest model available on the market, and the Atchisson just barely fit inside.

"Stay sharp," he added, opening the door.

"Born sharp," she answered. "I'll be waiting right here."

Exiting the plane, Able Team was getting its equipment bags out of the rear section when a man walked up to them wearing a dark blue suit and FAA cap. He had a radio clipped to his belt and a gun in a holster under his windbreaker.

"Stop right there!" the agent ordered, raising a hand. "This is an unscheduled flight, and I want to see your manifest and flight log right now before you go anywhere."

"We were told those weren't necessary here," Lyons said with a quizzical smile, as false as the dawn in Iceland. "This is a national park, not private property anymore."

"Then you were told wrong, asshole," the FAA agent said, sneering. "Papers. Now!"

"Of course." Blancanales smiled, passing over an envelope.

Warily, the FAA agent read the documents inside, then stuffed them into a hip pocket. "These look okay, but I still want to check inside your baggage."

"Whatever for, Officer?"

"Drugs, contraband, you know the drill." He snapped his fingers. "Come on, open them up."

Out of the corner of his vision, Lyons saw DeForrest lift a shotgun into view behind the windshield. He shook his head and she lowered the weapon. Lyons knew that it was probably loaded with a stun bag, but there was no sense in blowing their cover this soon.

With the warm sea breeze tugging at his white linen pants, Blancanales set down the golf bag as gently as possible, trying not to let it clank. "Perhaps we can come to some sort of an arrangement," he suggested, reaching for his wallet.

"Freeze! You're under arrest," the FAA agent declared, reaching for the radio on his hip. "You have the right to remain—"

Pulling out a stun gun, Schwarz jabbed the FAA agent in the side of the neck. As the prongs crackled blue, the man twitched wildly for a moment, then collapsed.

"I might have bought the act if he had gone for handcuffs," Schwarz said, tucking away the stun gun. "But a radio? He was a plant."

"Damn straight he was." Kneeling, Blancanales checked his pulse. "Okay, he'll live." Then he patted down the man and came away with a blackjack and switchblade knife. "Well, well, not exactly FAA issue, are they?"

"If he was under observation, then our cover is blown," Lyons snarled, looking around them. There was nothing in sight by cypress trees and a lot of white sand beach. "Check for keys. We'll borrow his car. Time is against us now."

"Check." Rummaging through the man's clothing, Blancanales found some keys and pressed the unlock button on the fob.

With a strident blast, the car exploded, flipping over onto

its back as flames and black smoke rose into the sky. It landed with a crumpling crash, the intact windows shattering and spraying glass squares across the landing field.

"Okay, now they know we're here," Schwarz said, lowering the arm in front of his face.

"Hell, everybody on the East Coast knows we're here," Blancanales said, tossing away the keys. "Another stinking trap! I only wish—"

"Madison!"

Spinning with a hand inside their jackets, Blancanales and Schwarz cursed at the sight of Lyons charging for the damaged SkyKing. The windshield was shattered, blood dripping from the frame, and there was no sign of DeForrest.

Yanking open the door, Lyons found the woman splayed in her seat with a long piece of metal sticking through her chest. Blood was everywhere.

"C-Carl…" she whispered, then went still.

Knowing it was pointless, Lyons checked her pulse just to be sure. Then closed her eyes. "God rest, soldier," he said softly.

As he stepped out of the plane, the others started to ask questions, then saw the answer in his face.

"Let's go," Lyons said in a voice from hell. "Five yard spread. I'm on point. Double time!"

Running in formation, a grim-faced Able Team left the airstrip and proceeded past a line of stately pine trees to reach Riverview Road. Several people were coming their way already, a couple of them talking on cell phones.

Lyons bit back a curse, then noticed the old-fashioned clapboard church across the road. There were several cars, a couple of horses and a dozen motorcycles in the parking lot, two with sidecars.

Without comment, the Stony Man Operatives dashed across the empty road, and went straight to the motorcycles. Blancanales stood guard, while Schwarz started checking for traps. The machines, every color of the rainbow, were covered with chrome and each had the owner's name painted on the side on the fuel tank in flowing script.

Placing the wicker basket on the gravel, Lyons pulled out his .357 Colt Python and racked the slide. At the sight of the handgun, the few people who had been headed their way abruptly stopped and turned to run away.

"Okay, these three are clean," Schwarz said, rising from alongside a sleek BMW motorcycle. "It was probably just that one car at the airfield that was rigged to blow."

"Good." Opening the saddlebag compartment built into the rear fender, Lyons threw out the blankets and fishing gear, and shoved in the wicker basket. It fit just fine. Stepping onto the bike, Lyons set it upright and pushed back the kickstand. The key was already in the ignition.

"Trusting folks," the big ex-cop muttered in disbelief. Twisting the throttle on the handlebars, he kicked the engine alive. The dashboard glowed into life, but the engine hardly made a sound, only a soft purr came from the twin mufflers.

"Got the directions?" Schwarz asked, going astride a Harley-Davidson. The huge Twin-V 88 engine burbled with raw power in the classic sound of the world-famous bike.

"Straight down Riverview to the mayor's office," Blancanales replied, draping the golf bag across the dilly bar rising from the rear of the seat like a mirrored-version of the St. Louis arch. "Then straight to the beach."

Swinging a leg over a Yamaha Speedster, Blancanales touched the ignition button. A plasma screen display, which served as the dashboard, pulsed into life with a bewildering array of VR meters and gauges that seemed to show everything but what the Stony Man operative had for breakfast. He felt embarrassed to be on the silly thing.

"Wanna trade?" Blancanales asked hopefully.

"In your dreams," Schwarz said, revving the Harley.

In a flare of anger, Lyons started to tell them to cut the chatter, then realized it was their way of handling the loss. They had to keep their minds clear and focused. This wasn't the time or place to grieve over a fallen comrade. They had work to do. People to kill.

Going past a marina, Able Team noticed a lot of sleek yachts of various sizes and makes, but there was nothing smaller than a hundred feet. The white beaches were lined with men and women laying on towels. A small kiosk was serving tropical drinks and doing a brisk business. Soft music played from somewhere. Kayaks knifed along the white-sand coast and occasionally a rider on horseback would gallop briefly into view, only to vanish again as the riding trails zigzagged behind the grassy dunes.

"Your vacation wonderland," Blancanales commented in passing. "A modern day garden of Eden."

"Complete with snakes," Schwarz reminded harshly, glancing in his sideview mirror. Nobody seemed excited, or upset. The blast couldn't have been heard this many miles away, and the smoke from the burning car couldn't be seen

from here. The wind had to be blowing it out to sea. That was
the first good thing that had happened to them since they'd
landed.

At the mayor's office, Able Team rode past a policeman
talking on a radio while pedaling his bicycle up Riverview
toward the airfield. Lyons snorted. If that was the local con-
stabulary, they had nothing to fear.

Leaving the beach behind, Able Team rolled along a two-
lane road that curled across smooth fields of grass, a few scattered trees and stately mansions offering the only breaks in
the beautiful scenery. But the sylvan view had no effect on
the three men.

Reaching a long bridge, Able Team traveled over a wide
marsh filled with squawking birds, then went back down
again to the road. Here the land changed to sandy grass, then
they passed a golf course. But past that, the island turned into
all sand again, the white shimmering from the ground giving the world an ethereal glow.

"There," Blancanales said, throttling down the Yamaha.

Up ahead was a small cottage situated near a wooden
dock, the wide Atlanta Ocean spread behind the Colonial-
style mansion. There was a satellite dish on the roof, but
Lyons knew it was too small to send a cohesive signal into
space, that it was built only for receiving cable TV. But nothing else was in sight. Where was the Sky Hammer maser?
Or the dish the NSA listening post used to record EM transmissions, like the feed from the tap? They had to be here. Unless he was horribly wrong....

Then Lyons spotted it. There was a wooden privacy fence
around what should be a swimming pool. It seemed normal

enough except that there was a guy sitting in a lawn chair on the diving board tower. He was dressed in regular clothes, not swim trunks, and had a yard-long something laying across his lap. It was covered by a towel, but the barrel showed a little in the bright sunlight and the shape was unmistakable.

Parking the bikes on the road, Able Team got off and pulled out their weaponry. With the need for secrecy over, Lyons got rid of the cumbersome wicker basket and draped a bandolier of spare shells across his white suit before taking out the Atchisson.

"Diving tower," Lyons said, arming the weapon.

"Roof," Blancanales added, jerking his chin in that direction.

"Car port," Schwarz said, heading that way.

As they separated, a man sunbathing on the front lawn looked up and jumped to his feet with a cry, pulling out a gun from under his Hawaiian shirt. Schwarz fired once, the short burst from the M-16 taking the guy out. Then Blancanales did the same to the guard on the roof, and Lyons fired a round from the Atchisson, killing the guard, then another to blow a hole in the privacy fence. The gunfire echoed across the sand dunes like thunder.

"What the fuck are you assholes doing?" somebody demanded from inside the cottage. The screen door slammed open and Bella Tokay stepped onto the porch, then stopped.

"You!" he cried, clawing for a gun behind his back.

Able Team put a triple blast into the leader of Blue Moon just as a window shattered and a lance of fire from a flamethrower danced across the front lawn toward them.

Paris, France

As THE GROUND shocks eased, Phoenix Force staggered from the Hummer and left the parking lot on foot. Driving would have been impossible as the electric gate was dead and the roads were jammed with running people and stalled cars, the engines dead from the cloud of powdered concrete.

Forcing themselves to ignore the cries of pain and calls for help, the Stony Man operatives grabbed each other's coats to keep from getting lost, and shuffled through the mounting chaos. The air was foggy with thick dust and everything was coated with gray. As they moved, cars crashed blindly into the sides of buildings, other cars and light poles. A truck burst into flames, gun shots crackled and a siren began to howl.

Crossing into an alley, the team shot the lock off a door and rushed inside a kitchen. The billowing dust cloud followed along with them. There was nobody in sight, but food was still sizzling on the griddle and in frying pans, a huge crock of soup bubbling away. As the dust filled the kitchen, McCarter threw open the door to the freezer and the team piled inside quickly. The dust flowed after them, but Hawkins slammed the door shut cutting it off. In clean air at last, the men panted for breath in the cold, and it took several minutes before they stopped coughing,

"Hello! Hello!" Price demanded from McCarter's jacket pocket. "Fire Bird One, this is the Nest. What happened? Repeat, what is going on?"

Lowering the handkerchief, McCarter started to speak, then turned to hawk and spit to clear his mouth. His chest felt hard, as if he had just smoke a thousand cigars. He may never smoke again.

"H-here—" McCarter coughed, barely able to say the word. Speaking was a major chore.

"Thank God you're alive." Price sighed. "I've been calling for half an hour!"

Had it really been that long?

"M-Meternich...hit...ESA," McCarter croaked.

"I understand, David," Price said in a calm voice. "Damn it, we were afraid that was what happened. Are any of our people hurt or killed?"

"No...breakage..."

"Good. Where are you?"

"Restau..rant...big freezer..."

"Ah, those are air-tight. Smart move. Okay, just stay where you are. We'll send help ASAP."

"Meter...nich..." Hawkins said, his voice full of hate. "Gotta...stop..."

Suddenly the lights in the freezer flickered and went out. A moment later the cooling fans slowed to a halt and the team stood in black silence. There was only the glow of the cell phone screen. Several of them pulled out small flashlights and thumbed them on, placing the lights atop boxes of hamburger or on the shoulders of hanging sides of beef. The freezer was filled with a kaleidoscope of shadows.

"Don't worry about Meternich," Price said. "We'll find him again."

"No...we won't," James declared gruffly. "Too smart...he'll disappear forever. Gotta get now..."

"Accepted. Any suggestions?"

"Track his…laptop," McCarter whispered, rubbing his aching chest. "Must have Internet account…he was on the computer when we passed…"

"I'm sure he has thrown it away by now," Price rejoined. "He is extremely smart."

"But not a professional…" McCarter said, starting to feel a little better.

"But his brother is trained by the NSA," Price reminded him. There was a pause. "No, we're in luck. An Echelon satellite has a location on wireless modem he's using. That was a mistake on his part. At the moment, it is moving due west thirty miles per hour. That's too slow for a plane or helicopter."

"He might own a yacht…" McCarter said, shivering slightly from the cold air in the freezer.

"Working…confirmed, the *Morning Star*," Price reported, looking off-screen. "In fact he just paid off a substantial mortgage yesterday from an account in Luxembourg."

"Does it have a lowjack?"

"Carmen?" Price asked.

A minute passed.

"Negative on a repeater signal," Price said. "He must have turned it off to prevent being found."

"Keep track of the that modem," McCarter said, wiping his dirty face with the back of a hand. "We'll get to the airport somehow."

"Hey!" Tokaido called. "The modem…the yacht…it just slowed to a stop."

"In the middle of the channel?"

"Yes."

"Think he threw it overboard?"

"Doubtfully. It's still working fine."

"Then the yacht has stopped," Brognola said off-screen. "Engine trouble maybe, or perhaps he's abandoning the ship and switching to another mode of transportation."

"That yacht looked huge in the newspaper clipping," McCarter said. "Any chance it has a helipad?"

"Checking… Yes, it does!"

"Then that's what he's doing," McCarter decided, standing a little straighter. "Contact Jack at the airport. We'll meet him there."

"Don't kill Meternich!" Brognola warned.

"Not until we get those target codes," McCarter agreed, then closed the phone with a snap of his wrist.

Taking a couple of deep breaths, the men of Phoenix Force braced themselves, then threw open the freezer door and moved swiftly into the swirling gray cloud.

CHAPTER TWENTY

The Morning Star

"What the hell is going on?" Meternich demanded, pounding in the control board of the yacht.

The magnificent vessel had been skimming along the waves, when all of a sudden the engines died. Angrily, he shoved the yoke and there was no response from the yacht. The great ship was coasting along on sheer momentum, going slower every second.

"Captain! Any word from the man you sent to check the engines?" Meternich demanded into the intercom.

"Nothing yet, sir," came the prompt reply. "I was just going myself when you called."

"Don't bother," Meternich said, flicking his wrist. The trick .32 pistol snapped into his hand, only to be tucked out of sight again. "I'll check myself. Radio the helicopter and tell them our current position. I want to be picked up immediately."

"Aye-aye, sir."

Starting for the engine room, Meternich knew that he could be overreacting. This might be nothing more than a drunken sailor, blown fuse or a clogged fuel line. These things did happen even on the best of ships. After all, the world now thought that he was dead. There was nobody chasing after him. That was flatly impossible. But a hard lesson the man had learned over the years was that when something odd happens, at exactly the wrong moment, it was almost always deliberate.

"You, you and you, come with me," Meternich directed, pointing out three crewmen. The men stopped watching the girls sunbathing on the deck below and followed him.

As the group descended to the main deck, two of the bikini-clad woman in the pool waved hello. Completely ignoring them, Meternich circled around to the main companionway, proceeded to the secondary stairs and then turned right, heading for the engine room. The door at the end of the corridor was closed.

Knocking loudly, Meternich stepped back as the door swung open and the chief mechanic leaned drunkenly against the portal.

"By God man, you're sacked!" Meternich roared. "Drunk on duty! Why—"

The mechanic smiled and red blood dribbled from his slack mouth. Moving fast, Meternich jumped back to avoid being hit by the grinning corpse. Shambling forward like a broken puppet, the engineer stumbled and fell flat onto the hardwood deck, the bones in his nose audibly breaking from the impact.

"You and you!" Meternich directed, the .32 automatic slapping into his palm. "Kill anybody in there!"

"That isn't our job, sir," one of them began hesitantly.

"Ten thousand dollar bonus. Fifty thousand!"

Now grinning in delight, the large men pulled wicked knives and charged into the dark room, one of them fumbling for the light switch along the wall.

"Lights are out" he reported, then went silent.

Meternich listened closely and there was only a sort of rustling noise, a scuffling, then a low groan of pain.

"What's going on?" Meternich demanded, fumbling for a cigarette lighter in his coat.

"There is no need for that," a low voice whispered.

Meternich flicked the gun into his hand and thumbed off the safety. "Who's there?" he shouted. "Show yourself!"

A young man of slim build dressed only in swimmer's trunks stepped out of the darkness, his face distorted by military night-vision goggles. A silenced pistol filled one hand and the other held a bloody knife, the tip reflecting the overhead lights like a demonic mirror.

"Murderer," the young man said in heavily accentuated English. "Monster! I'm going to kill you the same way you killed Kimberly. I loved her, you fiend! She was to be my wife."

"Who?" Meternich said, trying to sound puzzled. He knew exactly what bitch the insane Greek was talking about, but playing dumb would put the fool off his guard. Make him mad, and the moment he moved that pistol away...

"Liar," Kale Mikos said, his voice dropping to a whisper. "You know the name."

The young man smiled at Meternich now, and the Hungarian went cold at the sight. It was worse than that stranger he had glimpsed back in Paris. That man had at least been sane. This was no longer a human being standing in front of him, but a wild animal. A jungle killer.

"It took me so long to track you down," Mikos said coming closer, his bare feet patting on the bloody deck as he moved past the engineer. "I've been living in your boat for days. Days! Waiting, oh, just waiting, for you to come and meet my little friend."

The knife slashed and Meternich jumped back, but not fast enough to escape. He looked down and saw a red stain on his chest, the front of his silk shirt falling open to expose a shallow cut welling with blood.

"I have done nothing to you!" Meternich cried, swinging up the .32 pistol.

But Mikos fired first and the gun went spinning away, Meternich hitting the wall with a cry and cradling his crippled hand.

"Look, we can make a deal!" Meternich sobbed, raising the hand as protection. "I'm rich. More wealthy than you can image! I can pay anything! Give you anything!

"Thank you for begging, pig," Mikos snarled, raising the knife high. "The family of Miss Kimberly "Stone" sends their compliments!"

A gunshot filled the corridor and Mikos spun, collapsing the floor, his chest blown apart.

A dozen men charged down the stairs, their military rifles up and ready.

"Are you all right, sir?" Abelovsky asked, the other mercs standing respectfully behind their leader.

"It took you fools long enough," Meternich yelled. "You

and you! Stay with me until the helicopter arrives. The rest of you idiots search this ship from stem to stern! I do not want any more stowaways crawling out of the fucking wood-work!"

The mercs rushed to obey.

"And kill the rest of the bitches in the swimming pool," Meternich ordered, heading for the medical bay, holding his broken hand tenderly. "Kill everybody not a member of this crew!"

Working the arming bolt on the AMR-69 assault rifle, Abelovsky smiled widely. "With pleasure, sir."

Soon, the screaming started, but it didn't last for very long.

Jekyll Island

PATTING DOWN the sand over the shallow grave with a shovel, John Meterson looked up at the sound of gunfire. What the hell was going on here?

Dropping the shovel, he went back inside and rushed to the window. Behind the bulletproof glass, the man gasped at the sight of burning motorcycles on the front lawn and bodies strewed around everywhere.

Suddenly there was an explosion, and a moment later something wet smacked the glass. As it slid down, leaving a red trail behind, Meterson gagged and turned to retch in a wastebasket. An eye. That had been a human eye!

Wiping his mouth on the curtains, Meterson went to the computer and pushed back a panel on the side, exposing five switches. After flipping three of them in the correct order, a low hum came from the basement. It rapidly rose in volume until a crackling discharge surged through the machines below and on the desk. There was a puff for volatized circuits and the plastic casing began to melt, slagging down onto the eighteenth-century desk.

There, done. The files and targeting commands were gone. Meterson had done this before as an experiment, and there was no way at all to reclaim the lost data. Everything was now in his head safe and secure. Once he and his brothers escaped, they would be free from any possible retribution.

Another explosion shook the cottage and a machine gun chattered, only to be answered by two more, followed by screaming. Quickly he went to the closet. Meterson had no idea who was winning, but the wise course was to assume his people were losing. If he was wrong, no harm done. But if he was right, then every second he wasted was a nail in his coffin.

Inside the closet was an NSA wall safe. Pressing the dial to deactivate the defensive charges, Meterson merely rotated the dial twice to zero, and door swung aside. Yanking out a bulletproof vest, he tucked it under an arm and slid back another panel to expose five more switches. Tiny red lights burned brightly above each one. He flipped all five of them in the right order, then heard a solid clank of a solenoid engaging. The lights above the switches went dark.

Done, and done. There was no way to stop it now. Let the FBI or Homeland or Delta Force come, what did he care? The lumbering peasants would find only charred ashes with a body in the cellar whose remains perfectly matched his dental records. Did the Americans think they were dealing with fools? The Meternich family was royalty! There wasn't a dirt-eating peasant born who could outwit a Meternich!

Slipping on the vest, the former NSA agent grabbed a laptop from a bookcase shelf and left out the rear door. As she sprinted for the dock, something hit him twice in the back, the blows knocking the wind out of him. But he kept running until jumping off the dock and onto the deck of his yacht.

"Sir, I heard gunfire," the captain said. "What's going on?"

"Out of the way!" Meterson snarled, pushing the man aside.

Seizing the controls, Meterson flicked on the engines and then shoved the electronic speed controls to the maximum. The powerful Detroit diesels in the hold lumbered up to full power, then the hundred foot yacht moved away from the dock until the mooring lines were stretched tight behind them.

The lines! Shit, he had forgotten. Slapping a panel on the control board caused a panel to fall open, and Meterson grabbed an X-18 grenade launcher from the arsenal on display. Turning around, he stopped in the act of firing a 30 mm round at the docks, as he saw Bella Tokay slash the remaining mooring line with a large knife.

Leaping onboard, the man fell to a knee as the yacht leaped away from the dock, the powerful engines driving it quickly across the calm sea and toward the horizon.

"I thought you were supposed to stand by your brothers-in-arms until the end," Meterson said, the X-18 comfortable in his hands.

"Only a fool fights a losing battle," Tokay said, rising stiffly, his chest under the body armor a mass of aches from the savage pounding received from the Americans. "I would rather live and get new comrades than perish with the old."

Meterson smiled. "A very sensible attitude," he complimented. "Take a Stinger from the arms locker, watch for Coast Guard planes. We're not safe until we reach the twelve-mile limit."

"Do you think a legal nicety will stop these people?" Tokay asked, the wind ruffling his hair.

In the background the little cottage was ablaze, fiery bursts from automatic weapons dotting the smoke like blossoming hellflowers.

"By then, they will have other things to worry about," Meternich said, smiling, feeling an almost sexual release at the sight of the growing destruction. Then he looked skyward. There were sixty more minutes to go until Sky Hammer hit the United Nations and hell walked upon the world.

"Oh, yes, my friend," Meternich said, chuckling. "They will be very busy, indeed."

CHAPTER TWENTY-ONE

Heathrow Airport

As the helicopter landed on the roof of the main terminal, Attila Meternich stepped down with the precious laptop safely tucked into a designer carrying case slung over his good arm. His left hand was freshly stitched, wrapped in clean bandages and riding in a black silk sling knotted behind his neck. Even when ill, dignity and carriage were important to an aristocrat.

Mikhail Abelovsky and four members from the crew from the *Morning Star* stepped down next, all of them carrying gym bags that clanked slightly if they moved too fast. The Hungarian mercenaries viewed the hustle of the British helipad with marked disdain, but stayed with their employer. The Meternich family had ruled their valley in Hungary for centuries, and you forever served them, or were served to them on a platter. The men didn't like the options, but had made their choice. It was better to live at the right hand of the devil than to be trod under his hooves.

Abelovsky didn't share this opinion, but then, the others thought him insane.

Crossing the roof, Meternich and his bodyguards took the first elevator available, one of them blocking the other people from stepping inside.

"Full," Abelovsky said, his drooping mustache giving him an oddly sad expression that did little to beguile the diamond hardness of his black eyes.

"But there's plenty of space," a man started, then saw the other mercenaries looking at him closely.

"Right, full. I'll take the next one," he said with a smile, backing away.

"Coward," Meternich snorted, adjusting the sling.

"You would have fought for an elevator?" a merc asked pointedly.

"Everything is a battle," Abelovsky stated, looking over a wide shoulder. "Every loss is a step toward death."

The other men said nothing, their opinions on the matter kept private.

In the ride to the ground floor, Meternich took a chance to call his brother, but there was no reply. Not liking the sound of that, he took out a gold cigarette lighter and levered off the back of the phone to play the flame along the delicate interior. Wires crackled and the integrated circuit chip split apart, destroying the stored numbers forever.

As the steel doors opened, Meternich tossed the dead phone into a waste receptacle and checked his watch. Two hours until the remaining Thors were in range to hit the United Nations, then a final deposit of sixty-six million dollars from their client, and then gracious retirement. The man felt an odd mixture of elation and depression. Ten years in the planning, five days to complete. It was too fast, over too soon. He wanted more.

Trying to hide his irritation, Meternich, with his guards, headed directly to the gate assigned for private planes. Now that he was wealthy, a commercial flight was completely out of the question for several reasons. They were too slow, too crowded, too noisy, and there was far too much security. The owner of a private plane could go where he wished, and the security guards were far less stringent about following regulations. If the rich boy wanted to smuggle a bomb on board his own plane, what did they care? In fact, many of them were quite friendly to a millionaire with a pocket full of untraceable cash.

Only minutes later Meterson and his entourage were crossing the airfield toward a closed-off section, heading for his new plane, the largest that was available, a monster of the sky. His yacht had been one of ten largest private vessels in the world, as was this plane, the awe-inspiring, colossal, C-130 Hercules.

Unfortunately a military version of the craft had proved impossible to purchase without endless permits that would have taken months to obtain legally and weeks to forge properly. There were no gunports, no Bofors 40 mm cannons, no chaff and flare ejectors. Those were illegal and would have to be installed privately back in Hungary. The technicians were already waiting to begin at the newly built private airfield located at Meternich Castle.

This was the civilian model, but extensively modified. The interior was tastefully lined with decorative tiling to cover the control cables and air conduits. The sturdy military jumpseats lining the walls had been replaced with forward-facing rows of comfortable loungers, suitable for guests to relax in while enjoying a movie a mile in the sky.

The utilitarian, bare steel lavatory in the front of the colossal plane, located under the flight deck, was now tiled, illuminated with recessed lighting, and there were fresh-cut flowers in wall-mounted vases.

"I got your message, Mr. Smith," the pilot announced, standing in the open aft end of the plane. "I'm ready to take off as soon as you wish, sir."

The rear ramp was fully lowered to the tarmac, the carpeting covering the armored door so new it still carried the oddly pleasant chemical smell of the factory.

"Thank you," Meternich said, smiling graciously. "Please depart as soon as possible. I'm anxious to get back home." Actually, the plan was to fly to Switzerland first. There he would kill the pilot, get a new crew, some plastic surgery, and then eventually onward to Hungary. Briefly, Meternich wondered if he would recognize his brothers with their new faces?

"No problem, sir." The pilot touched his cap with two fingers. "I'll get clearance from the tower and we'll be on the way."

"Excellent." Meternich smiled as he walked up the ramp and into the mammoth interior.

Filling the rear cargo area was another new vehicle, something to replace the ESA limousine that he had been forced to abandon back in Paris. Pity about the driver, but these things happened. Walking past the machine, he ran fingertips along the satiny-smooth paint job. It was magnificent. A brand-new, Diplomat-class, armored limousine, the sticker still in the window. Armored top and bottom, bulletproof windows, air-tight as protection against gas attacks, electrified door handles, the Diplomat was as close as he could get to owning a private tank. The cost had been enormous, but he considered it well worth the expense. There was no replacement for safety.

"Is it securely fastened?" Meternich asked, plucking one of the wide canvas straps.

"Absolutely, sir," the pilot stated, holding a button to raise the aft ramp. The portal closed with a muffled boom. "I checked every one of them myself. Sure as hell don't want this behemoth rolling about loose while we're in flight."

"Quite so. Thank you…"

"Kossuth, sir. Janos Kossuth."

Meternich squinted at the tall blonde. "You are Hungarian?" he asked, surprised.

"Yes, sir, Mr. Smith. First generation raised in England," Kossuth replied, stroking his pale hair. "I guess my Swedish mother does show a bit strong."

The pilot laughed and Meternich smiled.

Abelovsky frowned. A dirty little half-breed. How disgusting. It would be a pleasure to kill the mongrel dog.

"Now, if you'll excuse me, sir," Kossuth said, starting to turn toward the front of the Hercules.

"Of course." Meternich waved him onward.

The pilot went quickly to the wooden flight of stairs that led to the flight deck and went inside.

Once the door was closed, Meternich relaxed slightly and waved his bodyguards toward the rows of loungers.

"Stow away your bags, gentlemen, and make yourself

comfortable," Meternich instructed, taking the largest chair for himself and buckling on a velvet seat belt. "We have a long flight ahead of us."

Jekyll Island

SWIRLING CLOUDS of acrid smoke covered the torn sod around the little cottage, with spent brass and dead bodies underfoot everywhere.

Moving through the bitter fumes from the burning motor-cycles, Zdenka Salvai limped along in her cast, the flame-thrower lancing out randomly across the battlefield.

With a sputter, the flamethrower died, and the redhead slapped the buckle on the chest harness to release the straps. The empty fuel tanks dropped off her back, and she pulled an antique Kalashnikov pistol from a holster.

"Okay, I surrender!" she shouted, trying to sound fright-ened, bracing the deadly weapon in a sure two-handed grip. "I give up! Please, don't hurt me!"

Striding through the smoke, the men of Able Team ap-peared with their weapons leveled. Snarling, the merc got off one shot before she was torn to pieces by the concentrated barrage. Behind her, the cottage was peppered with hardball rounds, the lead smacking into the bulletproof windows and staying there like flies trapped in amber.

"One down, two to go," Blancanales snorted, touching his shoulder. His hand came away red, but it was just a flesh wound. Repairs could come later.

"One to go," Lyons gruffly corrected. "We need Meterson alive."

Gingerly reloading the M-16 assault rifle, the Latino frowned. "Yeah, I keep forgetting that part."

"Yeah, me, too," Lyons admitted, visually inspecting the other man's wound. "Just a scratch, Rosario. You'll live."

"Never any doubt of that, Carl."

A sharp whistle caught their attention, and the two men joined Schwarz standing by the privacy fence. The gate was hanging from one hinge. Blancanales ripped off the splintered frame, while Lyons stood guard and Schwarz went inside.

"Bingo," he whispered, shouldering his M-16 assault rifle and starting down the ladder.

There was no water in the swimming pool, only a ceramic column that almost rose to the top of the fencing. The entire pool was the maser! Wary of booby traps, Schwarz went to the base of the column and fused a knife to force open an access panel exposing power cables and control lines. Moving fast, he snipped the controls lines, then attached a small relay box. The indicator light flashed and there was an answering beep of confirmation. He smiled. The maser was now under the control of the Farm. All the team had to do was find the access codes and Sky Hammer would be neutralized.

"All done?" Blancanales asked, lending his friend a hand to climb out of the pool.

"We own it," Schwarz said, getting to his feet.

"Good," Lyons answered grimly, studying the cottage. "Then let's finish this."

Going to either side of the sagging front door, the men of Able Team tossed in stun grenades and counted to six. On the mark, the charges cut with a sonic blast that temporarily deafened anybody within ten feet and released a thermite flash ten times brighter then the sun.

A man screamed and the Stony Man commandos swung into the building, weapons at the ready. In the living room, two men stood clawing at their eyes and cursing, AK-47 assault rifles hanging at their sides from the canvas straps. Blancanales and Schwarz stabbed them both with stun guns and moved on even before the mercs had mercifully dropped unconscious.

Sweeping into the kitchen, Lyons found a merc with a Neostad shotgun hiding behind the tipped-over kitchen table. Lyons dived out of the way as the merc fired the deadly South African weapon, the stainless-steel fléchettes blowing a hole in the plaster wall larger than a man's head. Blancanales and Schwarz appeared in the doorway to give cover fire, and the Able Team leader cut loose with a long burst from the Atchisson while on the floor. The hellstorm of lead chewed apart the thick wooden tabletop, then the merc behind. He dropped to the littered floor nearly cut in two.

Moving across the kitchen to the stairs, Lyons twitched his cheek and cursed. Reaching up, the man removed a dark wood splinter from his cheek, which had missed his eye by an inch.

Dashing down the corridor, a badly wounded merc stepped into view, loading a machine gun. Able Team turned, the three firing in unison, and the merc flipped backward, his lifeblood spraying onto the wall.

Doing a fast recon, Able Team couldn't find anybody else alive in the cottage. However, they discovered a set of locked sliding double doors at the end of a ground-floor hallway.

Pulling around his U.S. Army laptop, Schwarz slid the fiber optic camera under the doorjamb and twisted it about for a fast recon.

"Clear," he reported, reclaiming the probe.

Taking aim, the three Stony Man commandos fired in unison. The doors were blown off their tracks and Able Team stepped inside the cool office. They went directly to the smoldering remains of the computer.

"This is useless," Schwarz muttered, thrusting a EM probe into the ruined computer. "No way we're getting any data out of this wreck. Meterson knew what he was doing."

"Oh, hell," Blancanales said, stepping backward out of the closet. "Just as we feared, he's got a standard NSA self-destruct and it's alive."

"Kill it," Lyons ordered brusquely, dropping the spent drum from the Atchisson and shoving in his last reload.

Already moving toward the smashed doorway, Schwarz shook his head. "Can't be done, Carl."

"Okay, get moving!" Lyons decided, feeling the bombs in the basement ticking away.

The team hit the hallway moving and crashed through the back-door screen without slowing. Sprinting across the manicured lawn, the men tried not to think about the possibility of land mines as they headed for the low stone fence that separated the grassy backyard from the sandy beach.

Reaching the fence, they dived over and were airborne when the cottage violently exploded. Riding out the shock wave, they hit the sand rolling, the stone fence deflecting the brunt of the blast, a writhing fireball expanding above their heads only yards way.

"The maser!" Blancanales shouted over the detonation.

"Safe!" Schwarz yelled back. "Too low in ground!"

As the noise and shaking finally subsided, Able Team rose and picked its way through the burning debris to check on the swimming pool. The fence, the diving tower, everything above ground was gone, but the maser was undamaged.

"You were right, Gadgets," Lyons stated in relief. "They used a standard NSA charge. Just enough to blow the house, but not kill the neighbors."

"Yeah, very bad for public relations," Blancanales said, glancing at the empty dock on the beach. "But while we were busy with the mercs, Meterson took a powder."

"Speaking of the neighbors," Schwarz suggested, looking to the north. Rising behind a sand dune was the red-tiled roof of large house. "Think they might have a boat we can borrow?"

"Only one way to find out," Blancanales stated, already running in that direction.

CHAPTER TWENTY-TWO

Heathrow Airport

Smoothly, the Hercules taxied along the runway.

Settling into his comfortable recliner, Meternich had to admit it was a quality piece of furniture. Say what you will about British food, but they were master craftsman. He would even consider moving to the United Kingdom if necessary. England was clean, generally well run, and nice and cold. Rather similar to foggy Hungary.

Suddenly the Hercules started to slow down, and Meternich felt a stab of worry in his stomach.

"Something is wrong," Abelovsky stated, frowning.

"Captain, is there a problem?" Meternich demanded over the intercom built into the armrest of the costly chair.

"Sir, there's… Sir, there's a Black Hawk helicopter sitting in the middle our of runway and refusing to move!"

"A what?"

"A Black Hawk, sir. An American gunship."

Now, Meternich felt panic. "Is it armed?"

"Armed?"

"Is it armed, you idiot!"

"No, sir," the Captain replied. "No weapon pods in sight."

"Then run it down," Meternich commanded. "We're fifty times bigger. Brush it aside like trash."

"But, sir—"

"That is an order!"

There was a pause. "No, sir," Kossuth replied over the intercom. "I refuse. There are people on board that helicopter. They'd be killed! I'm powering down."

As the sound of the Allison engines got softer, Abelovsky started to angrily releasing his seat belt, but another merc stood first.

"I can fly this plane," the man stated, adjusting his wire-rimmed glasses.

"Then do it!" Meternich commanded with a wave. "Kill that fool and get us airborne!"

The merc nodded and started for the stairs when a series of holes appeared along the side of the fuselage, larger than closed fists. A split second later, matching holes appeared on the other side, but there was no explosion.

"Deer slugs!" Mikhail cursed. "Sir, they're trying to keep us on the ground.

"You, get to the flight deck and take command of this plane!" Meternich barked.

The merc turned to spring up the stairs. At the door, he paused and drew a knife. Stepping inside, there came cries of horror and then a brief gurgling scream.

"Get the guns!" Mikhail shouted, going to the luggage compartment.

Throwing open the door, he pulled out suitcases and passed them to the other mercs. The cases were yanked out and the guns quickly distributed. Kalashnikovs, Uzis, Skorpions, Magnum revolvers, shotguns and grenades.

Suddenly the Allison engines began to build tempo again, preparing for takeoff.

"The control tower has told us to stay on the ground," the pilot announced over the intercom. "Something to do about an incoming flight, sir. They were rather vague on details."

"It's a trick!" Meternich barked, leaning forward. "Keep going! Stop for nothing!"

"Yes, my baron."

In surprise, Meternich noted the added title. This was a man to watch. Many feared Meternich, but few showed proper respect. What was the fellow's name again? Rakoczy something. Dek, that was it. Dek Rakoczy.

"What do you want us to do, sir?" Abelovsky asked, slamming a clip into the grip of a 9 mm Uzi machine pistol.

"Kill them, my old friend," Meternich said, afraid to move from his chair. "Or it is back to the asylum for you."

Working the arming bolt, Abelovsky went pale at those words, then his face changed into an inhuman mask of feral delight.

"Cover all the doors!" he shouted, squeezing the pistol-grip safety of the machine pistol. "They'll try to get inside. We have to keep them out at any cost!"

"Sir!" Rakoczy shouted over the intercom. "The Black-Hawk…it's gone!"

"We ran it over?" Meternich demanded to know. He hadn't felt any jar. Surely there would have been some response when the Hercules plowed aside the American gunship.

"No, sir, it's just gone."

Just then, the Hercules bounced as if colliding with something large.

"Are you sure we haven't hit them?" Meternich asked, releasing his seat belt. The laptop was in the seat next to his, and he slid the strap of the case over his neck.

"Yes, sir! There's only clear space ahead of us."

"Then keep flying and your family will never know hunger!" he stated, feeling a trickle of sweat flow down his back. The damn Americans were up to something, some kind of trick, or trap. Blow off the wheels? Stall the engines? What could it be?

Suddenly there was an explosion and a gaping hole was blown in the side of the Hercules right alongside the hardened doorway. Before the smoke even cleared, a man in combat gear swung in through the ring of sharp metal at the end of a rope.

"Freeze, Attila!" McCarter ordered, leveling his MP-5 machine gun, the fumes from the C-4 breaching charge still swirling in the air.

Jumping from his seat, Meternich dashed around the chair and took cover as Mikhail and the others opened fire with their assortment of weapons.

Several rounds ricocheted off McCarter's body armor before he dived out the way and came up throwing a stun grenade. As it went off the mercs screamed and clawed at their faces.

A split second later the opposite side of the Hercules was blown open and Hawkins swung inside, his MP-5 firing in tight bursts at anybody that wasn't McCarter or Meternich. Blood sprayed into the air and the mercs dropped.

Laughing insanely, Mikhail stood up behind a chair holding a Skorpion and an Uzi, firing them both back and forth as if his ammo supply was unlimited. McCarter and Hawkins leaped for cover as James and Encizo swung in through the gaping holes.

"Sir, there's somebody on the windshield!" Rakoczy shouted, then there came strange banging noises and the intercom went silent.

Dropping to all fours, Meternich felt his heart pounding wildly as he scrambled for the armored limo. Staying low, he had to tap the entry code twice into the door handle before it was accepted and the vehicle unlocked. A hail of bullets peppered the black car and one grazed his arm before Meternich got inside and slammed the door.

Stretching to reach the dashboard, Meternich hit a switch and the vehicle locked every door, then sealed itself air-tight with a hydraulic hiss.

"Now, you die," Meternich snarled, starting the engine and throwing it into forward gear. He'd crush them against the wall! Crush them like bugs! The fight seemed to be going against his men, bodies and blood and smoke were everywhere, slugs bouncing off the armored hood of the Diplomat constantly.

But the limo didn't move, no matter how much gas he fed the engine. The wheels only spun around until smoke rose from the carpeting, and the engine gauges started to climb into the danger zone.

Cursing, Meternich beat his fists against the steering wheel as he remembered that the Diplomat was securely anchored to the deck. Then he jerked as something smacked against the driver's-side window.

In mounting horror, he stared at the sticky block of C-4 explosive clinging to the bulletproof glass, a radio detonator sticking out of the claylike material. Frantically moving to the passenger side of the limo, Meternich jumped as another block of C-4 was slapped onto that window. Then two more slammed onto the rear windows, and a fifth smacked onto the front windshield.

Staring through the thick glass, Meternich once again locked eyes with McCarter and finally recognized him as the fellow from Paris. My God, had they been that close behind him all this time?

Knowing the limousine was soundproof to prevent attack by stun grenades, McCarter lifted the radio detonator and motioned for Meternich to come out. The choice was obvious. Surrender or die.

Snarling in rage, Meternich pulled out the laptop and started contacting his brother. If he was going to die this day, then the price the Americans would pay would be beyond their imagination. There were dozens of major amusement parks across the United States. Switching Sky Hammer from hitting the UN, he could kill millions of their children in five minutes. He wished there was some way of telling the soldiers that, using the threat as a bargaining chip to gain his freedom, his life. But opening the windows even a hair would make him vulnerable. Meternich was trapped, and there was nothing to do but die. As he got an answering tone, Attila Meternich reached for the send button and the world seemed to explode as the five breaching charges detonated in unison.

To PHOENIX FORCE, the black limo crumpled inward as if crushed by an invisible fist. The noise inside the Hercules was off the charts, the men shook and then heard only silence, totally deaf from sonic bombardment.

The carpeting was ablaze and thick flames surrounded the smashed vehicle, the fumes reeking of chemicals. Weaving slightly, the team grabbed fire extinguishers from the wall niches and sprayed McCarter from head to foot, keeping the deluge of foam and CO2 going as the man walked directly into the flames and yanked open the sagging front door.

Covered with blood, Attila Meternich was sprawled on the front seat, pieces of armored molding from the frame of the windows obscenely sticking out his body. His arms and legs were bent at impossible angles, and McCarter realized they weren't broken, but pulverized. The man would never use any of his limbs again.

Taking the humming titanium laptop from the front seat, McCarter breathed in relief to find it still working. As he passed the U.S. Army computer to James, a noise came from Meternich, a pitiful whine of misery wrenched from the very deepest, darkest corner of hell. McCarter couldn't believe it. He was still alive?

Standing amid the dying flames, McCarter slowly drew his Browning Hi-Power and thumbed back the hammer. His face was a raging torrent of conflicting emotions, then he aimed and fired, the brains of the crippled ESA executive and terrorist splattering across the dented interior of the armored limo.

"It would have been more cruel to let him live as a help-less basket case," Hawkins said, his eyes intent upon the former SAS officer. "Thought we had lost you there for a second, David."

"Me, too," McCarter admitted honestly, holstering the hot piece.

"Oh, hell," James said, touching his ear. "We've got trouble."

CHAPTER TWENTY-THREE

Stony Man Farm, Virginia

"Got it!" Kurtzman shouted in victory. "Calvin just sent us the codes from Meternich's laptop."

"Something odd about this," Tokaido muttered.

"Thank God." Barbara Price exhaled, as if she had been holding her breath for hours. "Okay, send the Thors these new coordinates, latitude—"

"What the… Damn, this is the wrong code!" Kurtzman spit, staring at his monitor in disbelief.

"What?" Price demanded.

"Well, not quite," Tokaido said. "This is the communication code, the one that lets the maser talk to the Thors. But there is nothing here about targeting Sky Hammer."

"There are two access codes?" Price queried. Damnation, that brother of Meternich's really knew his job. This division of codes had to have been his idea of a failsafe, so that one of them could not seize control and kill the other. Nice family.

"Just like the Pentagon uses for the launch commands for the nuclear ICBMs," Delahunt stated from behind her VR helmet, her gloved hands gesturing in the air. "No good! This is 1,024-byte, triple-layer encryption. This can't be overridden or circumvented."

Price knew what she meant. The NSA had helped design "The Football", the briefcase launch computer that was never more than five minutes away from the President wherever he went. The Football could talk to the fire-control computers at NORAD, but only the President himself knew the launch code. That way nobody could simply steal the briefcase and start a nuclear war. You needed both. Man and machine together.

"Smart, maybe too smart," Kurtzman growled, rubbing his unshaved chin to the sound of sandpaper.

"Alert," Tokaido said calmly. "We have a problem."

The room seemed to chill with those simple words.

"Tell me," Price ordered, crossing her arms.

The young man took a deep breath. "According to the buffer memory of the Jekyll Island maser, the Thors are on a countdown," Tokaido reported. "They'll launch automatically as soon as the target comes into range above the horizon."

"Which is?" Price demanded, dreading the news.

The young man looked as if he was in pain. "The United Nations building in Manhattan."

Price couldn't believe it. The UN building? Hundreds of diplomats and ambassadors from every nation on the map would be killed. That would be more than enough to push the leaders of the world into full-scale war.

"How long do we have?" she asked, running her fingers nervously through her hair.

Wethers hit a button and a vector graphic of a clock appeared on the main monitor. "Sixty-two minutes."

One hour? "Aaron, crack the code," Price said urgently, going behind the big man and resting both hands on the frame of his wheelchair. "I'm always telling Hal that you're the best hacker in the world. Okay, prove me right. Shut the Thors down, or divert their flight path, drop them into the ocean, or something."

"I'll do my best," Kurtzman stated, his hands already moving. "But this kind if encryption takes time. I'm not sure it can be done by anybody alive in an hour."

"Try," Price urged desperately. They had gone so far and gotten this close, only to be stopped at the last yard. Unacceptable! America would never surrender, the Farm would fight until the last second.

Price put on a brave countenance, but down deep in her heart, the mission controller honestly knew that everything now depended on Able Team getting the targeting code from John Meterson in the next sixty minutes.

The wall clock blinked. Fifty nine minutes and counting.

SKIPPING FROM WAVE to wave, barely touching the water, the sleek speedboat raced across the azure Atlantic Ocean. There was no other craft in sight. Just the *Sister Sue* and endless miles of shimmering emptiness.

"Fifty-five minutes?" Lyons rumbled, his hair slicked back from the salty spray coming over the sloping windshield.

Schwarz nodded, holding on to the gunwale of the speeding boat. "That's what the lady said."

"Go faster," Lyons urged, leaning forward slightly against the sloping windshield.

"I'd get out and push, if I thought that would help," Blancanales said, steering with both hands tight on the controls. "But I've got this thing wide open now."

On the fancy dashboard, the digital fuel gauge was visibly dropping, and the team had started with only half a tank. The *Sister Sue* was designed for water-skiing, and it was incredibly fast, but she ate fuel at a voracious rate.

Lyons cracked his knuckles and tried to think. Slightly less than half a tank now and fifty-four minutes to go.

"Head north," he declared abruptly.

"North?" Blancanales said, changing directions.

"Trust me," Lyons told him, rocking to the motion of the speedboat.

A street cop often lost sight of a criminal he was chasing, that was when the good cops were separated from the men just walking the beat. Now you had to think like a criminal, get into their skin, and understand where they would run, and why. Attila had been in his yacht, but he had switched to a plane, so the brothers weren't going to meet somewhere at sea. After that, the logical decision was also a plane for Meterson, correction, John Meternich. A seaplane was possible, but unlikely. It was very difficult to get from a boat to a seaplane without going into the drink. Very undignified, and these assholes thought of themselves as royalty. So, no seaplane. Okay, there was nothing to the south but open water, which left north. There was an island located above Jekyll, just fifty or sixty miles away. St. Simmon. Small place. No homes or residences of any kind. Just a lighthouse and lots of flat land. Perfect for an oceanside rendezvous.

"You sure about this?" Schwarz asked, wiping droplets of salty water off his mustache.

"Hell, no," Lyons said honestly. "But a guess is all we got." The big man tried not to look at his watch, but the urge was irresistible. Fifty minutes to go.

Precious minutes and suddenly there were other ships dotting the horizon. Speedboats, yachts, sailboats, cabin cruisers, a fishing trawler! But none of them was the craft they were after.

There was a pair of binoculars holstered alongside the engine housing, low-power, but better than nothing, and Lyons used them to scan the horizon.

"Heads up," Lyons shouted, pointing to the north. "There she is! Right off the St. Simmon breakers."

Hunched over the wheel, Blancanales swung directly for the enemy ship, pushing the speed control harder.

"And here we go," Scwharz whispered, opening the breech of the M-203 and pulling out the antipersonnel shell. "We need him alive, right?"

"If at all possible," Lyons said, tucking away the binoculars and hefting the Atchisson. "But if he has a laptop, that's good enough."

"Until we know that for sure, yes, we take Meterson alive."

"At any cost."

The rest of Able Team nodded grimly. Their lives weren't a priority in the mission anymore. If they died taking Meterson alive, or obtaining his laptop, that was an acceptable loss. One man died to save a million. In the opinion of a soldier, that was a good trade, and they would pay that price any day.

"Fair enough," Schwarz said, dropping a stun bag round into the breech and closing it with a snap of the wrist. Then he changed his mind and inserted his only remaining HE shell.

"Hamstring?" Blancanales asked.

"Got a better suggestion?"

"Hell, no, just don't miss!"

"You'll be the first to know."

As the *Sister Sue* approached the enemy vessel, men began running about the main deck of the yacht, and suddenly the crew started opening fire with oddly shaped machine guns. The rounds forming little geysers as they tracked along the surface of the Atlantic, going right past the needle-sharp bow of the stolen speedboat.

Teeth bared, Blancanales kept going straight, and Lyons ripped half a drum of 12-gauge rounds over the ship, trying to drive the sailors under cover without hurting anybody.

It worked. As the crew dashed out of sight, Blancanales swung around the aft end of the yacht, while Schwarz braced himself and aimed his M-203. As the *Sister Sue* crossed the rear of the yacht, Schwarz fired the high-explosive round directly into the spinning propellers. The distance was good, the round had enough distance to arm, and the propellers exploded, steel blades flying into the air. A man with a shotgun standing on the rear deck screamed as a blade sliced off an arm, the weapon tumbling into the sea. He fell to his knees, trying to staunch the gush of blood with his other hand and having no effect whatsoever.

"Sure hope that wasn't Meterson," Lyons exhorted, watching the yacht lose momentum. The vessel came to a slow coast, only half a mile away from the sandy beach of St. Simmon Island.

"Surrender and live!" Lyons shouted through cupped hands as the speedboat circled the powerless yacht.

Several of the sailors raised their arms in capitulation, but one fellow lumbered into view holding a Sting missile launcher.

Blancanales swerved the speedboat.

Bella Tokay fired and the RPG flashed by, missing by only feet, then Lyons and Schwarz fired back. Blood sprayed high and Tokay stumbled backward to tumble overboard.

Throttling down, Blancanales cut in reverse and maneuvered alongside the yacht. Lyons kept the crew under watch while Schwarz threw a mooring line onto a deck cleat. Slowly he started pulling the two ships together.

John Meterson appeared on deck with an open laptop in his hands.

"Leave now, or I level Washington!" Meterson commanded, raising the laptop as if it were a bomb.

"Try again!" Lyons laughed. "We can't stop a maser, but this whole area is being blanketed by a jamming field. Nothing in the EM spectrum is coming or going."

Startled, Meterson glanced at the laptop, then looked up in time to see a stocky man with a mustache climb over the side of the yacht. Tricked! They had to know only he had the targeting codes. Damn them all! This is not how it was supposed to end!

Dropping the laptop, Meterson pulled out a gun from behind his back and opened fire.

Schwarz let go of the rope and dropped back onto the *Sister Sue*, just as Blancanales fired the stun bag loaded into his M-203. Made of wadded cloth and silicon jelly, it hit Meterson in the belly, knocking the breath out of the man. Doubling over, he dropped the gun and grabbed the laptop. Turning to run, the man tripped over his own feet and went tumbling, falling over the gunwale and into the Atlantic Ocean.

Instantly a shark appeared and Meterson's piercing shrieks rent the air. For a moment he surfaced, blood gushing from his mouth, choking the scream, and then he went down again and didn't reappear.

"Cover me!" Lyons yelled, dropping the Atchisson and pulling out a knife.

"Carl, no!" Blancanales yelled, reaching for the man.

But the ex-cop dived over the side and disappeared into the murky depths after the sinking laptop. The deep scratch on his cheek leaving a red contrail behind into the water.

"Shit!" Schwarz cursed, then pulled a knife and slashed his palm.

Bending over the side of the *Sister Sue*, he sloshed it about on the surface like a wounded fish. Sharks liked their food alive and kicking, so the more noise he made, the better was the chance that the man-killers would attack him and leave Lyons alone.

A gray shape ghosted past the speedboat and Blancanales started to hammer the water with rounds from his M-16. The shark curled back upon itself to bite the unseen enemy, and starting wildly thrashing around, bucking and heaving.

"Good sharky," Schwarz muttered, retrieving his hand and grabbing his own M-16. "Attaboy. Keep going!"

Two more sharks moved in, fast and silent, to attack their wounded companion. When they were all close, Blancanales and Schwarz both opened fire, stitching the monsters with hardball ammo and perfectly imbalanced tumblers. The soldiers didn't think the tumblers would do much the sharks, but the armor-piercing bullets would go deep at this a range. No matter what the creature was, if you poke in enough holes, it died.

But the sharks fought on, gashing and leaping from the water, going insane. Then one of them was in the clear and Schwarz fired the M-203. The shark shattered like a dropped china plate, bones and guts spraying out for a dozen yards.

As the pale gobbets of flesh smacked into the water, there were only two pale forms in sight, both of the sharks floating belly upward.

"Think we got them all?" Schwarz asked hopefully.

"Shove your head in and see," his teammate retorted, dropping a clip and then cursing to find his pocket was empty. Dropping the M-16, Blancanales drew his Colt pistol.

"Come on, Carl," he prayed, racking the slide.

Neither of the Stony Man commandos said anything as they watched the bloody water around the speedboat. A long minute passed and nothing seemed to move aside from the choppy waves slopping up against the two ships.

"I'm next," Blancanales said, kicking off his shoes and grabbing the anchor. The extra weight would send him down faster and every second of air counted underwater.

There was a clatter and the laptop landed on the deck between the men.

Spinning, they saw a trembling hand grab the gunwale of

the *Sister Sue* and Lyons rose into view gasping for air. As Blancanales helped his friend out of the ocean, Schwarz ripped off his white shirt to dry the computer before setting it on the dashboard and flipping up the screen. He typed for several moments then bitterly cursed.

"It's dead, shorted out!" Schwarz cursed. Taking out his pistol, he flipped it in the air, grabbed it by the barrel and started smashing the laptop apart.

Ripping out the hard drive, Schwarz pulled away the extraneous bits, and Blancanales passed over the U.S. Army laptop.

Lifting the interior cover, Schwarz slid out the hard drive and inserted the civilian hard drive into the universal mounting of the military model. Thank God, Army Intelligence thought about this as a way to read enemy computers in the field.

"We're in!" Schwarz grunted, his hands never moving faster. "Okay, Bear has the target codes and...done." The man sat back, breathing hard at the sky as if he had run a marathon.

"Talk," Lyons demanded, walking closer, water dripping off his torn clothing. There was a gash across his chest and the knife was gone. Obviously the man had seen some action himself.

"Bear and Akira seized control and managed to divert the Thors," Schwarz said, closing his eyes. "They're headed toward the Indian Ocean and detonation."

"Thank God."

EPILOGUE

The White House

The rain gently fell upon the porch outside the Oval Office, the open doorway letting in the cool, clean smell.

"Hal, you'll be pleased to know that I have begun a program to figure out how to deal with a Thor in the future," the President said, sitting straight. "It's headed by the fellow who invented the damn things."

"Mahone?"

The President nodded. "That's the fellow. He's got a wild idea about how it might be done, but it'll require money and time. Those we have."

"And I've had my contacts at Interpol and British Intelligence start a watchdog program to check on all steel foundries for any suspicious activities. Next time, we'll catch the bastards on the ground."

"The terrorists will only come up with something else."

"And we'll stop them again," Brognola stated firmly.

"And the next time after that, and so on. There's no other choice."

"We reach for the stars or grovel in the mud, eh, Hal?" The President smiled. "Who knows, maybe someday, the fighting may even stop."

"And we'll be there, too, sir," Brognola said. "To make sure it doesn't start again."

For a while, the two men listened to the gentle rain, then started to discuss other matters of national security. There was a time for battle and time for planning. Each had its place, neither lasted. Such was the way of the world.

Meternich Castle, Hungary

SITTING ALONE in the castle, George Meternich raised a glass to the pictures on the fireplace mantel and toasted his dear departed brothers. Both of them. He had lost both of them in a single day. His elder brother, and his twin. George hung his head, tears warm on both cheeks. Was the castle and the lands worth it all? Worth so many dead, so much destruction? The only possible answer was yes. Blood and family, that was what mattered. Nothing else.

Picking up the telephone on a nearby table, Meternich decided it was time to stop mourning, and dialed a number.

"Hello? Yes, I wish to hire a computer expert. A what do they call it? A hacker," the baron said, crossing his legs. "No, not somebody merely good, I want the best. The top in his or her field. Perhaps even so good they may be wanted by the police?... Ah, you do understand, excellent."

Watching the flames in the hearth, Baron Meternich

scowled. "That price is acceptable. Now have them get me all available information on the intelligence agencies in the United States, especially any counterterrorism forces."

James Axler
Outlanders®

Reborn as neogods, an anient race
begins its final conquest in…

RIM OF THE WORLD
Outlanders #37

An ancient artifact claimed to unlock secrets hidden for two
thousand years and restore the control of a ruthless Sumerian
god has the Cerebus warriors battling blood-thirsty rebels in their
determination to prevent such a destiny.

Available May 2006 at your favorite retail outlet.

GOLD
EAGLE®

GOUT37